Lynette
Ruth an
Marjorie

PRAISE FOR
RISK . . .

"DORIS PARMETT CONTINUES THE STANDARD OF EXCELLENCE IN WOMEN'S FICTION THAT SHE BEGAN WITH [*LIES*] . . . a believable, gritty, and exciting relationship drama . . . delightful . . . sure to leave readers completely fulfilled." —*Affaire de Coeur*

RAVES FOR
DORIS PARMETT'S *LIES* . . .

"AN EMOTIONAL ROLLER COASTER with plenty of twists and turns to hold the reader riveted . . . fast-paced, moving, and emotionally intense."
—Jayne Ann Krentz

"MASTERFUL STORYTELLING . . . one of those rare, meaty, can't-put-down novels we all look forward to reading. Superb."
—Fern Michaels

"DORIS PARMETT TRAVELS THE GLITTERY PATH FROM NEW YORK TO PARIS . . . captures the drama of politics and the glamour of the fashion world."
—Nora Roberts

"SUPERB . . . mixes po[...]
fashion glamour. A WINN[...]

"SPECTACULAR . . . a p[...]
emotionally charged, a[...]
passion."

D1205854

Also by Doris Parmett from Jove

LIES

Risk

Doris Parmett

JOVE BOOKS, NEW YORK

RISK

A Jove Book / published by arrangement with
the author

PRINTING HISTORY
Jove edition / March 1994

ISBN: 0-515-11333-6

A JOVE BOOK®
Jove Books are published by The Berkley Publishing Group,
200 Madison Avenue, New York, New York 10016.
JOVE and the "J" design are trademarks
belonging to Jove Publications, Inc.

PRINTED IN THE UNITED STATES OF AMERICA

10 9 8 7 6 5 4 3 2 1

For my son, Randy.

Acknowledgments

I AM INDEBTED to the following talented professionals for their patience and technical assistance:

Detective Sergeant First Class Lewis Trowbridge of the New Jersey State Police; Doctor Donn Hornick and Jeffery LeBenger; Chef Bruno Ellmer of the Culinary Institute of America at Hyde Park, NY; and Captain Robert Baker and Chef Mario Rotti of Princess Cruises.

Risk

CLAIRE JAMESON BRICE resisted the temptation to poke her finger through the *Los Angeles Times* to get her husband's attention. With his elbows propped up, the paper spread apart, all she saw of him was a narrow band of deeply tanned forehead, a crown of streaked caramel blond hair bleached whiter from the sun, his strong athletic hands, long fingers, and buffed fingernails, displaying perfect half-moon cuticles. On his left wrist, he wore a watch she'd given him for his thirty-fifth birthday, after he had admired her father's Patek Philippe.

They breakfasted in the solarium, her favorite room. French limestone flooring reflected blue tones through the glass-topped wrought-iron table. Early morning sunshine showered the glass-domed enclosure, splintering prisms of dappled rainbows. The view beyond the coved floor-to-ceiling windows framed a tranquil scene of rhododendrons, deodar pines, oaks, Norwegian maples, lacy pink-and-white dogwoods, a dwarf magnolia, and beds of periwinkles, impatiens, and caladiums. Despite five years of living in Beverly Hills, she often felt suffocated by smog, smoldering smiles, and sham kisses. When this happened, she closed her eyes and thought of Stamford, Connecticut, of sitting on the porch of her parents' home overlooking Long Island Sound. Her birth mother had died when she was an infant. While she loved Babs, her stepmother, it was her father,

Edward Jameson, her kindred spirit, with whom she enjoyed a special relationship.

From behind the paper came a disgusted snort. "Everyone expects a cradle-to-grave handout."

"*Everyone* is too strong a word. We're more fortunate than most. It's only right we help others."

The newspaper crackled at an angle, uncovering Colin's tanned face. Tall, broad-shouldered, the hazel-eyed future president of Brice-Jameson Developers possessed an air of leisurely confidence. The heir apparent, anticipating the day Edward Jameson stepped aside. His own father's retirement, following a mild heart attack a year ago, moved him one step closer to his goal.

He peered into sparkling emerald eyes that shone with brilliant clarity. "We do. You're active in your charities. I write checks."

"Dignity comes from within, from the ability to care for yourself. Jobs, food, clothing, shelter. Basics. That's what the people want and deserve."

He grinned. His wife's sultry dark-haired tresses, the fan of dark eyelashes surrounding her slightly almond-shaped eyes, and her red mouth excited him. "I want more of what we had last night."

Claire smiled in memory. Her tongue touched her upper lip. Shifting in her chair, her lace-trimmed peignoir parted, exposing creamy flesh. She saw the leap of interest in his hooded eyes, his slightly parted lips. "Stop it. You're forever doing that."

Colin lifted an amused brow. "Doing what?"

"Trying to distract me when I'm serious. Okay, if you like I'll change the subject. We'll discuss Marybeth Frankel."

His smile faded in a flash. He rattled the newspaper.

"Christ! For God's sake! I might have known you'd lead up to her. First you invited her Saturday night without checking with me. Now you're meeting her for lunch. For an interview yet! I don't relish reading about us in the gossip columns. We're not movie people."

Offered a movie career, Colin had flatly refused, joking with friends that in his opinion parading before cameras amounted to peasant fodder. Rather than repel talent agents, his sexual élan and inherent arrogance fueled more offers.

"Marybeth is down on her luck. I want to help her."

"No you don't, madame social worker. Our livelihood doesn't depend on social-climbing wanna-bes. We build shopping malls. Get out of the interview. Make up an excuse for the party."

He snapped up the *Times*.

"No."

Her dulcet refusal floated past the painted daisies in the sparkling Waterford vase centering the table, landing in Colin's ears. "You're serious?"

"Yes. Please don't blow this out of proportion. She's writing a piece on an illustrious California family. Brice topped her list."

Colin's arched blond eyebrows rose higher. "As long as this is my home, my life, I'll have a say in it."

"You do, but you know this town. After Charlie Frankel divorced her, her fair-weather friends dropped her. People were afraid to incur Charlie's wrath. She's talented. Did you know she wrote several of his sitcoms?"

He snorted. "The show's inane crap. When it's canceled, it won't matter. Tell her to be patient, she'll get plenty of offers."

"In the meantime she has to eat and pay bills. She signed a prenup. Charlie hired Brian Hickman," she said, mentioning one of the West Coast's top divorce attorneys. "He lived up to his reputation. Hickman bled her dry. When the *Carrier* offered her a chance, she grabbed it."

Colin folded the paper. "Who told her to marry that loudmouth comedian? I'm not running a charity for dumped Hollywood wives. I can't believe you'd compromise our standards."

Anger flushed through Claire. "You didn't mind my behavior last night. Did I compromise your standards?"

"Do what you did last night, and you can compromise them any day. Which doesn't change my mind."

"You're too late. We did part of the interview on the phone."

An irritated sigh tore loose from his lips. "What did you

tell her about us?" Colin sat tall on his chair, his blond hair neatly combed, his fingers tented.

"Very little. Your folks own a ranch in Palm Springs. You grew up in this house, your parents gave it to us for a wedding present, and when they're in town they use the Century City condo."

"What else?" He tapped his fingertips.

"She asked if we planned Thanksgiving with your folks and mine. I told her not this year, that your folks will be in Mexico City. My father's flying to London on the Concorde tomorrow to meet my mother. Oh, and I mentioned they're going on to Gstaad for a second honeymoon, where they met. She thought it very romantic."

Colin scraped back his chair. Hands in his pockets, he strode around the room. "Did you mention Yamuto's project?"

"Of course not!" Claire said stoutly. "I never discuss company business."

The newest, most advanced concept in malls, the one exciting Colin, would be the largest in California—a covered city of over three million square feet, with a nine-hole golf course, swimming pool, theaters, sports events, eateries, and hundreds of shops. Colin had accompanied Japanese financier Sam Yamuto and his acquisition team to the Sacramento site her father recommended.

"Sit down, Colin. You're not a prosecuting attorney. I'm not on trial. Marybeth already knew a lot about your family. Both sides, the Santiago-Garcias and the Brices."

Colin sat down. "What did she tell you?"

"She knows your mother, Angelica, descended from one of California's Spanish land grant families, that Juan Baptiste Santiago-Garcia founded Garcia cigars after he split with his half-brother, Ramon, who raised Arabian stallions."

"How the hell did she know that?"

"From books and magazines. You never told me your father's people made and lost a fortune in book bindery in England before your great-great-grandfather, Jacob, emigrated here."

Colin harrumphed. "Never mind. What did she ask about us?"

Claire folded her napkin. "Nothing. I wish you'd stop interrogating me."

His tone moderated. "I do it because you're too trusting. Marybeth came to my office, asking to interview me. My secretary sent her away. She's got gall, getting what she wants through you."

There was utter silence. Claire rocked back in her chair. "She never said a word." After a moment, she said, "Neither did you. Why not?"

"Why would I?" he retorted, exasperated. "She's irrelevant. You used poor judgment. It's a fixable error. Call her up. Say the party's canceled, say I'm going out of town. If you'd rather, have Essy phone. I don't want her here Saturday. She'll work the guests. Think how it would affect business adversely if she prints what's said in private. Incidentally, I gave Essy an updated list. She'll call the caterer."

His former nanny idolized Colin. She'd remained in the Brices' employ as housekeeper. Claire inherited her with the house.

In fairness, Claire asked herself if she could swear for Marybeth's discretion. No. Reporters squirrel information. Besides, she concealed the fact that she'd gone to Colin's office. Other than working on the Music Center's Blue Ribbon Committee when Marybeth was still Charlie's wife, Claire had seen her once or twice. Compassion prompted her to agree to the interview and invite her to their party.

"Do you think I'm a good wife?"

"I'm late for work. Must we start?"

A tiny breath exploded from her lips. "In my present mood, yes. Essy runs the house. You grill me as if I'm incapable of making a decision standing up, so, yes, I'd like an answer. If you need specifics, blame it on a marital itch."

He regarded her with alarm. Their personal and business lives were intertwined. "I hope that's a figure of speech. Does this itch involve another man?"

The concern in his voice had her shaking her head. "Of course not. I love you, but I'm suffering from arrested development. I traded a college diploma for a marriage certificate. It's not your fault, it's mine for coasting. I'm limited to charities, shopping, lunches, exercise, and entertaining.''

"Most women would envy you."

"Cee-Cee works." She missed her best friend. Their families represented the cream of Connecticut society— *real society,* not merely wealthy people who paid for a listing in the Social Register. Neither Claire nor Cee-Cee gave a waking thought to their distinguished heritages. They grew up in each other's homes, lived in the present, participated in activities, including community service organizations, attacking projects with youthful verve. Their temperaments balanced each other. Where Cee-Cee was outspoken, restless, and loyal, Claire, constant but calmer, willingly provided a cheering section to her friend's more daring adventures.

When their parents purchased telephones for them, they spent hours talking. They swapped homework, covered for each other, double-dated in high school, and roomed together at the Connecticut College for Women—"Co-Co Wo"—shortened to Connecticut College after it went coed.

Marriage separated the two women only geographically. The devoted duo spoke weekly, unless one or the other needed a sympathetic ear, then the transatlantic phone lines burned up. Cee-Cee converted a spare bedroom in her spacious Kensington flat into an office, where she wrote soap opera scripts, hoping for her first sale.

"Tom's a British diplomat. Cee-Cee maintains a full schedule, yet she finds time to be a gracious hostess. So will I."

"You worked. You quit after two months."

Beneath Colin's nonchalant response, his statement implied he hadn't pressured her to quit, when in fact he had. Subtly. He invited clients and their wives on midweek sailing or skiing excursions. He returned home in great spirits, bringing regards from everyone, planning more activities.

"I left the ad agency to please you."

Colin reached for her hand. "I appreciate it. We're a team, sweetheart. At our social and business level, it's important for you to be available when I need you. You're the Jameson connection. When I take over, it will be different. I'll move into my own. For now, I can't worry that you're busy or late or too tired. Besides, none of the other wives in our set work."

Claire clenched her teeth. "Is that why I'm a good wife? Because I stay home?"

He slid a glance at the newspaper article. "Of course not."

"Then why?"

He poured a cup of coffee. "All right. You're ideal. You're well-bred, beautiful, intelligent, a natural-born hostess, marvelous with people. You're ringside cheering me on when I play paddle tennis. I'm looking forward to the tournament in Hawaii next week. I'm anxious to test the Shamrock paddle. The waffle-type surface grabs the ball, gives it more topspin. I'm sure I'll win the doubles title this year."

With his penchant for speed and fierce determination, he grew bored with regular tennis and had switched to the faster paddle tennis. The court, two-thirds the size of a tennis court, made for faster play. The net was five inches lower than a tennis net, the ball slightly deflated.

"Colin."

"Sorry. Okay, you're faithful, loyal—"

Disappointed, she held up her hand. "I've heard enough. I sound like your lapdog or one of the rottweilers guarding the property. Look at me, Colin. At me, not your idealized version of me."

His smile vanished. "This is ridiculous! I see you. Fine. You fill in the blanks. What's with you today?"

"We're insulated. We need new friends. A breath of fresh air, not people who agree with each other over everything."

Not only his forceful speech, but his gesturing hands emphasized his commitment to his beliefs. "What's wrong with relaxing with people of similar background, good bloodlines?"

"We're not horses."

"Don't be cute," he said sharply. "Outsiders don't speak our language. They lack breeding. They're never fully accepted. Not even the ones who marry into great families. It takes generations."

Her gaze was drawn to a delicate white *Phalaenopsis* orchid nestled in a rare Ming vase. More and more lately she felt as confined as the flower. "In other words, you married me for my sterling family tree and my inheritance."

His head tilted back, his manner professorial, his tone enunciating, as if this time his lecture would make a difference.

"You hear what you want to hear. We're evenly matched, thanks to our forefathers. I love you for who you are, not in spite of it. This includes your heritage, your elevated status. It's intrinsic."

Flipping her mane of dark hair, Claire leaned forward. Talk of class distinction made her squirmy. She'd never heard it in her home. The soft sound of her voice registered her opposition. "We're born into families by accident. It doesn't make us better. What of the millions of others?"

He shrugged. "I wish them luck and fulfilling lives. They shop in the malls, line our pockets. If, as you say, we're accidentally born into an important family, then we're doubly obligated to keep out undesirables. I have an image of myself, of who I am, of who you are. We complement each other."

A bead of perspiration crept down the valley between her breasts. "I know you're proud of your family. I'm proud of mine, too. Don't you feel a twinge of guilt for having everything handed to you?"

Bristling, his expression hardened. "I work damn hard! Our ancestors' patina benefits us. Ask people which strata of society they'd rather belong to: lower, middle, upper, or rarefied. Don't knock the top. It's giving you a fabulous life. Stick to your charities. Don't spout nonsense to my folks. You'll start a needless argument."

Colin reminded her of his father's wedding toast. With her mother-in-law beaming at her husband's side, Simpson Brice had lifted his champagne flute.

"We can vouch for ourselves. We can vouch for who we are. Who our ancestors were. Our grandchildren will be prime."

Claire thought his toast resulted from too much wine. Cee-Cee drolly whispered in her ear that she had a mental vision of rows of infants, their diapers stamped USDA PRIME CHOICE! Claire had nearly spilled her drink.

Beyond the plate glass window, a hummingbird caught her attention. It flew to its teacup-size nest in a yellow hibiscus bush. Three babies, their beaks open, chirped for food.

Colin lifted his coffee cup to his mouth. He followed her troubled gaze. "This isn't only about Marybeth or your working, is it? Is there something else on your mind?"

She wasn't prone to tears, but now her eyes misted. Why did he act as if he hadn't a clue, as if he didn't know why?

"It's about our baby."

"Baby! What baby?" he cried, spitting his coffee in shock. He leaped up, snatched his napkin, dragged it across his mouth and chin.

"Christ, you're not pregnant? You're on the Pill, aren't you? You can't be tied down now. The timing is wrong. I need you. Damnit, did you pull a fast one? Was that gratitude last night?"

His indictment dissected the air, reverberating off the vaulted enclosure in a shocking chorus of harsh decibels. The swift condemnation left her aghast, momentarily stunned. In five years of marriage, sex was never a problem, as long as she faithfully took contraceptives. Smarting under his censure, she marveled at his priorities.

"You're amazing. Business first. Family second. No, I'm not pregnant. A deal's a deal. Although waiting until I'm thirty stinks. I don't care what I promised on our wedding night. I was a bride, unconcerned with my biological clock. Suppose your sperm and my egg are incompatible?"

The thin line of displeasure eased from his brow. "Never happen. If it does, think of the fun we'll have teaching them compatibility. For now let's stick to our plan, concentrate on each other."

He rose. "Have Essy stock the strawberry jam. It's thick and fruity, the way I like." Tucking the paper under his arm, he paused by her chair. He caught hold of her chin, leaned down, brushed his lips on hers. "Sweetheart, let's not argue. My mother defers to my dad. I wish you'd yield to me in these matters. We'd both be happier. Besides, you don't know what you want to do, so relax."

He asked when she was meeting Marybeth. She told him. "I'll pick you up after an hour. This way you won't get stuck."

He kissed the tip of her nose, patted her shoulder, then straightened up. Humming, he left the room.

Claire stifled the urge to scream. She loved him and wanted to kick his butt at the same time. She blamed his parents for his inflexible attitude, and vowed to keep trying to change it. In one respect she was lucky. He didn't philander. He'd planned his life and her place in it. Still, she wondered how many thousands of wives also subjugated their dreams for family and found a meaningful career in deference to their spouses. Plenty, according to the talk shows.

Absently she toyed with a lock of chestnut hair. She'd pushed at the wrong times, like now when he was on his way to work. When they returned from Hawaii, she'd find a time to earnestly, calmly, deliberately, diplomatically present her case.

Marriage involved compromise. Compromise and communication. For both partners . . .

At one o'clock Marybeth Frankel waited for Claire at a front table in the Cafe Rodeo across form Gucci's on Rodeo Drive. She wore her curly blond hair short, her blue dress short, her red nails long. She reviewed her copious background notes and sighed. There was a time she, like Claire, had lived north of the hotel, the golden triangle of exclusive real estate north of Sunset Boulevard, north of the famed Beverly Hills Hotel.

With luck she'd latch on to an influential, eligible man at Claire's party. To show her gratitude, she'd write a glowing article about the Brices. Even though she thought Colin was a pompous ass.

Fifteen minutes later, Claire entered the restaurant with eye-catching verve. In a fawn-colored silk dress, her leather purse slung over her shoulder, her rich dark tresses shifted in harmony to her gently swaying hips. Male patrons paused to admire her as she strolled by their tables with undulating, sensual grace.

After greeting Marybeth, Claire studied the menu, while Marybeth talked about the latest gossip making the Hollywood rounds, her lively blue eyes matching her animated chatter, halting when the waiter took their orders.

"Tell me about your necklace," Marybeth said at one point during their lunch of shrimp salad and iced tea. "Is the heart an heirloom?"

Claire fingered it. "My father gave it to me when I was little. It's my good luck charm."

"You don't need it. I can't imagine anyone living a more charmed life than yours."

"Please don't say that."

"Why? Are you superstitious?"

A frisson of fear ran through Claire. "I told you my father's flying to London in the morning. CNN's weatherman predicts snow for New York. I hope it holds off until after the plane departs."

"I hope so, too," Marybeth crooned sweetly, reaching into her large purse for a mini tape recorder.

Repeating her mantra that she'd do this galling thing to preserve marital peace, Claire trailed a finger down the side of her frosted glass and hoped her nose didn't grow like Pinocchio's.

"Before we begin, I hate to be the bearer of bad tidings. The party's canceled. It's last minute, but it's unavoidable. Colin's going away on business."

Disappointment drained the pink from Marybeth's round cheeks. Filled with remorse, Claire offered to tell anyone she knew connected with show business to contact Marybeth. Mouth pouting, blond curls bobbing, Marybeth said she welcomed any help she could get.

Marybeth conducted the fact-check with all the buoyancy of a rock at the bottom of the ocean. She'd charged a fortune on a new outfit to wear at the party.

"Claire, is there anything else I can use to flesh the article? Something current?"

Claire searched her brain. "I know!" she said with false bravado. "Highlight the charities. You'll help them, too."

For the next fifteen minutes she made an impassioned plea for her pet children's charities, citing statistics on poverty as it affected learning, the need for educational reform. Relief flooded through her when Colin pulled up to the curb and honked the horn.

"My master's voice." She bid Marybeth good-bye, then left money for the bill on the table. "Let me know when your article runs. I'm sure it will be wonderful."

Marybeth promised to send her free copies. She watched Claire get into the car, and her gaze locked with Colin's. The hairs on the back of her neck rose. He looked through her as if she weren't there.

She'd bet her bottom dollar that Claire hadn't canceled the party! Snatching the tape recorder, she dumped it back into her purse. If her editor heard the dullsville crap she'd listened to, she'd heave her and her fledgling career out the door.

Snapping her fingers to get the waiter's attention, she ordered a bourbon, then headed for the phone booth past the bar. Flipping through the yellow pages, she found the listing for caterers. On the third call, she hit it lucky. Saying she wanted to write an article about his firm's careful attention to exquisite detail, she asked which parties he was doing next.

"The Brices' tent party on Saturday."

Her fingers squeezed the receiver. Claire had lied. She knew intuitively that Colin was behind the ruse. According to the bragging caterer, the Brices' housekeeper had just phoned with additional names.

Steaming mad, Marybeth returned to her table. She tossed back the drink and gave herself a moment to calm down. She'd made a mistake going to Colin's office first. Now what? Damn, she needed a break. She ordered a second drink, sipping it slowly, wishing for a way to make the Brices pay for slighting her.

Two

THAT EVENING CLAIRE sat in front of her lighted mirror, a cup of chamomile tea on the dressing table. While she felt better for her decision to stop complaining about double standards and act, she had lingering guilt feelings with regard to Marybeth. Lunch went well, until she had nearly choked over her lie.

Tonight they were entertaining Sam Yamuto, and his adorable wife, Lia. Uncle Sam and Aunt Lia. She'd known her parents' friends since childhood. Fifteen years earlier at Pebble Beach Golf Club on the Monterey peninsula, the golf starter teamed Edward Jameson with Sam Yamuto. Following the round, the men made their way to the clubhouse, where, to their surprised delight and amusement, they found their wives gabbing like old friends, having introduced themselves in the lounge. The foursome ordered drinks. The conversation proved so enjoyable they met again for a leisurely dinner. In subsequent years, they planned joint vacations. While the avid golfers teed up at St. Andrews in Scotland; Dorado Beach, Puerto Rico; Hilton Head, South Carolina; and Brisbane, Australia, the women explored the countryside.

Colin slipped his cuff links in his shirt, knotted his red silk tie, then sat down to put on his shoes. "By 1990 it's projected there will be four point five billion square feet of shopping space in the country or eighteen square feet for every man, woman, and child. Sam's vital to my long-range

13

plans. Through him, I'll sign other Asians. They're the ones with deep pockets. Sam owns a large chunk of Tokyo's astronomically expensive Ginza district, more than Akio Sony. He thinks globally, but he's worried about a backlash toward Japanese investors. He's as publicity-shy as your father."

"Can you blame him?" Claire said. "Think of the threat of kidnappers." She outlined her lips with a lip brush, switched to a larger brush, blending shades of crimson and coral.

Colin stood behind her. The master bedroom suite had French skirted chairs, silk wall covering, and furniture upholstered in serene tones of peach and off-white.

"Which is another reason I didn't want Marybeth writing about us. I tried contacting your dad today. Have you spoken with him?"

She blotted her lips and discarded the tissue. "He's probably on his way to New York. Did you try the car phone?" When he nodded, she added, "He's spending the night at the Plaza. We'll catch him later. Why? Is there a problem?"

"Nothing major. The lawyer called this morning. There's a glitch in the zoning law. A section of the property backs a residential zone. You know me. I'll feel better once we clear the legalities and Sam signs the final papers."

"Don't fret. I know how hard you've worked, but I wouldn't worry. Sam's a true friend."

Colin stood, shaking down his pant leg. "Sweetheart, friendship has nothing to do with money."

He caressed her cheek, fleetingly, possessively. She gave him a tender smile, letting her gaze linger on his face. No wonder women envied her. He looked splendid in his navy blue custom-made suit and, she thought, fabulous without clothes. His hands were powerful, his fingers long and lean, his palms hard from years of playing paddle tennis.

As if sensing her thoughts, he squeezed her shoulder, his eyes sending hers a heated message. "Later," he said huskily. He'd made reservations at Wolfgang Puck's Spago, the noisy, popular Sunset Strip eatery that attracted movie stars, agents, and moguls.

"You know Lia. A trip to the States isn't complete unless she sees movie stars. She's anxious to taste the Jewish pizza she's read so much about in movie magazines."

Even people who gagged on caviar ordered the upscale pizza to be "in." Not listed on the menu, the pizza featured salmon, caviar, and crème fraîche.

Claire nodded. She dabbed perfume behind her ears and wrists, picked up her brush, applied long, vigorous strokes to her thick hair, deftly styling it in a chignon, and secured it with a clip.

She stepped into a pair of black pumps and checked her hose which contained tiny particles of shimmering gold threads.

"Earrings? Yes, no?"

His eyes skimmed over her beaded silk-georgette skirt and gold chiffon blouse with its softly draped halter top. "No. You're gorgeous. You do me proud."

She stroked his cheek. "Stop frowning. Don't worry about the zoning glitch. I'm sure Sam isn't."

She scooped up her leather purse and strode from the room, her hand in Colin's.

Across the continent in the South Bronx, in the section that Colin had read about in the *Times* that morning, Dr. Wendall Everett-Lawson studied his face in the cabinet mirror above the sink in his cluttered office. His patients knew him as Dr. Lawson. He had dropped the Everett for their benefit.

"Too much of a hyphenated mouthful," he told his parents.

Slashed across his forehead, beneath a shock of wild auburn hair that in the past year had started graying, two parallel psychedelic green lines ran approximately one inch apart. He dipped his index finger into a jar of red water-based paint. Letting the excess paint drop into the container, he drew a red line from the outer tip of his right eyebrow, down his right cheek, curving it slightly around his full-lipped mouth to end at the cleft in his square chin.

He duplicated the procedure on the left side of his face

and wiped his finger on the lip of the pot, saving each drop of paint for future use. Humming off-key, he washed and dried his hands and pitched the crumpled paper toweling over his shoulder into a wastepaper basket.

"Okay, how do I look?" he asked the man slouched on a brown Naugahyde couch amid piles of diapers.

Detective Sergeant Vito Malchesne extracted a tiny pink sneaker buried between the cushions. He put it into one of the shoe boxes on the floor, beneath a rack of children's clothes. Wendall's gifts for his poor patients depended on donations and job lots he purchased at discount.

Wendall preened. "I'm waiting. How do I look?"

He wore a white cotton coat studded with multicolored glass stones. A rubber-tipped tomahawk stuck out of the lower right pocket. A leather tie hung loosely from his neck. So did a stethoscope.

Vito snorted. "Like an unrefined jerk." He left the sofa for a chair and propped his feet on the edge of the nearby desk. "Why wear a costume?"

Wendall chucked him under the chin. Any other man who tried that would get his finger broken. "You, my precious, are tasteless. You are not a social arbiter. I happen to look terrific. See these glass beads?"

He pointed to his studded white doctor's coat. "The blue brings out the color of my sexy aquamarine eyes. The red adds drama. The green have pizzazz. The yellows are snazzy. My patients expect this fashion flair. The tomahawk is extra. Rosaria is bringing in Juanito. If I wear this getup, he'll let me give him his measles shot. So will the others. For that I let them bop me over the head. Fair payment. Needles hurt. So there."

"You're nuts. What did you make today?" Vito asked. A large pot of soup simmered on the electric stove in the corner.

"Mushroom barley."

"Give me some. I'm famished."

Wendall closed his eyes, breathing the aroma with a happy sigh. He dipped in a cup, wiped the sides, and brought it and a spoon to Vito.

In 1978 Vito Malchesne met Wendall in the emergency room of Columbia-Presbyterian Hospital in New York. Vito sat sketching a dying John Doe for possible identification. The artist was a shade under six feet tall, with a powerful frame and penetrating dark eyes. Vito earned the distinction of being the first male in his family to graduate from college. The word on the crime-infested streets was, "Don't mess with Malchesne." Despite the wry sense of humor, he was hard as nails if the situation warranted it.

Born with a photographic memory, Vito savored minutiae, collecting minuscule facts. He melded them into mental mosaics, stored them in his fertile brain. He relished solving old cases. He haunted dead police files the way other people voraciously devour mystery books. His IBM clone maintained a mountain of meticulous records. Magazines were piled high in his bachelor apartment. His dogged determination turned disparate facts into hot trails. His pursuits paid off. He helped send more than one long-time fugitive to the slammer. For this he'd earned a drawerful of police commendations.

He also taught composite art for the FBI and the police, familiarizing his students with the skills for reconstructing a skull from bone fragments and anthropological skills. This included head training, measurements of face, full and profile, position of the nose, set of the eyes, and dimensions of twenty-one facial points to determine skin thickness and race.

Wendall, whose curiosity and thirst for learning matched Vito's, pierced his concentration by pulling up a chair and asking a slew of questions. To get his job done, Vito humored him. Gradually the tolerance changed to respect. The men continued their discussion over lunch.

Afterward, Vito learned what he could about Wendall. The staff idolized the sunny icon. He boosted medical students' lagging confidence and dispensed tender loving care to his patients and their families. A twentieth-century Pied Piper, he gathered lifelong friends, especially among the female population, a talent that escaped Vito and one he desperately envied.

Within a week of their meeting, Vito dragged out the scrapbook he kept in his car. Knowing a picture was better than a thousand words, he used the graphic stills of the horrors that befell the South Bronx in it to enlist the help of good Samaritans. One picture, taken in 1977, showed President Carter at Charlotte Street amidst a sea of rubble and burned-out abandoned apartment buildings.

In the sixties and seventies, arsonists demolished businesses and over one hundred thousand apartment units and other dwellings, transforming neighborhoods into instant war zones. The peak year, 1976, recorded more than 33,465 fires of all kinds. By 1985, despite renovations and progress in rebuilding, the *Times* reported snafus. As in many cities, pockets of human misery served as mute testimony to society's ills.

"The fires," Vito explained to Wendall, "started for all the usual reasons: gang warfare, drugs, crime, the energy crisis, greed. Welfare families withheld rent. Landlords faced rising costs in rent-controlled apartments. Many withheld taxes, cut services. Arson let them scam insurance companies. Engine Company Eighty-two was kept busy. Druggies set fires to pick the bones—pipes, anything salable—of burned-out buildings."

Vito was assigned to the Forty-first Precinct, which by 1985 sat on a renovated block. Back when the torches were set, the precinct, the only building left standing, earned its nickname, Little House on the Prairie. In his office, above his cigar-burned oak desk, Vito hung a plaque with the official motto of Bronx County: *Ne Cede Malis:* Do Not Give Way to Evil.

"When my dad was a teenager, he slept beneath a shady oak in Crotona Park on hot summer nights. Our family picnicked on the banks of Indian Lake. The national and foreign media called the South Bronx a peacetime holocaust. How would you like it if the *Dictionary of American Politics* awarded your neighborhood the dubious distinction of 'the nation's most famous slum'?" he had asked, driving Wendall to the Bronx for a guided tour of the area under discussion.

Despite freezing cold weather, Wendall insisted on walking. He commiserated with doctors in nearby Lincoln Hospital. Fighting insufficient funds, mountains of red tape, urban violence, and the myriad illnesses that struck the poor, they were heavily overworked.

Over coffee, Wendall outlined his concept for a clinic. The facility would represent the first of other community health centers in the inner city and suburbs, where many poor people also lacked adequate health care, but didn't get media attention for their plight. It would treat walk-ins, accept those who fell through the insurance cracks.

During the dedication ceremonies, Wendall sat on a green metal folding chair, enjoying the sunshine. His proud parents, Ron and Kitty, sat beside him. Wendall inherited his passion for community service from his mother, his decisiveness from his father. From both he learned not to waste energy suffering fools. He lived by his code: People who breathe air without making a contribution on earth were self-indulgent. He had no use for snobs.

Seated on the dais, he chatted with Ed Logue and Father Gigante, two men committed to effecting change. He listened to Mayor Koch and Congressman Herman Badillo's laudatory speeches. In his remarks, Wendall stressed jobs, vigilant corporate, city, and government cooperation.

His blunt message: Cut the bureaucratic bullshit. Speed the pace of redevelopment.

Vito anchored idealism in reality. Let the big shots spout reform. The politicians left by stretch limo. Vito showed up at the clinic the following day insisting it have round-the-clock protection. For this he sought only one man.

Franklin Paggliani.

Twenty-two-year-old high school dropout Franklin "Piggy" Paggliani eminently qualified. His face, knifed in a fight, could give anyone a heart attack. A menacing scar, sliced grotesquely, started at the outer edge of his right eye, arced downward, and ended at the right corner of his mouth. He fine-tuned his powerful frame pumping weights. He streaked across a basketball court in Nikes, zapped opponents in Nintendo games, shot pool like a tiger shark.

"He's my man." Vito punched Wendall's arm.

Aghast, Wendall said no way would he let Piggy near the place, let alone protect Daria, the young receptionist whose job description covered just about everything, or him. He knew Piggy's reputation. "He's a thief. He steals what he wants."

"Shhh. Watch Papa and learn."

Vito, carrying a large taped carton, escorted Piggy into Wendall's office. The building reeked of fresh paint and disinfectant. The structure resembled a concrete bunker flanked by empty lots Wendall purchased from the city. The waiting room had blue metal folding chairs, children's toys, and a low table with crayons and coloring books. Barred windows faced the street.

Vito locked the office door, dragged a chair over for Piggy, and politely asked him to sit. He placed the carton on the desk. He asked Wendall for a knife. With it, he slit the tape.

"Okay, take a peek," he said to them. "Go ahead. Pick it up, Piggy. It's yours."

Piggy and Wendall peered inside. "Jesus!" Wendall cried.

Both men eyed Vito as if he had taken leave of his senses. A New York City cop freely offering an AK-47 assault weapon to a truant whose record dated back to elementary school didn't happen every day. Unless the cop had gone over the edge.

"You think I'm nuts?" Piggy snorted. Wendall breathed a huge sigh of relief and almost kissed his scarred cheek.

Vito had read Piggy's spotty school record, knew he had an IQ of 140, figured it was probably even higher. Piggy was a rare gem. A street fighter with smarts. Prepared to shoot mental craps, Vito unhitched his gun belt and laid his weapon on the table.

Wendall prayed they'd walk out alive, that the gun wasn't loaded. It was. Deadly proof Vito had lost his marbles. But then as he witnessed the dawning admiration on Piggy's face, he realized he was privy to a contest of wills between two mental gladiators.

"Anyone can whack a guy with one of these things.

Brains." Vito tapped two fingers to Piggy's head. "That's the trick. Some of us got them, some of us don't. Some of us got brass balls, some of us don't."

Piggy, a virtuoso with a wad of bubble gum, fired off a round of machine gun pops. Nervous and edgy, he danced away from the desk. "Yeah. Well, some of us are too fuckin' smart to let a cop slice his balls off."

Wendall danced over to his side

Vito shot Wendall a dirty look. He trapped Piggy's shoulders with an arm vise. "I'd hate to think of you as stupid. The doc can't operate without protection. Drug addicts will rob the place. Daria will get raped. It's a good bet they'll be murdered, not to mention innocent kids and their mamas. That's where you come in. You support the police. With your guys you're top gun. They don't know this shoots blanks. You do. There's the ultimate thrill, Pig Man. You work with us. You keep this place safe from a bunch of fuckin' losers. Give them your special look, Pig Man. Scare the shit out of them with that pretty mug of yours. Pass the word you command a specialized army."

Wendall rolled his eyes. He'd die caught in one of Piggy's gang wars. He might as well be measured for a coffin.

Vito removed layers of blue tissue paper from the box. He took out a black leather bomber jacket and held it up for inspection. First the front, then slowly turning it to the back. A dagger dripped bloodred leather drops, and *Wendall's Warriors* was emblazoned in big gold lettering.

"Try it on with these." He handed Piggy a pair of wraparound blue mirrored sunglasses.

Piggy put them on. As tenderly as you'd pick up a newborn, Piggy received the jacket from Vito's proffered hands. He sniffed the leather. His fingers caressed its soft skin. Closing his fist, muttering he didn't want his hands to dirty the lining, he slipped on the jacket.

Wendall was flabbergasted. He saw a fleeting flash of yearning in Piggy's eyes. Orphaned Franklin Paggliani stole with impunity. Yet he treated Vito's gift as if Christ himself anointed it and him. He seemed to sense Vito was doing more than giving him a present. He offered him a chance to

change his bleak destiny, find a meaningful future, not the
hopeless one bequeathed by his dying mother, who delivered him on a filthy back room cot in a dirty tenement after
a botched abortion attempt.

Franklin Paggliani was passed around, then dropped by
age ten. He lived by his wits. He thirsted for recognition, for
the intrinsic value of self-worth. Wendall bet the jacket was
the first gift he'd ever received in his life.

Piggy rolled his shoulders and cocked his head to glance
in the mirror. "Shit. You're asking me to head a fuckin'
Rambo platoon with my brains. Is that it, Detective?"

"That's it," Vito confirmed cheerfully. "Sly Stallone's an
actor. You're the real Rambo. Without you, the clinic's
doomed. Dead. Rigor mortis. Finis. Kaput. Made. I appreciate what the doc's doing for us. But you and I know he
doesn't know squat."

Vito shot Wendall a warning look not to interfere.

"Hell, Pig Man, you remember the blackout back in July
of 'seventy-seven. Here's a few stats. Looters stormed four
hundred seventy-three stores and started three hundred
seven fires. The doc's anesthetized for life without your
protection. There is no one who can touch you. Not for
brains. Not for balls. Not for leadership. You're my choice,
Franklin. My only choice." He slapped Piggy's back.
"You're the king."

Piggy's salvation notwithstanding, Wendall didn't want
any part of his pal's insanity. Let him play social worker on
someone else's turf. He hoped Piggy would steal the
jacket—after he told Vito to fuck off.

Piggy didn't. Born and raised in purgatory, Piggy and
Vito understood each other. Wendall, for all his noble
intentions, hailed from the wrong side of the tracks, too far
up the societal scale thanks to a warm belly, hot meals, and
loving parents who nurtured him from conception. He had
never been bitten by rats as he lay in a crib. Never been
passed around, then told at ten he'd worn out his welcome.
As heir to the Everett-Lawson fortune, Wendall had
achieved his majority blessed with a brilliant mind and
healthy body. After a private-school education at Choate, he

enrolled in Columbia. His flawless skills displayed his surgical expertise. But it was his great heart, his ability to care and listen, to devote several afternoons a week in the practice of family medicine in the South Bronx clinic, that set him apart from others, that made him celebrated.

A child of the ghetto, Piggy understood, without knowing Wendall's privileged background, why Vito excluded him from the decision. He didn't belong. His eyes lacked the wariness of a street fighter.

Vito leaned forward, his piercing eyes pinning Piggy's dark irises.

"For you?" Piggy asked. His liberation teetered on a spiritual high wire.

Vito gripped his hand. "For you, too. I believe in you."

They shook hands. *Mano a mano.* In many ways they shared similar values and views. Wendall witnessed a rare rapprochement of kindred souls. After the handshake the men rapidly settled the details. Piggy promised to muster his army from among his loyal gang. Vito reserved final approval.

"No murderers, Pig Man. No one who tasted blood." Vito promised that when possible, he would defer to Piggy in front of his troops.

Wendall offered to remove Piggy's scar.

"Nah. Thanks anyway, Doc."

Wendall understood another fact. Piggy's puss was his trademark.

Piggy's and the Warriors' esteem rose in direct proportion to the compliments Vito and Wendall heaped upon them since that day.

Two months ago, Wendall had sat with a *Post* reporter, who interviewed him when the clinic marked its sixth anniversary. He called Piggy. Affectionately clapping his broad shoulders, he credited Franklin Paggliani for the clinic's excellent safety record. He praised him for earning his high school GED. He omitted saying Vito badgered Piggy into it.

Piggy mugged for the camera. His one moment of depression came when Wendall seized the gun he cradled in his arms. The chary cameraman, who accompanied the reporter, set his eyes to the viewfinder. He jumped as if shot when Piggy rat-a-tat-tatted a wad of bubble gum.

Right now Piggy was outside. Vito finished the soup with lip-smacking appreciation. "It's good."

Wendall snatched the empty cup. "That's the best you can say? 'Good.' It's a nutritional masterpiece. I'd like to remind you that considering your volatile occupation, you should kiss the ground I walk on. You never know when it'll be you I sew up."

Vito snatched a lollipop from a plastic jar on the desk.

Wendall rapped his knuckles. "Leave the red ones for the kiddies. Are we meeting Louisa and her friend at Harry's?"

"No. Louisa's sick," he said glumly, choosing an orange lollipop. "So's her friend."

Wendall's brows hiked, rearranging the green lines on his forehead. "Sounds like Louisa's sick of you."

"I'm sick of her, too. I'm sick of all women."

Wendall tutted. "Impossible. Lust lines your loins. Not to worry. I'll play soothing music for you tonight."

Vito rolled his eyes. "Soothing! Harry should toss the Baldwin for his own safety. One of these days some doper will hear you play and pull a gun. I'll have to shoot him. Dead. That leads to a shitload of extra paperwork. And me testifying. For what? To hear your lousy renditions of the 'Wedding March' or 'Chopsticks' or Brahms' 'Lullaby.' Harry bribes his patrons with free drinks whenever you play. It's a wonder they don't demand bicarb and earplugs."

Wendall grinned. A lot Vito knew. He paid for the drinks, not Harry. Harry, the genial redheaded owner of Harry's Bar, emigrated to the United States from Ireland at the age of twenty-six. He removed all traces of the previous owner's Italian affiliation, painted the walls white and decorated them with Irish and American flags. Travel posters beckoned the patrons to Ireland, and the place mats were shaped like four-leaf clovers.

Harry, his wife, Molly, and their two grown sons operated the thriving family establishment. Due to its postage-size dance floor, he advertised his establishment as a cabaret.

Several nights a week, patients permitting, Wendall ended his day entertaining his cult following. The faithful gleefully gasped, groaned, clapped, and cheered. He played so badly, and he loved the piano so much, he was a legend in his own time.

The *Village Voice* ran an affectionately glowing article about him. The conclusion, generally conceded as on the money, read: Humor the plastic surgeon, the city needs him.

"You play for stoned sickos," Vito grumbled.

"They adore me. So does Harry. I'm practicing a new piece. The *Appassionata.*"

"You're looney. How did you ever graduate Columbia? With honors yet?"

Wendall's glance was swift, encompassing, the bond between the two strengthened by their common concern for life. "Same way you fooled the John Jay College of Criminal Justice. How did it go today?"

Vito leaned his head back. "Normal shootings and robberies. We fished a murder victim out of the East River. A boy. He couldn't be more than ten." He sighed heavily. "Some schmuck officer didn't protect the crime scene. Tomorrow I'll sketch the corpse, fix his little smashed face, eliminate the knife cuts, put back his missing eye. I'm going to get the person who did this. What about you? Did you interview Peter Ramirez?"

Wendall maintained a private practice. He kept a thin roster of assistant doctors, welcomed more. "Peter's good. Next year he'll give us two days a week. If things go okay, he may sign on full time. I hope so. Daria's dying for him to come here. She nearly fainted when she saw him."

"With all the crap that loudmouth wears on her face, I bet he fainted."

"Don't be nasty. Daria's a little loud, that's all. She'll learn. Be nice to her. Help her gain confidence. Her father never married her mother."

"So what else is new? I can't help it. She bugs me. She reads your medical journals, spouts off like she's a doctor. If she's not doing that, she's reading a tabloid."

"What's it your business?"

"She talks about everything she reads. She's hooked on Hollywood. Tell me something twice and it's memorized. I dream about it. I'll buy you a subscription to one of those rags. You'll know what agony is."

"Wear earplugs."

Now twenty-one, Daria Flores had walked into the clinic the week before its dedication ceremony, said she lived in the area, knew most of the people. Could he use help? For a good salary, of course.

Wendall checked out the lacquered beehive hairdo, heavy blue eye shadow, Cleopatra black eyeliner, tight skimpy clothes, and platform heels. He saw a short girl trying to look taller, and beyond that the terrified hope she failed to hide in her dark eyes that unless she raised herself out of a horrible situation, she'd be stuck forever. He asked two questions: Did she like children? Did she do drugs? She said yes to the first, no to the second with such haughty disdain he believed her. He hired the sixteen-year-old on the spot, paid her handsomely, never regretted it. She worked part-time until she graduated high school.

He couldn't imagine the clinic without her services.

Wendall opened a locked desk drawer, then retrieved a manila envelope containing an empty revolver, three loose bullets, and his accident report. He slid the envelope across the desk.

"Larry Golden shot himself in the thigh cleaning his unlicensed thirty-eight."

Vito took the envelope. "Tell me some good news."

"I delivered a fat baby boy and treated six pregnant girls."

Vito sucked the lollipop. "Just what the taxpayers need. Six more child-mothers on welfare."

Wendall poked his head out his office door and asked Daria to send the first patient into the examining room.

"Come on, Vito. You entertain the monsters' mommies while I work."

At nine-thirty that night Wendall's beeper went off. At first he thought his stomach was rumbling. He called the hospital.

"Chuck asked me to stop by," he said to Vito, speaking of their mutual friend, radiologist Chuck Morino. "A man wrapped his Mercedes around an abutment going forty miles per hour. The air bag didn't open. He wasn't wearing his seat belt. It's a miracle he's alive."

Vito put on his overcoat. "Call Chuck back. Tell him I'm going into shock. I need food."

Wendall locked the medicine chest. "You're a bottomless pit. I said I'd come. The patient's lucky the trauma team reached him during the golden hour—the sixty minutes when his chances of survival are greatest. You go ahead. I'll meet you at Harry's." Vito refused.

Wendall removed his war paint, washed, combed his hair, and put on his coat. They came outside to falling snow.

"Have you heard the weather forecast, Piggy?"

"Yeah. We're in for an inch or two by morning. They're calling for slippery road conditions. Drive carefully."

"Yes, Mother." Wendall stowed the medicine chest on the backseat. He drove the old Pontiac into the city. To the casual observer, the heap looked ready for the junkyard. Beneath its hood, the engine purred. He stored his snazzy, sparkling clean white Corvette, affectionately named Ludwig for his idol, Beethoven, in his family's garage in Groton, Connecticut.

Considering the transport of drugs risky, Vito put his gun on his lap. He ripped off the paper on a Hershey chocolate almond bar, stuffing the wrapper into his pocket that bulged with candy wrappers. He snapped the chocolate in two, sharing half.

"I've known you for years. How the hell do you do it?"

Vito interrupted Wendall's mental keyboard finger exercises. He usually warmed up with one or two mental selections from Czerny's *Practical Method for Beginners on the Pianoforte*. Maneuvering around ruts and potholes, the Pontiac bounced and bumped along the Cross Bronx Expressway.

"What's your problem?"

"Women adore you. You love them. Take Marilyn, for instance."

"Ah, yes. Sweet Marilyn, a gorgeous chorus girl whose shapely legs go to her armpits."

"I hate you. Marilyn proposes to you. You refuse. You offer to end the relationship. She refuses. She takes you however she can get you. She's not the only one. Once an affair ends, you and the lady remain kissing friends. You don't brag you're stinking rich. Women love you for yourself. So what am I doing wrong? You're a skinny, ugly thing. What's your secret?"

"I'm a devotee of Dr. Ruth's sex talks," Wendall said, deadpan.

"This isn't funny. I need answers."

Vito's bravado masked a basic shyness with the opposite sex. Beneath his macho facade beat the heart of a sensitive artist. His sporadic love life formed a continual topic of discussion.

They crossed over the Harlem River into Manhattan. Wendall cracked the window. "All right. The idea is to show a woman your compassionate nature. Romance her. Before I make love I need to like the woman. If she feels liked and loved, it helps her relax."

"What the hell kind of secret is that?"

Wendall chuckled. "You miss the point. If you help her relax, she's ready. Then she helps you. It's a stimulating, satisfying scenario. Quality not quantity counts."

Vito scowled. "Are you saying I'm a wham bam, thank you ma'am type?"

Wendall gasped in mock horror. "Please don't ask me to visually confirm or deny your technique. You might try dropping the term *gioia*. Calling a woman a little onion isn't a term of endearment. *Picola* sounds better. In matters of love, a woman prefers to think of herself as a man's treasure, not an onion in need of peeling."

Vito colored. "What do you call a woman?"

Wendall chortled. "Anything but wife."

Vito switched the topic to Wendall's mother, Kitty, whom he had met helping the Children's Fresh Air Fund, one of her pet projects. She had adopted Vito as her second son.

"Better start thinking about it. Kitty wants to be a grandmother."

Wendall sighed. "She knows better than to hound me." He turned left onto Broadway. "I've never met a woman I'd want to marry."

Vito reached in his breast pocket for a cigar. Wetting the tip, he broke the end, twirled it in his mouth, sniffed it, then applied a match. Contentedly puffing, the acrid cigar smoke swirled around his face, softening it. A 747 jet swooped low overhead, heading into Kennedy Airport.

"You're an only child, Wendall. You're thirty-six. It's no wonder she pesters you. I have brothers and sisters for buffers."

Wendall peered warily at the pistol, at the cigar's glowing tip. "Put the stinking cigar out and stash the gun. Those things tend to fire."

He parked in the lot at the corner of 165th Street and Fort Washington Avenue. With the brisk wind whipping them, they sprinted across the street, passing the site of the Milstein Hospital scheduled to open in 1990. They hurried into Presbyterian Hospital, taking the stairs to Chuck's third-floor office. Wendall tossed his coat onto a chair. "Okay, we're here. Who's the patient?"

"Edward Jameson. He's from Connecticut. Do you know him?"

"No."

Three

"WHERE IN CONNECTICUT?" Wendall asked.

"Stamford. We found Jameson's airplane ticket, dated tomorrow morning, in his coat pocket. He was going to London. It's with the rest of his personal staff in the envelope."

Wendall read the trauma team's reports, scanned the medications given, noting an injection of lydocaine one percent to numb the wounds. "What about the surgical release?"

"He signed it."

Vito emptied the manila envelope, poked through Jameson's belongings: a wallet containing three thousand dollars, Visa platinum, more credit cards, a pair of broken eyeglasses, the airplane ticket, and a picture. He held it under the desk light. The snapshot portrayed two women. Dressed stylishly, the attractive blue-eyed older woman's blond hair was pulled back, framing a delicate face. She had an arm around the waist of a grinning, younger woman with dark, shoulder-length hair. Barefoot, she wore skimpy white shorts, a halter top, and a necklace with a gold charm.

Vito whistled. He flipped the picture over, whistled again. "Taken at Claire's in Beverly La-de-da Hills. Picture this, guys. A ten-bedroom Mediterranean-style villa, leaded beveled windows, atrium, private security guards, rottweiler attack dogs, security cameras facing the street, maids, butler, four full-time gardeners, and a chauffeur to cart them around in their Rolls when the poor darlings tire of driving their Bentleys. Oh, yeah, an Olympic-size pool with its own guest house for changing clothes, clay and grass tennis courts, a temperature-controlled wine cellar, screening room, modern gym, and gourmet kitchen off the master suite."

"Jesus! What wound him up?" Chuck asked, clipping a set of X rays on the lighted viewer box.

"He's a fan of the tabloids." Wendall took the picture from Vito's hand.

He glanced briefly at the older woman, longer on the curvaceous younger woman. Compelling eyes, slim waist, softly rounded hips, long coltish legs. Sandals. Painted toenails.

He handed it back. "Lovely. Who is she?"

Vito swiped the snapshot. "*Lovely*. Notice the interest, Chucko. Winnie's on the prowl."

"Oh, shut up. I never mix business with pleasure. Bad form. Who's the beauty, Chuck?"

"Jameson's daughter. Claire Brice."

Vito sighed theatrically. "The best ones are taken."

"Make allowances for him, Chuck. Vito thinks below his belt. Did you call London, tell Mrs. Jameson?"

"Jameson nixed it. I've got the daughter's phone number. He said he'll phone tomorrow. Fat chance in his condition. He's neuro stable. As we speak, he's in OR having his spleen removed. He's got a broken nose."

"Telescoped?"

"Yes."

"Too bad. He'll need a skin graft in about six months. Bones are easier to fix than cartilage," he explained when Vito asked why.

Wendall studied Jameson's body and skull X rays. "Okay, gentlemen. Mr. Jameson also has four broken ribs. He suffered a Lefort Two fracture of the midface. The orbital floor fracture is responsible for the dropped eye socket. ER's report cites extensive lacerations, contusions. The patient's had prior implants. That accounts for the opaque areas on the films over the malars and jaw." He checked the report. "The trauma exposed the implants. They need to come out to prevent infection. Besides being black-and-blue with a face as fat as a beach ball, raccoon eyes, pain from his broken ribs, fractured tibia, cuts and lacerations, and recovering from a splenectomy, I'd say Jameson's in excellent shape."

Vito said he didn't envy him.

Wendall agreed. "Who wants to look forward to six weeks with his teeth bound together? He'll sound like a ventriloquist, drink through a straw, swear he resembles his worst nightmare."

Vito checked the driver's license. "Hell, he's fifty-five years old. He wears a gap filler," he said, holding up the denture. "He's not an actor, not in public life. I can't imagine a man being so vain as to have a face-lift and wear a gap filler."

Wendall helped himself to a cup of coffee from the machine on a table in the corner, then stirred in two teaspoons of creamer. "Vanity isn't necessarily the determining factor for facial surgery. Lots of men have it done. It's possible he's had a prior accident."

Vito showed a professional's interest in the medical narration. He stared at the areas of lucency on the X rays.

"Male vanity sucks. You wouldn't catch me dead getting a face-lift."

Wendall sipped his coffee. "It wouldn't help you."

"Thanks," Vito said wryly. "I need a favor. I'd like to draw Jameson at bedside, record him on my camcorder."

"What for?"

Vito sat on the desk. "Practice. Before you say no, there's a psychological plus for him, too. I'm scheduled to teach a course on computer imaging, which is cute since I need more training myself. Your guy's alive. He's an ideal subject. Suppose he decides he doesn't want another face-lift? I'll show him how he'll look without it, but healed. The software's amazing. I saw a demonstration at a computer convention and ordered the program. Given police paperwork, I should have it next week. What percentage of Jameson's original face would you expect to see without facial reconstruction?"

"Factoring for age, eliminating the malar, jaw, and chin

implants, the chin and jowl formation will recede. Once the swelling goes down . . . about eighty-five percent."

"I bet the computer gets closer to ninety-five. The program takes a subject to any age, forward or backward. What do you say?"

Wendall hesitated.

"Look, it's worth a try. I'll show you how to work the program. It's good experience."

Wendall used computers as a tool to help patients decide on elective surgery, and for other reasons. If the software was as good as Vito said, he'd buy it.

"Okay."

He finished the coffee, switched off the X-ray viewer box, slipped the films in their protective jackets, then dialed OR for an update on Jameson.

"His spleen's out. They're traching him for me now. I'll contact his daughter later."

Taking Jameson's envelope, he asked for Claire's phone number, then glanced out the window. "Snow's heavier. What do you think, Vito? Harry's or home?"

"Your call. You're driving."

"Harry's," he said, pocketing the slip of paper with Claire's phone number. "I'll meet you in the cafeteria."

Wendall stared at his patient and shook his head at the waste. Jameson had lost a fair amount of soft tissue. His puffy face did justice to a Hollywood makeup artist's rendering for a color horror movie. Had Jameson worn his seat belt, he wouldn't be in this fix. Working efficiently, he removed the exposed implants and wired the jaw. Later he joined Vito until ICU called to say his patient was out of anesthesia.

Jameson's bed was in the far corner. He was hooked up to an IV, dripping four mg's of morphine for pain. Wendall drew up a chair, leaned forward, and identified himself and his medical speciality. Wendall repeated the name of the hospital, knowing that memory lapses and shock often carry a patient over the first hurdle. He assured Jameson he would recover, then told him why he wired his jaw.

"Your family needs to know."

Jameson lifted his right hand, motioning with it as if writing. Wendall handed him a pencil, found paper and a magazine to lean it on, while a groggy Jameson scribbled.

"Not Babs." The letters wobbled. The pencil slipped through his fingers.

Wendall lifted Jameson's hand. "Tap your finger on my hand if Babs is your wife." Jameson tapped. "Sir, we saw the airplane ticket. We know you planned to fly to London in the morning. You told the doctor that your daughter lives in California. I'll phone her."

Jameson drifted in and out of consciousness. Wendall waited. He repeated much of what he had said, adding, "I'll phone Claire. Please tap my hand if you understand."

Jameson moaned. A tear rolled down his cheek. His finger tapped Wendall's hand. Assuring he would get better, Wendall left his patient. He found an empty office and dialed California. A maid said Mrs. Brice was out for the evening. Rather than scare her, he didn't identify himself, said he'd call back later.

A half-inch of snow covered the ground when he and Vito got into the Pontiac for the drive to the Village. Vito accepted Wendall's invitation to spend the night at his house.

Wendall had purchased his two-story, four-bedroom house on the Upper East Side near Sutton Place from his good friend and former colleague, David Orchin, after the man Orchin thought would buy it couldn't meet the loan requirements. David practiced medicine in San Francisco.

"Two steaks, medium rare," Harry said to his son, greeting them. "I had the piano tuned."

Thinking about playing, Wendall doubly enjoyed the steak, steaming-hot baked potato slathered in butter, green beans, and salad dripping in Roquefort dressing. Draining his beer, he wiped his mouth, ascended the tiny platform, and sat down on the piano bench. He ran a chord over the keys. He was in heaven.

Vito and Harry fled to the kitchen.

Half an hour later, Vito couldn't stand any more. He

dragged Wendall off the bench to good-natured applause. "I was really good tonight, wasn't I?" Wendall teased.

Vito shoved him out the door.

The slippery roads looked deceptively serene. The sky looked light. People crunched by in boots. The *Daily News* delivery truck driver tossed a bundle of newspapers in front of a corner stationery store.

Once home, the tired duo headed for separate rooms. Wendall undressed, then dialed the hospital to check on Jameson's condition. His temperature had gone up to one hundred one degrees, not unusual after his experience. Opening the envelope containing Claire's picture and phone number, Wendall touched something Vito missed before. A second picture.

Taken when she was about ten, her dark hair braided, she wore a finely tailored red dress, shiny patent leather shoes, and white, lace-trimmed anklets. She looked seriously into the lens. Her large green eyes challenged the viewer to see beyond her pretty dress.

He flipped the picture. There was writing on the back.

I love you, Daddy.

Not more than I.

Yes.

No!

Yes! Yes! Yes!

IMPOSSIBLE!!!!

Stubborn, he thought, imagining her dashing off the script like a game they played.

He dialed. A woman answered.

Wendall identified himself and asked to speak with Mrs. Brice. A honeyed voice said she was Claire Brice. He introduced himself. As gently as he could, he broke the news.

"Accident! Oh, God, no! Is he dead?"

"He's alive," he stated firmly. "He is in no imminent danger."

"Imminent?"

"Based on my experience, I expect him to fully recover.

He's in intensive care. The surgeon removed his spleen." He explained it stopped internal bleeding.

"Oh, dear." She gasped.

He said the ICU staff was monitoring him.

She asked when she could speak with him.

"Wait until tomorrow. He'll be happy to hear from you."

"Please tell me everything."

A phone was a miserable way to hear about an accident. Had he been with her, he could have made it easier. Eye contact helped.

"His car has an air bag. How could this happen?" she asked, perplexed.

"He didn't wear his seat belt. Without it the air bag doesn't open."

"He's usually so careful." She took a sharp breath, and he imagined her struggling for composure. "Did you know my father before tonight?"

A blast of icy air shot through the window. Wendall hiked a blanket over his shoulders. "No, I was called in on the case."

"By whom?"

"The radiologist, Dr. Morino."

There was a pause. "What's your speciality?"

"Plastic surgery."

Her voice cracked. "Oh my god. My father's handsome face."

"He'll be fine," he assured her, speaking quietly, hoping to temper her agitation.

"Please tell my father I love him. Tell him we're coming. Naturally we'll expect him to receive the best medical attention. We'll need second opinions. Please prepare a list of physicians you would use for yourself or a member of your family. My father prefers light, airy, cheerful surroundings—a suite or a room with a view of a grassy area and the Hudson River. He'll need round-the-clock private nurses. Would you see to it, Doctor? May I have the correct spelling of your name and your office address?"

His trouble, he decided, after the call ended, was his active imagination. Show him a beautiful woman's picture, and he built a whole movie script around her. Claire Brice disappointed him. She robbed him of his warm, budding speculations. He'd seen promise in her eyes. He felt cheated, sorry he'd wrongly interpreted her pictures, ascribing qualities she didn't possess. He vowed to conquer his bad habit of letting his fertile imagination run rampant.

He lowered the window, then got into bed. He looked hard and long at Claire's pictures one last time. A suite with a view of the river! He chuckled. Who did she think he was? A hotel reservation clerk?

Yawning, he switched off the light.

Dr. Lawson's phrase "no imminent danger" burned in Claire's brain. She had a mental picture of her father fighting for his life, his jaw muzzled, unable to speak, to ask for help. Sobbing, wishing a magic carpet could transport her to his side, she dropped her head against Colin's chest.

"Dr. Lawson wired Dad's jaw shut. I don't trust the phrase 'no imminent danger.'"

Colin's lips brushed her forehead. "You're driving yourself crazy for nothing. If he says your father's doing a jig, would you believe him? He gave us encouraging news. Let's be grateful he's alive."

Putting her arms around Colin's waist, she lifted her sodden lashes. "I am. It's such a shock. I have you, thank God, but Mother's alone. Overseas yet. How will I break the news to her? She'll ask if I know Dr. Lawson. I can't recommend him. I don't know him or his reputation. We don't know the surgeon who removed Dad's spleen. We know nothing of the care he's receiving. First the shock of the fire, now this." She was referring to an electrical fire that had gutted a room in her parents' home six months earlier. "I remember how upset she was when the fire destroyed all her picture albums. She's never forgiven herself for not putting the negatives into a vault for safekeeping. That's minor compared to this." She sighed. "I wish you'd come with me."

His expression was compassionate and loving. "I'll join you as soon as I finalize things with Sam. If he learns your father suffered a serious accident, he might want us to wait. The Japanese are a cautious race."

Baffled, she shook her head. "He's Dad's friend."

"Don't swear for Sam. There's too much at stake. Your father wants this, too. We both see the Japanese investment as important to the future."

She sniffled. "You keep saying that. What does one thing have to do with another?"

He wiped a tear from her cheek. "I learned a long time ago not to leave things to chance. To increase our profit margin and assure prompt delivery, I prepaid many of our suppliers. Considering the size of the mall, that's a huge investment. I'll pay us back when the loans come through, but I'd rather not have a delay." Colin brushed the hair from her forehead. "Sweetheart, I'm not saying Sam would cancel, only if, God forbid."

Frightened, her hand tightened on his arm. "Say it. You mean if God forbid my father dies."

He gathered her close. "There's the possibility Sam might think the company would hit a quagmire without your father's orderly transference. He sees him as the head of the firm. I know you love Sam and Lia. Set that aside and listen. Orientals have zero loyalty in business. They think they're superior. They're suspicious by nature. You can't tell what they're thinking. I know more than you in these matters. We can't jeopardize this deal. We've got to do whatever it takes."

Shaking her head, she eased from his embrace. Despite Colin's impassioned plea, his argument didn't feel right. Sam was a dear man. He okayed the specs. Knowing him, she couldn't accept Colin's argument. Not this time.

"Sam's not heartless," she said, arguing against his fixation. "This could backfire, work against you. He'd be shocked if you weren't with me."

Colin's tone took on an edge of controlled exasperation. "You're understandably upset. Just this once, see this from my viewpoint, without a debate. Understand when I tell you that friendship and business don't mix. We're talking about our future. It's what I've worked years for. A foothold in the door with Japanese investors. I'll finally be out from beneath your father's shadow. It's time for the next generation."

She stared at him, seeing his vision for himself burning brightly in his eyes. "Is this all you think about? How it relates to you? Never mind family or being there for me when I need you. This morning you spoke about us as a team."

"We are," he said swiftly. "I am thinking of us, and of your parents, too. It's my job to carry on."

She shuddered. "If Dad dies, you'll be president. You'll need an heir then, won't you?"

"We planned on children," he said evasively.

Her eyes narrowed. "Does this mean I won't have to wait until I'm thirty?"

"It would change things," he said cautiously.

"I thought so!" She fumed. "Let's not worry about making a good impression on clients. If Dad dies, you'll be president. If he lives, we stick to your timetable. Why make me or him happy until you decide it's expedient for us to start a family? I'll tell you what! If he dies, we'll crown you company president at the gravesite. That way we can go from the open grave to bed!"

Colin gripped her upper arms, shaking her. "Claire, goddamnit, stop!"

She shook him off. "I have to pack."

She threw a suitcase onto the bed. Yanking open a bureau drawer, she snatched lingerie, slammed the drawer shut, and tossed the garments into her luggage. From the temperature-controlled cedar chest she took her sable and dropped it onto a chair.

"How did we get from the accident to this? I'm going to overlook your insult. You're upset."

Tears blurred her eyes. "Don't patronize me. Do you think I'd let anything stop me if the situation was reversed? My priorities are straight. Are yours? What's to stop you from asking your father to fill in for you?"

"It's unfair. He's never been a part of this mall. He'd have to study the specs, meet with me to know what's been going on. Does compounding the tragedy make sense? Stop and think. Your father initiated the project. I'm carrying the ball. Ask yourself if he'd want me to drop everything and fly to New York. Dr. Lawson said he's in no imminent danger. Don't twist his meaning. Believe the man."

Claire halted. The bed was strewn with clothes she didn't intend to take. She was too distraught to think straight, and she realized it. Perhaps Colin was right. She'd been hard on him, unfairly taken her worries out on him.

She dragged a hand over her forehead. "You're right." Her voice faltered. "It's no excuse, but I'm so scared."

Colin heaved an audible sigh of relief. His voice was now a rich, mellow caress. "I'll come as soon as I can. I promise."

He dialed London. Unable to reach Babs at the Claridge Hotel, they decided against leaving a message with the concierge or with British Airways at Heathrow Airport for fear of scaring her.

Claire computed the time zones. "I'll be airborne when she's due to meet Dad's plane. It arrives six-twenty P.M. London time. That's ten-twenty our time, one-twenty New York time. Her friends live in the Mayfair section. She could be spending the night with one. Try Cee-Cee. She'll help us. We'll ask her to be with Mom when we tell her the news."

The housekeeper informed them the Evanses left town for the day. They were due back the following day. Colin left word about the accident, saying it was vital Mrs. Evans not mention it to Babs should she phone. He stressed it was urgent they speak or, if they missed each other, would she please contact Claire at the Plaza Hotel in New York?

"I promise I'll keep trying until I get her. It's going to be all right."

"I worry about Mom."

"Are we okay?" he asked, tipping up her face.

She nodded, letting him wrap his arms around her. A flash of unaccustomed alarm went through her as if she were about to sail alone on an uncharted sea. It was a strange feeling. Her heart pounded. Her mouth went dry. She started shaking.

"Easy," he murmured. "You're so tense."

He kissed her forehead. He kissed her lips, delving his tongue into her mouth. He kept on kissing her until he felt her awakening response. He cupped her buttocks, bracing her tightly against him. His lips found the pulse at her neck. He licked it, felt her involuntary tremor. She let him undress her. He undressed, too, slipping into bed beside her, drawing her naked body next to his beneath the cool silk sheets. His skillful hands massaged the tense knots in her back, relaxing them one by one, replacing it with a different kind of tension.

His kisses took on a lover's ardor. She could feel the frantic clamor of her heart, and she squeezed her eyes shut, kissing him with a wild intensity, as if by doing that she'd stop time, blot out reality.

Arching her hips, she let him love her, acutely aware that life was precious, snuffed out in a precarious instant. Instinctively her body responded to his in an ancient rhythm. Quelling her lingering doubts, she tightened her arms around him. The labyrinth of despair slipped from her shoulders.

Colin was her husband. He anchored her hopes and dreams. She loved him. They cared for each other. Nothing was more precious, not even her restless desire for a career.

Digging her fingernails into his muscled back, she welcomed his plunging prowess. Each masterful stroke brought her more outside herself, further away from her terrible pain.

Her whole body trembled as he caressed her secret place, working his magic to rob her of thought. His strokes came faster, deeper. Desperate to reach the place where conscious thought disappeared in exquisite ecstasy, she clung to him.

He didn't disappoint her. He made it happen. She burst apart. She came and came, the shock waves bucking her lissome body. He held her close, his breath mingling with hers. He dropped a kiss on her forehead.

"Thank you," she murmured.

"My pleasure," he said warmly, holding her until the aftershocks subsided.

He rose from the bed, coming back with a damp washcloth and a towel. "Stay in bed. This is the best sleep you can have. I promise to come as soon as I can. We'll talk daily until then."

Her heavy eyelids drifted shut. "I lied to Marybeth for nothing."

He drew the covers over her shoulders. "Not for nothing, sweetheart. I've been thinking. We invited the Yamutos to the dinner party. You heard Lia when we were with them tonight. When she found out we expect Bob Hope, she couldn't wait to accept."

"But if I'm not here?" Claire mumbled

"I'll say you had root canal, you're running a fever. I'll make some excuse. Essy will help. In a week or so it won't matter. We'll have the agreement locked up. The Yamutos think your father's leaving tomorrow for a second honeymoon. If Sam learns the truth, we tell him we didn't want anyone to know until we knew the extent of your father's injuries."

She yawned. "Okay, don't cancel. Make my apologies. Handle it however you think best."

"You looked very beautiful tonight, darling. Lia looked at movie stars, but Sam's eyes were on you. I'm glad. You're mine. It makes me proud for people to see my beautiful wife."

It seemed as soon as she closed her eyes, the alarm clock went off. Waking instantly, she jumped out of bed. Colin was already dressed. Hearing a familiar humming noise, she peered out the window. In an area close to her favorite flower garden, the gardener mowed the lawn in neat crisscross rows. On a wrought-iron patio table there was a basket of freshly cut red- and apricot-colored roses.

She showered, coming back into her room with the scent of French milled soap and Arpege lingering on her skin. Essy brought a tray of coffee, juice, and rolls. Although in her early sixties, her smooth olive complexion and lustrous black hair made her look only fifty. Colin briefed her on the situation. Upon hearing the shocking news, she assured

Claire not to worry about a thing at home. She'd care for Colin.

Claire turned the TV to the weather station. New York was gripped by cold weather. Snow covered the ground and more was predicted. For the trip she chose a peridot green cashmere sweater, black woolen slacks, and comfortable shoes. She brushed her hair, leaving it loose so that she could rest her head comfortably on the seat.

Colin dialed London's Claridge Hotel. The concierge reported that Mrs. Jameson left a while ago.

"We'll try again from the car. If I can't reach her," Claire said, "please keep trying. Don't tell her about Dad's accident. Find out her itinerary. We'll make sure Cee-Cee's there, too."

"I will. I'll call my parents, too."

At LAX, she hugged Colin, asked him to join her as soon as he could, then rushed for her plane. She gave herself a good mental shake. She was Edward Jameson's daughter. The Jamesons were made of sterner stuff.

"Welcome aboard, Mrs. Brice."

"Junie!" she cried, delighted to see June Lamont, the stewardess. They'd spoken enough times at thirty-seven-thousand feet in the air to qualify as more than acquaintances. "I'm so glad to see a familiar face."

"Let me hang up your fur. You'll be glad for it. New York's freezing. It snowed yesterday. Today it sleeted. Kennedy says it'll be clear by the time we arrive. Aren't we lucky to be flying there?"

"I wish I didn't need to go."

"Still time to change your mind," the perky blonde said.

Claire smiled bleakly. June followed her to her seat. "It's not a pleasure trip. My father's been hurt in an automobile accident."

"Oh, dear! Not bad, I hope."

"Bad enough. He's in Columbia Presbyterian. I'm still in shock. He was set to fly to London to join my mother for their wedding anniversary. A sentimental journey to Gstaad where they first met."

"I'll pray for him."

Claire attached her seat belt. "Thanks. What about you? How's Tony and the boys?" June Lamont had married a struggling actor, and a year later she'd given birth to twin boys.

"The kids are great. Tony had a small role on *General Hospital*, but they killed his character. He worked on a couple of *Dallas* episodes. He's up for a small part in an ABC movie of the week. He needs publicity. One of these days he'll hit it big. When he does," she said, "I'll stay home, be a mommy."

Claire fumbled in her purse for a pad and pen. "Maybe I can help," she said, writing down a number. "I know a columnist who'll welcome your call. Her name is Marybeth Frankel."

"Frankel. Is she the one who was married to Charlie Frankel, the comedian?"

"Yes. She's restarting her career. Call her, use my name."

"Thanks, I will."

Once airborne, Claire skimmed through *Redbook* and *People*. Unable to concentrate, she stared out the window.

"Why do people think food's the answer for every catastrophe in life?" she asked several hours later when June brought a lunch tray to her.

June shrugged. "Beats me. Maybe it takes our mind off our troubles. If you plan on eating in the hospital cafeteria, our first-class food beats it. Where are you staying in the city?"

"The Plaza."

"On second thought, maybe I should eat this."

"Be my guest."

"That was a joke. You need your strength."

"I'm scared. My father is so handsome. My mother says he resembles Rossano Brazzi, the actor who played opposite Katherine Hepburn in *Summertime*. God knows how he'll look. It doesn't help that we don't know his physician."

"Where's your husband?"

"Busy. And I haven't been able to reach my mother in London." Claire sighed. "Can you imagine her shock?"

After June left, Claire lifted her glass of Beaujolais.

Swirling the deep red liquid, she took a sip. Although she wasn't hungry, she forced herself to nibble part of the meal. With a pleasurable start, she realized Colin hadn't mentioned Hawaii. Without a word her sweet, generous husband had given up the tournament, promising that as soon as Sam Yamuto signed the final papers, he'd fly to New York. He'd put her first.

She wondered when her father would be well enough to be discharged. She had grown up on the Denison estate, Babs's childhood home. Located on Long Island Sound, her grandparents had moved inland because of her grandfather's advancing arthritis. The one time she heard her parents argue over money was after her grandfather's death. The day, she recalled, had been as cold as the weather in New York today.

The lawyer had read her grandfather's will. As expected, her grandfather left everything to his wife and daughter, with a stipend for Claire. Exhausted from her ordeal, her grandmother rested upstairs. Her parents were on the terrace, bundled up in winter coats, talking. When she came outside she heard her mother asking her father to commingle the Denison funds with theirs. He refused, which surprised Claire. He rarely refused Babs. He offered to act as an advisor.

"Nonsense," Babs said in her low, cultured voice. "Mother trusts you as I do. The money will be ours and Claire's. Currency of this magnitude is too tempting to allow a bank or lawyer to oversee. They might rob us blind. You'll make life easier for me if you do this. Pay Mother's bills. She'll live in the life-style she's accustomed to without worrying about money. She's never understood it anyway. It saves me the headache of explaining things to her after you've explained them to me. She and I will drag our feet over decisions you make in a minute."

Claire recalled them halting their discussion when Ruth and Jimmy Fortune, the caretaker couple, on their way to the supermarket, asked if the family wanted anything special.

"Trust isn't a commodity Mother and I pass out lightly,"

Babs said after they left. "Please, Edward. I can't understand your reluctance. Do this for me. For our daughter, too. To protect Claire's inheritance."

He resisted for another few minutes, saying if anything happened to the fund, he'd never forgive himself.

Babs beseeched him. He finally said yes.

Her grandmother lived out her days in peace and tranquility, her financial needs cared for. Her father was the most caring, kind man she knew. Now it was her turn to help him. What puzzled her, what she couldn't understand, was his forgetting to buckle his seat belt. A stickler for safety, he had purchased the Mercedes for its added air bag protection, and he had had one installed on the passenger side as well.

The plane landed on time at 3:15 P.M. In the baggage claim area, she gave a skycap her claim tickets. Despite the late afternoon hour, shafts of brilliant sunlight glinted off the windows of cars and patches of snow and ice. A policeman with cherry red cheeks exhaled puffs of air as he barked orders, pointing his finger, keeping traffic moving.

Two months earlier she'd been in New York to celebrate Babs's fifty-fourth birthday. Her father surprised them with tickets to Ringling Brothers Circus, which delighted Babs, who had once confided to Claire that as a little girl she'd dreamed of being a trapeze artist. Babs looked on in awe, leaning forward so as not to miss anything. Claire couldn't imagine her conquering her natural timidity to brave the high wire. It amazed her that fastidious Babs yearned for the pungent smells and noises of a circus. Afterward they dined at Lutece. For dessert they munched chocolate-dipped strawberries and sipped Cristal. Babs wore her birthday gift—a diamond-and-sapphire necklace with matching earrings.

The baggage carousel started moving. The skycap retrieved her luggage and carried the bags to a waiting taxi. She tipped the man and then rode to her hotel. There was a message from Colin waiting for her. He'd contacted her mother, not to worry. Anxious to speak with Colin, she dialed his office. His secretary said he was out.

She tossed her coat on the chair, unpacked, washed, put

on fresh makeup, and emptied a dozen American Beauty roses from the vase in her bedroom. She wrapped the stems in paper toweling, put on her fur coat, picked up her purse, then dashed out the door for the elevator. The doorman hailed a cab. She climbed in, gave her destination.

After she saw her father, she wanted to meet Dr. Lawson.

Four

CLAIRE STOOD TRANSFIXED in the doorway of the wrong hospital room. Her feet refused to move. Her gaze was riveted to the man on the bed. When she'd asked the information clerk for her father's room number, the woman was chatting with a friend. Stating her request twice more, the receptionist rattled off a number as though she were doing her the biggest favor. She'd obviously made an error.

Whoever this poor creature was, he had her sympathy and her prayers. He lay deathly still: covered by a light blanket, hooked to an IV, and connected to a machine by various tubes. An overhead light shone brightly on his swollen face. A sickly, bluish purple, ghoulish Halloween mask face. His puffed eyes were swollen shut. A bandage hid his nose. His right leg stuck out the side of the bed. A cast kept it stiff. His toes were swollen.

The patient wasn't alone.

A dark-haired man with thick wrists sat by the bedside drawing the man's face on a vellum pad. He raised and lowered his head as he switched his attention from his subject to his drawing. A camcorder lay on the floor near his chair. The man paused. He put his pad on the bed and slipped off his brown suit jacket, which he lay near the camcorder. The rustling noise he made didn't disturb the patient.

Claire's eyes widened. The man wore a gun holster strapped to his chest. *Police.* Who else would openly wear a weapon? Her gaze darted to the patient. He must be a victim of a hideous crime. Or a criminal. Whichever, he was in terrible shape. Thank God, she thought, thank God Babs wasn't with her. She would have fainted.

Claire heard a moan. A pitiful, thin wail of sound.

She knew she should leave. She had no right intruding on the man's privacy, yet in an awful way, seeing him helped prepare her for her father.

The man moaned again. If she were his doctor, she'd sedate him, take him out of his agony. He had a right to die with dignity. Die in peace. When her grandfather Denison died, he'd looked shrunken. Her father had said that when the quality of life is gone forever, death is a blessing.

She surveyed the room. Blue walls matched the two chairs. There was a single sink and mirror outside the bathroom. Two windows faced the street. She saw no flowers, no get-well cards wishing for a speedy recovery. She was glad she'd requested private-duty round-the-clock nurses and a cheerful room with a decent view. Wishing the poor man Godspeed, she strode briskly down the hall to the nurses' station.

Nursing Supervisor Molly Steinfeld put down her pen. "May I help you?"

"Yes, please. I was told Edward Jameson is in room five-oh-six. He's not in there. May I please have his correct room number?"

"And you are?"

"His daughter. Claire Brice."

Molly came around to the front of the desk. She was two inches shorter than Claire, four dress sizes larger. Her big, soft brown eyes filled with compassion. "I'm Molly Steinfeld. Let's step in here where we can talk."

Claire stilled. All she asked for was her father's room number. A simple request requiring a simple response. Trepidation and panic shook her voice. "Where's my father? Is he dead?"

"No. Your father is the man in room five-oh-six," she said gently.

Claire sprang back. She dropped the roses. Her first

thought was that there must be a horrible mix-up. It wouldn't be the first time a hospital was negligent. "He's not. He doesn't look anything like him."

Nurse Steinfeld picked up the flowers. "It's always a shock the first time."

No imminent danger. The phrase whirled in her brain. Dr. Lawson had lied. How could the pathetic mass of immobilized flesh, hooked up to machines with tubes running out of him, be her father? The man Dr. Lawson diagnosed as in *no imminent danger* looked hideous. Worse than her stone-cold dead grandfather laid out in his coffin!

Molly saw the myriad emotions: denial, doubt, and the terrible growing awareness that Molly had nothing to gain by lying crossed the young woman's face in a deafening silence, confirming the unrecognizable man as her father.

"It's always a shock the first time," the nurse repeated.

"You mean you get used to this?"

"It's my job."

Claire's voice was barely a whisper. Her lips trembled. "When is he going to die?"

"He's not." Molly Steinfeld put her hand on the young woman's arm. "He's not going to die," she repeated. "He's going to live."

"Please don't lie to me," Claire begged, gripping her hand. "I have to know. For my sake, to prepare my mother."

Molly smiled. She could report good news. "I'm not lying. I know it's hard to accept seeing him in his condition, but it's true. His vital signs are stable. He's alert. He's taking nourishment."

Claire shook her head. The revulsion and horror that made her want to flee also made her stay to verify the truth.

"He can't lift his head to sip water. He's not alert. I don't believe you."

"Your father's groggy from the pain medication. He takes nourishment through the IV. Once his facial swelling recedes, you'll recognize him. He'll be so glad you're here. Patients always do better with loved ones nearby."

Claire dragged the backs of her hands across her cheeks. They came away wet. Seeing the nurse's calmness and hearing her assurance, she asked, "Who is the man with him? Why is he wearing a gun?"

"Detective Malchesne's a police composite artist."

Claire reached into her alligator shoulder purse for a tissue and blew her nose. "I surmised he's with the police, but I don't understand why he's in the room. Why is he drawing my father's picture? Why the camcorder?"

"Vito needs the practice. He's teaching a computer composite course. Wendall—I mean, Dr. Lawson—said it was all right."

"Did my father okay it?"

"I doubt it," Molly said with a sunny smile. "He probably won't remember last night and today."

That stunned Claire. Aghast at the doctor's blatant disregard for her father's fundamental rights, she forced her dazed brain to check. "You're sure the doctor gave his permission?"

Looking at her face, Molly thought Jameson's daughter was very pretty and remarkably resilient for one who had had the life scared out of her. She'd been a nurse for all of her adult life—twenty-seven years—and she still hated seeing accident victims.

"Absolutely," she assured her, mistaking her outward calm. "The doctor gave his permission. He's close friends with the detective. You have nothing to worry about on that score. Detective Malchesne is a fine artist."

A fraction of a second later, Claire exploded. "How dare Dr. Lawson allow him free access to a private patient's room! What gives him the right to infringe on my father's privacy? Why wasn't I asked first if he's too medicated to understand what's happening? Where's the private-duty nurse I requested? The room with a view? What kind of good-ole-boy institution do you people operate, Miss Steinfeld?"

Molly's smile faded. Her features sobered instantly. "We operate a fine hospital."

"You wouldn't know it by me. At this moment my father might awaken. If he sees a man wearing a badge, carrying a gun, drawing his picture, isn't it conceivable he might think he killed an innocent person in the accident? Could even be awaiting arraignment on a vehicular murder charge?"

Molly met her battering with stoic resolve. The young woman was nervous. Upset. She'd had a shock. With cool equanimity, she waited for the wrath to run its course.

Fear for her father propelled Claire. "I'm holding you, Dr. Lawson, and his detective friend responsible if my father suffers a heart attack or a stroke from unnecessary shock. Is this the way you administer patient care?"

Molly Steinfeld paled. The veteran nursing supervisor loved her job. She had trained at Columbia's School of Nursing and worked her way up through the ranks. She'd spent her entire career within the Columbia-Presbyterian complex, moving from Babies Hospital to Neurological Institute before assuming her present position ten years earlier. She couldn't envision another profession. Many physicians, Wendall included, were her close friends. Vito, too.

She'd seen it all. Done it all. Comforted accident victims and their families. Held the hand of the dying. Rejoiced with the living. Threats? Never. Not until now. She pitied Wendall. Chuck Morino had dumped Jameson's case into Wendall's lap. The overworked doctor didn't need the hassle from this infuriated daughter. Molly signaled a nurse. In moments a student nurse joined them.

"Frances, please phone Dr. Lawson's office."

"In case he's too busy to come," Claire lashed out bitingly, "kindly inform Dr. Lawson that at the very least he can expect to be sued. He, this hospital, and every staff member involved in this reckless invasion of privacy, which adds undue emotional distress to my father, thereby jeopardizing his life. That includes his police buddy and his superiors."

The nurse scooted. In minutes she reported Dr. Lawson's nurse said he could be reached at his clinic in the South Bronx. Cheated of giving him a piece of her mind, Claire turned on Molly.

"Why is a light shining on my father's face? Is everything

around here done for the benefit of Dr. Lawson's artist friend? I demand you remove him from the room *now*!"

Molly sent the nurse scurrying.

Claire shrugged out of her fur. She slung it over her arm. She blew hair from her face. Her eyes glittered as shiny as the gold charm on her necklace.

Vito, his brown suit jacket buttoned, took his time walking down the hall, getting a long look. The nurse had warned him.

"How do you do. I'm Vito Malchesne, Mrs. Brice. I understand you'd like to discuss a problem." He spoke in a deep baritone, his calm dark eyes meeting her defiant green eyes.

He appeared so casual that she wanted to throttle him. Her lashes whipped up. "Haven't you left something out?"

He cocked his head. "Out?"

"Yes, Mr. Detective. Out! Is my father under arrest?"

"Of course not."

"Is he suspected of a crime?"

"No."

"Is it true it was a one-car accident?"

Vito's eyes narrowed slightly. "Yes."

"Did he kill, hurt, or maim anyone in the accident?"

Her clipped delivery fascinated him. "No."

"Then may I assume your police department superiors didn't request that you invade my father's privacy?"

"Now see here—"

"No." She moved closer, giving him a whiff of perfume he could swear was one hundred dollars an ounce, not the cheap toilet water his last girlfriend wore. "You see here! Did you film my father with your camcorder?"

He snapped to attention. "Yes, I did, but—"

She cut him off. "May I also assume your superiors don't know you filmed him and drew his picture? The picture of a man so disfigured by an unfortunate accident he wouldn't want anyone seeing him in this condition. May I assume that?"

His lips thinned. "You may."

She nodded briskly. "Then I assume Dr. Lawson collects portraits of people too ill to grant their permission."

"No, you may not assume that." Vito glanced briefly at Molly Steinfeld, standing a little behind Claire. Palms outward, she rolled her eyes heavenward as if to say, "It's your turn. Good luck."

Suddenly the word "pacemaker" boomed over the loudspeaker, signaling a life-threatening episode. Two residents and a nurse flew down the hall.

Claire flattened her back to the wall. Attendants raced past her, speeding after the medical personnel, pushing a stretcher loaded with high-tech life-saving equipment. Her heart pounded, and her knees buckled. Squeezing her eyes shut, she prayed they'd pass her father's room.

"They're not going to your father's room," Vito said. When she opened her wide-set green eyes, he used her fright to his advantage. He extended his hand.

"Let's go in there, where we'll be out of the way. I'm sure I can clear this up." Not giving her a chance to object, he walked ahead of her.

She had no choice but to follow him into a small waiting room. Vito closed the door. He laid his things on a chair.

"Won't you sit down?" he asked, indicating a red couch.

"I prefer to stand." She did, near a wilted philodendron plant in a horrid brown plastic pot. She put the roses on an end table littered with magazines. A lithograph of a schooner hung above the couch. The ship briefly captured her attention. She choked back precious memories of hours spent aboard her father's yacht, hours when she poured out her wounded heart at some boy's slight or a tiff with a girlfriend. Never too busy for her, Edward Jameson soothed her around rocky shoals. Tearing her gaze away, she found the detective's dark eyes on her.

"I understand why you're upset."

She tried to control her shaking. "Detective Malchesne, you can't begin to understand how upset I am. But you will. So will Dr. Lawson. Trust me."

He didn't doubt for a minute her ability to make good on her threat. "I asked to draw your father's picture."

Her eyes flashed. "So I'm told. Are you some kind of ghoul?"

He owed it to Wendall to exercise patience. She had a legitimate complaint. One that could land him in hot water with his superiors. If she complained to the medical board, it could haul Wendall before an inquiry.

"Give me five minutes. Please."

"Two. On the clock." Her tone dripped ice.

"I accompanied Dr. Lawson when he reviewed your father's X rays. I draw composite pictures of the deceased or dying in order to get a positive identification. Many people can't view pictures of accident, murder, drowning, or suicide victims. They're too graphic."

"What does this have to do with my father?" she demanded, her sympathy with those people.

"I think it will comfort him to see how he'll look when he's better." He indicated the camcorder. "By transferring his picture onto my computer, I can generate his image, remove his facial swelling, eliminate his bruises. He should be happy to have a print of himself healed."

"In other words," she spat in disgust, thinking him a vile self-serving, opportunistic liar, "you're pitching your Good Samaritan routine. I don't buy your pseudoaltruism, Detective. My father knows how he looks. If he needs pictures, my husband will bring them."

Vito passed his hand over his chin. "That's my point. He isn't going to look the way he did before, not without the implants. You saw him. I see how it's affecting you. Think of his reaction when he sees himself in a mirror. My picture will lessen his shock. When your mother arrives, it will help her, too."

Claire felt like smashing the man's face. "Is this how you spend your spare time? Do you give all the families this pretty speech, then make money on the side peddling pictures to distraught patients and their families? What a scam! What do you do with your videotapes? Sell them to underground movie producers?"

Vito gritted his teeth. He had a tiger by the tail, and her name was Claire. "No, I don't do any of those things."

She arched a refined brow. "Detective Malchesne, stop wasting my time."

He unbuttoned his jacket and shoved his hands into his pockets. The action flipped back the material, showing the gun. He ran a hand through his thick hair.

"All right. I'll level with you. I'm scheduled to teach a course in computer art to fellow policemen and FBI agents. I asked Wendall's permission to draw your father's picture. I want to compare it with the computer-enhanced pictures I'll get from using the video. Dr. Lawson is completely blameless. I needed the experience."

Claire's opinion of the loathsome man and his friend, Dr. Lawson, scraped bottom. She hadn't arrived in New York a moment too soon. Her helpless father needed an ombudsman, and by God she was it.

"The truth is you're an opportunist who isn't above using an unconscious man for a guinea pig to line your pockets. Dr. Lawson is as guilty as you are."

"Just a minute—"

"Are you paid to teach?" she asked, interrupting him with an icy blast.

He flushed guiltily.

She gave him a smug look. "I thought so. Obviously, Detective, it doesn't bother you or Dr. Lawson that you're both breaking the law. Or am I naive? Do the laws of privacy also apply to New York City cops and their friends?"

Vito wondered if she was a lawyer or a law student. He made the mistake of estimating her one-hundred-thousand-dollar sable, two-karat flawless diamond earrings, the thousand-dollar designer slacks and sweater, pegging her for a rich, spoiled airhead. Wow! Was he ever wrong!

Claire Brice reeked of class. Of money. Of brains. Of righteous determination. As much as he pitied her, knew the cost of her fraying emotions, he prepared to strip her of even that. He had let her rattle on long enough.

"Your father slept during the time I was in the room."

"That doesn't excuse you."

"Think what you will of me, but don't blame Dr. Lawson.

Your father is fortunate to have you for his protector. Can you honestly say he'll object to seeing himself healthy, without the swelling and without the implants? Shouldn't you let him decide? He's competent. Is it better for him to remain depressed, let him think the disfigured apparition he'll see in the mirror is the way he'll look permanently? I've seen pictures of his mangled car. It's a miracle he's alive. I'll show them to you. Let Dr. Lawson help him through this."

She sucked in her breath.

"In your place, I'd be upset, too. I understand your anger at me. But please don't take it out on Dr. Lawson. He's a fine doctor, the best. Your father needs him. Please let me complete my task. Yes, it benefits me, but more importantly it helps your father. If he's displeased with his healthy likeness, take legal action. I'm not running away."

Her troubled gaze focused on the picture of the ship. For a moment she could almost feel herself aboard her father's yacht, the warm trade winds at her back, the sun on her face, experience the sea's rocking motion. Her father's guiding hand at the helm, his other arm draped around her shoulders.

She choked up.

Quick to take advantage of the softening in her demeanor, Vito led her to the couch. They both sat down, but when he tried to take her hand, she leaped up as if burned. She paced, letting him know that as far as he was concerned, the jury was still out. A temporary truce was the most he could hope for until he got her to Wendall.

For a while neither spoke. From the hall came the clatter of food carts. From the other side of the door, they heard an ambulatory patient asking what the cook had ruined for dinner.

The answer was given in good cheer. "Last week's leftovers."

"My father enjoys good food," Claire said finally. She mentioned the fire in her parents' home. She said Babs burst into tears at odd times. She said that her father had dealt with it better than her mother. He'd hoped a change of scenery would do her good. Babs had gone on ahead to shop and see friends. Her father had planned to join her in London.

Claire shuddered. "The trip was supposed to be a second honeymoon. After England, their itinerary included Gstaad, where they met when I was nine months old. When my mother sees him, she'll crack."

"She could surprise you."

Claire kept pacing the small room's perimeter. She didn't trust the detective's motives, didn't know why she bothered talking. She circled the floor, her shoes beating the beige carpet. She halted midstride, rubbing the bridge of her nose between her thumb and forefinger.

Vito took advantage of his opening. "What happened to your birth mother?"

"She died when I was two months old."

"I'm sorry. But your parents will have a delayed honeymoon. Wendall won't let them down."

Reaching into her purse, Claire took out a tissue and blew her nose. She was mentally weary. Suddenly a word Vito had used replayed itself in her brain.

"*Implants*. You mentioned implants. What implants? What were you talking about?"

He saw the confusion in her eyes. Alerted, he realized she didn't know about her father's face-lift. Her parents must not have told her. Shit! He'd said too much. This was Wendall's domain, not his.

"Dr. Lawson will explain better than I can. He knows the medical terms, why he did what he did. I'm on way to my precinct. Would you like me to drive you to his clinic to meet him?"

She touched her gold charm. Yes, she wanted to meet him. The sooner, the better. As Colin would say, be cool. Don't go off half-cocked. Think of your ultimate goal. God, she missed Colin.

"On one condition."

Vito waited. "Yes?"

"No phone calls. I don't want him knowing that I'm coming."

Vito almost smiled. He knew why. It was written in the

tight set of her shoulders, the taut line of her lips, the fiery condemnation in her eyes, and the agitation in her voice, but he wanted to give her the satisfaction of venting more of her spleen before she lit into Wendall.

"Why, Mrs. Brice?"

"I don't trust you. If he knows I'm coming, he'll dummy up an excuse for giving you permission to be where you didn't belong. I don't want Nurse Steinfeld knowing where we're going either. Is that clear?"

If he weren't worried about Wendall, Vito would have applauded her gutsy bravado. His reprieve over, he nodded.

"Perfectly. But you're making a mistake. You couldn't ask for a better surgeon or a more caring doctor. He's rare. Everyone respects him. Ask the people of the South Bronx."

She collected her things. "It's not my job to conduct a popularity poll. No doctor with integrity allows a patient to be used for a friend's personal gain. Regardless of your argument, he should have asked my permission. He knew I was coming. One day wouldn't have mattered."

Vito granted her the point.

"He didn't get the private-duty nurse I requested. I asked him to have ready a list of doctors for a second opinion. I'm willing to bet he hasn't."

Vito was tempted to ask why she would accept Wendall's recommendations if she disapproved of him, but he didn't want to fan the flames. He didn't envy Wendall. He'd seen Wendall pocket her picture when there was no reason for him to do so.

"You'll have to judge him for yourself."

Claire looked directly into Vito's dark eyes. "I intend to."

Taking the upper hand, making her meaning crystal clear, she swept out of the room, leaving him to follow. They rode down the elevator in silence. He led her to the car, saw the candy wrappers on the passenger seat, picked them up, and shoved them in his pocket. She snagged a Mars candy wrapper, dropped it into his palm, got in the car, swung her fur away from the door, and slammed the door.

Damn, he thought, backing out of the parking space to roar out of the lot. The Beverly Hills beauty was recharging her batteries. By the time she met Wendall, she'd be on full power. They'd both be lucky if she didn't sue them right out of their professions. He felt terrible for dragging Wendall into this mess. He hadn't wanted to teach the damn computer course in the first place. Now it looked as if he'd get his wish for all the wrong reasons. If Wendall couldn't deter her from hauling their asses up on charges, he could kiss his police pension good-bye.

Realizing this was her first time in a police car, Claire huddled in misery, her shoulder pressed against the door, the roses lying on her lap. She noted the gun rack, CB, mike, portable lights, and phone. Vito clipped a canister, the size of a large cigarette lighter, to a holder beneath the dash-board.

"What's that?" she asked.

"Mace."

"Oh." Tear gas. *Mace*. The word hung in the car's close confinement, rising and expanding with the temperature thrown off by the car's heater. "Why is the rifle rack empty?"

He reached into his left pocket for a Mars candy bar. "Would you like some?"

She declined. He took a big bite. Working his mouth around the gooey chocolate, he crumpled the wrapper and glanced at the overflowing ashtrays. He tossed the paper over his shoulder. She counted ten wrappers on the floor.

"I inherited this car. It belonged to a marked unit. They repainted it for me without the numbers. The mayor declared a budget freeze. The rack stayed. It's a good thing. In case a marked unit needs a car."

"Marked unit?"

The sweet disappeared in three bites. He lit a cigar, took a few satisfying puffs. The smoke drifted to her side. "The numbered cars with the bar of lights across the roof. The numbers aid police helicopters in a chase."

The police dispatcher streamed a steady dialogue: accidents, knifings, family disputes, fires, murders. There was no shortage of violence. Vito responded to a call sending him to a crime scene. He had to refuse to go.

"Have you ever killed a person?"

"No, and I never want to. I like sleeping at night. I don't feel like facing an inquiry from Internal Affairs. The unit guys and patrol people deserve the credit. They put their lives on the line every day."

"You don't?"

He flexed his left hand. "No. My work comes after the crime is committed. People who live outside the area tend to let you know right off the bat they don't live in the South Bronx."

"Where do you live?" she asked, hearing the slight swagger in his tone. Litter was too polite a word for the wind-tossed garbage skimming over the streets like flotsam from a floating wreck.

"Here. In the South Bronx." She raised her brow. "Some of us have this urge to give back. Make life better."

He explained about the fires that sent people fleeing for their lives. He spoke about the reconstruction, slowed the car to a snail's pace, and pointed to a row house. Behind sheer curtains, lights blazed in the front parlor. Claire spotted a red couch, a framed picture above it, a standing lamp with a ceiling fluted glass bowl, and an upright piano.

"Are you making things better?" she asked, skeptical.

"We try. Sadie over there crocheted doilies." Vito indicated an elderly woman on a stoop. She was swallowed up in a man's navy peacoat and yellow plastic knee-high boots. Sprouts of gray hair stuck out from beneath a red babushka. Pumping her arms up and down, she held a dripping soap sponge in one hand, a towel in the other, scrubbing and wiping her wooden front door with the precision of one who had repeated the act thousands of times. A sheet of newspaper blew onto the stoop. With a firm kick, she sent it on its way, never breaking stride.

"Hey, Sadie," Vito shouted. "I see you made it to another day."

A hitch of her shoulder let him know she heard.

"She shouldn't do that. She's old. She'll catch pneumonia."

"Naw. Sadie's tough. She lived through the bad times.

Her house was torched in the sixties. This one's her pride
and joy. She washes the door, scrubs the stoop every day."

Vito smiled. "Her husband owned a deli. I wish I had a
nickel for every hour I spent watching whitefish and carp
swim in his fish tank. Sadie made the best pickled herring in
the Bronx. The old man had huge wooden barrels filled with
brine." Vito ran his tongue over his lips as if he tasted it, and
smiled in reminiscence. "Customers came from all over the
five boroughs for her crunchy half-sour pickles. I loved her
pickled celery. Sadie's brother, Moishe Gold, owned a
hardware store over on One hundred-seventy-fourth Street.
If he didn't like you, or if he was in a rotten mood, he
wouldn't sell you that day."

Intrigued, Claire asked how long Moishe stayed in
business with that attitude.

"Till the day he died of a heart attack at ninety. He keeled
over at the cash register. Had one of the largest funerals I've
ever attended. With as many dignitaries as a police captain's
or a mayor's. It's a good thing he died when he did."

"Why is that?"

Vito increased the car's speed. "In the 1960s life as the
oldtimers knew it fell apart. Kids used to play jacks, jump
rope, stickball, handball, roller-skate, shoot marbles, basketball." He shook his head. "Today they worry about
staying alive."

"And Sadie? Who watches out for her?"

"We do, but life's a crap game when you get down to it."

Claire felt grateful for the elaborate security Colin had
installed on their property.

"Gangs and drug addicts descended here, spreading fear
in epidemic proportions. Your parents lost your baby
pictures. These people lost everything, some including their
lives."

They passed groups of men dealing drugs under a street
lamp. Vito didn't phone it in.

She was amazed at their brazenness. "If I weren't here,
would you arrest them?"

He puffed the cigar. "Not me. I told you I like to sleep
nights." Smoke made the car stuffier.

"You're a policeman. Isn't it your sworn duty to uphold the law?"

He could tell she lived in fairy-tale land where the law of the jungle didn't apply. "My sworn duty is to stay alive so I can draw corpses, reconstruct their faces for identification, so the other cops can make the arrests. There are fewer artists in the department than other police personnel. They can't do what I do. I prefer not doing what they do."

She noticed his use of the word *prefer*. Needing to clear the air of cigar stench, she rolled her window down all the way.

"Believe it or not, at one time *bad* meant snitching cigarettes, sneaking drinks at the Zombie Bar on Boston Road. Kids attended school. Good schools with good teachers. Principals held parents responsible. God help the child if the truant officer showed up. In Sadie's day, the greatest sin was getting a girl knocked up. If a boy stayed too long on the stoop, parents embarrassed him by shouting the time out the window. They kept it up every few minutes. In those days parents had control. Today it's the opposite way around. Grown-ups afraid of kids."

She counted her blessings. For all her fussing, she led a charmed life, and she knew it. Tonight she would sleep in a king-size bed on silk sheets in her Plaza suite. Missing Colin, she swore never to complain about her rarefied life in Beverly Hills. The stench of garbage came through the window. She willed herself to imagine the scent of newly mown grass on the lawn outside the solarium.

Wendall wagged his finger, warning three-year-old Juanito for the fourth time to quit screaming. Wriggling his butt, he bounced on the examining table, kicking his chubby legs. He needed a measles immunization shot. After six girls, his mother finally gave her husband a son. Spoiled rotten, the rascal demanded attention. Wendall wondered if there was a screaming contest he could enter him in. He'd be a sure winner.

Daria stormed in, establishing her territory by a quick

shake of her beehive hairdo. She shook her fist at Juano. He plopped a thumb between his lips.

"Mama! You're raising a brat. You should smack his mouth!" Short in stature, her dark eyes level with Juano's, she tipped her forehead to his. He was her favorite. She'd assisted in his birth. "You bad boy! Ten years no popcorn. No soup. No cookies. No lollipops. Forget me reading *Bubbles the Whale*. I can't hear myself think."

On cue from the waiting room, a chorus of five children who'd had their shots and stayed for snacks and story time added their voices to Juanito's devilish antics. She roared at them to shut up. They did. Once they did, Juano howled.

Wendall nodded. "That's it." He had been on the go since five-thirty, sitting with Edward Jameson for half an hour before starting rounds. They communicated in the fashion that worked best for them. Wendall spoke. Jameson wrote or tapped his finger on his palm. He assured him he was making progress. Wendall left, promising to see him when he returned from his clinic. Which wasn't going to happen until he stabbed Juanito.

"Knock it off, Juano."

"No." He stuck out a pink tongue.

Wendall ripped off a generous length of adhesive tape. "Fine with me. How about you, Mama? Okay if I bind Juano's mouth so he can never speak again?" Mama grinned. Doc Wendall was a pussycat. Under his direction, the clinic had evolved into a social way station.

Juanito's large dark eyes went wide. "I want Piggy."

Wendall put on a stern face. "I'll get Piggy. I'll ask him to shoot you, how's that?"

Juanito's eyes went wide with hero worship. "Goodie."

Piggy basked in his role of cult hero. He swung giggling kids over his shoulder like gunnysacks. Tickling their tiny behinds, he sauntered down the street. Parents treated him as a kind of benevolent uncle. They saw past his florid scar to a big-hearted savior. Wendall's Warriors, under Piggy's guardianship, had created a safety net—a neutral zone. But it took practice to protect his flock.

At the moment, given a wide berth by a circle of

Warriors, Piggy curled his upper lip in a menacing snarl. Assault gun cocked, he stalked an imagined enemy. He wore black leather boots and tight leather pants molded his rock-hard thighs. He defied the elements in an unzipped bomber jacket and a slit-to-the-waist black shirt that displayed a rug of dark chest hair. With his jagged facial scar, he was the ultimate street predator. Gleaming. Sinewy. Muscular. Deadly.

Wendall tore out of the clinic.

"Freeze or you're dead!" Piggy boomed. The sound ripped the air. He pointed the AK-47's barrel at Wendall's forehead.

Vito drew up to the curb, took in the scene, chomped down on his cigar, and muttered, "Aw, shit."

Claire gasped. A berserk, armed animal was about to commit murder, egged on by a wildly cheering mob. In seconds the man's brains would be splattered on the filthy ground. Blood drained from her face. Ashen, shaking, her eyes signaled a wild kind of terror. She could almost feel the cold steel, the barrel's icy circle signaling her for its next victim.

Vito dropped his head on the steering wheel.

"Detective, do something," she screeched. She couldn't believe her eyes. He sat there, shifting his head from side to side.

"My God! Do something!" In a flash she knew why Vito wasn't moving. He himself admitted he stayed clear of violence. He said he liked to sleep at night. He said he avoided Internal Affairs!

"Coward!" She screamed at the top of her lungs. Her frantic eyes darted up the stark street. A trio of metal cans ricocheted down the road, pinging off curbs, ramming crazily into hulks of cars, machine-gunning onward as if symbolically clapping approval to the Kafkaesque melodrama.

Outlined by a gloaming sky, Piggy heard her. He swiveled. Claire dove for the tear gas. Vito galvanized into action.

"Jesus, don't! Stay back. Mace!" He manacled her wrist.

Paralyzed by a steel arm wedging her chest to the back of the seat, she yelped in pain as she felt him pull her thumb outward.

"There's no danger. The gun's not loaded. Damnit! Loosen your grip on the canister!"

Shocked by his violent attack, she dropped the Mace into Vito's hand. He spit out a mouthful of fur. Breathing hard, he said, "I'm sorry. Are you okay?" Allergic to fur if he came in close contact with it, his apology ended in three humiliating sneezes.

Scared, her adrenaline surging, she pressed her hands to her temples. With supreme effort she quelled her stark fear.

"There's no danger," Vito kept saying.

She gaped at him in disbelief. She plucked a rose thorn from her hand. Rage vibrated through her. Cell by cell her core imploded, gathering small dynamite charges to form one giant explosion.

"You bastard! I don't believe you. You nearly give me a heart attack, then ask if I'm okay?" She pointed outside. "You call *them* normal?"

"They guard Wendall. Piggy's the leader. The gun shoots blanks. The clinic couldn't operate without him."

The backs of her eyes stung. Her heart raced. Her thumb hurt. "Piggy?"

Vito unbuckled his seat belt. "Franklin Paggliani. Don't let his looks scare you. He's harmless."

She released her seat belt. The metal buckle slammed the door frame with a resounding crack. "Detective, I'll have your badge for attacking me! No, I take that back. I'll have your badge for my father, too! You're going to jail, you bastard!"

"I said I was sorry."

Her chest heaved. She stared out the window. "You're all insane. The lot of you. Who's that other one? The one in the crazy getup? What's he supposed to be? A barbershop fixture?"

Vito wanted to cry. He ran a hand through his hair. "That's Wendall," he mumbled.

Her eyes widened. "Who?"

"Dr. Lawson. He's wearing makeup."

Her head whipped around. She whacked Vito's face with the roses, sending him into a sneezing fit. The more he sneezed, the more she belted him.

He held his hands up to ward off her blows. Realizing what she was doing, she stopped. "Let me make sure I understand you. You're telling me that painted farce is *Dr. Lawson*? The man you tout as the beloved, highly respected, skilled surgeon who wired my father's jaw shut?"

Vito stared at Wendall, who waited for his all-clear signal. He groaned. The doctor he'd praised as the Albert Schweitzer of the South Bronx looked freakish. Awful. An insult to all proud Native Americans, even the ones who weren't proud. Wendall insulted makeup artists worldwide. His red and green steaks wobbled. Instead of two evenly spaced parallel lines on his forehead, the colors dipped, kissed, danced off, giving the impression Wendall was either inebriated or suffered from some gross neurological impairment. No patient in his right mind would allow him to touch him with a knife, let alone his rubber tomahawk. The subliminal message screamed: Trust me with a scalpel at your own risk.

Vito felt violently ill. The candy bar clogged his throat. He pulled at his shirt collar—his noose. He glanced at Claire's furious face and kissed his pension good-bye. She'd hire a high-priced lawyer to handle her case, and he'd be in deep shit.

Thanks to him, so would Wendall.

Five

WENDALL RECOGNIZED CLAIRE from her picture. He was fascinated. She was out for blood. From the looks of it, his blood.

She carried herself in regal fury. Fire danced in her eyes as she threw back her shoulders, lifted her determined chin, and swooped toward him swathed in sable, spurning Vito's attempts at conciliation.

"Wow!" Piggy jabbed his nearest buddy. "Any of you ever see a dish like that?"

Standing in a mismatched row, five little noses pressed against the windows, their welfare mothers awestruck by the lady in fur. Feeling utterly preposterous, Vito trotted at Claire's side, bemoaning his fate. Two lousy minutes! If he had arrived two lousy minutes later, this wouldn't be happening. He introduced her to Wendall, whose sharp blue eyes catalogued every detail about her: oval-shaped face, flawless skin, thickly lashed emerald green eyes, attractive mouth, long dark hair.

"Mrs. Brice." He offered her a smile.

"Dr. Lawson." Claire offered him a tone of quivering steel. Incensed, shaken, her thumb throbbing, she dismissed the gawking guards, bars on the plate glass windows, empty lots, and the street-out-of-hell, inwardly fuming that if this location was where the celebrated shaman, Dr. Lawson, hung his shingle, it said a lot for his level of success!

An enthralled Piggy elbowed in for an introduction. She

made a swipe at touching his fingertips, while her other hand clutched her alligator shoulder bag and roses.

Daria slammed out of the door, cursing the pest who interrupted her storytelling time. When she saw Claire, she stopped in midsentence.

Her breeding helped Claire hide her shock. The young woman in an outrageous lacquered beehive hairdo wore a skimpy orange skirt, a bright yellow sweater, and black knee-high boots. She'd outlined her shiny red lips well above the natural line. Defining her dark eyes, overdrawn eyebrows crested with midnight blue eye shadow. A cascade of silvery stars dangled from her earlobes.

Vito cast a glance at the two women, mumbled an introduction, and yanked Wendall aside. "I can't stay. She's steamed. She caught me drawing her old man. Jesus Christ, my career might go up in smoke!" he charged with a disgruntled finger wag. "I drove here so you could charm her out of suing us, and look at you! You're a fucking disgrace." Disgusted, he flipped his cigar into the rubble-strewn street. The fiery tip died in a fizzle of slimy water. He drew a miserable breath.

"Take it easy, Vito."

"Yeah, sure. Wait until she starts on you, then tell me to take it easy. She gave Molly a conniption fit. You better call her, see how Jameson's doing before you speak with his daughter."

Wendall scowled. He was very protective of the nursing staff. "Thanks for telling me." He rejoined Claire, who was answering Daria's question, saying she lived in California.

"Is this sable?" Daria asked.

Claire flushed.

"Franklin," Wendall interrupted smoothly, "please keep Juanito quiet for a few minutes while I speak with Mrs. Brice. Ladies, shall we go inside?"

Wide-eyed youngsters, their faces splattered with cookie crumbs, jabbered noisily. A blond-haired boy bounded over to Claire. He proudly displayed a Band-Aid on the inside of his elbow.

"Doc Wendall shot us. It hurt," he said, his blue eyes solemn.

Not to be outdone, another showed his bandage. "Doc Wendall killed us. Don't let him touch you."

That disarmed her in ways nothing else could. She hid a smile. "I promise he never will. You're very brave boys." She solemnly shook five damp hands. A boy stroked her fur.

His mother flushed in embarrassment. She snatched his hand away. "You'll dirty the lady's coat."

Claire saw the distress in the boy's eyes. She assured the mother it was all right, then took the child's sweaty hand, letting him stroke the fur. The other children took turns.

Wendall excused himself. "Daria, entertain Mrs. Brice for a few minutes. I have to make a phone call." He slipped into his office and dialed the hospital. He got an earful from Molly Steinfeld, hung up, and returned to the waiting room.

"That's enough, kids. Mrs. Brice."

He steered her into his office and closed the door. She brushed the crumbs from her hand, removed her coat, then put it on the sofa.

He regarded her somberly, thinking she treated the children with kindness. She seemed a darn sight nicer than the woman Molly described.

"My patients have no loyalty." He cleared a seat for her to sit. "You made quite an impression on the little turncoats. Would you like coffee? It's no trouble to fix a cup."

She sat. Her thumb throbbed. She rested it in her other hand. "Nothing, thank you. After we speak, I'll phone for a taxi."

He put his stethoscope on the desk. "Sorry, you're out of luck. Cabs avoid the neighborhood. It's against the law to discriminate, but they do. I'll drive you back when I'm finished. Too bad you caught Franklin practicing. I can imagine the scare you had. Anyway, it's nice to meet you."

She gave his facial stripes a stare. When he turned away to stir the soup, she mumbled, "Certifiable."

He heard her. "No, I'm not crazy. I do what works for my patients. When I schedule vaccinations, I sometimes put on makeup. Some doctors perform magic tricks. It's not easy to make frightened kids comfortable. What's jerky to you often does the trick, especially in this harsh neighborhood. It's a tough environment."

She bristled. "You're preaching. You don't know me or how I think. How would you like being greeted by that welcoming committee?"

"Piggy didn't know you were coming. If he had, it wouldn't have happened. The gun isn't loaded. This is a tough area. As for Daria, you saw the way she looked at you, at your expensive clothes. She's self-conscious about her height. She hates being a shrimp. The hairdo adds height. She used to wear spiked heels, but her hammertoes threw her feet forward, pinched her toes. In time she'll learn character is what matters. She hasn't had your privileges. The fur you're wearing costs more than she or the women inside will see in a lifetime. Daria lives in a rent-controlled housing project. Her mother's dead. Her father disappeared when she was little. Her grandfather was a peddler, an I-Cash-Clothes man."

Seeing Claire's confusion, Wendall said, "He pushed a wooden cart in the streets, clanged a bell for attention, and sang, 'I Cash Clothes.' Customers ran to the window yelling they'd be right down. Daria's grandfather was one of many immigrants who bought discarded clothes for pennies, eked out a tiny profit selling rag dealers the clothes for second-hand stores."

"Why are you telling me this?"

"So you'll understand. You strike me as a caring person. I saw you with the boys. Not everyone takes time for them."

"They're innocent children."

"You'd be surprised how many people look right past them as if they didn't exist."

Like Colin. Ashamed, she quickly quelled her nasty thought. *Of course he would take time for the children.*

"I sympathize with the plights of the people in your community, but I didn't come for a sermon. Frankly, Doctor, you look ridiculous."

Cupping his chin, he peered in the mirror, examining his

sloppy handiwork. "Hmmmm. I see your point. I was in a hurry today. I messed up the forehead." His finger trailed to the midpoint below his bottom lip. "No matter what I do, a dab of paint always finds a way to get stuck in my cleft."

She regarded him in amazement. "I don't believe this conversation," she muttered.

He spun around, braced his palms on the desk, and regarded her with intensity. "I spoke to Molly Steinfeld. You chewed out a decent, overworked professional. I gave Vito permission to be in your father's room, not Molly. She carries out my orders. If you want to get angry at someone, take it out on me. Your father will be fine. I know he looks awful, but that will pass. If you have a problem in the future, discuss it with me. One last thing. I didn't ask for his case. I told you last night I was drafted."

She felt her cheeks burn with embarrassment. The room grew warmer under the powerful draw of his scrutiny. She regarded him with equal intensity, his strong jaw, firm mouth, the lean taut line of an athlete's frame, letting her eyes come back to his. She was annoyed that their breathtaking aquamarine shade reminded her of the shimmering depths of Magens Bay in St. Thomas. Her favorite bay in the entire world!

Her thumb throbbed, and she winced.

"What's wrong?"

"Your friend wrestled me for the Mace. He nearly broke my thumb. Shaking hands with the boys aggravated it."

Wendall took her hand. He gently tested the thumb's rotation. He gave her an ice pack. "This should help. Give me a minute to shoot Juano, then we'll discuss your father's treatment. Hold your ears. Juano's training for the Met." He scooped an armful of children's clothes from a chair, told her to make herself at home, then left the office.

Taking him at his word, she examined the crowded office. Spanish and English comics and paperback books crammed a shelf. A toaster, tagged with the name *John* sat atop a small refrigerator. A pot of purple and white silk hyacinths—tagged with *Mary, widow of Ben*, in parentheses—sat atop a gun-metal gray, four-drawer metal file cabinet, next to a pair of Priscilla curtains, neatly folded in a plastic cover, tagged with the name *Lavinia*. An ironing board and iron were propped near the refrigerator and were labeled *Frank*. Cartons of diapers buried the brown couch. It was hard to believe Dr. Lawson practiced medicine in a flea market.

Drawn by the aroma of chicken soup on the stove, she lifted the lid and sniffed. Steam misted her face. She turned her attention to a metal clothes rack, the type used to transport merchandise in New York's garment center. It held snowsuits. Double rows of shoe boxes lined the floor. She opened one. It held a pair of yellow baby sneakers with matching shoelaces. Replacing the top, she peered into a cardboard box topped full with loose crayons. From there she studied a corkboard displaying children's pictures. A few children wore clothes far too big for them. The header sign read *Hall of Fame*.

She paid particular attention to one picture. Swathed in a blue bunting, a sleeping infant dozed with a pacifier in its mouth. Chuckling, she moved, studying each picture.

On Wendall's desk there was a plastic jar filled with lollipops, a plastic bag with pacifiers, and near that an open red plastic pirate's jewel chest tagged *Joey*. She peeked in. A folded dollar bill lay beneath a baby tooth. Hurriedly she opened her purse, dug into her wallet, folded a ten-dollar bill, slipped it under the dollar bill, then snapped shut the lid.

Wendall leaned on the doorjamb, his legs crossed at the ankle. She was unaware that he'd been studying her. He'd seen her slight of hand routine. "I was lucky. Juano was on his best behavior."

Startled, the smile left her face. "Your office is a surprise. It looks like a thrift store. Sorry, I didn't mean to snoop."

She was dying to snoop; she knew he knew it. "I invited you to make yourself at home. We solicit donations of clothes and household goods for our clinic's patients. As you can see, we lucked out today. But don't worry, we fumigate regularly, so it's safe to sit. Besides, there are a couple of cats around here. They keep the mice away." He went to the sink, ran water in the enamel basin, splashed his face, and scrubbed off the paint.

Claire hoped he was right. "I commend you for coming up the hard way, Dr. Lawson. I compliment you for giving your expertise back to your neighborhood. Is there a reason you haven't removed Franklin's scar? He might be able to get a better job if you fix his face."

Wendall gave her a bemused look, not bothering to correct her wrong assumption that he'd lived in the South Bronx before getting his medical degree. If she wanted to think he was a hometown boy who made good, let her. "It's Piggy's badge of honor, his protection."

"It sounds to me as if you've been lucky."

"We have been. Vito and the police keep an eye on us, too. But Piggy and his Warriors deserve most of the credit. Few know the gun shoots blanks. The word's out we don't keep drugs here overnight."

He dried his face, combed his hair, removed his white coat. When he faced her, she was surprised by her reaction. She reordered her first impression of the broad-shouldered, lanky physician, dressed casually in a plaid shirt and corduroy pants. His hair wasn't bright red as she originally thought, but more of a honey auburn, toned down by a sprinkling of gray. A square chin etched his rugged face. Straight thick eyebrows enhanced his incredible blue eyes. His mouth was well defined. As he jotted notes on a chart, she noticed his expressive hands.

He brought out a silver flask from the bottom drawer of his desk, poured a small amount of whiskey into two paper cups, and put one before her.

"After what you've been through, this will do you good."

She declined. "Please tell me about my father."

"Doctor's orders."

To humor him, she lifted the cup and took a sip. She stopped entirely as he discussed her father's accident. The extent of his injuries devastated her.

"Will he be crippled?" She lowered her head as if to prepare for the anticipated blow.

Wendall's gaze descended slowly from the light shining

down on her bowed head, to her quivering chin, to the cashmere sweater clinging to her breasts, before coming back to rest on her face as she lifted it. Tears brimmed her eyes, deepening the color of her irises.

"He'll receive hydrotherapy for his leg. That helps the healing process. He'll be back at work soon, good as new. Your being here will speed his recovery."

Her shoulders relaxed. Her fingers opened. "Thank God. I was so worried. My father loves the outdoors, especially sailing and golf."

"You know him better than I. He struck the trauma team as a man used to being the boss. If he's too impatient, it could prove difficult. Be prepared for him to look different."

Her fears laid to rest, the fire came back into her voice. "Why did you give the detective permission to draw his picture without his knowledge? He stands to gain from this. Don't deny it. He told me he's teaching a computer imaging course."

"I wouldn't dream of denying it. I was skeptical at first, but Vito pointed out the psychological benefits. He has a good point. A patient's recovery depends on many factors: family, friends, but mostly the positive attitude the patient brings to the recovery process." He smiled. "After all, I can't put on facial makeup for adults."

The liquor burned a warm path to her stomach. "The detective mentioned implants."

Wendall raised his cup. "That's right. The silicone implants cracked when your father's face hit the steering wheel. That's why I said he'll look different for a while. I guess you can say he's getting back his old face. Older by some years, but recognizably the one he would have had if not for the implants."

"If you're implying he had a face-lift, you're dead wrong."

Wendall steepled his fingers, peering at her over their tips. He tore his gaze from her lips. "I'm not implying it. I'm stating a fact."

She put down the cup. Her hair went flying as she gave

her head a belligerent toss. "He didn't. I would know. He's never gone more than two weeks."

Wendall lowered his arms. "He did," he said firmly. "I know implants."

She leaned forward. "I intend to seek other opinions."

He drew back his hand, reached into a drawer for a legal-size envelope, slid it across the desk. "Be my guest. I've written down the names of six fine plastic surgeons. I've also given you the Medical Society's phone number. Before you act, ask your father. His mind is sharp. He's capable of making decisions. Don't treat him like a baby. He has rights. Let him exercise them."

She snatched the envelope. She searched his face for signs of anger and found none. "Why is he alone? I had hoped you would have ordered him a private-duty nurse."

Wendall studied the stubborn set of her mouth. "I did."

Her eyes flashed. "I didn't see one in his room."

He eased back in his chair. "The nurses' registry is backlogged. By the time you return, one should be on duty. Sorry about the view. There aren't any suites overlooking the river," he said blandly. "If you want your father moved, ask the supervisor."

Claire felt her cheeks redden. She'd lost another round. He'd done everything she'd asked. She faltered. "Thank you."

Wendall choked back a laugh. Her "thank you" sounded more like "damn you." She was young, spoiled, and pissed, and too damned beautiful for him to sit there wasting time on impossible thoughts. He checked his watch.

"After we see your father, we'll stop by my office. I'll show you his X rays. He had prior nasal surgery. He had implants in his malars—those are the cheekbones—and his jaw. It's a matter of surgical record, observed by the entire surgical team. I removed the exposed implants to ward off infection. No prudent surgeon would start reconstructive surgery until it's safe."

"My parents would have said something," she argued. "We don't keep secrets in our family. My father was thirty-one when he married my stepmother. She's never said anything about his having had a face-lift. Besides, wasn't he too young to have had one at that age?"

Wendall tipped back his chair and crossed his legs. He pulled up a sock. Idly tapping his foot up and down, he sipped his whiskey. "There could have been extenuating circumstances. Think back. Was he ever in an accident?"

Resting her chin on her forefinger, she searched her memory. "No, never. He's rarely ill."

"We're talking accident, not illness. Are you absolutely certain? The team checked him thoroughly in ER. There's a faint X-shaped scar below his right shoulder blade, and he wears a gap filler."

She lifted an eyebrow. She knew about the gap filler between his teeth, and she'd seen the faded mark, too. "So?"

"There could be a connection."

"There just as easily couldn't."

"True." He noted her habit of rubbing the charm suspended from the delicate chain around her neck. He put it down to nerves. "It could have happened when you were a baby."

Her hand dropped. She sat up. "My real mother died when I was two months old. That's the only accident I can think of."

"How did it happen?"

"A ski lift cable snapped."

"I'm sorry. Where was your father?"

She turned her palms outward. "On the ground. Helplessly watching."

"That's awful. If he were on the ski lift, too, it could shed light on the implants. Where did the accident happen?"

She shook her head. "Switzerland, where I was born. It doesn't make sense. There's no reason to keep it secret."

Wendall wondered. It helped explain the closeness between father and daughter. He'd seen evidence of their love for each other in the teasing messages on the back of her picture.

"Suppose it didn't occur the way you said?"

The ice pack dulled the throbbing in her thumb. "What do you mean?"

"For argument's sake, put yourself in his shoes. Do you have children?"

"Not yet." She replied more harshly than she intended. "Not yet," she repeated more softly.

The yearning in her eyes left him curious. He'd hit a raw nerve. "For argument's sake, if your father was on the ski lift, it's a sure bet he'd have been injured, too. It would account for the face-lift. In accidents involving more than one person, recovering victims often experience periods of depression. Take wounded Vietnam veterans, for example. On the one hand they're grateful to be alive; on the other hand, they ask why God spared them. Imagine how your father felt losing his wife, the mother of his infant. I suspect he'd feel guilty whether my theory has merit or not. There's your welfare to consider. Burdened by the emotional aftershock and your day-to-day care, isn't it natural to assume he'd worry about the long-term psychological damage to you?"

"That's conjecture. I know how my mother died. I've always known."

"You know what you've been told. Consider your father's mental state then. Suppose he was advised, by a doctor or a friend, not to let you know you almost lost your father that day, too. We're merely exploring why he did his prior face-lift. An extensive one at that."

"Go on."

Wendall watched the myriad emotions on her pretty face. Body language told him as much, sometimes more, than speech. He'd jogged her memory.

"Many children lose a parent," she said. "What about orphans?"

"People adapt, but they also carry scars. Do you mind my asking if you have a good relationship with your stepmother?"

"Excellent," she replied quickly. "I love her dearly. She's a wonderful mother, a special person. She relies on my father for most things. We're very protective of her."

"Like father, like daughter. I think it's admirable. He couldn't know one day he'd be in an accident."

"It still sounds farfetched."

Wendall continued to observe her reaching for the gold charm. If he were to chronicle his thoughts, they'd take a distressing turn. He didn't mix business with pleasure. Ever. Claire Brice was a patient's daughter. Married. He would have preferred it if she were a snob. A spoiled brat. She wasn't. She had been severely rattled, reacting from a long trip, fear, and probably little sleep. Vito's pulling the Mace from her hand hadn't helped.

"It's solvable. We'll ask your father."

"Absolutely not!" She sounded shocked at the mention of it.

He leaned forward. "Why not? It can't be easy to live with a secret."

"We don't know if there is a secret."

"There's no doubt he's had a face-lift. For whatever reason. It could be as simple as his not liking his looks, or as a result of his being in the ski lift accident with your mother. Or any other reason."

"I don't care. If he wants the past buried, that's okay, too. I love him. I respect his motives. I don't need to know his reasons. Wouldn't the stress of telling me impede the recovery process?"

Wendall scraped back his chair, stirred the soup, sniffed. "There's good stress and bad stress. Bad stress suppresses action, good stress energizes it. How's the thumb?"

"Much better." She handed him the ice pack, which he returned to the freezer. "I don't buy your theory. It's too hypothetical."

He tilted his head and forcefully advanced his position. "Whether it is or it isn't doesn't change my obligation. I've informed your father of his surgical procedure. He knows I removed the implants. Once the swelling subsides, if he looks in the mirror, he'll know anyway. He might request his original plastic surgeon. Any reputable surgeon discusses the time frame for the various reconstructive procedures with his patient. Incidentally it could take up to six months."

"That long? Six months?"

"That's due to the type of nasal fracture he suffered. But as for the rest, if Vito shows him how he'll look without reconstructive surgery, he may decide not to bother with surgery after I plate the cheekbone to set the eye."

"You sound so matter-of-fact."

"We're coming from different paths. This is my job. He's your father. I won't tell him we discussed this. That's for you two to work out."

"Thank you. Six months. One hundred seventy-six days. Half a year," she computed sadly.

"Don't play with math. You'll drive yourself nuts. In the meantime, he can resume his duties. If he wants me, I'll be there for him medically. We've spoken twice."

"I thought he can't speak?" she said swiftly.

"Of course he can. His throat is sore, so we're giving it a rest. He'll sound like a ventriloquist, but you'll understand him. For now I ask questions, and he taps yes and no answers on my palm. I spent half an hour with him this morning. You'd be surprised how many good friends I make at five A.M."

She locked gazes with Wendall. *His eyes could mesmerize a person.* The blue pulled you into their persuasive depths. He looked tall sitting down. It was a curious sensation to discuss the intimate details of her father's life with a stranger. A silence passed as she digested the idea that her long-held beliefs might be open to interpretation.

Could there be a kernel of truth in the doctor's hypothesis? Her father was protective of his family. Could his grief contain remorse, a component of lasting guilt he himself was unaware of, thus preventing him from psychologically healing? Whenever she spoke about her mother, it was as if his whole body sighed in sadness.

She dredged her memory, pulling from it a fact she hadn't consciously admitted. Whenever they spoke about her real mother, she initiated the discussion, not her father. Had she unwittingly kept his painful memories alive? In a very real

sense, Nancy Jameson still lived. In the poems she had
written that Claire saved. In the stories about her that she
cherished even more as she grew older.

"Where are you staying?"

"The Plaza."

He checked his watch. It was half past eight. By nine or
so they'd be in his other office. He'd go over the X rays.
Allowing for her questions—nine-thirty. "It's eight-thirty
now. Visiting hours are almost over. Since you're with me,
we'll break the rules."

"Thank you. I'm very anxious to see my father."

"Inasmuch as this concerns him, I'd appreciate it if you
would tell me what you think I should know about your
stepmother. You've indicated you treat her with special
consideration. If you don't mind plain food, we can see your
father, grab a bite later, talk, then I'll drop you off at your
hotel."

She had the feeling he was as wary of her as she was of
him. "My mother isn't your patient."

His smile crinkled his eyes, making him appear boyish.

"There's where you're wrong. She's vital to his recovery.
If she's not up to caring for your father, I need to know.
You're returning to California. The more you help me, the
more I help them."

Her first reaction was one of gratitude, then she questioned his motives, refusing to let the whiskey's mellowing
effects lull her into complacency. She had seen the detective
take him aside. She didn't doubt he and Molly Steinfeld had
warned Wendall she had threatened to sue.

"Do you ask your other patients' families to dinner?"

Wendall eased his chair away from the desk and stood.
He stomped his foot, shaking down a pant leg. "That
depends."

"On what?"

He locked his portable medicine chest. "Any number of
things. If I'm on a tight schedule. If I'm available. If the
person is alone, three thousand miles from home, and had a
hell of a shock. If I think a little cheering up is good
medicine. That's what holistic doctoring is all about."

She rose, lifted her hair from her neck, tipped down her chin, smoothed her sweater. "What about your wife?"

"If I had one I'd bring her along."

She looked up. "You think I need emotional support?"

He turned the burner off under the soup. "You're too smart for me. I think we all need emotional support. I told you, I'm an old-fashioned doctor."

That drew a hoot. "I thought you said you're a holistic doctor. That's relatively new, isn't it?"

"It's the modern-day version of the family practitioner."

"You're a plastic surgeon."

"True, but as you can see from my thrift store," he teased, deliberately using her words, "I'm also a family doctor. After you visit your father, you'll need a bit of cheering up, or your stomach will be in knots. Then you won't eat. How do you think I'll feel knowing you're pacing your hotel room, fighting jet lag on an empty tummy, dwelling on his condition, returning tomorrow with a face full of worry and gloom?" His wicked grin was so full of tomfoolery, she couldn't help smile at his scenario that held a grain of truth.

"So terrible you won't be able to sleep for a week?"

His smile blazed. "Correct. This is a simple case of preventative medicine. Comes under the heading of boosting patient morale. It's too bad your husband isn't with you."

Something in the way he'd said it made her wonder if he thought her incapable of managing without a man. The me-man/you-woman syndrome.

"I'm a grown woman, Doctor."

Aquamarine eyes met green. And saw right through them.

"I can see that. If I were distraught I'd want my loved one to comfort me. If I were married, the person would be my wife. I'm speaking about myself, you understand."

Reaching for the charm, she rubbed it, releasing it hastily when she saw his gaze drop.

"I've got to speak with Daria. Be back in a minute. Then we'll go."

All of a sudden, she desperately wanted to hear Colin's

voice. "May I use your phone? It won't take long. I'll use my credit card."

She dialed home. From the outer room she heard children jabbering to Wendall. She heard Daria shushing them. Then Essy answered. Colin was out. The tents for the party were up. The grounds looked particularly festive. "The reporter you lunched with called. She didn't leave a message. If she calls again, Colin said to say you're ill."

Wendall found her sitting quietly, her hands folded in her lap, her shoulders slumped. "Better?"

She swung around. "Fine."

He placed one hand firmly on her shoulder, causing her to look up. "You're sure?"

"Positive," she replied, shaking off her pensive mood. If she were gone for months, Essy and Colin would have matters under control.

"Good. Let's go. I'm starved."

"Why not have a bowl of your soup?"

"No time. Besides, that's for Daria, the guards, others if they want. We're expanding. We're building a kitchen."

He dipped a spoon into the soup, tasted it, then rinsed the spoon. "Delicious. In winter I make a different soup each day."

"Are you a frustrated chef or is this more of your holistic doctoring?"

"Both. I'm a regular holier-than-thou."

She smiled. "And modest, too."

She has a nice smile, he thought. The sound of giddy youngsters saying good-bye to Daria filled the outer room. Taking his medicine chest, he led Claire out of the office.

Daria hopped off her chair to say good night.

Piggy blocked her path to apologize for scaring her.

What a difference between her life and theirs, she thought.

Her home was guarded by an elaborate security system in a wealthy neighborhood, patrolled by an elite police force.

"Franklin, both Detective Malchesne and Dr. Lawson told me how valuable you are to the clinic. You're very brave."

Piggy choked up. His entire body flushed. By her simple

statement, by her reaching out to him, by her taking his hand to shake it, she made a devoted friend for life. "If there's anything I can do for you, Mrs. Brice, anything at all, ask me."

"You're very kind, Franklin. I'll remember that."

With Wendall's warm hand protectively splayed on her back, and for the first time since she learned of her father's accident, she didn't feel as if the world had crashed down upon her shoulders. When she saw his old red Pontiac, she thought that Essy drove a better car.

"Piggy's in love with you," he teased.

"No girlfriends?"

"No. Neither he nor Daria have luck in that department. She needs someone like you to teach her how to dress, tone down her makeup. She's a bit short on style."

"Is this a request?" Claire asked.

"No. It's a compliment. I never tell people what to do." She cocked her head. "Never?"

He smiled. "Rarely. I merely suggest."

She couldn't help smiling back. "I'd be honored to buy subscriptions to a few fashion magazines for your office. That way she can read them and learn more about applying cosmetics."

He grinned. "That's very kind of you. I appreciate it. For reasons I can't figure out, Daria never painted her face the way I paint mine."

Claire scooted onto the car seat, tried and failed to close the misaligned door. "It's stuck."

"Temperamental. Watch your coat." He lifted the door slightly, then kicked it shut. "There, now you know the secret combination."

Maybe, she thought as they rattled down the street, there was something to his holistic doctoring. . . .

Six

CLAIRE MET ABIGAIL Goodman, her father's private duty nurse, as the diminutive widow bustled down the hall. Seeing Wendall, her brown eyes crinkled in pleasure. He enveloped her in a bear hug. Claire's stomach sank. If Abigail weighed ninety-five pounds, she weighed a lot. A stiff wind would blow the wisp of a woman away.

Abigail had been a nine-pound baby, convincing her ruptured mother she had given birth to a giant. The infant's blue eyes changed to brown, matching the cap of curly ringlets on her head. A joyful child, she grew slowly, stopping by the sixth grade, proving her mother's feared prediction wrong.

In 1947 Abby's ebullient personality earned her the title "Miss Personality" in the Erasmus Hall High School yearbook. Marriage to a fellow Brooklynite, Ralph Goodman, a cardiologist who practiced on Empire Boulevard, followed two years after she obtained her nursing degree. A quarter of a century later, she retained her peppy personality, Clairol retained the soft nut brown shade of her youth, and she'd moved to the city to be closer to work.

"I know what you're thinking," she said, seeing the question in Claire's eyes. "Don't worry. I may not have the pectorals our good doctor has, but I've yet to lose a patient."

"Abby's the best," Wendall assured her when the nurse scurried away for supplies. "Before we go into your father's room, be prepared if he doesn't want you seeing him in this condition."

"You're wrong. Of course he wants me. I'm over my shock."

"But he's not over his," Wendall said gently. "It happens. I only want you to know, in case he's not ready."

Claire gave a quick shake of her head. A memory of when she was six and suffering with itchy measles flashed before her mind. Miserable, confined to the house, her father had taken time from work to be with her. By diverting her with games and stories, he got her over the roughest part.

"Then I'll simply have to help him, won't I?" She strode past Wendall, tossed her coat and purse onto a chair, and approached the bed, her fist clamped around the roses.

Her bravery dissolved. She recoiled. Engulfed in shock, she bit down hard on her lower lip. Close up, her father looked worse, if that was possible—from his smashed pulpy nose, the massive black-and-blue marks on his swollen face, puffy raccoon eyes, wired jaw, to his pained expression as he exhaled each labored breath.

She felt faint. Light-headed. The bouquet of flowers hung down at her side. "I . . ." She swayed.

Wendall placed his hands on her shoulders, imperceptibly drawing her full body weight to his chest, cushioning her wobbly legs with his. He lowered his head. His breath warmed her cheek. Trembling, she felt his lips close to her ear.

"Do you want to sit down?"

"No, I'm okay," she whispered. But she wasn't, and her quaking body communicated that to Wendall. He slid his hands down her arms, keeping them there should she need him. When he felt her trembling cease, he released her.

She thanked him with her eyes, then spoke to her father.

"Daddy, I'm glad to be here. I've brought your favorite American Beauty roses. Aren't they a gorgeous shade of red?"

Jameson lay still, silently screaming. Air rattled through his lungs with excruciating pain. His entire body felt as if a sixty-ton truck had rolled over it. His puffy tongue hit a wall of IMF bracing. Witnessing Claire's anguished horror, he didn't blame her. Neither did he acknowledge her presence.

He had seen himself in the mirror. A repulsive mass of flesh. Why had he swerved to avoid hitting a rangy, soaking-wet mutt? The stupid dog triggered his past. He felt sorry for the skinny stray. Why hadn't he the common sense to buckle his seat belt? He knew the air bag in the Mercedes wouldn't work otherwise. Three miles. How ironic! How blasted ironic! After all these years, he had stupidly let down his guard. Played Russian roulette with his life, his family's security. A lousy three miles from his destination. Played and lost.

"I know what you're thinking," Claire said, not having a clue to his chaotic thoughts. "It doesn't bother me. I was here before when you were asleep. I understand. Truly I do."

He picked up the chalk and scribbled, "Leave."

Claire shook her head. "No. I flew here to be with you. I'm staying."

The chalk banged out, "You're different."

Claire refused. "No, I'm not."

"Go!!"

"No! Doctor Lawson says you'll be fine. That's what we should concentrate on. Remember when I had the measles? You told me to think of tomorrow. In a few days the swelling will go down. Isn't that right?"

Wendall flicked the IV tubing. "Yes. Mr. Jameson, as I said to you before, it may not seem that way or feel that way to you now, but your daughter is right. You're going to get well."

Claire tried to wipe his father's drool. With surprising strength, Jameson shoved her hand away.

She kept the smile plastered to her face. "All right, you do it. You're not helpless."

Jerking the tissue, he dropped it on the floor. Unused to controlling the trachea to speak, he sounded like a mewing cat. Beaten, he jabbed one word on the chalkboard. "GO!!!" He tossed the slate off the bed.

"You'd be with me if I had been hurt."

She picked up the board and erased the slate as if nothing happened. "Babs will be here tomorrow. Colin sends his love. He'll be here in a few days. We're a family. We stick together."

The chalk scratched. He pushed the board at Wendall. "Get her out of here!"

A cry of protest lodged in her mouth. She lost her smile. Her chin quivered. Her voice broke. "Don't shut me out. I love you."

His good eyelid batted furiously. Dismissively he turned his face to the window.

She ran to the other side of the bed. "I love you. Why are you doing this? I've seen you."

He turned his head back toward Wendall. She resumed her spot near Wendall. He let her protests fly as long as he dared. The tension darted from Claire's mouth to Edward's chalkboard, reminding Wendall of the headstrong missiles father and daughter had written on the back of her childhood picture. With duty to his patient paramount, he wrapped his arm around her shoulders, tugging her firmly aside.

"Mr. Jameson, I know you're concerned about your appearance. I don't blame you. In a few days, I'll replate your cheekbone, fix your eye socket. Hang in for a few more days, sir, until the swelling subsides."

Abigail came in with new bottles for the IV. She hooked them on the IV stand. She wiped Jameson's drool. He slapped her hand.

Claire gasped. Her polite father, who normally treated women with courtesy, was gone. In his place, a helpless, angry stranger rejected everyone.

"Go." The *o* hissed like evaporating steam, escaping through the wire cage, whistling through the air, piercing her breaking heart.

Shattered, her brimming eyes huge in her face, she apologized, not for knowing what she'd done, but for upsetting him. Blindly she raced from the room.

Wendall nodded to Abby, hurried after Claire, and took

her in his arms. Her slender frame vibrating, she welcomed the safe haven he offered.

His big hand cupped her head. As she burrowed against him, pressed to his chest, her delicate perfume wafted to his nostrils. He rested his chin on her shiny hair. Letting her cry her pain out of her system, he thought of the vibrant fire in her eyes as she slammed Vito's car door, ready to do battle, then waiting in ladylike fashion for privacy.

Wendall fumed. Where the hell was her husband? How important could his business be that he couldn't be with his wife? It wasn't as if he couldn't get away from his job. Her husband should hold her, not a stranger. A husband should wipe her tears and make love to her tonight; give her something good to dream about, not let her see her father's god-awful face in her nightmares.

His hand came up to stroke her spine, soothing the tense knots. "Shh, don't blame yourself. He needs time to adjust. Come with me." He guided her into the little room where she'd spoken with Vito. He shut the door.

"Please believe me. This is the worst of it."

She drew a forlorn breath. She looked at him in misery. "But what happened? What did I do? Why doesn't he want me?"

"He does. Don't blame yourself. He hates you to see him like this."

"But I must," she argued. "I can't turn off loving a parent. I won't leave him alone. Who else is there if not me? Please, tell him it's okay." She squared her shoulders. "I'm through crying. I promise. It's over. Not one more tear."

It was impossible to look into her beseeching eyes and not be moved by her plea. But he resisted. "Not tonight. I'll give him a sedative. It's been a long day for you, longer for him. I'll speak with him tomorrow."

"Do you promise?"

Stubborn, just like when you were a kid writing messages to your father. "I promise to do my best." She breathed a sigh of relief he felt to his toes. "I'll need a list of the things he likes: movies, food, TV shows. Whatever you can think of. If we occupy his mind, he'll do better." He said this as much for her as her father.

"All right. I'm sorry for wetting your shirt."

He smiled at her. "Consider it my baptism." He hoped to elicit a smile in return. When he failed, he reminded her to start on the list, saying he'd be back in a few minutes.

Composing herself, she walked down the corridor. Hearing laughter, she recognized comedienne Rita Rudner's droll delivery. Slowly passing the room where it came from, she saw a man, his eyes bandaged, his hand in a woman's, sitting side by side near a radio. Their hilarity sparked an idea.

Her father adored Abbott and Costello. He owned eleven of their movies: *Abbott and Costello Meet the Mummy*; *Abbott and Costello Meet the Keystone Kops*; *Abbott and Costello Lost in Alaska.* Babs considered them crude louts. Claire loyally echoed her father. She liked the comedy duo. Babs told Edward he gave their daughter the wrong message, but she softened her scolding with a huge bowl of buttered popcorn.

Claire was glad she thought of the films. She would leave *Abbott and Costello Meet Frankenstein* on the shelf in the screening room. In her father's depressed state, he'd claim Frankenstein looked better than he did. Two days ago he could have modeled for *GQ*, impeccably tailored in a Savile Row suit, the confident picture of a successful businessman.

First she'd arrange for a private room. The view didn't matter. Once she installed him in it, she'd buy an entertainment center for him to see his movies, play radio tapes of Fibber McGee and Molly, George Burns and Gracie Allen, Bob Hope, and Eddie Cantor. Because of his eye, she'd start with books on tape. She'd read him Ogden Nash's humorous poetry. To keep abreast of business, the *Times* and *The Wall Street Journal*. When he improved he could summon Irwin French, his director of operations in his Connecticut office. Resuming work, as Dr. Lawson said, was good therapy.

Her father probably wanted to bar her permanently. She paced the hall, then rushed to meet Wendall.

With long-legged strides, he met her halfway. Wearing his blue overcoat, he carried her fur and purse over his arm. At her worried expression, he said he'd given her father a sedative, and no, he hadn't barred her from the room as she feared.

"Why don't we skip the X rays? You've had enough for one day."

"No. I'd rather get it over with. I'm fine."

He gave her a long steady look. "You're sure?"

"Yes."

His spacious office in the next building was a far cry from the one at his clinic. Unlike the flea market atmosphere in the South Bronx, this office had sleekly modern lines. The club chairs and his desk chair were upholstered in expensive Italian black leather, contrasting with the beige Berber carpeting. Medical diplomas and professional certificates hung on the wall. Another held a bookcase of medical books.

The office was as neat as a pin. Including his desk.

He hung her coat up in the closet, slipped the X rays into the viewer box, and flipped on the light switch. Step by step, he explained each film, pointing to the opaque areas. He held nothing back, giving her a simple explanation.

"I see what you're saying," she said, comparing the films of a patient's without facial augmentation. "I'll take your word he's had a face-lift. I swear I didn't know. My parents never let on. Perhaps your theory is plausible."

"If you refuse to ask your father, it's fairly easy to check. You know when the accident happened. The Swiss hospital saves old files. If not, the police have a record of accidents. Chances are the local newspaper does, too."

"What would it prove?" she asked.

"Don't you want to tie up loose ends? I would."

"Why bother? Babs will be here soon. I'm sure she knows. She'll tell me now."

He heard movements outside the hall, signaling the start of the night cleaning crew. Wendall dropped the discussion. He put a picture album and a stack of loose pictures from inside its back cover down on his desk.

Seeing the first color glossy of a person missing part of his face, she cringed. "Easy." His hand lightly draped her shoulder. "Now look." He matched it with a picture taken of the man after reconstructive surgery.

Her head swung up to face Wendall. Once again her perfume swirled beneath his nostrils. He inhaled her fragrance. "But he looks wonderful!"

"That's why I showed it to you," he said gruffly. "Look at these." He turned the pages.

"You operated on all of them?" she asked in a voice thick with emotion.

"Yes, but other doctors do the same thing."

"All of them," she repeated, humbled by his, not another doctor's, skill. "You'll do the same for my father? You'll give him back his dignity?"

"He already has that. I'll make him gorgeous. You said he likes Abbott and Costello. How about if I make him into Costello's double?" He made the joke hoping to coax a smile from her.

In the face of his awesome talent, she couldn't be dissuaded by humor. Wendall's before and after pictures did the trick. She turned an emotional tide, leaping forward in a mental bridge of faith in his expertise. Her father's situation no longer seemed bizarre or frightening. She held on to the knowledge his future was bright.

Staring at a picture, she said, "You're a miracle worker." Dewy-eyed, she impulsively hugged him.

Feeling his pulse race, his throat knot, and that it had suddenly become very hot in the room, he left her to put the album away.

"I see Detective Malchesne's point," she went on. "A picture is worth a thousand words. I don't care about his personal motives. It will help my father enormously. Unless you're going to show him these?"

"No, this isn't the time. It's better to stick to a picture of himself. You saw his strong reaction. Vito's way is better. He'll be relieved when I tell him you've agreed."

"I owe him an apology." She went to her purse. "Take this

back," she said, offering the envelope he'd given her containing names of other surgeons.

"Keep it. Your parents may want it."

She nodded. "Okay, but I doubt they'll use it. I can't tell you how much better I feel, thanks to you."

He took a bottle of wine and two glasses from a cabinet.

"In your clinic you pushed whiskey. Here you push wine. Are you by any chance a lush?"

"Absolutely. You'd be surprised how liquor steadies my hand in surgery."

Her jaw dropped open. "You are teasing, aren't you?"

No, damnit! I'm flirting with you. "Yes, I'm teasing. Can I help it if people shower me with gifts?"

She dropped onto the leather sofa.

"A toast." He held up his glass.

"What shall we toast?"

"The hope in your eyes. The bright light at the end of the tunnel. The fact that when you speak with your mother, you'll pass on the hope. To you, Mrs. Brice."

"That's very sweet. And to you, Dr. Lawson. I'd like you to meet my husband. You'll like Colin. If it weren't for Mr. Yamuto, he'd be here." As she sipped, she told Wendall about the shopping mall, that Colin preferred Sam Yamuto not know of her father's accident. "Colin knows the Japanese mind."

"Does he really?" Amusement danced in Wendall's eyes.

"Colin's worried Uncle Sam may postpone signing the final papers."

"Why?"

"Sam's my father's friend. Colin's concerned he might put a hold on the mall or use another company if my father is impaired or, God forbid, if he died."

"And you believe that?" he asked, thinking it ridiculous.

"I have to admit I disagreed. But Colin is the businessman in the family, not I."

As she spoke, Wendall entertained himself by studying her delicately drawn features. The slightly arched brows followed the contour of her wide-set eyes, which were a teensy bit almond-shaped. A widow's peak, its tiny mole centering her forehead at the hairline, hadn't shown up on the snapshot. He came around to perch on the edge of his desk. Leaning forward, he rested his glass on his thigh, continuing his leisurely perusal. There were flecks of gold in her green eyes. Gold dust. Figures, he mused. Gold, the precious metal. Nothing fake about her.

"So you see, this means a lot to him," she was saying.

Caught musing, he grinned sheepishly. "Sorry. You were saying?"

Tilting her head, she asked, "Are you sure you want to hear this? It's not as exciting as what you're used to."

"It's fascinating," he lied. Her husband's opinions didn't interest him. The one he had heard was enough.

She moistened her lips, giving Wendall another focus for his attention. "Colin hopes—no, he *expects* the mall to open doors for foreign investors. He's gone way over specs to make it spectacular. Tomorrow night while my guests wine and dine in billowing tents, Colin will circulate my excuse. He thought it up."

"Oh, and what excuse will he give, Mrs. Brice?" he asked to be polite. He pictured her circulating among her guests in a diaphanous designer gown, dripping in jewels, charming the men, making the women green with envy.

"Mrs. Brice sounds so formal. Call me Claire."

"In that case, call me Wendall. What's your husband's excuse?"

She tipped her glass. Wendall's searing gaze was a tactile reality that landed in the pit of her empty stomach. She warned herself to ease up on the wine.

She giggled. "I'm ill. Hidden from sight. Languishing in my bed, suffering from a horrid case of root canalitis. I ask you, isn't that sad?"

"It's awful. Shall I offer my condolences or shoot you with cortisone?"

"Condolences," she said, horrified. "I avoid doctors. I'm a certified coward."

He doubted that. "Do you care if you miss your party?"

"Mmmm. Yes. Mostly watching Lia—Mrs. Yamuto—ogle the stars. She's not jaded." Claire accepted a refill. "Aunt Lia is the genuine article. She's not a bit like the other wives who go from power party to power party."

Without realizing how much she was telling him about herself, Claire chattered on about Yamuto's star-struck wife.

A pleasant glow warmed her toes. She caught him watching her sip wine. "Are you trying to get me foxed?"

Wendall roared. "You're too smart for me."

She held up her glass. "You're right, Dr. Holistic. This is excellent Beaujolais."

In a theatrical voice, she recited:

> *Which cheers the sad, revives the old, inspires*
> *The young, makes weariness forget his toil,*
> *And fear her danger, opens a new world*
> *When this, the present, palls.*

"Shelley," she bragged.

"Byron, *Sardanapalus*," he amended.

Amazed, she bolted upright. "You don't say!"

He smothered a laugh. "I just did."

She squinted. "How did you know?"

"A friend gave me an illustrated guide-to-wine book. It's in there. I like poetry. I memorized it."

She flopped back on the sofa. "Remarkable. We have something in common."

"We both like children."

"Yes, but I didn't mean that," she said wistfully, confirming his earlier opinion.

"What else do we have in common?" he asked.

"Poetry. I love poetry. My mother was a poet."

Her voice, he thought, was low and soft, like a throaty caress. "Mine's one terrific lady. We call her the do-gooder."

"That's where you get it from, then."

He was a whirlwind—with serendipity. The detective praised him for being a rare human being. Ms. Steinfeld agreed. Franklin adored him. She imagined Daria did, too.

"Talking about mothers, may I use your phone?" She removed her right earring, found a pencil and paper, dialed the hotel, and asked for her messages. Cee-Cee and Babs had called. Each insisted she call when she got in, despite the six-hour time difference.

Claire gave the overseas telephone operator her credit card number and called Cee-Cee. Her friend's gravelly voice answered.

"Cees, I'm sorry to wake you. I wanted to talk with you before I call Mom. Thanks for being with her when Colin broke the news. How is she?"

"Hysterical at first. Better when I left her. Poor dear's got a horrid cold. Could be flu. She said it's going around Connecticut. London, too. She's stuffed up, hacking. Ask the doctor if it's safe for your mother to see your father."

Claire asked Wendall. "He advises she stay away. We don't need Dad getting pneumonia in his weakened state. Between us, he didn't want to see me. You know how proud he is. He's not easy to look at. Her cold is a valid reason for her to stay in London."

Cee-Cee promised to keep tabs on her. "You'd better phone her. Forget the time difference. She's up, trust me."

She was.

"Tell me everything," Babs demanded. Claire assured her she had. "You're keeping the worst from me. I know it."

"I'm not. Dad will be fine."

"If he lives!" The retort was swift, censorious. "Your father and I brought you up to tell the truth. Don't lie, Claire. I won't have it. How could you dishonor your father?"

Praying for patience, she said, "Mom, if Dad's life were in danger, Colin would be here with me."

"Why isn't he?"

"He's waiting for Sam to sign the final papers, then he'll be here. It proves I'm right."

"It proves nothing of the sort," Babs said, coughing. "It proves Colin is honoring your father's wishes."

Claire brought the receiver to her forehead, moving the cool plastic from side to side. "She refuses to believe he's not dying. Or dead."

"I heard you," Babs shrilled. "I'm surprised at you. Turning on me when I'm so upset."

"Mother, please!" Claire pleaded. "I know you're scared. I was, too. I'm not now. Dad's in good hands."

"All I ask for is the truth."

At her wit's end, Claire didn't know how to convince her. A hand tapped her shoulder. Swiveling her head, she looked at Wendall in dismay. He wiggled his fingers, motioning for the phone. She relinquished it gladly. Pinching the bridge of her nose, she silently wished him luck. As she listened, she realized he didn't need luck. He assessed her father's condition and assured her mother he didn't expect complications. Her husband had the option to choose facial reconstruction. No, he wouldn't be an invalid. The sooner he resumed work, the better. After the delayed honeymoon, of course. Where did they plan to go? He praised her choice of itinerary.

He smoothly switched the conversation to Babs's cold. By focusing on her health, rather than her husband's, Wendall gave her the impression her primary worry should be herself. He upgraded her cold to a possible flu or bronchitis, advised fluids and bed rest. As if he had all the time in the world, he leisurely took a case history, replying to her questions about dry skin, bouts of insomnia, arthritis in the hands, and the safety of hormone therapy to ease the discomfort of menopause. The list—Babs was good at lists—went on.

He meandered far afield from her father's injuries. He grinned wickedly and gave Claire a broad wink. The action was so unexpected she clapped her hand over her mouth to keep from laughing aloud. He gestured for his wineglass. Tipping back his chair, he propped his legs up on his desk. Keeping Babs talking, he punctuated her replies with appropriate comments.

Claire marveled at a master at work. Shy Babs, who rarely spoke with people she didn't know, was chatting away as if he were an old and trusted friend. Claire was stunned to hear that Wendall had broken through her reserve so effortlessly.

"Mrs. Jameson, colds can be tricky. We don't want yours to settle in the ears and pop your eardrums." Wendall gently but firmly advised her not to fly until she was completely over her cold.

"You're terrible," Claire whispered.

Arching a brow, he cupped his hand over the phone. "Behave yourself. I believe everything I'm saying."

"Including Vaseline for dry skin?"

His gaze drifted over her elegant face, one that didn't need cosmetics for beauty. "Absolutely," he whispered, cupping the phone. "Cut it with water. Why pay for expensive cosmetic packaging? Vaseline's as good as anything else for soft skin. I know Park Avenue women who nightly apply lemon juice and snippets of peeled aloe leaf they blend in an electric mixer. Daria passes on the tips to my South Bronx patients."

"Does it work?"

"No, but the women swear by it, and it saves them money."

He promised to check back with Babs to see how she felt, adding he would update her on her husband's progress.

"Don't worry, Mrs. Jameson. Claire and I have everything under control."

"He sounds nice," Babs said to her. "Should we trust him?"

She glanced at the lanky redhead, slouched in the chair with his legs draped over a corner of his desk. She recalled the pictures of children, the shoes, clothes, soup, tooth money, and now she added cosmetologist to his list of credits.

"Yes, Mom. We can trust Dr. Lawson. He's a holistic doctor."

"What's that?" Babs asked.

"Old-fashioned with modern skills. Bye, Mom."

"Thanks for the compliment," he said after she hung up. "That was a compliment, wasn't it?"

Flushed from the wine, embarrassed for her earlier condemnation, she gazed into his smiling aquamarine eyes. A little-boy grin lifted the corners of his lips. Seeing him in action, hearing him allay her mother's fears, remembering his coming to her aid in her father's room, she decided the family was fortunate.

"Yes, it was a compliment."

"In that case," he quipped, "next time tell her that I'm also a great cook."

The truth was she had never cooked a complete meal, scrubbed a floor, vacuumed a carpet, dusted a house, washed a stack of dishes, or cleaned a toilet in her life. She never had to. The closest she ever came to domestic arts had been sharing a college dorm with Cee-Cee. Their idea of cleaning was to hurriedly drag on bedspreads and hide things in closets when their parents visited. A maid vacuumed and scrubbed the toilets.

"When I was little I sometimes made Jell-O or baked cookies."

"Cooking's therapeutic. Besides soup, omelettes are my specialty."

"What's so hard about whipping eggs?"

"Spoken like a novice. Consistency for one thing. I bet you don't know to test for stiffness?"

"Who cares?"

"I'm shocked at you."

She gave him a mock look of hurt.

"The test," he said with eager boyishness, "is to invert the bowl on your head."

"That's the nuttiest thing I ever heard!" she protested. "Who wants an egg bath?"

"You've had a sorry education, Claire. You whip egg whites, not yolks. The idea is for the whites to stay in the bowl, not drip on your head."

"I suppose you were perfect from the get-go?"

"Naturally," he said with pompous conviction. His eyes held hers in a teasing smile. "I'm a surgeon. Therefore, I'm an expert with kitchen tools."

"One doesn't necessarily follow the other. You could be a butcher."

He looked appalled. "You should see me carve a turkey. Cooking is restorative. It's fun sharing the results."

"I couldn't displace Essy." She explained her long-term relationship to the Brice family, that she was Colin's nanny. When his parents moved, giving them the house for a wedding gift, Essy had stayed on as housekeeper.

Wendall regarded her with perceptive eyes. "Most women stamp their personalities on their house. It helps make it into a home. Do you like her?"

"In fairness, I do. There isn't anything she wouldn't do for Colin."

Wendall tipped down his head. "Then why am I getting the impression you would prefer choosing your own home, that Essy's more than a housekeeper, that's she's a second mother-in-law?"

"If you are, it's my fault," Claire objected loyally. But she was thinking that Wendall absorbed information like litmus paper. "I'm not complaining. After I return home, I'm either returning to school for an advanced degree or getting a job. I'll doubly appreciate Essy."

There was no reason to stay in his office. He helped her on with her fur. It held the fragrance of her perfume. In a spiral of sensation, he lifted her thick brunette hair over her collar, letting his fingers linger briefly in the silky strands. He switched off the lights and locked the door. They strolled to the elevator.

"So that's what you do," she summed up. "Doctor and cook."

"And play piano. When I can, I drop by Harry's Bar in the Village. Harry's a big, redheaded Irishman. He serves Irish soda bread with everything, hamburgers included. If you don't like it, don't come back, is his motto. Harry says white bread is pasted sawdust bound in a mushy brown tasteless wrapping."

"He's right. Is he a good cook?"

"His wife is better. She knows it. Harry knows it. His sons know it. We don't rub it in. I taught *her* to make omelettes. Harry wastes too many eggs."

"You must love eggs."

The elevator door opened. He punched Lobby. "Not

particularly. I like making omelettes. I do a mean backhand flip."

"Please don't think of this as a compliment," she teased, "but I think you're daffy."

"Certified." The jest reminded her she had called him nuts.

She peered at him. "Were you ever married?"

His gaze dropped to her red lips. "Aristotle said men should wait until they're thirty-six and then choose a wife half their age, young enough to be biddable."

"He wouldn't get far on his philosophy today. Feminists would crucify him." A coy smile lit her eyes. "Am I to assume you're hunting for an eighteen-year-old?"

The elevator halted at the ground floor. "No. I like my women seasoned," he said impenitently. "You may assume I'm a fabulous cook, modest piano virtuoso, bachelor. Never married. Now you know my life story."

She doubted that. Strangely saddened by his admission, she couldn't imagine a more lonely existence. She had always lived surrounded by a loving family. How awful to come to an empty house night after night, to hear the sounds of silence.

No longer used to icy winds plunging the chill factor to minus zero, Claire's spine knotted. She felt cold in her bones. Head down, she strode briskly to the corner and stepped off the curb. Not checking for cars, she failed to see one speeding toward Riverside Drive.

Wendall did. Alarmed, his throat went dry with fear. "My God!" He bolted forward into the traffic. Seizing her arm, he hauled her to safety. The car narrowly missed them.

He began yelling the moment her feet touched the sidewalk. "That was dumb!" he snapped furiously. "Didn't anyone teach you to cross on the green and wait for a red light in opposing traffic? What the hell were you trying to prove?"

"Nothing," she stammered.

"Suppose he hit you?"

"I didn't see him. I'll be careful. I don't want to give Colin or my parents grief."

That set him off. He shook a finger in her face. "Oh, wonderful! Very considerate! What about me? Do you think I want you splattered all over the ground? If you don't care about yourself, what about me? I've been up since four-thirty. The last thing I want tonight is another patient. You especially!"

She staggered backward. Minutes ago they had enjoyed a budding friendship, teased good-naturedly, exchanged confidences. Smarting under his surprising tirade, she stammered another apology.

"I'm sorry. You're right. Forget dinner," she said hastily. "I'll phone for a cab from the phone in the lobby. You go ahead. I'll be fine."

"Don't be ridiculous."

"I'd rather."

He opened his mouth to say something and appeared to think better of it. "I'll drive you to the hotel."

She didn't argue. There were too many knots of apprehension paralyzing her vocal cords. The swiftness of his unwarranted attack had her reeling. Neither of them had gotten hurt.

In the dimly lit cold garage, their heated breaths shooting short bursts, their footfalls echoing off the cement, their emotions skidding, they walked in silence to his car. He unlocked her side. She quickly buckled her seat belt.

When her door stuck, he lifted it, kicked it shut. He got in and yanked the door closed. Revving up the motor, he pulled out of his parking spot, jerked to a halt at the gate, slapped a receipt in the security guard's palm, and whipped out of the lot.

For reasons he couldn't explain to himself, even now after the danger had passed, his heart lodged in his throat. He gripped the wheel tightly. When he trusted his hand not to shake, he switched on the radio to a talk show.

Claire kept her face averted. She stared out the window. The day couldn't be over fast enough for her.

Wendall saw her aristocratic profile, her firmly clasped hands. He heard her ragged sigh. Great! He'd frightened her. What should he say? She'd done worse to him. The thought of her hurt with God knows what kind of serious internal injuries, or worse, had aged him ten years. How would he have broken that news to her mother? Her father?

He pulled up to the Central Park South entrance of the Plaza. A uniformed doorman approached the car. Wendall signaled him to wait. Swiveling round, he angled toward Claire, who sat rigidly still. He thought of Jameson, of her going back into his hospital room in the morning, trying to radiate cheer. Some healer he was.

He tapped the steering wheel. "We could eat in the Oyster Bar."

Her hand on the doorknob, she faced him fully and declined. Gritting her teeth, she politely thanked him for speaking with her mother, for spending valuable time explaining the X rays. Leaving nothing out, she enunciated each kindness, ending with a thanks for driving her to the hotel.

"Damnit, stop thanking me for doing my job."

Her nerves scraped raw, she exploded. "Fine! Have it your way. I take it all back. How dare you yell at me? I'm sick to death of men telling me what to do, when to think, how to act. Just be good to my father. I'll keep out of your way."

His fist hit the steering wheel. "Claire, for chrissakes!"

Motioning to the doorman, she scrambled out of the car. She didn't look back.

Wendall fumed. What the hell was that all about? So he may have overreacted. Big deal. Damnit, she was too touchy. He never claimed sainthood. He needed a vacation. One of these days he'd take one, combine it with checking his microchip plant in California. No, he wouldn't. Bad idea. Claire lived in California. So what? So he'd think of reason later.

He rolled down his window, cleared the scent of perfume from the car, and rolled the window back up. He'd spent entirely too much time with her. Claire was a grown woman. A happily married woman.

When he got home tonight, he would call Marilyn. Set up a date with her. Get back to basics. A weekend in bed with her was exactly what he needed. Marilyn wouldn't go stepping off curbs! Marilyn took good care of herself. She took good care of him, too. If he had a brain in his head, he'd marry her.

Except he didn't love her.

For once the gods were kind to him. He found a space in front of Harry's. The affable Irishman greeted his favorite physician with a broad sweep of his arm, ending with a generous pat on the shoulder. "How are you, Wendall?"

"Terrific."

"You look tense."

"I'm fine. Never better." He slumped moodily into a chair. "Just a hamburger, Harry. Burn it."

"You want to play piano until it's ready?"

He leaned back in his chair and fiddled with a paper napkin.

"Not tonight. I don't feel like it."

Harry raised his brows. "Jenny's making dumplings. You want to watch? If you ask her real nice, she'll let you help."

He shredded the napkin in rows. "Nope. Thanks anyway."

The robust proprietor rushed to tell his wife the shocker. Wendall said no to his two favorite pastimes! Jenny wiped her hands. She picked up a ladle. She filled a bowl with chicken soup.

"Give him this. He's coming down with the flu."

Seven

HER STOMACH ROILING, her heart pounding, torn between shock and incredulity over Wendall's mercurial behavior, Claire hurried through the hotel's lavish lobby, past a strolling violinist. Her face a taut mask, she kept her eyes straight ahead, strode to the elevator, punched her floor. How dare Wendall reprimand her! To think she had felt a kinship—a camaraderie—toward him. She'd pitied him for living alone, for not having a loving wife to tend to his needs. No wonder the man was a bachelor. What sane woman would put up with his pendulum moods?

Her fault. She fell for the patient-doctor-family psychology trap, cast him in the role of father confessor. So much for infringing on the great one's precious time!

Unlocking the elegant suite, decorated in the Victorian period, she tossed her fur and purse on the sofa, then checked her phone for messages, hoping Colin had called. Until this moment she hadn't realized how much she missed him. Her hand hovered over the phone. Resisting the urge to figuratively cry on his shoulder, she decided to soak in a hot bath, forget the whole awful day.

Fireplaces and crystal chandeliers lent old-world charm to the sitting room and bedroom. She lifted the sweater over her head on the way to the bedroom, where blue- and white-striped wallpaper covered the walls, femininely softened by the use of flowered fabric swags on the windows.

Snow gleamed pristine on untouched trees across the street in Central Park.

She kicked off her shoes, sat down, and snagged a new pair of panty hose with her fingernail. "Naturally," she muttered, watching the run slither over her kneecap. She threw the ruined pair in the wastebasket. She stripped, scratched her breasts, and sighed. She took out a bottle of aspirin tablets from her makeup case, popped two pills into her mouth, filled a glass with water at the wet bar, swallowed, and headed for the sumptuous bathroom. Except for the mirrored backsplash, the walls were cream white, the ceiling border trimmed with a strip of roses to complement the trompe l'oeil screen of cherubim and roses. A crystal carriage lamp hung over the bathtub. She turned the gold fixtures on full blast, emptied a packet of Chanel bath bubbles, creating thousands of inviting scented bubbles in the swirling waters. Sinking into the frothy foam, she inhaled the perfumed scent, lay back and waited for the tension to slip from her shoulders and neck.

It didn't happen. Her mind wouldn't rest. What had set him off? Wendall's temper and her disillusionment aside, several indisputable facts emerged. One: She stepped into oncoming traffic. Two: Wendall placed himself in personal jeopardy to save her life. Three: Her brush with danger scared him. Four: He could have been hurt. Five: Who would care for his patients?

She blew bubbles from her breasts. Lifting her leg, she idly stroked it with the loofah sponge. Assuming she was the only one hurt, he'd have snapped her picture for his rogue's gallery, looked at it guiltily for not saving her in time.

He still had no right to yell at her.

On the other hand, she glimpsed the real Wendall, not a godlike figure, but a man. Flawed, human, weary after a long day. According to Molly, he made rounds at five A.M. and kept up a killer pace until nighttime. Seen in this light, coupled with his fear for her, she forgave him.

But he still had no right to yell at her.

Her internalized debate over, the tension eased from her

shoulders. Cee-Cee hated it when she took both sides of an issue.

"You drive me crazy, Clarissa. What's wrong with a good healthy sustained mad? Nice is unnatural. It's too timid. You're a born earth mother, kid. Be a bitch. It's infinitely more satisfying, more rewarding."

Groggy, she closed her eyes, drifting to sleep. The cooling water reminded her to get out. She dried off, put on a long-sleeve cotton lavender nightgown. Her tummy rumbled. The suite was stocked with fresh fruits, nuts, sodas, and wines. Carrying an apple and a club soda into the bedroom, she folded back the bedspread, angled the feather down pillows, slipped contentedly between the lace-edged bed linens, and clicked on the television. The phone rang as she finished the apple.

She dove for the receiver, praying it wasn't the hospital.

"Hi, sweetheart."

"Colin!" she cried happily. "I miss you."

"I miss you, too. What's going on?"

Muting the TV, she filled him in on her conversations with Cee-Cee and Babs, saying her father's physician impressed her mother.

"He showed me before and after surgery pictures. He's got an excellent reputation. Dad's in good hands."

"That's a load off my mind."

"Mine, too." Claire went into great detail telling Colin about the South Bronx clinic, Wendall's Warriors, Daria, even mentioning the elderly woman scrubbing her front door in yellow boots and a babushka on her head.

"Thank God we don't live in the Bronx," he said, dismissing the subject as inconsequential. "You don't need to go back there, do you?"

"There's no reason to," she said, switching subjects when she heard the hint of disdain in his tone. "The cold snap should end by morning. How is it at home?"

"Balmy, as usual. They expect the same tomorrow night. Perfect night for a garden party. The grounds look fabulous. The new firm you hired outdid themselves. If it impresses me, it will move the Yamutos. By the way, Marybeth

Frankel phoned. Essy told her you were out. One of these days she'll get the message." Claire felt a twang of conscience. He promised to take a roll of film of the party.

"What's happening with the mall?"

"The lawyer counsels patience for a few more days." He chuckled. "I'll take a page from the Oriental's book. It'll work out fine. Sam and Lia are leaving for Northern California after the party. They'll be gone for a week. Lia wants to tour Napa Valley's wineries, and from there they'll go to Twain Harte to see the gold country."

"Colin, that's wonderful! There's no reason you can't fly here. We'll have the week. Honey, I'm in our old suite."

There was a telling pause. "Sweetheart, as long as things are under control, I'll fly to Hawaii for the tournament."

She sat silent.

"Did you hear me?" Colin asked.

She couldn't hide her dismay. "Yes. When did you decide?"

"Just now."

Her joy fizzled. "I thought you didn't want Sam knowing about Dad?"

"He won't. He knows I'm a competitor. If you're in New York after the party, it shows you're well and flew to the Big Apple to shop, see friends, whatever. It's perfect."

"For you, not for me."

"Dr. Lawson expects your father to make a full recovery."

"Wendall also said if he were married he'd want his wife with him during a crisis."

"How chummy did you get with this doctor today, Claire?"

She bristled. "I resent that!"

His tone grew cold. "I resent you holding him up as a paragon. I can't figure you lately. You spend the better part of a half hour wasting time, telling me about a clinic that doubles as a Salvation Army department store, guarded by a thug with the barnyard name of Piggy, who carries an automatic weapon that shoots blanks."

"That's unfair." She pictured the nerve pulsing in Colin's cheek, the firm line of his sensual mouth.

"No, you're unfair. You turned this into a confrontation. You know how much I want to win the championship. It's not as if your father is dying. He has you, his private nurse, plus the staff. What can I do there? Sit with you?"

She hadn't expected the idyllic bliss of their courtship and honeymoon to continue, but she hadn't expected disenchantment to set in after nearly six years of marriage.

Colin's frosty voice came back on the line. "You're angry."

"What do you want, Colin?" she asked tiredly. "A puppet in fancy clothes you trot out at parties for a fancy backdrop?"

"I'd like a compassionate, understanding wife. A woman who knows this is a tense time for me. Who appreciates Yamuto's mall is the key to my dreams. Hawaii will take my mind off it for a few days. It'll do me good."

She touched the frown line between her eyes. Was she unfair? Selfish? Why was it always his dream? His tension? I, I, I, me, me, me. Not *us*.

"Uncle Sam's basing his signature on Brice-Jameson's reputation, not his friendship with my father."

"You know nothing about the Japanese mind-set!" Colin snapped.

Tension cramped her neck. "I know a few universal truths regarding people." Her voice vibrated with emotion. Disregarding the disastrous consequences, she asked, if it were his father lying in a hospital bed in New York, where did he think she'd be? New York or Hawaii?

"I'll come when I can."

"So what's different?" she grumbled.

"Claire." He clipped her name. "You're tired. Get a good night's rest. Don't sit in a hospital room the whole time. Take breaks. Buy yourself a wardrobe. Charge it. Treat yourself to a few Broadway shows."

"Stop trying to placate me!" Incensed, she slammed down the receiver, plowed her fingers through her hair, and threw her head back on the pillow. Her husband hated her.

Why couldn't she communicate? With others, she acted prudent. She'd swear to be diplomatic, then do the opposite. Stymied, she knew she loved him but couldn't talk to him. Not the way husbands and wives should. Like best friends.

A wave of anguish washed over her. She was window dressing. A pretty mannequin, nothing more. When she told Wendall Colin's root-canal party excuse, she'd been giddy from wine. She wasn't giddy now. She was stone-cold clearheaded.

She'd come east to assist her father. In large measure, his recovery depended on the strength and stability of those around him. Everything else would wait. She wanted Colin to win the championship, yet perversely she would have been thrilled if he had chucked it, if he had acknowledged her importance over his damn paddle tennis!

She lustily blew her nose. "That's it," she muttered, determined to stay focused.

The following morning, Claire apologized to Molly Steinfeld. She didn't see Wendall, nor did she attempt to contact him. She learned from Molly he made rounds early, well before visiting hours. When several more days passed with no change in her father's worrisome demeanor, she met with Molly and Abby to discuss her concern. Molly attributed it to rage.

"How can this be? He knows he's getting better."

Privately the nurses wondered the same thing. Each communicated this to Wendall. Jameson's shutting Claire out disappointed the nurses. They observed him pretending to be asleep when Claire spoke with him.

After four days of silent treatment, Claire's sympathy changed to annoyance and frustration, and the awful worry that if he treated Babs the way he treated her, she'd have two patients on her hands, not one.

"Don't spend so many hours in the room," Abby said, reminding her of Colin's advice. "You'll get cabin fever."

Lunch consisted of an apple or a banana, eaten in the room. Claire didn't give up, nor did she sit passively. She tried to spark her father's interest in news, books, business, and Abbott and Costello's movies.

She failed.

She tried harder. Determined, she chattered on at great length about anything and everything. She yakked about the Sacramento mall. She talked of the pleasant evening she and Colin spent with Sam and Lia at Spago, that Lia saw Clint Eastwood, Robert De Niro, and Barbara Streisand, her favorite singer. Nothing. Her father hid in his shell.

Get well cards poured in from Babs, Cee-Cee, Colin, her in-laws, and from herself. They overflowed the bulletin board opposite his bed. With the facial swelling subsiding, the underlying bony structure of his face grew more visible. His eyelids lost their raccoonlike bulge.

"Can you blame him for being depressed?" Abby said in the hall. "His right eye wobbles. He says it looks like a damn fish eye."

Abby spoke with Wendall. "It's a crying shame. The poor darling bounces in each morning with a cheerful smile, looking gorgeous for him. I thought for sure by now he'd turn the corner. It's days since the accident. Molly and I can't figure out why he's reclusive. Claire won't leave the room."

"She goes out for lunch, doesn't she?"

"No. She's as stubborn as her father. She's determined to reach him. She doesn't know what she'll do if he gives her mother the silent treatment. Do you have any suggestions?"

A muscle tensed in Wendall's jaw. He was dealing with tormenting primitive male emotions. He owned up to it. He wanted her. Without rights, he kept away. He'd spent Sunday night between Marilyn's thighs, thinking of another man's wife.

Sick.

"Tell Claire I'm setting his eye socket tomorrow. Tell her I said she's not doing her father any good cooping herself up in his room all day. When is her husband coming?"

Abby made a sour face. "He's not. He's in Hawaii, having a blast." At his raised brow, she scoffed, "The man plays paddle tennis."

"What does Claire say?"

"Nothing. She's loyal. Her eyes say it all."

Wendall scowled. He left strict orders: No visitors between noon and two.

"He means strangers, not me." Claire stayed.

"Who else visits him?" Abby asked.

"In case." Claire ended the discussion.

Wendall quietly asked Molly to keep tabs on Claire. She made an appointment for lunch.

"I can't get my father to understand I love him unconditionally. I thought we were close," Claire told Molly.

"The other patients look forward to their families' visits. I see how many hang around the elevators. Did you ever feel as if the walls were closing in on you? That's me."

Their argument notwithstanding, she missed Colin. She slept poorly, her hand seeking his side of the bed. The "watch-and-wait patrol" hours in the hospital room amounted to a standoff. When Colin finally phoned, she asked about his tournament.

"This is my year," he said warming to her reception. "Sweetheart, I'm sure to win. The spectators sense it. I'll bring you the trophy."

She gritted her teeth. *Don't start!* she told herself. It was a good thing Sam Yamuto vacationed in Northern California, not Hawaii. She wished Colin luck. He asked about her father. Without going into detail about his depression, she said he'd been moved into a private room with a view of the river.

Often during the ensuing days she wondered how Colin spent his evenings in the tropical paradise. To boost her morale, she adopted a routine. She took brisk walks before breakfast. After visiting hours ended, she shopped. The stores stayed open late for Christmas. At F.A.O. Schwarz, she loaded up on stocking stuffers for Wendall's young patients.

Remembering that Daria needed help selecting her clothes, Claire bought her a red silk blouse. Wendall could say he'd bought it. For Franklin—she refused to call him Piggy—a Pulsar watch with a tachymeter and chronometer.

At a Lladró shop she bought "Sleigh Ride" for Cee-Cee's collection. For Essy, Abby, and Molly, gold pins from Tiffany's. For Babs, an heirloom locket from the estate collection. For her father, a suit. For Ruthie and Jimmy Fortune, the caretaker couple in Connecticut, she bought sweaters. For Colin, Gucci's two-button linen sport coat, straight-collared linen shirt, and pleated linen trousers. For Wendall, a peace offering. An omelette cookbook. For Vito—her conscience hurt for causing his allergy attack and for calling him a bastard twice!—*Thomas Hart Benton: An American Original* by Henry Adams.

She bought herself a psychology book. She had reached a plateau with her father. Babs was due back as soon as she felt better. Claire wrote Wendall, asking if, as a result of the trauma, her father subconsciously feared the pain of more surgery. She suggested if he could see himself looking well with the aid of Vito's computer-enhanced picture, it might help his depression.

Wendall sent word he'd talk to Vito.

At night she curled up on the sofa in her silk pajamas, her face scrubbed free of makeup, a pencil and pad on her lap, jotting down questions. She drank too much coffee. She slept fitfully, awoke cranky, her nerves jittery, her stomach queasy. Her phone conversations with Babs drained her. She was tap-dancing faster and faster. During the day, she updated her father on family news.

Then a small miracle happened. Her persistence paid off. Her father squeezed her hand! It lifted her spirits. Her frowns changed to smiles. Another time he held her hand when she brought flowers. Buoyant, she bubbled all day. He wrote a message for Babs on the chalkboard. Claire put the psychology books away.

Wendall repaired her father's eye socket. He requested a typewriter. Her hopes soared anew. Thrilled, anxious to speed his recovery, she repeated what she knew about Vito's computer program.

Her father reverted to his former silent self.

She dragged out the psychology books.

On Friday, Vito called Wendall to say he'd received the

software program. They met in Wendall's office Saturday night. He supplied ham and turkey sandwiches and beer. While they ate, Vito studied the instruction manual.

"How's Claire holding up?" he asked.

"I'm sure she'll be glad when you're finished." He didn't tell Vito he was avoiding Claire. "Jameson's asked for a typewriter. He types after Abby leaves."

They finished eating. Vito reached into his case for a thick loose-leaf book. "My costume library of clothing styles and hairstyles," he said, working the computer.

Jameson's face, realigned for bone structure, jowls, and age lines at the eyes, mouth, and forehead emerged on the color monitor. Vito clicked on a moustache, fooled around with handlebars, twirls, stubs, droopy ends.

The men loosened their ties, rolled up their shirtsleeves, learning. Focusing raptly on the screen, they acted like adolescents at an arcade. Vito zapped off Jameson's age, shaving off a decade at a time. They joked and laughed and shook their heads, zapping out pictures.

Both agreed he made a crappy-looking hippy in long, straggly hair. "How's this?" Vito added an earring and an eye patch. Then he substituted a monocle for the eye patch. "Okay, I've got the hang of the program now."

Working in earnest, he consulted his loose-leaf book for ideas. He painted on various noses, adapting them to different thicknesses, shapes, and lengths.

"My turn to learn." Wendall narrowed the cheeks, raised the eyebrows, thinned the jawline.

"Holy shit! Freeze that!" Vito barked suddenly.

"What?" Wendall peered at the screen. Jameson was approximately twenty-five.

"Let me." Excited, Vito shoved him aside. In swift strokes, he added sideburns, sculpted the cheeks, added a mole to his lower right cheek. He slapped his thigh. "I knew it! I've seen his face before."

"Where?" The phone rang. Wendall let the answering machine take it. Vito stared at the screen, rubbing his neck.

"I'm not sure. It'll come to me." He closed his eyes as if sifting dusty files.

Wendall dragged his gaze from the screen to Vito who was attacking the computer "paintbrush" with gusto. He executed a series of printer commands. The machine whirred. Beginning with Jameson at approximately age twenty, it printed his image at ages thirty, forty, fifty, and forward to age sixty. Except for his eyes and ears, the man bore scant resemblance to Edward Jameson.

"What do you suspect?"

Vito leaned back, tapped the side of his nose. "I've seen his picture. Don't ask where yet. Thank you, Lord, for making my day interesting."

"Christ!" Wendall groaned.

Vito barely controlled his excitement. "What's with you? This is when humdrum police routine heats up. Now I play Sherlock Holmes. What could be better?"

Wendall's serious expression contrasted with Vito's glee. "Better for you, not Claire or her mother."

"Yeah, well I'm sorry about that, but if my hunch is correct, it explains Jameson's behavior. Let's go to Harry's. I'm starved. Tomorrow I'll lift Jameson's fingerprints from a glass, which you'll make sure I get. So what did you do last Saturday night?" Vito asked, turning off the computer.

Wendall marveled at how easily he switched subjects. "I dated Marilyn."

Vito shot him an envious glance. "Lucky you."

"Mmmm." So lucky he saw the wrong woman's face when he came. Now a chill raced down his spine. Vito honed his photographic memory, hunting files of unsolved cases. Knowing him, he rarely got excited for nothing.

He returned from Harry's to find a message from Edward Jameson on his answering machine. Jameson apologized for disturbing him at home, said it was urgent he see him. Wendall's premonition of impending disaster heightened. The switchboard lines to the patients' rooms had shut off for the night. Grabbing his car keys, he raced out of the house, got back in the Pontiac, its engine still warm.

He found Jameson cloaked in shadows, seated by the window, his foot elevated on a footstool, his hair slicked back, his face washed.

"Thanks for coming. Please close the door."

Wendall switched on the light and closed the door. Jameson said he'd speak with the aid of the typewriter. Wendall helped him over to the machine. Jameson handed Wendall a legal-size envelope.

"It's addressed to Claire," Wendall noted out loud.

"Please read it. Then give it to her."

Wendall's sense of foreboding increased. He guessed the contents confirmed Vito's suspicions. Without preamble, he asked whether it had anything to do with Vito. Jameson nodded. The affirmation reverberated through him like a bad omen.

"Do you say why you had a face-lift?"

Edward's fingers raced over the keyboard. "Yes, it's all there. And more. If I hadn't tried to avoid the stray mutt, if you hadn't let your detective friend in here, we wouldn't be meeting now." His shoulders sagged. "Life's a roulette wheel," he typed. "You ought to know. Those patients of yours in the South Bronx do. My leg itches."

"It's healing. Why do you want me to read this?"

"I'll tell you after you read it. It's confidential. Consider it doctor-patient privilege. Understood?"

Wendall gave him a hard stare. "Mr. Jameson, you're in no position to dictate terms."

He quirked a brow. "Trust, Dr. Lawson?"

"Exactly."

He nodded.

Wendall sat. In increasing shock, he read the long letter, a neatly margined, single-spaced chronicle of a man's life, without comment. He handed it back.

"I can't be a party to this, Mr. Jameson."

The typewriter clacked. "You already are. You involved yourself when you allowed your detective friend in here without my permission. You involved yourself further when you told me what he planned to do with the computer. I love my daughter. She may doubt it based on my recent actions, but it's true. Had I died in the accident, she and Babs would have been better off."

"Why did you steal the money?"

Jameson's hands hovered over the keyboard like a pianist awaiting his cue. He brought his fingers down. The pads raced over the keyboard. "I didn't. My friend Carmine Rossa did. We grew up in public housing in the Bushwick section of Brooklyn. We had big dreams. Carmine, the math whiz, and me, the business brain. He worked for a bank. He drew the attention of the bank president. After a few years, he sent Carmine to Switzerland as his courier. Carmine loved it. It gave him a chance to see the world. When the bank installed computers, he took to it like a duck to water. He hacked for the learning experience. He accessed files, never altering any, merely getting the thrill.

"Two years earlier the press carried a detailed account of a twenty-million-dollar robbery. The robbery took place in another bank. Carmine hacked away. One night he stumbled on the truth. The banker he idolized set him up. He and a police captain stole the money, set themselves up with their own private pension fund. Over a period of months, with Carmine's help, they diverted twenty million dollars to a Swiss account. The Swiss were used to seeing Carmine. When he realized the banker tricked him, he opened another account. He transferred half the money."

"Jesus! Then with his knowledge of computers, he cooked the books."

Jameson nodded. "Right. Unearned income is an aphrodisiac. I have no idea how the cop and the banker discovered Carmine had taken half the money."

Wendall whistled. "Do you have a criminal record?"

"No."

"Then why is Vito sure he recognizes you?"

Jamson coughed, then wrote, "After Carmine's death— they car-bombed his Buick—the police circulated his picture. They questioned everyone for leads. People knew we were friends. They found my picture among his personal effects when they searched his apartment. I had access to the numbered account."

"Why would Carmine give it to you?" Wendall asked, skeptical.

"Business. Friendship. You have to trust someone. We trusted each other. We planned on working together."

"Then Nancy was really Claire's mother?"

"Of course. We met in Switzerland. She was an *au pair* for a wealthy Swiss family. Nancy was the sweetest girl in the world. I loved her. She quit work, came to the United States. After Carmine's murder, I became frightened for my family's safety. I used her homesickness as an excuse for fleeing the country. She knew nothing."

Jameson's confession stunned Wendall. He studied him carefully. "Did she die in a cable accident?"

"Yes. She loved skiing. I don't ski. What Claire knows is true. After the accident, I almost lost my mind. If it weren't for Claire needing a father, I would have. We were adrift in a foreign land. A Swiss doctor performed the necessary surgery. I met Babs in Gstaad when Claire was nine months old. My real name is John Sheldon."

"I wish you hadn't told me."

"I wish it weren't necessary. Is Vito checking me out?"

"He asked for a set of your prints. Ten million dollars bought you a new life. Does Babs know about you?"

Jameson said no.

Wendall snorted. "You're a chameleon. You got yourself a new face, married respectability, hid behind Babs, used her and Claire for a cover, only you did it with your family. The banker used Carmine. The difference is, you've given yourself a noble excuse."

"Don't moralize, Doctor," Jameson typed. His fingers raced across the keyboard. "The money is a curse. You try returning ten million dollars to a closed Swiss account. I couldn't go to the banker. I'm certain the police captain murdered Carmine, then made it look like a mob hit. How long do you think he'd let me and Claire live? Her life was in as much danger as mine. I love her. Don't preach to me."

Wendall saw his point.

"I made an awful error in judgment. I don't have the temperament to be a successful thief. I've done penance for three lifetimes thinking about Claire and Babs, what this will do to them."

"What happened to the police captain and the banker?"

"The police captain died six years ago, the banker eight."

"Then you've lived worry-free," Wendall scoffed.

"Free! If you call looking over my shoulder free, I guess I did. The fact is I didn't know if either of them told anyone, or if anyone else took part in the theft. Who's to say Carmine knew the extenuating facts? If this gets out, there'll be a media blitz. My family doesn't need that, nor does my business. I own the majority stock of Jameson-Brice construction."

Wendall urged him to cooperate with the authorities. "You're wealthy. Make restitution, for Claire's and your wife's sake, if not for yours. Have your lawyer arrange it quietly."

Jameson pounded the keyboard. "Don't take my word for it. Get a calculator and figure the penalty for tax evasion on ten million dollars for twenty-six years. I'd have to rob Fort Knox to pay the fine."

Lord in heaven, he'd opened Pandora's box. "What did you do with the money?" Wendall asked.

"I set up a phony Swiss corporation, used part for collateral, part to finance my first mall, let the remainder earn interest. I paid taxes on the interest. In the sixties and seventies the tax laws were very lenient. The government encouraged people working overseas. Today the law allows a maximum of ten thousand dollars. I always paid my full taxes, rather than chance calling attention to myself or the business. In cases of intentional misrepresentation, the statute of limitations is voided. Once Vito figures this out, and if the IRS gets wind of it, they'll slap liens on everything with my name on it. They'll comb records for the past twenty-six years—business and personal. Insurance companies don't have limitations. When they get wind they'd settled the original claims, they'll line up in a heartbeat. Simpson Brice isn't involved. He retired with a golden parachute. His personal money is safe."

Jameson stunned Wendall. No wonder Jameson had spent a depressing week. He controlled vast funds, business and personal. Family funds. Stocks. Bonds. This could send untold shock waves.

"How do you finance malls?"

"Through bank consortiums. *Conservative* bank consortiums."

Wendall stepped over to the window. Jameson had handed him the information to help destroy not only him, but also Claire and her mother. Why?

"You haven't been charged. Vito's my friend. There's a chance he won't find out. Aren't you concerned I'll tell him?"

Jameson covered the trach hole. "I'm gambling you won't tell him."

"Why?"

"You're a man of conscience. You know Vito will find out on his own if he snoops long enough. He's a born hacker, like Carmine. I'm your patient, swearing you to confidentiality. Claire and Babs will need you."

Wendall's expression hardened. "Don't make a bid for my sympathy. What about Claire's husband?"

Edward made a sour face. "Colin's in Hawaii. She needs you now. Tonight."

Wendall thrust his hands in his pockets, a grim look on his face, his heart thrumming. "Level with me. Claire visited you earlier. Why didn't you tell her yourself? Why not let her decide who she needs?"

Jameson covered the breathing hole. "My daughter is a wonderful, loyal, caring woman. Thanks to her parents, she's lived a sheltered life. Before this is over, she'll change, much to my regret. You opened a clinic in the South Bronx. This makes you special, a man with a heart. Please, I beg you. Be with her when she reads this letter. Don't wait. See her before Monday. Help her. I'm worried."

Wendall understood his fears. For Claire's sake, he pocketed the envelope. Christ! He had triggered a Shakespearean tragedy. Vito would capture his quarry and in the process hurt Claire, her mother, and God knows who else. Him, certainly. By avoiding Claire to protect his bleeding heart, he shirked his professional duty. Short of tranquilizing himself into a spaced-out zombie, he'd allowed her to remain front and center in his mind—fringed lashes, emerald eyes, burnished brown hair, creamy skin, and a kissable mouth he had no right to taste.

As a toddler, he'd been afraid of the dark, thinking monsters lurked in readiness. His mother cured his fears with a magic potion—the same potion he advised mothers to use today: Fill a bottle with colored water, preferably inky blue or purple, label it "Monster Bomb." Spray the doorsills and windowsills, while chanting "Take that, monster!"

It worked for him. After two weeks of water-bombing, he had slept like the baby he was. But he wasn't a baby now. He was a grown man wishing for a magic potion for Claire. Sighing, knowing he couldn't offer her an abracadabra cure, he picked up the phone and dialed.

Livid, Colin Brice flung the *Carrier* across the hotel room, toppling a vase filled with orchids. The vicious headlines screamed at him.

Real Estate Tycoon Edward Jameson Critically Injured in Auto Crash. Her Marriage in Shambles, Heartsick Heiress Claire Brice Maintains Lonely Vigil at Her Father's Bedside. Playboy Husband Colin Parties in Hawaii.

He shook with anger. He'd played masterfully. Never missed a serve. A perfect forehand. The crowd roared its approval. And why not? He kept his head perpendicular to the court surface until his racket contacted the ball. He kept his weight on his toes, not his heels, achieving maximum power. He could teach a class on backhand. He kept the paddle head slightly behind his left side, perpendicular to the ground until he hit the ball just behind his right knee. He had used a short, low backswing. He won the championship! Could he savor his victory? No! Whose fault was it? Claire's.

Marybeth Frankel should be shot. Between her poison pen and his wife's gullible assistance, they jeopardized the most important, career-defining deal of his life. He fervently prayed Sam Yamuto didn't read the *Carrier*. Claire's business acumen fit on the head of a thimble. Why couldn't she be like his mother? His mother would never shoot her mouth off to a reporter or befriend the wrong sort.

Claire had defied him. First the nonsense about working, as though she had to find herself! For what, for God's sake! For a paycheck he'd have to give back in taxes? Then she nagged him about a baby. Blaming him for his sensible timetable. Now this!

Her lack of discrimination, accepting people at face value until proven otherwise, had backfired. He had to put out the fires she started rather than go home and rest up in California, before he met with Yamuto on Monday. Zoning glitch or no zoning glitch, he'd try to get his signature on the dotted line without delay.

He glanced at the time, snatched the garment bag, and raced out the door. He had a day to fly to New York and bring Claire home. He didn't care if he propped his eyelids open with toothpicks to prevent Lia, who avidly read the papers, from thinking things amiss. Now wasn't the time to gamble with his future or the fortune at stake. With the huge sum of money he laid out to his suppliers, not one damned thing in the world mattered more than Sam Yamuto's signature on the dotted line.

Then he'd take care of Marybeth Frankel.

But first he'd deal with his blabbermouth wife!

Eight

CLAIRE HURRIED. WENDALL had phoned an hour earlier, asking to meet with her. He mentioned his tight schedule, and if she were free for dinner, he'd like to discuss her father. If not, he'd try to see her the following week.

"Tonight is fine," she said quickly, then raced to dress. Half an hour later, she had on a white silk blouse trimmed with signature gold buttons on the cuffs and also flowing down the sides of her black velvet skirt. Her hair fell in soft waves, framing her face. She completed her makeup, added pearl earrings, dabbed Arpege to her wrists and the pulse point at the base of her neck, patted her gold charm, and gave herself a critical glance. She put her list of questions for Wendall on the coffee table near a plate of Godiva chocolates.

Wendall rode to her floor, stepped into the long corridor, and knew how a condemned sailor felt walking the gangplank. He hoped her husband won his damn paddle tennis game, cut the deal with Yamuto, and got his ass to New York on the first available flight. When the shit hit the fan, Claire would need all the support he could give her.

What a mess. He stood outside her suite, dreading the evening. He pivoted on the ball of one foot, retraced his steps down the hall, pivoted again, retraced his steps. Rubbing the back of a stiffening neck, he hesitated at the door, took a deep breath, and knocked.

He heard her call out. The door was flung open, and he looked into a pair of beguiling green eyes smiling up at him in shy greeting. He felt like running, beating the clock, hightailing it out of there, rather than be the bearer of bad news.

"Wendall." She ushered him in. "Don't you look nice." She was thinking how wrong she'd been about redheaded men. Or else about one in particular. His brown suit fit his broad shoulders as though tailored expressly for him. He didn't have the pale coloring of a redhead. There was something very appealing about a man's after-shave.

"I thought we were meeting downstairs."

"Sorry." His voice sounded husky. He coughed, clearing it.

"Are you coming down with a cold?" she asked.

"No." His collar suddenly felt like a noose. She was the innocent angel, he the hangman. "I . . . I must have gotten our signals crossed. You look better than nice."

She dimpled. "Thank you. There's wine, beer, Perrier, sodas, that's about it. Oh, and this is for you." She gave him an ornately wrapped Christmas gift from a stack of presents near the fireplace.

"I know it's a bit early for Christmas, but please accept this with my thanks for caring for my father."

He looked down at her. "This isn't necessary," he said gruffly. She pressed the box in his hands, their fingers touching and holding as Wendall's emotions careened.

"Please take it with my gratitude. It's my small way of thanking you for pushing me out of harm's way. These," she said, pointing to a huge stack of gifts, "are for you to bring to the kids at the clinic. There's something for Daria and Franklin, too."

Caught off guard by her generosity, aware that before this evening ended her life would change dramatically, he decided to wait until after dinner to give her the letter. The symbolism of a last supper wasn't lost on him. She was so beautiful with her shiny dark hair, luscious red lips, and the lush curtain of long, dark lashes sweeping upward over clear innocent green eyes that he hurt to think of tears replacing her happiness.

Thanks to him.

"May I open this now, or do you want me to wait for Christmas?"

"Don't you dare," she said with a laugh. Her feet shifted impatiently when he took his fingernail to separate the tape and carefully save the wrapping. She dashed into the kitchen, bringing him a knife.

"Wendall, stop making neat surgical cuts."

He was thinking how different it would be if she weren't married, if they were going on a bona fide date, if her father weren't his reason for seeing her. He would tell her she was breathtakingly lovely, take her in his arms, and thank her with a kiss. A long one.

He unwrapped the cookbook. "Sorry, force of habit. We save everything for the clinic. Thank you."

She hovered close by, looking concerned. "Do you already own this one? If you do, we can return it for another one."

He flipped through the colorful pages. Even if he owned ten copies of the book, he'd never tell her. She'd made the selection, that's what mattered. She'd thought of him.

"No, it's wonderful," he said, and grinned when she sighed in relief. "It's my first omelette cookbook."

"I'm so glad. I have to confess I adore receiving presents, but giving them is nicer. Your eyes lit up, so I know you like it. Now, if you're not worried abut cholesterol, you can eat an omelette a day."

At the moment he would give the moon not to tell her about her father. He much preferred seeing her saucy smile light her green eyes, hear her silky voice trade teasing quips with him.

"Do you want to eat or talk first?" she asked.

"Eat first," he said quickly. "I'm famished." It wasn't true. The lump in his throat was the size of a golf ball, but anything to delay the inevitable. He glanced down at her feet.

"No shoes?"

"Oops! You've caught me. I hate shoes." She giggled. Claire dashed into the bedroom, put on her shoes, took her purse from the bed, and joined Wendall.

"Ready?" he said quietly, gazing at her.

Her hand went to his arm. "You seem worried. If you'd rather stay and talk, I'm a good listener."

He took a deep breath and smiled. She had no idea what she was doing to him. What it did to him to carry a sinister secret, know he'd share it with her all too soon.

"My prescription for what ails this doctor is pleasant company. That's you. A fine meal and putting aside the events of a rough day."

"Sounds good to me. I made reservations in the Edwardian Room. But with what you've just said, you might prefer a livelier atmosphere. It's up to you. Before I talk with a psychiatrist, I want to compare notes with you, and if you prefer, we'll come back afterward for our discussion."

Wendall jumped at her offer. "I'd like that. Do you enjoy Northern Italian food?" She said she did. "All right, we'll go to Asti's. Have you eaten there?" She said she hadn't. He squeezed her hand. "You're in for a treat." He made a quick phone call to the restaurant, reserved a table for two, while Claire slipped on her fur.

"Lead on," she said happily.

Asti's opened in 1925 and was known as the birthplace of the "singing waiters." Even the bartenders joined in, offering up a musical menu: opera arias, pop standards, Broadway tunes. Asti's encouraged diners to let down their inhibitions and sing, too.

Claire did. "Hold your ears, Wendall."

With the waiters cueing the words, she warbled a theatrical rendition of "Anything Goes." Giggling like a schoolgirl, having a grand time, she held up her hand for the waiters' kisses, winking and bowing to the people at the nearby tables. Her green eyes sparkling, her cheeks flushed, she scolded Wendall for not singing.

He ran his finger around the rim of his empty glass. He leaned back in his chair. "I'm a piano player, not a singer. I'd rather watch you. You're more interesting than the waiters," he said, safely falling short of confessing he thought her the most beautiful woman he'd ever seen. That her burnished hair fell to her shoulders in shimmering waves. That her jade eyes reflected the candlelight. That he wanted very much to drag her out of there, devour her lips. That he dreaded the end of the evening.

He didn't like what he was feeling. He sternly reminded himself he wasn't on a date, but sharing a temporary respite with her before her father's world turned hers upside down.

Their gazes locked. And held. Then skirted away.

She flushed as if suddenly questioning if they were sharing more than a dinner of Mediterranean grilled swordfish nestled in olives, capers, tomatoes, garlic, and oregano. Cee-Cee would call his eyes to-die-for eyes. She chose topics such as raising flowers, movies from the fifties and sixties, life in Tinseltown. She praised Colin. She entertained Wendall with amusing anecdotes, but couldn't help noticing every once in a while he seemed distracted.

Throughout the meal, he chose safe topics. He talked about ice-skating at Rockefeller Center, summertime excursion boat rides up the Hudson River, movies, art, anything pleasant.

Anything to stay where they were.

She checked the time. "Goodness! I've been having such fun, I hadn't realized I'm keeping you past your witching hour."

Wendall forced a smile. He heard his outer voice say, "They close in a half hour," while his conscience cursed him.

He paid the bill, and they left. The taxi driver spoke terrible English and didn't know his way. Wendall leaned forward with his arms on the front seat, instructing him in Spanish how to reach the Plaza. Claire studied the back of Wendall's head, noticing his hair curled up at the ends. She had become engrossed in thinking Wendall could solve everything when she looked out to see they'd reached the Plaza.

"You did the work," she quipped, stepping onto the sidewalk. "You should have tipped yourself. Would you rather do this in the morning? I could come in early if you like." She spoke as they threaded their way through the lobby.

"No, it's okay."

She nodded, and they rode upstairs. She halted in the foyer of her suite, tipped her face up, put her hand on his arm, and smiled. "Thank you for a delightful dinner and marvelous company. I babbled, you listened. In my book, that makes you a perfect companion, Wendall. I can't believe I've never been to Asti's. I'm so glad you thought of it."

Helping her off with her coat, his gaze narrowed on her face. He couldn't resist putting his hand on her soft cheek.

"I'm glad you enjoyed the evening."

"How cozy!" a masculine voice boomed. "Take your filthy hands off my wife!"

Wendall whirled around.

Claire blanched. "Colin I . . . I didn't expect you."

"That's obvious," he said with a sneer. "While I sit here cooling my heels, worrying about your whereabouts, you're out on a date!"

She ran to him. "Colin, please. Meet Dr. Lawson. We're here to discuss my father."

"Despite how this looks, Mr. Brice, your wife is right," Wendall said evenly, despising Colin on sight. Colin Brice was a tanned, muscularly built man with a sheaf of wheat gold hair, who glared at him with cold brown eyes.

"You keep unusual hours, *Doctor*. Is this an example of your bedside manner?"

Claire winced. "Colin, for goodness' sake! What's gotten into you? You're deliberately embarrassing us for no reason. I promise you, nothing happened. Wendall, please go."

Hating to contribute to her discomfort, he stayed put. "I'll leave in a few minutes. First, I have something to say."

Colin gave him a suspicious stare. "Whatever it is can wait." He thrust a newspaper in her hand. "Your friend Marybeth sent the *Carrier* to Hawaii. Read it. She sent a copy to the house. My folks received a copy, too. The whole town's talking about us."

Claire's eyes nearly bulged as she read the damning headline. She scanned the article. A blatant fabrication, it carried Marybeth Frankel's byline. Nothing she wrote remotely resembled the interview.

"This is trash. What's more, I can prove it," Claire said, loyalty to her husband paramount. How awful for him to read this contemptuous lie, fly to New York to be with her, only to have him see her walk into their suite after midnight with another man.

"June Lamont, the airline stewardess, knows why I flew here. You remember June. We've flown with her often. She's Tony's wife? Tony, the actor."

"My God! You're responsible for this entire mess. You blabbed to an airline stewardess. I'm surprised you didn't take out ads. Or call Sam and Lia personally. If Yamuto gets wind of this, you can give yourself credit for putting the deal in jeopardy. I packed your suitcases. The Yamutos will be in L.A. Tuesday. We'll entertain them. They'll see a loving couple. Once he signs the papers, you can fly back."

Mortified, humiliated, Claire's eyes went wide with hurt. Colin hadn't come to be with her, then suffer a disappointment she wasn't there. Worried for himself, for his precious mall, he'd come to haul her back. Not one question about her father's health.

"I can't leave," she said, mustering her tattered dignity. She wished Wendall hadn't witnessed Colin's outburst. "There are things going on with my father that won't let me leave now. Also my mother's due in from London. I'm needed here to prepare her for what's been happening."

"That's true," Wendall said.

Colin didn't hesitate. "Claire, this is a crisis. Your mother will understand."

Wendall smoothly interjected before Claire could reply. "Mr. Brice, I'm advising your wife to remain in New York."

"Who the hell are you to advise her? She's not your patient, or is this personal, Doctor?"

"I won't dignify your remark."

"Whatever she wants to discuss can be said on the phone."

Claire blanched. "Wendall, please go. I'll see you in the morning."

Colin growled, "No, you won't. You'll phone him from home. Which is where you're going. Excuse us, Doctor."

"Mr. Brice," Wendall said tightly, "there's no pleasure in listening to you try to humiliate your wife. I'm here as Mr. Jameson's messenger. He entrusted me with certain information—vitally important news that can't wait. I advise you to rein in your misplaced temper, sit down, and cool off. This concerns you, too."

Wendall's stern visage, cold tone of voice, and icy demeanor held Colin in check and stunned Claire.

But as he spoke to her, his bearing and tone softened. "Your father sent for me last night. We spoke for a long time. He's written you a letter. At his insistence, I read it."

Clearly puzzled, she said, "I . . . I don't understand. You said he's improving. Isn't he?"

Wendall removed the letter from his inside jacket pocket. "Physically, yes. He's making an excellent recovery, but there's a problem, a serious one involving his past. Vito discovered it with his computer. Your father surmised Vito would find out. He wants you to know beforehand."

"Before what? What the devil are you talking about? Who's Vito?" Colin simmered with unconcealed irritation.

"I told you about him," Claire said quickly. "He's Detective Vito Malchesne with the NYPD."

Wendall kept his attention on Claire, holding her with his eyes as he handed her the letter. He crossed the room, sat in abject misery, and watched the expression on her face change to incredulity.

Colin and Claire sat side by side, their heads bent, sharing the letter. She uttered cries of disbelief, while he shook his head, cursing. At the end, a stunned silence filled the room.

"It can't be true, can it, Colin?" Claire asked.

Knees bent, elbows propped on his thighs, Colin held his head in his hands. When he didn't answer, she touched his hand, repeated the question. He pushed her hand away.

"Colin, talk to me," she pleaded.

He cocked his head, his mouth twisting in grim irony. "If this doesn't beat all. I'm involved with a fucking impostor. A goddamn thief!"

Cold numbed her spine. "You can't mean it. The business

is honest, there's never been a hint of scandal. You see the books. This," she said, waving the letter, "isn't true."

He jumped up, towering over her in his rage. "Don't be stupid. You read the letter. Do you doubt he's telling the truth? Did he confess to a fantasy? How much more is there to know? This skeleton in your father's past threatens to destroy me. Are you so naive you think we can keep this a secret? Jesus! The papers will have a field day!"

Nostrils flaring, he slapped his fist in his palm. "I flew from Hawaii worrying about Marybeth's article. Once Yamuto gets wind of this, he'll cancel the contract, and I'll be left holding the bag. For millions of dollars. I've got you to thank for ruining me."

She didn't know which fire to put out first, only that she didn't want Wendall witnessing it. "Sam wants the mall as much as you."

"You didn't trust my judgment when I told you friendship flies out the window in business. Do you think he wants his name linked with a crook's?"

She flinched. Her cheeks flamed. Wendall's lips thinned. Her frantic look begged him not to interfere.

"You knew I prepaid a fortune for materials," Colin stormed, sucking in a furious breath. "The trucks are loaded, ready to roll. Thanks to you, my smooth operation is turning into a disaster."

"What about me?" she cried angrily. "I'm more hurt by this than you. He's my father. I'm the innocent party."

"What am I, Claire?"

"A first-class shit!" Wendall said.

"Shut up!"

"Please, Wendall," Claire implored. "Colin, what do you want me to do?"

"Do?" He snorted. "Leave the bastard. Cut your losses. Get out while you can. You don't owe him anything."

"No. I won't abandon him while he's ill. He's my father. I haven't heard his side."

"You read his side in the letter!" Colin shouted in disgust. "What more do you want? I'm telling you to get out now. It's better than having our name associated with a thief."

Wendall heard all he could take. His jaw taut, he said, "Leave her alone."

Colin ignored him. He stuck his face in Claire's.

"Please, we've both suffered a shock. Can't we reserve judgment? Dad's been good to us. You've always admired him. I can't leave without talking to him. Think of Babs, if not my father. She'll need me, too." She put her arms around him.

Colin yanked her arms away from him. He fretfully ran his hand through his hair. "Your father duped my father. He tricked me. I hope he's locked up for the thief he is. How dare he lead us to believe we're equals? Jesus! The money I laid out for supplies. Babs is in for a shock, but now I understand why you fought me whenever I said class tells. How could you possibly understand its intrinsic worth?"

"Stop it. You're saying hurtful things you'll regret later."

"Christ!" He slapped his forehead, paced the room, then hurled another insult. "Your mother was alive when this happened. She condoned the robbery, too. She lived off its spoils. She couldn't know she was going to die. That makes her an accessory." As if struck by a daunting thought, he said, "I married the daughter of two thieves, not one."

"What are you doing to her?" Wendall demanded. He couldn't stand by. "You're destroying her. You're speaking about unimportant crap! Have you any idea what she's facing? Damnit, man, she's your wife! Show some backbone. Stick by her. You owe her."

Colin whirled. "For the last time, you shut the fuck up! Don't preach to me. This is none of your business!" He flung the *Carrier* at the pile of Christmas gifts. "Thank God we don't have children. With your genes they couldn't miss growing up to be criminals. I thought I married a pedigree. It turns out I married a mongrel."

He never saw Wendall's fist shoot out. It came at him too quickly. The blow sent him crashing backward, toppling a chair, scattering the pile of Christmas gifts.

"You slimy bastard! You're not fit to wipe her shoes."

More shocked than hurt, Colin scrambled up. He swung. Wendall ducked. Colin's fist closed.

"No!" Claire shouted. She grabbed a fire poker and threw

herself between the two men. Her hand shaking, she aimed the poker at her husband.

"Stop it! Stop it! I won't let you hit him. You'll have to hit me first."

Colin lowered his arm and unclenched his fist.

"You're crazy," she said, weeping. Wendall pried the tool from her grip, dropping it onto the green carpet.

Tears spilled down her face. "Colin, don't you see what you're doing? How you're acting?"

Wendall shielded her. "Don't waste your breath on him. The bastard's not worth it."

She sagged against him, a broken doll, her arms limp at her sides. "Just go, Colin."

"Don't worry," he spat. "I'm leaving. Stay with your precious doctor, your thief for a father. I'm filing for a divorce. I loved the woman I thought I married. I don't know you."

"Get out before I tear you apart," Wendall snarled.

The door slammed behind Colin. Claire's brokenhearted gaze was on the floor near the fireplace, where Colin had flung the *Carrier*. Its front page ripped, the banner headline blared the truth.

Claire Brice's marriage to Colin Brice was indeed in a shambles.

Wendall's right hand hurt like hell. He sat on the sofa, hunched over the glass coffee table, dunking it in a bowl of ice water. He'd split his knuckles. Vito and Piggy should see him now. They'd be struck by the absurdity of it. For a man who preached peace while patching up bruised bodies, he had violated the rules of civilized behavior. Despite the pain, he felt pretty damn good. In fact, he amazed himself at how good he felt, except for wishing he had broken the bastard's jaw.

If he ever saw the shit again, he would. Gladly.

Claire sat next to him, her face drawn, her lips pinched. She looked ill, shell-shocked. Every light in the room blazed. Only hours earlier her sea green eyes had sparkled.

He had listened to her praise her precious, paddle-tennis-playing prick of a husband.

The horse's ass.

He patted his hand dry, rose, and set the overturned chair upright. He stacked the presents in a neat pile near the fireplace and hung the poker on its stand.

Claire heaved a sigh. "I'm sorry about your hand."

"Will you be all right?"

Her bottom lip quivered. "Yes, I'll be fine. Haven't you heard? Youth is resilient. Life goes on. It's always darkest before the dawn. Fifty percent of marriages end in divorce, but maybe not as spectacularly as mine. . . . Pick a cliché. It's late, Wendall. You ought to leave. Go get some sleep."

He had scheduled surgery for nine, rounds three hours earlier. "I've got a light day tomorrow."

She touched her gold charm. "Colin hates me."

"Men say things in the heat of anger."

His lame excuse sounded in stark contrast to his private thoughts. As he studied her woebegone expression, her sad face and reddened eyes, he wanted to tell her she was better off without him, convince her Colin was a first-class shit.

Instead he blew on his hand, reached for the wine, and poured two goblets full. "This time," he said with a wry chuckle, "it really is for medicinal purposes."

She drained half, took a breath, then drained the rest. "You heard Colin. I'm a thief's daughter. What venal sin did my poor dead mother commit, other than have me?"

"Listen to me," Wendall said sharply. He cupped her chin, forcing it upward. He looked directly into her teary eyes. "Your mother did the world a big favor giving birth to you."

"Why are you so nice to me?"

He wiped her cheek. The corner of his lip twitched. "You've discovered my darkest secret. Nice is my lot in life. My mother tells great stories about our ancestors."

"Don't tell me they were crooks, too?"

He loved her spunky attempt at humor. "Only the favorites. My folks live in a big old house with hand-me-down furniture. One of the Lawson wives started the tale that if the mistress of the house gave away old furniture, she'd anger the ghosts who live there. Each generation of wives added pieces and passed them on. My mother likes sitting on old Uncle Charlie better than on Uncle Frank."

Claire sniffled. "Who is Uncle Charlie?"

Wendall poured her more wine and handed her the goblet. "Uncle Charlie is the piano bench. Uncle Frank's the rocker. Aunt Harriet's a wingback chair. She's the one with loose springs. We call her Saggy Bottom. The other wingback chair is her proper twin. Stiff as a board. We prefer Harriet. Harriet married Frank. We think he helped sag her tushy."

"I like you," Claire said softly. "You tell the nicest lies." She knew he said them to cheer her. He was a good friend. "Your mother is lucky to have you for a son. You're a special person."

"So are you," he said fiercely, so furious with her asshole husband he wished he had wrung his lousy neck. "Now you listen to me. I know people, and believe me, Colin's not worth it. Why the hell did you marry him?"

"I loved him," she said, beginning to blubber. "Oh, nuts. I'm better off without him."

His eyes hardened. "You got that right." He didn't for a second think she believed it. "Your father should cut a deal with the government."

She sniffled and reached for her drink. "Why would the government do that? He's not a spy. He's not connected to organized crime. What's in it for the government?"

Wendall wondered about that, but kept his counsel. "Rich people cut deals. Your father paid taxes on the money he earned over the years. Tax evasion cases are customarily handled as civil matters. He's not a violent felon. If a lawyer convinces the government to prosecute whoever set the car bomb for the police captain, they'll plea-bargain for your dad's information. Sticky fingers is bad police publicity. Knowing a police captain masterminded this crime with the banker adds to the reasons for plea-bargaining. It's a safe bet to assume the other ten million is long gone from the Swiss bank. The bank's insurer will want to recover whatever it can of the claims it paid. The other half of the twenty million dollars is nothing to sneeze at."

"Pipe dreams," she muttered. "My father stole money, then he set himself up in business. It makes no difference if he paid taxes. He's heading for jail. Which penal institution remains to be seen. Colin is divorcing me. That's reality," she said bleakly. His betrayal brought on a fresh onslaught of tears.

Wendall put his arm around her shoulders. "If the government sells off your father's assets, they'll come up short. The taxes must be staggering. I think it's better if they let him stay in business, keep a small salary, earmark the profits for back taxes."

"What we think isn't the point. Face it, he's looking at a conviction for tax evasion."

He took her hand. "I won't lie to you. I don't know what will happen. I only know plea-bargaining is worth a shot."

She wanted desperately to be convinced. "I can't think of him as a thief or my mother an accessory to a crime."

Wendall's throat suddenly went dry. He wouldn't want her problems. "Don't do this to yourself. Your mother didn't know."

"Her daughter is stupid. I told Colin I couldn't abandon my father. But let me tell you something. He's right to be upset. This morning I had a life. He had a life. We had a life together. Now what do we have? Our lives are in shambles. Wrecked. The irony is my father abandoned his relatives — for money. Colin's done the same thing to me. Only worse."

She thrust out her right arm. "With my father there's a paper trail. I'm fighting an invisible enemy. My genes. I can't see, touch, taste, feel, or hear them. But they're there. My stamp of disapproval. My father taught me values. Among them, honesty. So you tell me, Wendall, how can I blame Colin when my own father is a liar?"

Determined to narrow the issues for her sanity, Wendall charged off the sofa and loomed over her. Tonight he'd seen her husband's true character. His attitude defied understanding. Anger boiled up inside him.

"Colin's a selfish prick! An asshole. The shithead thinks only of himself. He wants you to feel guilty. That way if anything goes wrong with his precious deal, he blames you.

I thought it crazy all along to hide the accident. I bit my lip, keeping still when you said he claims to know the Oriental mind. What arrogance! Does he have all the facts? No. None of us do. We have your father's letter. Yes, he made a whopping mistake. He'll pay for it. Him. Not you. Colin is wrong. One day he'll find out how wrong."

Incensed, Wendall crossed over to the window to calm down before he said more. In the street below, a hansom cab, drawn by a horse wearing a flower wreath, plodded along toward the entrance to Central Park. Its passengers sat bundled with blankets over their laps. The man put his arms around the woman, tipped up her face, and kissed her.

"Excuse me." Claire rushed from the room. She reappeared ten minutes later in pajamas, bathrobe, and slippers, her face washed. She knelt on the floor, stuffing a plastic laundry bag with Christmas gifts.

"Take these. Please go. I need to be alone."

He had no intention of leaving her with Colin's ghost. He removed his tie and jacket and tossed them over a chair. "Thank you for the gifts. Maybe you'd like to give them to the children yourself. There's plenty of time."

He stalked to the middle of the room. His mouth tasted bitter. He felt sick to his stomach. He kept reminding himself she loved her husband. If he crooked his finger, she would run.

He drew a careful breath. "Come home with me."

She shook her head, pushed her hair out of her face, and told him to go home. He'd be damned if he was leaving her.

"I'm not going. I don't want to leave you alone tonight."

"I'm fine. You have rounds early. You need your rest. Please, go home."

She wasn't fine. Far from it. She was upset. In two strides he closed the distance between them, crushing her in his arms. "Let me stay. Don't send me away. I won't sleep worrying. I'm a terrible worrier. If I leave I won't be fit for work tomorrow. I'll use the sofa."

Too tired to argue, she shrugged her shoulders. "Suit yourself. You're awfully tall for the couch. I'm going to bed." She started to say good night but the words disintegrated. "I was going to have the perfect marriage. Like my parents. Oh, God. Wait until Babs finds out. Colin meant every word. You're a scientist. I've heard there are people who carry bad genes. How can I find out if I'm one of them?"

Wendall gathered her in his arms, brought her to her bed, and held her while she sobbed. He had a frantic urge to get Colin back if it would make her happy, although he couldn't see what she saw in him.

She held onto him, wracked by gut-wrenching sobs. He stretched out fully on the bed. Her tears drenched his shirt. He murmured over and over that Colin didn't know a thing about genes. One day she would make a fine mother of beautiful, healthy children.

He blamed himself for showing Vito her father's X rays. He hated himself for bringing terrible heartache into her young life. When exhaustion overtook her, he stayed with her through the night. She twisted and turned and cried in her sleep. He murmured healing words of praise. He kissed her tears, knowing she would never be the same again after last night. Even he couldn't imagine the consequences of the scene with Brice. As the first rays of dawn peeped through the window, he relinquished his vigil.

Nine

CLAIRE AWOKE, NOT slowly or languorously, but wide-awake in a flash of jagged memories. Colin's rejection was a daytime nightmare. The bed was warm, the spare pillows indented from Wendall's head. Poor man spent the night holding her, rather than getting the sleep he needed to perform his duties.

Her jaw felt sore from grinding her teeth. She rubbed her gritty eyes, held up her left hand, and stared at her wedding band. Set in platinum, the circle of diamonds represented five years of a failed marriage. The grounds for divorce. Wrong genes, your honor.

She licked her dry lips, pulled at her pajamas, went in search of a glass of ice water, then wandered into the sitting room. Without the Christmas presents the room was an impersonal, elegant salon for transients. She, too, was a transient.

The only sound she heard was the soft ticking of the clock on the marble mantelpiece. For the past week she hadn't noticed its sound. Today it was an anvil. Do all people who live alone hear sounds magnified? she wondered. This was the first time she had thought of herself as truly alone.

Because she was. Forever. Unless Colin changed his mind. If he did, would she want him?

No.

She dialed room service and ordered a huge breakfast: orange juice, a dish of fresh strawberries, a pot of coffee, eggs Benedict, a rasher of bacon. No more picking at dry bagels so Colin could compliment her on keeping her figure. Fat lot of good that had done.

She slumped dejectedly onto the floor, wrapped her arms around her knees, hung her head down, and cried. She chastised herself for crying, then cried more. She felt as if she were on a roller coaster. One minute she pumped herself up, the next she plunged into despair.

At the knock on her door, she dragged the backs of her hands over her face. The waiter delivered the linen-covered cart, set with a bud vase and a rose, gleaming crystal, and silver service.

She caught the young man staring. "I have allergies," she said, adding a fifteen-dollar tip to the tab. After the food smells made her gag, she wheeled the food cart with the breakfast into the hall. She didn't eat it. Assailed by a fresh wave of nausea, she dashed back through the suite and hurried to the bathroom. When the feeling passed, she concentrated on her future. Her real future. Not the fairy tale she'd made up in her mind, then watched disintegrate as Colin's ambition consumed him. Bursting into tears, she grabbed a tissue, wiped her eyes, blew her nose. Her head ached. She hated Colin's guts. She missed Colin. She loved Colin. She hated him. A sob worked its way up to her throat, starting another waterfall of tears.

Her father had brought Colin onto the flagstone terrace of their Stamford estate, introduced them, winked at her, then left. She sat atop a stone balustrade, the picturesque Long Island Sound at her back, the soft summer breeze teasing her hair.

At nineteen, a junior in college, she had had flirting, not marriage, on her mind. She'd promised to call Cee-Cee to tell her about Colin. Her father said he felt sorry for him. She'd planned the scene, imagined viewing herself from above, approving the effect of a glamorous girl in a sequined red bolero over a classic black dress, her shapely legs crossed.

Colin didn't look impressed, which piqued her interest,

made her remember in California glamour was the norm, not the exception. Suntanned, handsome, he carried his broad-shouldered physique with masculine grace.

"Relax, for goodness' sake. It's one dinner," she said, startling him.

He chuckled. "Am I so obvious?" His sexy teasing voice made her heart melt.

"Yes. You look as if you need a stiff drink."

His brows pulled together.

"Oh, dear, I never thought . . ."

"What?"

She wet her lips. "Are you gay?"

He didn't answer at first, but gave her a slow, scorching look. "No."

She thanked God, and wondered what it would be like to kiss him. "You obviously don't want to be here. Why did you fly all the way from California to meet me? Did your father force you?"

He leaned forward, blocking her view of the house. She caught the clean scent of his cologne.

"You're a very forthright young lady. Would you believe me if I said I came for the Broadway shows and made a side trip to Connecticut?"

"No. I may believe you if you said you came here to date chorus girls."

He leaned a hip on the rail, amusement alive in his eyes. "Business with your father brought me here. How would it look if I refused his invitation to dinner? To meet his only child."

Delighted, she nodded sagely. "I see your point. Our fathers who art in business together and all that." A giggle escaped her lips. "You acted prudently. Refusing one of Daddy's command performances is dangerous. He might chop off your head, then where would you be?"

"Why are they anxious for you to marry? You're a kid."

She tsked. "Bite your tongue. I'm nineteen, going on sixty."

He trailed a finger down her cheek, her neck, halting at

the pulse point, then downward to touch the child's charm she'd forgotten to put inside her dress. "So I noticed."

A thrill raced through her. "I graduate from college next year. Besides, this isn't about marriage. If it were, I'd be a wreck. Who wants to be saddled with a man as old as you at my age? That's why I told you to relax. This is about exposure."

Colin burst out laughing, a nice deep rumble of sound, and his eyes crinkled in the corners.

"Stop. You're hurting my feelings. Suppose you tell me why I'm here."

She flirted outrageously. "You're part of my mother's game plan. She's afraid I'll be tempted in the future to pick from the wrong pile. You see, I refused to be a debutante. Mother's a Denison. Very old-line. Stodgy people. Very proper. Even Grandmother Denison got into *this* act. Consider yourself lucky you made the cut."

Colin focused on her lips. "I do. From what I know of your family tree, we're blessed. Coming from exalted ranks is a burden, isn't it?"

"It's best not to dwell on it. Our family doesn't. This is an exception. Mother's desperate."

"As long as this isn't about marriage, we're safe. If you don't mind supporting Methuselah, how about going out with me? If I don't put you to sleep, we can try for a second date. See a few shows."

She fell for him like a ton of bricks. His molten hazel-brown eyes and his mature Cary Grant charm captivated her. He showered her with flowers and token gifts, and delighted her with surprise visits.

And now, she cried, it's over. *It never began, you dope. We both married figments of our imaginations.*

She wished Vito had never seen her father's X rays. Concentrate, she scolded herself, shaking her jumbled thoughts into order. Okay. First things first. A place to live. She scratched living in California or Connecticut. Where, then? If she couldn't live on the moon and never see another soul she knew, she'd buy a terraced apartment overlooking

Central Park, live here in impersonal New York. Until she located a suitable place, she'd stay in the hotel, pay by plastic. Good. What about a job? What were her qualifications? The "hostess with the mostest" also knew her way around computers. She'd write a first-class resumé. Transportation? No problem. During the week she'd rely on taxis. She'd ship her Jaguar to New York for weekend getaways. Good progress. She congratulated herself.

If she was making progress, why did her head throb? Her eyes sting? Did discarded wives always have the terrible feeling of being alone?

An hour later, dressed in a pink mohair-and-wool suit, her hair in a chignon, she applied makeup to her pale face, then went downstairs to the Edwardian Room for coffee and a roll to quell her queasy stomach.

"Good morning, Mrs. Brice. Is Mr. Brice joining you? I spoke with him yesterday," the maitre d' said. "He told me he won his tournament. You must be very proud."

Her throat constricted. "I . . . I beg your pardon?"

He smiled. "Is your husband joining you?"

She looked at him in misery.

"Are you all right?" he asked. "You look pale. Would you like to sit down?"

Sweat broke out on her forehead. She felt nauseated. Her hand flew to her mouth. "Excuse me. I left something in the room."

She fled to the elevator. Rolling her lips inward, she kept her hand over her mouth. When she reached her floor she raced down the hall. Her hand shook. Pushing open the door, she ran to the bathroom. Her stomach empty, she heaved dry heaves.

Her head hurt. She stripped to her bra and panties, bathed her face in cold water, brushed her teeth, and rinsed her mouth. Shivering, she curled up on the bed in a fetal position. She didn't want her marriage ended. She wanted it fixed. She loved Colin. She thought long and hard about the previous night from his perspective. He had flown in from Hawaii. He was tired, suffering from jet lag, understandably upset over Marybeth's vile lies. He walked into an empty suite, waited hours, only for her to show up with Wendall.

Of course he would be jealous. If she saw him with another woman, she would hate it.

It didn't matter if she disagreed with keeping her father's accident a secret. Colin had a right to his opinion. When he told her he needed her at home, she refused. Even after they read her father's letter, he had asked her to come home. But no. She refused, exacerbating the situation. He never would have said those awful things if he weren't provoked.

Seen in that light, she had wronged him. Husbands said things they didn't mean in the heat of an argument. So did wives. Marriage meant compromise. Communication.

She phoned American Airlines and booked a seat on the red-eye to Los Angeles. Then the phone rang.

Colin's voice came on the line. Thrilled and delighted that he'd reached out to her first, Claire felt relief surge through her.

"Claire, are you okay? I'm sorry about last night."

"Me, too. I'm glad you called. It's mental telepathy. I was about to dial you."

"I phoned earlier. You were out."

"I went for breakfast," she said remorsefully. She'd wasted time worrying. "You were right. My first duty is to you. I booked a flight for tonight." She rushed on. "Postpone the meeting with Uncle Sam for one day. I'll go with you."

"It isn't necessary. I thought it over, and I'm fairly certain he'll sign. Your father isn't likely to broadcast this. His case won't come to trial for at least a year. By then we'll have broken ground."

Colin had lifted a thousand pounds from her shoulders. "That's wonderful, darling. We think alike."

There was a long pause.

Suddenly she realized she hadn't mentioned the *Carrier* article. "I'll take care of Marybeth. I'll speak with her editor, demand she fire her."

He cleared his throat and said, "What I said about our having children—"

"Don't apologize," she interrupted. He *was* sorry. She

closed her eyes. *Thank you, God, for helping Colin realize his error.* "We both said things we regret."

"I meant what I said."

She froze.

Colin raised his voice. "Claire, are you there?"

She twisted the phone cord. "Yes, I'm here."

"Look, this is hard for me." He sounded tense, angry. Irritated. "I was and am terribly disappointed. After I calmed down and thought about it, I realized how far we've grown apart. On important issues, we don't think alike, never did. We're fundamentally different. In a way your father's letter is a blessing in disguise."

"A blessing in disguise," she repeated.

"Your father's a liar and a cheat. I invested five years of my life in our marriage, more in my work with him. My name is linked with his. My dreams are wrapped up in a business headed by a crook. There is no greater tragedy as far as my family and I are concerned."

"Your family?" she said dully. She thought *she* was his family.

"My parents are cutting short their vacation. They're sick over this. Essy's on her way to Palm Springs to care for them. If we had children, I would always wonder which bad traits they carried through you. Please don't make this more difficult. The awful thing is that I love you. I have to stop loving you, go on with my life."

Trembling, lights flashing before her eyes, she gripped the phone with both hands. *He had to stop loving her. Cold turkey. Like taking the AA cure.*

She felt like screaming. "Why did you call me?"

"I forgot my trophy. I won the tournament. When I packed your things, I put the bag in the closet. Be careful when you ship it, it's crystal. You'll be in New York for quite a while, I suspect. I'm sorry it turned out this way."

She clenched her teeth. "Wendall said you're a first-class prick! A shithead and an asshole. He was wrong. You're a selfish, pompous prick."

"Be careful who you call names," he warned. "We'll let our attorneys handle the particulars."

The line went dead. Flat. Dead flat. *Flat!* Flat when she wanted to tell him off!

She was steaming mad. All motion, she cancelled her airline ticket, then she dialed Bloomingdale's, asked for a personal shopper, and spent a long time telling the woman her requirements. She ordered twenty couture outfits, a selection of Karan, Versace, Lagerfeld, Armani, Ellis, and Klein.

"No, I don't want to try them on. Send them over, and send one of each style number you stock of your most expensive lingerie. I wear size seven shoes and want matching pairs. Chanel, or another designer. Thank you. Charge this account." She gave Colin's Visa number and hung up as the woman gushed her thanks.

"I may not have designer genes, but I'm sure as hell going to wear designer clothes. Thank you very much, Colin."

She swept into the living room, found the Godiva chocolates, and devoured the top row, chewing over the amount of money she'd receive from the sale of their community property. The house would bring a tidy sum. Beverly Hills north of the hotel brought a fortune. Her jewelry collection was another small fortune. Money wouldn't be a problem. She'd have more than enough to live on.

For five years she had blinded herself with her rosy marital vision, a figment of her imagination. She qualified as the world's most colossal idiot! How could she ever trust her own judgment again if—she found a piece of paper and multiplied—for one thousand eight hundred twenty-five days, give or take the nights he was away, she'd slept beside Colin, made love with him, attributed to him qualities he never possessed? She married a fill-in-the-blanks nonexistent hero! God, how could she be so dumb? When he didn't live up to her romanticized fiction, she quelled her thoughts.

Colin freely admitted he had married her for status.

Thanks to private schools, clubs, the trappings of privileged lives, they traveled freely amongst the exalted "tribe," xenophobic, insulated clans, perpetuated by generations of glorified ancestors. Except she hadn't a clue to her ancestors. If Colin maintained she carried tainted genes, she couldn't dispute him.

All the genetic research proof in the world wouldn't matter under his qualifications. For the first time in her life she felt the heavy ax of prejudice and exclusion. If she were brutally honest, the one element she never factored into her future was her genes. But she knew one thing. Colin taught her a bitter lesson. She didn't know what her future held, only that she'd steer clear of associating with men from privileged backgrounds.

Had she used better judgment, she would have listened critically to Colin's recent breakfast speeches. As he grew more rigid, she'd made excuses for him, telling herself he was stressed, overworked, anything rather than face the truth.

Brilliant at nineteen! Who else but a kid cites her parents' marriage as her role model for her own success without looking long and hard at her intended groom *before* marriage?

Poor Babs. The sweet, gentle woman her father loved and protected would see her fairy-tale marriage go down the tubes, too. She thought of Sadie on her stoop in the South Bronx, wearing her navy peacoat and babushka, scrubbing her front door, and of Daria's eyes when she saw her sable, of the children stroking the fur, and of Wendall's revolving flea market. For all she knew, these people were her relations. She spied Colin's Christmas gifts. She'd give them to Franklin. She got a charge out of the symbolism. Colin paying for Piggy's clothes.

Over is over. Life goes on. She'd make it as surely as the sun rose in the heavens.

She only wished she wasn't terrified.

Claire found Colin's trophy, a pyramid of Baccarat crystal. The inscription on its base proclaimed Colin Brice a champion. She glowered at the inappropriate accolade. Plagued by a dull headache, she set the trophy on the mantelpiece and walked to the window. Yesterday's pearl

gray sky had given way to sunshine. On impulse, she
decided to spend the day in Connecticut. After her hellish
experience she wasn't ready to face her father. The bad-
news details could hold off until she was in a better frame
of mind. She phoned Babs.

"I'm better, darling," her mother said. "I'll be home
tomorrow."

She pretended to be thrilled. She took down the flight
number, then dialed Abby.

"I was about to dial you. Your father is anxious to see
you."

Claire pursed her lips. "Please tell him I can't today."

"After all you've done to lift his spirits, it's the break-
through we've been praying for. Could you manage a short
visit?"

She pinched the bridge of her nose. "No, I'm sorry." Not
wanting Abby to think she was selfish, she added, "I'm not
well." *Understatement of the year.*

She phoned the concierge and rented a Jaguar. She
couldn't wait to see Ruth Fortune, whom she considered her
second mother. For as long as she could remember, Jimmy
and Ruth Fortune were family. Ruth was a fabulous cook,
the best buttermilk biscuit maker in the world. Nothing
rattled Ruth O'Shea Fortune. The brown-eyed dimpled
colleen from County Cork, Ireland, had married an ex-
boxer. Ruthie, as they fondly called her, had put her foot
down.

"It's either me or the ring. Boxing is no life."

Jimmy loved her madly. He wisely knew his limitations
as a pugilist. He was good, but not good enough. When the
Jamesons hired Ruth, they asked if she knew of a good,
honest handyman with a strong back, a man who loved the
land and the sea. She said she knew just the man.

The delighted Jamesons gave them a six-room apartment
above the six-car garage. Jimmy, a stocky, sandy-haired
thirtysomething Irishman, said he'd died and gone to
heaven. He planted the apple orchard with the help of his
employer, Edward Jameson. They discovered they shared a
love of the soil and the sea. The apple trees flourished, and

so did the Fortunes. Ruthie showered her love on Claire, whose sunny disposition drew people to her from infancy. When the toddler scraped her knee, she flew to Ruthie, carrying her Boo-boo bunny—a washcloth Ruthie folded and decorated to hold Band-Aids.

The phone rang four times. Claire disregarded it. Her father was okay. She'd talked with her mother. With that under control, she dressed warmly in beige slacks, beige sweater, and walking boots. It rang a fifth time. She put Essy's and her in-laws' Christmas presents into a Tiffany shopping bag, sat down, wrote out a generous Christmas check for the Fortunes, slipped into her fur, grabbed her purse and the Fortunes' gifts, and left.

While waiting downstairs for the car, she chatted with the concierge. When she mentioned she was taking the Merritt Parkway to Stamford, he cautioned her to keep an eye out for the Connecticut State Police. "They're ticket-happy on the Merritt Parkway."

Once she left Manhattan, the traffic moved at a steady speed. The wind flowing through the window cleared her head. An hour later she turned off exit 35 in Stamford, the land sold by the Siwanoy Indians to Nathaniel Turner, an agent for the New Haven Colony in 1640.

She stopped at the entrance to unlock the wrought-iron gates to the thirty-acre Denison estate before noon. Like many spectacular waterfront properties nearby, the land bordered Long Island Sound. She passed a line of sturdy poplars and pines as she drove down the winding road.

Driving partway down, she braked the car and turned off the motor. The snap of the wind coming off the water ruffled her hair. In the distance a fishing boat plied its course in the inky waters, the ship's horn breaking the stillness. Sniffing the salty air, she lifted her head, watching as a flock of birds veered off to the right.

Home was a three-story white Colonial with a white-pillared porch built in the eighteenth century. Babs's father had added a rear terrace. There were high ceilings, molded and stretched over twenty-five rooms, fireplaces in the upstairs bedrooms, two at either end of the thirty-by-eighteen ballroom where she and her friend Cee-Cee practiced the latest dance crazes. One particular day, they caught her father lounging in the doorway, looking amused.

His thirteen-year-old daughter challenged him to do better than they.

"You're on!"

He yelled for Babs. "Count me out!" she said, coming downstairs.

He winked and changed the record. Babs's size-five feet started tapping. He grabbed her hand. Before two wildly clapping youngsters, proper Babs gyrated to the Lindy Hop. When the song ended, she breathlessly clung to Edward.

"What was that?" Claire asked when she stopped laughing.

"Cutting a rug."

Sometimes Babs let loose. It happened infrequently, but when it did, she astounded Claire with glimpses of her personality she normally hid behind ladylike decorum.

Babs had converted the second-floor bedrooms into suites, assigning the third-floor bedrooms to storage. Guests occupied a Cape Cod cottage located about two hundred yards from the main house.

The first time a horrified Babs saw her seven-year-old daughter zip down the curving mahogany banister to the left of the entrance hall's mantel, she hid her face in her hands. Her father applauded Claire's efforts and whipped down behind her.

Babs had a hissy fit—a fit that would pale in comparison to the one she was about to have.

Dry leaves crunched beneath Claire's boots as she made her way to the bare-limbed apple trees. *We've done a lot of celebrating,* Claire thought glumly. She picked up a twig, tossed it. In spring, the orchard's delicate blossoms scented the air. Nothing tasted more succulent than a freshly picked, vine-ripened apple.

When she was little, the entire family planted the vegetable garden. Jimmy marked off precise rows. Babs and Ruth studied the previous year's growth records, offering advice. The men—with Claire—planted zucchini, tomatoes, green peppers, cucumbers, corn, broccoli, lettuce, and asparagus. She scattered radish seeds. The radishes sprouted quickly, thus giving her the thrill of harvesting *her* crop first. The last task, patting mounds of earth at the base of the marigolds planted to ward off foraging rabbits, signaled a warm buttermilk-biscuit-strawberry-topping-and-milk celebration.

Her father's first-floor library was next to the music room where she'd taken lessons on the concert grand Steinway. She played for her own enjoyment. Certainly she couldn't compare herself to Wendall, who admitted he played well.

The library contained three thousand books. The shelves reached the ceiling, the higher titles obtained by climbing a movable ladder. The room smelled bookish, a mixture of old and new leather. In a place of honor, near rare volumes of Keats and Shelley, her father kept her birth mother's slim volumes of leather-bound poems. Claire's row, designated with a small gold-lettered sign, filled with books *after* she completed them. *Before* books she kept in her small library adjacent to her bedroom, next to her former playroom. Whenever she finished one book, a new one replaced it.

A horn honked. She swiveled. Coming toward her, in a gray Range Rover, Jimmy Fortune screeched to a stop, spewing gravel.

"Claire!" A smile creased his craggy face. When she was little she had thought him a giant. She rode his colossal shoulders, wrapped her pudgy arms around his thick neck, and straddled his broad back, ordering him to giddyap.

Lithe and limber with a rugged complexion, he hopped down from the cab. He wore jeans, work boots, and a lumber jacket; the crisp Connecticut air lifted the ends of his sandy hair.

"How's my girl?" He gave her a big hug and kiss. "What are you doing here? Not that I'm complaining, mind you. Where's Colin?"

Her eyes filled. She swiped at them quickly. "He's in California."

Jimmy cocked his head. "What's wrong? Your eyes are red. It's not that cold."

"Dad's been in an automobile accident." She told him the details. "That's why I'm in New York."

"Lord, child. Is he going to be okay?"

"He'll be fine."

"Where's your mother?"

"She's in London. She had the flu, but she'll be home tomorrow." She gave him her best smile, tucked her arm through his, and clung tightly to his hand. "How's Ruthie?"

"Great. As usual. She'll be shocked, but she'll be thrilled you're here. House gets lonely. The day help comes and goes. I'll be glad when your dad's well enough to come home. Ruthie's baking pumpkin and blueberry pies. The freezer's stacked, but you know her. Cooking and baking makes her happy. Leave the car. I'll put it in the garage."

Above the ornate central doorway, a Christmas wreath hung in the Palladian window. As she stepped inside, the tantalizing aroma of fresh-baked pies drifted from the kitchen, at the rear of the house.

"Ruthie! Claire's home."

Letting out a squeal of delight, Ruthie came on the run, wiping her floury hands on her apron. "This is what I call a nice surprise!"

Claire hung on to her, never wanting to let go. She told her about the accident. As shocked as Jimmy, Ruthie wanted to know what she could do.

"Nothing until he comes home. He's improving each day. Oh, Ruthie, you smell so good."

"It's apple, cinnamon, and raisin."

Wrapping an arm around each other's waists, they strolled into Ruthie's modern kitchen which was equipped with gleaming Hobart equipment. The windows above the double sink and the rear door overlooked a trellised eating area, redolent in the growing season with the scent of tea roses.

Claire wondered what would become of the Fortunes. Of all of them.

Ruth turned on the faucet containing boiling water. She steeped the tea, poured three cups, sliced portions of warm apple pie, dusted sugar on top, and brought everything to the round table.

"I'll make a nice dinner. Steak. Potatoes. The works."

Claire's stomach tightened. She hadn't eaten. Ruth had always served portions fit for an army to everyone except Babs. "I'm not hungry. Don't trouble yourself. I'll have a salad or soup."

Ruth lifted a forkful of pie. "You have your choice of split pea, chicken, or tomato. I keep soup on hand in the winter."

So does Wendall. "Chicken's fine."

Jimmy poked his head in the doorway. "Where's your overnight bag?"

She glanced down at her teacup. "I didn't bring one. I made a spur-of-the-moment decision."

Something in her tone of voice made Ruth give her a sharp look. She finished chewing a piece of pie. "Here, let me look at you."

Claire lifted her head.

Ruth thought Claire had never looked more fragile. "You're exhausted. I see it in your eyes. You're too pale. Have you lost weight?"

"Not that I know of."

"You're sure you've told us everything."

"I've got allergies," Claire lied.

Jimmy's eyes narrowed. "Since when?"

She shrugged. "Lately."

Ruth cupped her chin. She stroked her hair. If her father was getting better as she said, then why didn't she have her old spark? "Allergies in the dead of winter when nothing grows?"

"Have you seen a doctor?" Jimmy asked.

Suddenly Ruthie's eyes crinkled. Smiling, she asked, "Is there anything we should know?"

She swallowed hard. The cup rattled on its saucer.

"You know what I mean," Ruth prompted.

"I'm not pregnant."

"Don't bother the girl with a lot of questions, Ruthie. How's your handsome husband?" Jimmy asked, disregarding his own advice.

She fingered her gold charm. "Fine," she said with false heartiness. Avoiding the truth, she spent a torturous half hour bringing them up-to-date on her marvelous life in Beverly Hills. Ruth asked about her in-laws and Essy, peppering her with questions about her real love: movie stars. Claire said she'd seen Clint Eastwood at Spago the night they'd dined with the Yamutos.

"Clint's hair's receding a lot." Ruth chewed on another mouthful of pie. "He should wear a hairpiece, like Charlton Heston's. It'll make him look younger."

Jimmy asked about Colin's paddle tennis game. Claire pictured the inscribed crystal trophy he'd wanted packed carefully. God forbid it shattered like their marriage. Her misery resurfaced with a vengeance. She didn't have the energy to put up a cheerful front. Plagued by a feeling of hopelessness, lying about her charmed life, holding back the full truth about her father, she felt suffocated. Coming here was a mistake. There was no place for her. None. It didn't matter where she was. She was alone with her emotions. Her earlier bravado left her. No matter what she did or said from now on, a whole segment of society, especially people like Colin, would view her as a pariah.

She pushed back her chair. "Thanks for the pie. I'm poor company. I think I'll go upstairs, see my old room." She fled.

The Fortunes exchanged grim looks. Claire's slice of apple pie sat untouched on her plate, along with three-fourths of her tea.

"I get the feeling it's more than Mr. Jameson. She's not herself, Ruthie, she's unhappy. What's she doing here alone? Why isn't Colin with her? I saw her hands in her lap. She squeezed them so hard her knuckles were white. I'll clean up, you find out what's troubling our girl."

"Maybe we shouldn't intrude?"

"Strangers intrude. We're family. Family helps family. It's better if you talk woman-to-woman. Otherwise I'd go."

She removed her apron, patted her brown hair, and marched upstairs. She hesitated at the bedroom door, despite Jimmy's orders.

Claire stood at the window, her arms wrapped around her waist. She was crying. "God, what should I do?"

Ruth flew in.

Claire swung around, too late to hide her tears. "I didn't hear you. I can't stay. I've got to get back to New York."

"You'll go nowhere, darling girl. Nothing is so bad it can't be fixed. Tell Ruthie."

Sobbing, Claire buried her head on Ruthie's chest. In fits and starts, she said Colin asked for a divorce, but she didn't say why. Ruth silently cursed Colin to hell, assuming he'd found another woman. She never trusted very good looking men. Especially blonds. She unequivocally took Claire's side.

"There, there, darling girl, you're home now. We'll take care of you. When your father recovers, I hope he hangs Colin."

Much as she wished to remain, she said she had to get back, worried that if she stayed she might blurt out the truth.

"I must leave."

"Nonsense. You're exhausted. Take a nap or rest for an hour."

Claire gazed longingly at her inviting bed. She didn't relish driving in rush-hour traffic to New York. If she left later, she'd miss it.

Ruth opened a dresser drawer, still filled with Claire's lingerie. "Take off those clothes and put this on. You'll rest better."

Claire changed into a low-cut, white silk nightgown. Ruth folded the bedspread, turned down the covers, and placed the dressing gown at the foot of the bed. The room featured white Battenburg lace. Claire's stuffed animals and Madame Alexander dolls had been moved into another bedroom formerly used for Cee-Cee's overnights.

Claire had spent hours curled up on the wine-colored velvet window seat, a pink Princess phone at her ear, yakking to Cee-Cee. Often on blustery days her young, boy-crazy heart churned like the waters on the Sound. Now Colin had broken her adult heart.

"Wake me in an hour," she said.

Ruth kissed her, stroked her cheek. She pulled down the shades and closed the drapes.

"Colin's divorcing Claire. She's brokenhearted," Ruth reported to Jimmy.

He gasped. "But—but," he stammered, following her into the kitchen. Six apple and six blueberry pies cooled on the counter. "They were here two months ago. They seemed so happy then. Did she say why he asked for the divorce?"

"No, and I didn't press her. It's got to be another woman. The man's an idiot." In no mood to bake now, she wrapped and labeled the pies. Jimmy carried them to the pantry freezer.

"Her parents will be so upset, coming right after the accident. I can tell she's troubled by how this will affect them. Colin's in business with her dad. What a mess! No wonder she's pale and withdrawn. How could Colin pull such a dirty trick? I made her lie down. She said for me to wake her in an hour, insists she's going back to New York."

"You going to wake her?" Jimmy asked, taking his lumber jacket and work gloves from the closet and putting them on.

"Why would I? What's waiting for her other than an empty hotel room?"

Jimmy squeezed her hand. Twenty-one years of marriage. Ruthie and he got along like two peas in a pod. "That's my girl. I'll be out back. I'm going to chop wood."

"There's plenty."

He planted a kiss on her neck. "I'll pretend I'm chopping Colin's neck."

She squeezed Jimmy's fanny. "In that case, chop a cord."

A commotion awoke Claire. In the pitch-dark room, the digital clock read ten minutes past midnight. She'd slept the day away! Her fingers groped for the lamp. She switched it on. Just as she got out of bed, the bedroom door burst open.

She blinked. "What the . . . ?"

Wendall strode in. His hair was disheveled, his face haggard from lack of sleep. He trained his red-rimmed eyes on her, took in her near-naked condition, the warm bed she'd gotten out of, and her bare feet.

"Great!" he yelled. He wagged his finger, then ran both hands through his hair.

"Wendall, what's wrong? Is it my father?"

He was incensed at her, a muscle jerking in his lean jaw.

"No, it's not your father. I *know* where he is. It's me, you selfish girl. Me! Did you once consider me when you skipped town? You're bound to give me a heart attack. First you run into traffic, now this!"

Her jaw dropped open.

Ruth and Jimmy rushed into the room. Oblivious to his audience, Wendall railed at her.

"After we spent the night together, what was I to think?" he scolded, his blue eyes accusing her of insensitivity. "I left you this morning sleeping. Did I see you all day? No. Did I hear from you? No. What was I to think? I phoned five times."

She swallowed hard. "That was you?"

"You're damn right it was me. Why didn't you answer your phone? Or have the courtesy to leave a message? I told you I'm a terrible worrier. Why do you think I slept with you last night?"

"I told you to sleep on the couch."

"Couch! I couldn't leave you alone after the way that arrogant ass treated you. You needed me. I held you while you cried in your sleep. You soaked my shirt. What's the thanks I get from you? You skip town! Did I deserve it? No, I most certainly did not! I'll have you know, young lady, that I had surgery this morning. Thanks to you, I nearly built the woman an ear instead of a nose! I swear to God I don't know what I'm going to do with you."

"I'm sorry I wet your shirt," she said meekly.

"You should be. Shut up. Let me calm down. I'm having a heart attack. A major coronary. Thanks to you! I can't take this." His gaze slid to her breasts. "Oh, hell!" With no warning, he yanked her in his arms, bracketed her head with one hand, pulled her close with the other, and covered her mouth with his. Too surprised to protest, her arms flapped at her sides, giving Ruth and Jimmy a view of Wendall's back.

He kissed her as a man possessed. He kissed her until the surprise left her. He thrust his tongue into her mouth and kissed her until she trembled. He kissed her until her arms wound around his neck, and she pressed closer. He groaned, lifted his head, muttered his litany about being a terrible worrier, pulled her back, kissed her again. He was a man in distress, scolding her, scolding himself, muttering he'd never done anything like this before, not in his whole professional life. His rapt audience heard and saw a man in the throes of a terrible problem.

He held her face with both hands. "Oh, God, I nearly died with worry. Did I go to Harry's tonight? No. I missed my piano recital. Have you any idea how many people I disappointed?"

"I'm sorry."

He kissed her cheeks. "You're not fair. Not a bit. I didn't want to fall in love with you. But there it is. I did. I am. Jesus, this is terrible. It goes against my principles. It violates everything I teach my students. Christ, this is awful. Kiss me."

He didn't wait for her answer. He wrapped his arms around a dumbfounded Claire, pulling her up hard against him. He kissed her so thoroughly and so deeply that Jimmy coughed. A thunderstruck Ruthie whispered that the tall drink of water was a crazy man. As if aware of his audience for the first time, Wendall swiveled. "It's okay. I'm her father's doctor."

The flabbergasted looks on Ruthie's and Jimmy's faces said they were dead sure he was nuts. Struck by the ludicrousness of her situation, her husband dumping her one night, Wendall attacking her the next, Claire started laughing.

Wendall scowled. She brushed a lock of unruly hair from his forehead and stared into his confused blue eyes. The more he frowned, the more she laughed. She held her sides as a great, big belly laugh overtook her.

"Oh, Lord, did you wear this blue sweater all day?"

He blinked. "Yes, why?"

"And your patients saw you in it?"

"Sure, when I wasn't wearing my white coat over it."

"Did your secretary see you in it, too?"

"Of course she did."

She pressed a hand to his heart, and she giggled. "It's inside out."

He looked down at himself. "Figures," he muttered.

She glanced over his shoulder, speaking to the Fortunes. "This is Dr. Wendall Lawson. He practices holistic medicine. It's okay. He didn't mean a word he said. It's part of his treatment. He dresses up like an Indian, paints his face, makes soup, gives away free clothes. Last night he punched Colin's jaw."

The Fortunes hadn't the foggiest notion what any of this meant, but their faces reflected their approval of the crazy galoot who brought the bloom back into Claire's cheeks. If the big, wild redhead had a new way of doctoring, that was okay with them. They didn't understand it, but hey . . . whatever works.

It dawned on Wendall that he'd made a prize ass of himself. It also dawned on him that if he stood this close to a nearly naked Claire, in a few more seconds the things happening to his lower body would be downright impossible to conceal, especially with her nipples clearly showing through her gown, and him dying to taste them.

He shoved her bathrobe at her. "Put this on." He shook hands with the Fortunes.

Claire pulled on the robe and tied the sash. She found a pair of blue mules for her feet. "Now that the hellos are out of the way, what made you think of coming here?"

He grinned sheepishly. "I didn't know where else to look. I'm hungry, and I haven't eaten. Feed me, please."

Ruth interjected that if he had punched Colin, she'd make him a feast fit for a king. Jimmy wanted a blow-by-blow accounting.

"You can sleep here tonight," Claire said. "We've plenty of room."

Wendall leered at her bed.

"Not there." She shoved a teddy bear in his hand. "So you won't be lonely later. Come on, I'm starved, too. I swear,

Wendall, you're a piece of cake. You're better than aspirin."

He wasn't amused. In fact, he was furious with himself. Like a fool he had blurted out the truth. He was in love with her. It had hit him like a bolt of lightning. For now it was fine she thought it a big joke. When the right time came, he would show her he meant it.

Until then he would probably worry himself to death.

Ten

WIDE-AWAKE NOW, Wendall leaned against the kitchen counter sampling Ruthie's cooking. He licked his lips over her apple pie, said her flaky crust was superb, took a whiff of her chicken-vegetable soup, then said he was a soup maven. He added fresh dill and sprigs of parsley to his, although it didn't really need perking up. She suggested a drop or two of lemon juice as an enhancer.

He asked for her recipes, she asked for his. Insisting on helping, he ladled out generous portions of soup.

"That's too much," Claire protested.

Three people admonished her to eat.

Wendall and Jimmy discussed Jimmy's passion for deep-sea fishing. Wendall led him smoothly from question to question, asking about lures, live bait, test lines, where the best fishing places were. Claire put down her soup spoon. With a little start, she realized he used the same method on Jimmy he'd used on her mother, relieving her of making small talk when she was upset. He avoided mentioning her father, letting her conclude he'd leave it to her to bring the subject up. Every once in a while, as now, she sensed him watching her. She recalled the pressure of his lips on hers.

Their eyes met. She felt his gaze whisper like a summer breeze on her lips. Her fingers tightened on the spoon. She carried it and her bowl to the sink, rinsed them off, then stacked them in the dishwasher. Excusing herself, she walked past the darkened living room, into a room deco-

161

rated with splashes of yellows and greens on the sofas and chairs, its color scheme taken from early nineteenth-century wallpaper panels. A pastoral watercolor painted by her birth mother occupied a place of honor above a Carrara marble and lapis lazuli mantelpiece. She strode across the parquet floor, coming to stand in front of the French doors that overlooked the terrace, where her father had introduced her to Colin. *It was all an illusion.*

"Claire."

She turned at the sound of Wendall's deep voice. He strode out of the deep shadows toward her. "Do you want to talk?" he asked gently.

She peered at his hands. He kissed her, she kissed him back. If pressed for a reason, she'd attribute it to surprise, his blocking out the pain. As for his saying he loved her, she didn't doubt he was sorry, that he'd meant it for a lost soul, in the same way he rescued other lost souls like Daria and Piggy.

With desperate determination, she drew in a calming breath, then slowly exhaled. "About your hello," she began, "I realize the way you greeted me, the things you said to me, were to lift my spirits. I assume Abby told you I refused to see my father today."

He caught the hand nervously playing with her sash and brought it up to his chest. He knew the womanly charms beneath the silk robe clinging to her willowy form. He didn't dare do what he yearned to do, carry her upstairs, strip off her clothes, and show her how wrong she was. He let the first part of her statement go.

"Your father's riddled with guilt."

"He should be," she tossed back. "Look what he's done to my life. What he's doing to my mother's. We're all swept up in this mess, even Ruth and Jimmy."

For a moment Wendall studied her face, noting the delicate facial structure. "He's a shattered man. He understands the enormity of his actions. He says if he'd died in the accident, this wouldn't be happening."

Her eyes glistened. "Then why didn't he have the sense to wear his seat belt? The air bag would have opened.

Furthermore, we'd all still be living in our comfortable dream worlds if you didn't show Vito the X rays, wouldn't we?"

Wendall didn't deny it or the remorse he felt.

Her eyes started to water. "For all intents and purposes my father ruined my marriage."

That he couldn't let slide. "He did you a big favor."

"Favor! How? I spent a week begging him to speak to me. I tried enticing him with movies, with a room with a view. Abby and Molly wasted their time, too. He suckered us. No wonder he hid behind his wired jaw. As if it mattered. As if my sitting on tenterhooks in his room all day getting cabin fever mattered."

"Marrying Colin was a mistake."

"How dare you?" She pushed past him.

He caught her arm. Whirling her around, he forced her to look into his eyes. "I dare because you're important. If you start believing Colin's ethics, it will destroy you. He's a shallow shit. What man turns on the woman he loves on the strength of a letter? Did he show good character? If the situation were reversed, would you act the way he did?"

She'd said the same thing to Colin. In the past she commiserated with friends whose husbands left them. All the empathy she'd felt for them hadn't prepared her for this raw rejection. Her marriage wasn't perfect. What marriage is? Now she faced a painful dissemination, picking out who gets what.

Moonlight spilled through the French doors, bathing her in a silvery glow. Her eyes were huge, luminous. Her breath came in short pants. She twisted out of his grip.

"Stick to my father. He's your concern, not me. Yes, I'm furious and hurt. But I understand Colin. He can't separate himself from his heritage. His values are ingrained in him. Before you came in, I was wishing a geneticist could test my genes, tell me if I'm cursed. Tell me whether I should be sterilized. Colin called me. Would you believe he said he still loves me?" Her laughter echoed in the room. "He's taking the cure to get me out of his system. I'm a disease.

Can you beat that? Regardless of what you think, this is hard for him, too."

Wendall cursed liberally. "Jesus! You're doing a great job deluding yourself. You're on an emotional roller coaster. You're up one minute, down the next. That's understandable. But don't make excuses for Colin. He shot his mouth off with no scientific basis. The world's populated with millions of decent men and women, many of them offspring of people who ran afoul of the law, others of parents who never get caught. Don't confuse your father's mistake with Colin's reprehensible stupidity. His character is flawed. He is a product of a narrow-minded upbringing. I told your father what he said. He blames himself for introducing you two."

She sniffled and wiped her eyes. "I'm very good at misjudging men. I can't face Ruth and Jimmy, knowing I withheld the entire truth. This affects them, too. My mother's flying home tomorrow. I'm petrified she'll have a nervous breakdown. I want to hide, lick my wounds, yet I don't have that luxury. I thought coming here would do me good. I was wrong."

The simple white dressing gown accented her slim figure. Her hair tumbled down her shoulders. Backlit by moonlight, her face pale, tears tipping her long eyelashes, she appeared ethereal. Vulnerable. Fragile.

"I'll pick your mother up at the airport."

"She doesn't know you. Besides, you've spent too much time on us. You're a busy man. I'll be okay. You said yourself I'm up one minute, then I'm down. You caught me in one of my downers."

"Don't make me go into my worrywart routine," Wendall coaxed. "I'll say I saw a friend off. It saved you a trip, you're with your father. I'd rather answer her questions while she's calm."

Claire wavered. "Much as I'd like to, I can't let you."

"Why not? I offered."

Tears sprang to her eyes. "Don't be so good to me. I can't return the favor."

"Sure you can."

"How?" she asked, giving him a wary look.

He opened his arms. "Give me a hug. I'm in desperate need of a good hug."

She tipped down her chin, shook her head, but didn't argue when his hands on her shoulders tugged her forward, aligning their bodies.

"Hugs," he instructed gently, "involve two. Put your arms around me. There, that's better," he said, when the skittish beauty's arms hesitantly circled his waist. "Hugs communicate better than words. I'll get a doctor to cover for me at the clinic. Let me go with you."

She tilted her head, flashing him a watery smile. He knew the shoddy details. His offer meant a lot. It would lift a troublesome burden. His presence would soften the blow. She felt the power of his eyes and nodded. With a little shudder, she melted against his chest, soaking up his warmth and protection.

"Give it time," he murmured. His lips brushed her forehead. Heat stirred his loins, sending an insistent message to his brain. He released her. "Bed. Doctor's orders."

After they bid good night to Ruth and Jimmy, Claire showed Wendall the bedroom next to hers. He took one look at the room and gave her a lopsided grin. "If I fall asleep, don't dare take a picture of me."

The four-poster bed's frilled canopy matched the white eyelet ruffled curtains at the windows. A lacy ruffled overskirt draped a small round table, set with a miniature china tea service, decorated with pink tea roses. White-painted bookshelves, framed in borders of pink, contained sets of Nancy Drew, Louisa May Alcott, and an assortment of books whose authors he didn't recognize. A full gumdrop machine stood next to a doll cabinet chock-full of Madame Alexander dolls. The bedroom was a typical girl's confectionery boudoir.

She smiled. "This was my first bedroom. I adored this room, especially the sleigh bed. Jimmy painted the pink roses on the headboard."

Wendall pulled the gumdrop machine's lever. Two pink

and two white gumdrops slid down the tiny chute. "Color-coded gumdrops. It's amazing. How old are these?"

"They're fresh. Everyone uses the machine. Did you always want to be a doctor?"

He popped the candies into his mouth. "In the interest of truth, for a long time I thought the life of a bum sounded more enticing."

"Oh, when was that?"

He tapped his cheek. "Mmmm. Let's see. Four years in premed. Four years in med school, during my entire internship, and most of my postgraduate work."

She saw the amusement lurking in his eyes. She didn't doubt he was brilliant. "Seriously, did you become a doctor to help your people?"

"My people?" he repeated with a blank look. This was the opportune time to tell her he had grown up in Connecticut, in a mansion on one hundred acres of prime property King George III of England deeded to an ancestor. He sat on the boards of various companies, including ownership of a microchip facility near San Francisco. Thanks to Colin's devastating remarks, he kept quiet, fearing she would erroneously conclude his parents held the same self-serving beliefs as Colin and his parents. He would tell her when the time came, when her wounds weren't so raw.

"You know," she prodded. "In the South Bronx where you grew up. Daria. Franklin. Vito. The kids at the clinic."

"Nothing so character-defining. My heroes were Louis Pasteur and Jonas Salk. I kept frogs in formaldehyde. You'd be surprised how many tough boys stay clear of you when you stink worse than they do."

Her hand slipped to his arm, and when his muscles leaped reflexively, her voice sounded shyly tentative. "I'm sure you didn't keep them or the girls away. You nourish souls. You're wonderful to the people who need you desperately. I appreciate you."

Wendall wished she wouldn't see him as a medical Pied Piper, but as a man. For one brief moment, he let his gaze travel downward from her face. "You liked this lacy stuff, didn't you?" he asked, quelling his riotous emotions.

"I spent my childhood in ruffles and bows. In what I call my prolonged curly period. My parents sentimentally kept this room intact when I moved into the larger one next door. I guess they figured one day a granddaughter would use it. Silly, isn't it? Some parents save mementoes like hobby horses, dolls, baby shoes. Mine preserved an entire room. The mattress is new. We teased Cee-Cee that she wore out the old one. She and I practically lived in each other's houses. If these walls could talk." She shrugged

"What would they say?" he asked softly.

She gazed at him through wounded green eyes. "They'd applaud Cee-Cee's happiness with her husband, Tom."

"And you?"

"I'm a foolish dreamer."

Her suffering tore at his heart, filling him with rage at her bastard husband. He gathered her to him, and his soothing fingers rubbed her spine. "I promise you," he said, fiercely willing her to believe him, "it will get better."

"That's what I tell myself. I've cried more since this happened than in my entire life. That's not me."

She eased out of his arms. Leaving the room briefly, she returned with a pair of Colin's green silk pajamas and the teddy bear she'd teased him with earlier. Wendall declined the clothes. He refused to put anything next to his skin that Colin had touched except Claire herself.

"If you need anything, I'm right next door. If you get scared in the night, hug your teddy bear."

He tossed the stuffed animal she'd given him earlier onto a chair. Frustrated, he stripped, washed in the adjoining bathroom, found a new toothbrush in the medicine cabinet, brushed his teeth, and got into bed. He stared into the darkness, thinking his parents would love Claire. His mother would spend one day in her presence and count grandchildren. For the first time in his life, he wanted to give them to her.

Lately his father echoed his mother. "Get married, damnit. Give me a grandchild."

I'd love to, Pop. As long as the mother's name is Claire.

He couldn't believe he'd told her he loved her in front of

Ruth and Jimmy. He'd never win an award for subtlety. Not only did his timing stink, but Claire herself hadn't taken him seriously. He should be grateful she thought him a benevolent looney tune.

With the single women he dated, restraint wasn't necessary. With Claire it was an absolute must. Shifting uncomfortably, he fought his natural instinct to barge into her room and make such passionate love to her that he would wipe Colin's face from her memory. He conjured up visions of huge icebergs instead.

My dreams weren't supposed to die like this. Exhausted but too keyed up to sleep, Claire sank back on her pillow. She lay awake for a long time. On a shelf in her cedar closet, layered in blue tissue paper, she sentimentally saved her wedding dress and veil for a daughter. Angry and miserable, she muffled her sobs, stuffing her fist in her mouth to keep Wendall from hearing.

At first light she dragged the down comforter off the bed, wrapped it around her shoulders, put on her slippers, and stepped onto the second-floor balcony. A cold blast of air chilled her face and her exposed legs, sending shivers through her. On clear days the breathtaking panoramic view let her see for miles. As the mist rose, she could see boats heading for the channel. Anchored alongside their redwood dock, her father's Hatteras bobbed gently. They had sailed it often to the Caribbean, anchoring at St. Thomas's magnificent Magens Bay. *The color of Wendall's eyes!*

She considered his blunt opinions. Her marriage had failed for reasons beyond her control. From now on she would control her life, set and achieve her own goals. As soon as she could arrange to leave, she was going to California to claim what was rightfully hers.

Next door, a fully clothed Wendall, his hair damp from a hasty shower, sat at a phone speaking to Vito.

"Jameson doesn't have a police record." Vito explained what had triggered his memory, confirming what Wendall already knew.

"It's an unsolved murder case. Goes back twenty-seven years. Murder doesn't carry a statute of limitations. At the time the police investigated Carmine Russo's murder, they found Jameson's pictures in Russo's house. A detective tossed it in the file, but the leads went cold."

"What now?" Wendall asked, afraid of the answer for Claire's sake.

"Now we reopen the case. Why did Jameson alter his appearance? Change his name? How did he finance his business? Who killed Cock Robin? What do you think we're going to do? It's a full-blown police investigation."

"Hold off. Jameson's ill. He's emotionally fragile. His wife doesn't know the extent of his injuries, let alone this. I'm taking Claire to meet her plane today. Question him after he's released. His jaw won't be wired."

"I'd rather not wait."

"I'll pull rank," Wendall said tersely.

"Don't give me that crap!" Vito shot back.

"I mean it. Jameson's under my care. The man's in psychic agony."

Vito hooted. "The man's a crook. I'd be in psychic agony, too, if I were caught living the free life for nearly thirty years, buddy. Where do you come off giving me that shit?"

"He's not going anywhere. He's in a hospital bed with his jaw wired shut. His leg's busted. Why give his family grief before it's necessary?"

"Hold it! Time out! You do your thing. I do mine. For starters, we're talking heavy-duty fraud. Plus withholding information in a murder investigation. That's my end. When the IRS and the bank insurers get wind of this, they'll have a field day. You can bet Jameson's lawyers will make him clam up. What happens to my investigation?"

"For God's sake! You're resurrecting the dead. The case is nearly three decades old. Do you honestly think a few more days matter?"

"Since when do you interfere with a police investigation?" Vito went on brusquely. "I don't tread on your turf. This man's lived off the fruits of a poisoned tree. The sooner I cut the branches, the better."

Wendall clenched his teeth. "Get off it. Don't be a bloodhound for once."

"What makes this so fuckin' personal?" Vito demanded.

"I told you, I'm his doctor." The excuse sounded lame.

Vito cursed, then stopped abruptly. "Where are you?"

"In Connecticut."

"Give Kitty my love. Better yet, put her on. She's an early riser. I miss her."

Wendall inwardly groaned. Vito's bloodhound nose smelled clues miles away. "I'm at Claire's house."

A protracted wolf whistle came over the line. "You arrived early or you slept there?" After a ripe curse made him hold the phone away from his ear, he said, "That's a hell of a house call. So she's the reason for your impassioned plea. What's going on with you two?"

"Damnit! Nothing's going on!" Wendall said savagely. "I feel responsible. I opened this Pandora's box. I let you see the X rays. Jameson wrote her a letter. It's all spelled out."

"Why didn't you say so before?"

"Don't split hairs."

"I'll split anything I want, hot shot. You're acting mighty strange. Tell me the truth. Are you in love with Claire?"

"Leave my feelings out of this."

"Bullshit! You're involved."

"Christ. Get off it! If Jameson's told her the truth, he'll tell you. He's not hiding. After Carmine's murder he altered his appearance out of fear for her life."

"If you buy that I'll sell you the Brooklyn Bridge. I'd alter my puss for ten million dollars, too. I'd do it for half."

"He doesn't know who killed Carmine."

"He may not know who set the car bomb, but he knows who was responsible. Carmine stole money. Carmine died. Jameson helped himself. He's been living right under our noses—mine included!—thumbing his finger at the police."

Wendall tried another approach. "Claire's husband read the letter. He's filing for a divorce."

"That should make you happy."

If it weren't partly true, Wendall would have cursed him out. Instead he repeated Colin's ugly statements.

Vito's attitude underwent a dramatic change. "Fuck the bastard! He's got no balls. I ought to sic Piggy on him. Let him squeeze his exalted genes. By the way, Piggy told me the kind things Claire said to him. He's got the hots for her."

Join the club. Hoping to capitalize on Vito's sympathy, Wendall told him about the ten dollars Claire slipped into the tooth-fairy chest. "She's not conceited. She's sweet, loyal, and she's hurting. Bad, Vito. Think of the living nightmare this is for her. She's afraid of telling her mother. Please hold off. Jameson's on an emotional tightrope. He blames himself for introducing her to Colin. You and I may disagree on his motives, but consider this. Given the length he's gone to in the past to shield his family, the man's a ticking time bomb. He's liable to do anything to avoid public shame. That's a psychiatrist's opinion, not just mine. Give him time to heal physically, and he'll be stronger mentally. He'll be more help to you."

In the ensuing silence, each man knew their friendship was at stake.

"You're in love with Claire, aren't you?"

"Yes."

"Is it too late to change your mind?"

"Much too late."

"At least you didn't tell her."

There was a dramatic pause.

"You told her!" Vito sounded astounded. It violated the first cardinal rule of conquest. *Never play your trump card too soon.*

"What did she say?"

"She laughed."

"Thank God you didn't have a witness. You scared me to death. You can claim temporary insanity."

Another dramatic pause.

"Wendall, Wendall, Wendall," he clucked. "What am I going to do with you? I've written down your pithy sayings in a little red book. For six years I've patterned my life according to your sage advice. Now I'll have to toss the book. How did the witness react?"

"Witnesses. The Fortunes who work here. Claire told them I practiced holistic medicine. For your information, she didn't believe me. Okay! Now get off it. What are you going to do?"

"For you, in memory of the brains I thought you had, I'll sit on this with the department. For myself, I'm going to find out everything I can about Colin and his family, after I take Jameson's statement."

"Why can't it wait?"

"Too many variables. Colin's a loose cannon. The man's bound to protect himself. I want the record showing I proceeded in a prudent manner, otherwise it's my ass."

Wendall had done all he could. "I owe you one," he said. He picked up the teddy bear, then knocked on Claire's door. Hairbrush in hand, wearing a lavender lace-trimmed teddy, she ushered him in and closed the door.

As his gaze moved down her creamy skin, past the tops of her breasts to her slim waist, the curve of her hips, the length of her thighs and legs, his senses resonated with need. But then he saw the dark smudges beneath her green eyes, their sparkle dulled by worry and fatigue. She'd been crying.

"Did you get any sleep?" he asked gruffly.

"Some. How about you?"

"The teddy bear isn't quite the same as a warm body."

She slipped on her slacks and sweater, applied makeup, and blotted her lips. "I'm going to see my father. It'll make it easier dealing with my mother once I've gotten that out of the way."

"I think you're wise, not only for your sake but for his. We'll speak to your mother in the hotel. It'll be quiet, private. If she needs a mild sedative, I'll give it to her."

She sat down and pulled on her boots. "I'm going to California as soon as I can."

A muscle flexed in his jaw. "I see."

"No, you don't see. I'm not running away. I need cash to pay for an apartment. My jewelry is worth a small fortune.

I don't intend to live like a pauper. Colin certainly won't."

"Where will you live?"

"New York. The city's impersonal. There's anonymity in New York. I'll get a job and go on with my life. But first I have to help my mother."

Wendall heard the hard edge in her voice. When she strode from the room, she did so with her head high, a sense of purpose in her step.

As a parting gift, Ruth gave Wendall her pie recipes on five-by-seven cards. "Next time," she beamed, handing him a package of buttermilk biscuits, "I'll fix roast beef. The secret is basting the meat with fresh rosemary dipped in olive oil."

"Thank you," he said. "I'll mail you my recipe for salmon and leeks baked in parchment." He gulped down a glass of fresh-squeezed orange juice, munched another biscuit, and drank a quick cup of coffee.

He squeezed Claire's shoulder. "I'll see you later."

"I like him," Ruth told her. Jimmy echoed her opinion. "He's real. He knows what's important. Not like some men I know."

Molly stopped Claire in the hall. "I'm glad you're here. Your father missed you yesterday. He spends hours at the typewriter. More than is good for his leg in one position."

"I wasn't well. Also, my mother's flying home today. There's lots to do."

Despite her resolve, she approached her father's room with leaden steps. Her heart pounded so loud she thought he could hear it over the clacking typewriter. Bracing herself, she walked in. He was alone. His crutches lay on the floor. A strong sun flooded the room, accenting his hospital pallor, his increased weight loss. His hair was dull gray.

She shut the door.

"Claire." The tenderness and loving in his eyes was full of despair. "I'm so sorry," he said, speaking with his fingers covering the breathing hole. "Wendall told me about Colin."

"I don't want to talk about him," she said sharply.

He sighed. He gave her a typed sheet of paper. "Would you read it, please?"

"No," she bristled, fighting the wave of pity washing over her. She stared angrily at the man she had trusted more than anyone in the world. Her moral, upstanding father. "I want you to tell me. Maybe I'll read it later. Maybe I won't." He urged her to read it. "It explains a lot. Things I wish I said."

"Say them now," Claire demanded. "Talk. Tell me why you did it. Don't leave anything out. I drove home yesterday. Ruth and Jimmy were shocked, but not as shocked as they're going to be. Ruthie's baked your favorite pies. Jimmy's hung the Christmas wreath. Can you imagine how rotten I feel for my part in this charade? Mom's due home today. Wendall insists on taking me to the airport. He wants to be there in case she needs a sedative. I'm not reading letters. Talk. I want to see your eyes. Who are you?"

She tossed her fur on the bed and drew up a chair.

"John Sheldon."

"Where did you live?"

He spoke with great difficulty, saying he had grown up in Brooklyn. "My father was a motorman on the IRT subway. My mother cleaned houses."

"Did they love you?"

His expression grew pained. "Yes."

"What did they think happened to you? And to my real mother? They knew Nancy. They knew me. Did they think we fell off the face of the earth?" She found it difficult to comprehend. The father she thought she knew was a total stranger. Like Colin, another figment of her imagination!

"They knew Nancy was homesick. They knew she died in Switzerland."

"That was then," Claire said angrily. "But afterward? Did it once occur to you they might like to know their granddaughter? I might like to know them. How dare you play God? When I think of my father-in-law's wedding toast I can puke! You seconded it!" she said scornfully.

"I'm sorry," he said.

"I bet you are! 'We can vouch for ourselves,'" she

mimicked. "'We can vouch for who we are. Who our ancestors were. Our grandchildren will be prime!'"

"Don't."

"Prime," she said bitterly. She stalked the room. Her eyes blazed, her hands beat the air. "While you lived in splendor with your new face, how did your parents live? Did you try to find out?"

Jameson covered his face. When he lifted his hands, tears spilled down his cheeks. She slapped a box of tissues in his hand. "Answer me, damnit!"

After a moment, he typed. "They lived near Hopkins Vineyard on Lake Waramaug."

"That's near us!" Her voice rose. "How do you know?"

The keys clacked. "I visited them regularly. So did you. The apple farm."

Her eyes nearly popped. "Good God! Your mother's the fudge lady. The candied apple lady! The tall man, the one who let me ride on his shoulders to pick apples from the high branches, is my grandfather. He used to come to our orchard, too."

Shock made her dizzy. She trembled. "How could you be so cruel? I don't know you, do I? How could you let your parents mourn a dead son and granddaughter, be so ghoulish as to visit them in disguise? Let them visit us? I wanted to marry a man like you. You know what?" Her voice rose to a hysterical shout. "I did. I married your clone. All you and Colin care about is social position and money. What a colossal fool I am! He's convinced I carry tainted genes. He's right. I do," she said bitterly.

Jameson's hands stretched out to her. She jerked away, her fingers clenching and unclenching, her eyes pained, accusing.

He typed rapidly. "My folks knew we were alive. They've always known. I couldn't let them think we died."

"They knew?" she asked.

He smiled wanly. He tried speaking. Frustrated, he banged the keys. "Yes. Grandma made the best fudge and candied apples in the world, but I'm no fudge freak or candied apple lover. That's how we started the tradition of giving fudge and apples for Easter and Christmas. It gave us a legitimate excuse for visiting. I planted the apple orchard so my father could see it, give him a legitimate excuse for coming to us. I pretended I needed his advice."

"My God!"

"I bought him his farm. My dad despised working underground. He missed sunlight, fresh air, rain. When I sent my folks to Paris for a vacation, he refused to ride the Metro. My mother never cleaned another person's house." There was a proud, defiant look in his eyes. "The gold charm you wear. She owned a duplicate."

Claire's jaw dropped open in amazement. She sat. She was forced to digest the newest shock. She hadn't seen the elderly couple since her marriage.

"You told them everything? The reason you had plastic surgery?"

"Yes. They knew I did it to protect you. They knew about Carmine's murder. Fear makes you accept the intolerable. They accepted my new face and new name. We let our relatives think I decided to live in Europe, that I did well and sent them money to buy the farm. With both the police captain and the banker dead now, the fear no longer exists."

"Remarkable." She'd been caught off guard, and her shock registered on her face. "Then I can't understand why you wrote the letter. You're not charged with a crime. Why didn't you wait?"

"The mind goes through strange things after an accident. I saw Vito. I saw his police badge. I freaked out. The swelling in my face started going down, and I figured it was a question of time. Everything piled up. Living a secret is hard. I thought it best you hear the truth from me."

Visibly tired, he needed a break. He asked for water, and she complied. Her mind agog from processing so much startling information, she went to the window to think. The trees in the park were barren, but she was seeing other trees. An orchard of apple trees. A tall man with dark hair was opening the door of a white station wagon with wood panels. He asked how his little lady felt.

"Fine," she had said.

The man hugged her, kissed both her cheeks. People were always kissing her. Ruth. Jimmy. Babs. Grandma and Grandpa Denison. She was used to it. As long as it wasn't on the lips. Her mother said she shouldn't catch germs, always turn her cheek.

Her father walked with them while she picked apples. Spotting a squirrel, she scampered after it. Her braids came loose. Her father asked the apple lady if she wouldn't mind braiding his daughter's hair. The lady held out her hand, saying she'd be delighted.

"I've always wanted a granddaughter your age," she said, taking the little girl into her bedroom to braid her hair.

On subsequent visits, they sat around the big oak table with the claw feet, drinking hot chocolate. The table's top fascinated her. The woman called the round dish a Lazy Susan. Light and dark green dishes—sections—curved snugly against each other, formed a circle around a light green bowl filled with scented brown balls. She touched one. It felt funny. Prickly. Uneven. But it smelled delicious.

"They're pomanders," the lady said, giving her one to hold. "The cloves hide an orange."

The little girl disagreed, very pleased she couldn't be fooled. "Oranges aren't hard."

"Dried ones are," her father explained. The apple man added that without juice, fruits dried up.

"Would you like this pomander for a souvenir?" the lady asked. Claire looked at her father. Her said yes. She spent the next hour learning from the apple lady how to make a pomander.

The clove stems kept breaking in her little hands. The lady kissed her cheek and gently took the orange.

"We'll do it together." She pierced the rind with a darning needle. "There, now try."

After that, the cloves pushed in easily.

"May I have this one?" the lady asked her when she was through. Claire hesitated. She wanted it for her mother.

"Let's make a second one," the lady suggested.

That brought a smile. How could she say no? The nice lady

braided her hair, gave her hot chocolate, fudge, a candied apple, and taught her the secret of making pomanders.

"You take one of mine," the lady said, kissing her in thanks. Her father praised her. The apple man beamed.

Claire closed her eyes. To this day she could bring back her grandmother's unique scent. Somewhere in her house in Beverly Hills she still had the pomander. She'd kept it all these years without knowing its significance.

"Your parents are good people."

"They loved you. My mother treasured your pomander."

"I saved hers, too. Once I told her she smelled like chocolate apples." She paused. "Does Babs know?"

"No."

"Well, she's going to be in for an awful surprise," she said, flabbergasted. "In more ways than one."

Her father's face grew strangely contorted. "I've relived the accident every minute of every day since it happened. I've had a good life. I wish I can say I'm sorry for all the years we and my parents lived well, but if I did, I'd be a hypocrite. The real tragedy is what this is doing to you, will do to Babs, thanks to me. I love you both dearly. Nancy was my first love, and then I was lucky to meet Babs. Some men don't find happiness once. I've been doubly blessed."

"Tell me about Carmine."

"His parents were nasty alcoholics. Both beat up on him. He stayed with us a lot. Or he escaped to the library to avoid beatings. He consumed books and magazines. He grew tall. Strong. After a few street fights, gangs left him alone. Eventually he got a job in a bank. He was dedicated, excellent in math. He got ahead. The bank president trusted him. He sent him to Switzerland as his courier. The Swiss knew him. He had access to a numbered account. He returned with receipts. Then the American bank installed computers. Carmine spent hours at his. Unfortunately he learned the banker he idolized had used him to ferry stolen money."

"If Carmine was so smart, where did he think the money came from?"

"I'm certain he thought the banker was hiding money he

had earned. Then the sum became staggering. Carmine didn't want to believe anything bad about his mentor. But then it all came together. We all knew about the big bank robbery. Through Carmine's computer hacking, he put two and two together. The insurance companies made good on the robbery. It was the perfect white-collar crime. Carmine didn't get mad, he got even. He bided his time, made more trips, opened a Swiss account. He transferred half the money into his account."

"Carmine was a thief."

"Don't judge him too harshly. There were many forces at work, pulling him in different directions. After his murder, I was frantic. I knew your life was in jeopardy. Carmine stole from dangerous men."

"And now?" she asked.

Jameson inserted a clean sheet of paper, began typing. "It's Vito's move."

"Colin knows. He worried Sam Yamuto wouldn't sign the final papers if he learned about this."

"Colin's shown his true colors. He doesn't upset me. He can't shift large sums of money without my signature. My biggest regret is introducing him to you. One day you'll meet a man worthy of you. Next time you'll pick each other."

She gazed down at her wedding band. "I married too young. Like a blind, trusting fool I allowed Colin to make the major decisions. I focused totally on my marriage. It was an easy trap to fall into. We lived well. We traveled. We entertained friends and business accounts. I buried my twinges of discontent for the sake of peace. I lived vicariously through my husband. It's a mistake. I'm going to make something of myself so this will never happen to me again. And I'm going to visit my grandparents."

A low cry erupted from Jameson's mouth. "You can't. Didn't you hear me use the past tense? My father died four years ago of emphysema. A year later my mother passed away."

Claire could feel her heart beat in dismay. She disapproved of his act, but she couldn't hate him. He was already paying a heavy price for his wrongdoing, would pay an even greater one soon—the inevitable loss of his good name. Others would judge him in a court of law. Right or wrong, he was her father. She couldn't abandon him.

"Are you afraid?" she asked, reaching for his hand.

"Yes. I hate what I've done to you, what this will do to Babs. Neither of you deserve this kind of notoriety."

"Wendall thinks you should plea-bargain."

"White-collar crime takes a long time to investigate, longer to prosecute. Don't let him blame himself for showing Vito the X rays. I think this is God's way of closing the account."

He sounded prophetic, and she looked at him sharply. Warning bells sounded in her head. "I'll stick by you."

He squeezed her hand. "Hearing you say that means more than you know. But I don't want you hanging around when the vultures start picking apart my bones."

Amidst the swirl of conflicting emotions, she wanted to cry for him. She was all too aware she couldn't kill a lifetime of love. "Don't tell me what to do." She kissed him, then fled from the room, rushing down the stairs to hail a cab back to the Plaza.

At the far end of the glittering lobby she passed the spacious old-world European elegance of the Palm Court, with its Four Seasons marble statues gracing the walls. The room hummed with guests, a few of whom paused to study the sumptuous desserts displayed on a table near the entrance.

In the elevator, one couple linked fingers, another carried on an animated conversation. Once inside her suite, she gave Colin's trophy a sour look.

It symbolized the final insult.

Eleven

FRETTING, HALF HOPING her mother had missed the plane, Claire sat in a maroon seat in the British Airways terminal, staring at a monitor listing the Concorde's arrival. In the past half hour, she'd stared at gray walls, leafed through four magazines she'd brought with her, and used the ladies' room twice.

Wendall slouched in a chair, dozing. She tapped his arm. "Let's go. The plane's in."

He cracked open an eye.

"Relax. She's got to go through Customs."

"How do you do that?" she asked.

He stretched his long legs. "What?"

"Nod off in public."

"I survived medical school. I sleep standing up." He leaned down, reaching for a container of coffee he'd brought along. "Want some?"

"It'll go though me like a sieve. What can I say to her? First, I mean."

"Try hello," he said, and Claire rolled her eyes upward. "Stick to small talk. Wait until we're in the hotel."

"Right. Did I thank you for coming?"

He ran his index finger down her right cheek. "Mmmm. Yes, three times."

Her hands flew to her face. "My eyes! Do you see smudges under them? Mom's very observant. It'll be a dead giveaway if she notices."

Her dark hair shone. Her eyebrows were full, shaped dramatically above luminous green eyes. He saw no signs of worrisome purple smudges. Her cheeks were flushed, her lips slightly parted. All he could think about was kissing her.

"Come closer." He settled for an intoxicating whiff of perfume. "Delicious."

"Well?" she demanded. "Do I pass?"

"Stand up. Here, give me your coat." He put down his coffee, helped her off with it. His lips curved into a smile. The coral woolen dress accented her curves. Tan high heels and sheer stockings emphasized her long, slender legs.

"You're fine. How do I look?" He gave her back her coat.

"What?"

"My suit. Will it make a good impression?"

She angled her head. Her gaze swept the length of the navy pin-striped suit. "You're fine. Blue's your color."

He lifted his chin. "How's the tie?"

"Okay," she muttered.

He raised a pant leg, wiggled his foot. "Do my socks match?"

She glanced down, heard him chuckle, then whipped her head up to see him grinning. She whacked his arm. "Beast! Don't tease me. Oh, God. I'm a faucet." Thrusting the coat at him, she flew into the ladies' room. She returned in seconds.

"That was quick." He finished the coffee and tossed the empty container into the trash.

"There's a long line."

"You're a bundle of nerves. That's all your mother needs. She'll assume your father is worse. Calm down. It's going to be okay."

"Easy for you to say." Claire shifted feet. "Can you guarantee my father won't pull another surprise?"

No. Wendall turned her forcibly in the direction of the ladies' room, giving her fanny a little push. "My Pontiac may be a relic, but it draws the line at letting you pee on its upholstery."

Twenty minutes later, Babs fell into her daughter's arms. Wendall studied the pair. Both were striking women, yet totally different. He reminded himself they weren't blood relatives. While Claire was vibrant and colorful, Babs was petite and delicate. Unlike Claire's lush dark hair, Bab's hair was spun gold. Both dressed elegantly. Babs wore a stylish mauve suit under her mink.

After the introductions, he asked them to wait while he got the car. When Babs saw his Pontiac, she murmured beneath her breath, "Oh, dear."

Wendall winked at Claire. "We're off to a smashing start." He shoved aside a stack of AMA medical journals on the rear seat so Claire could sit there. "She likes my suit."

"You're mad," she whispered, bowing her head to sit down.

He rolled up the window, shutting out some of the airport noise. Chatting as if he'd known Babs for years, he discussed her husband's continuing progress, saying he was getting therapy to strengthen his leg.

"Is swimming good for him?" she asked.

"Water therapy is good for everyone."

"It's settled," she said with a little trill of happiness. "I'm building Edward an indoor swimming pool. We've talked about it over the years. It's time we did it. I know a fabulous architect. Dick Harris will design us a showplace. He did Princess Thelda's. Just think, Claire, when you and Colin visit, you can swim year-round."

Claire blanched. "The ground's too frozen to dig."

"No matter," Babs said. Used to luxury from the moment of birth, her wealth permitted her to satisfy every extravagance.

"I'll custom-order the furniture from Kenneth Naples," she said, mentioning a well-known posh outdoor firm. "Wait until Dad sees the George the Third library table I found for him. And, lucky me, I found a George the Third lady's writing desk, plus a marvelous Continental rococo painted chest of drawers for our bedroom."

Wendall caught Claire's eye in the rearview mirror.

Sheer will put a smile on her face. Determination kept it there until she arrived in her hotel suite. She dropped the pretense, waiting for her mother to come out of the bathroom.

Wendall squeezed her icy hand. "You only have to do this once."

Her mother joined them. Her heart thumping, Claire sat down next to her mother. In a quiet tone, she told everything she knew, including what her father had said earlier. She handed Babs his letter.

"Preposterous!" Babs flung it aside. "My Edward's the most honest man in the world. I'm shocked you'd fall for this hokum. Your father's hallucinating. The accident temporarily rattled his brains. Isn't that right, Dr. Lawson?"

Wendall was incredulous. Of all the reactions he expected, this wasn't one of them. She hadn't believed a word! Keeping his tone devoid of judgment, he confirmed the damning evidence.

Agitated, she demanded proof. "Doctor, I'm surprised at you. You should know if a man's face hits the steering wheel, it jars his brains. He's liable to spout nonsense."

Wendall and Claire exchanged guarded looks.

"Mother, there's more."

Babs's complexion paled. "I don't want to hear it."

"Colin's divorcing me."

"God in heaven! Why? You were here for my birthday. Everything was fine then."

Out of the corner of her eye, Claire saw a muscle in Wendall's jaw tense, his fists flex at the mention of Colin's name. "He and I read Dad's letter together."

"He was here?" Babs said.

"Briefly. He feels cheated."

"Cheated? How?"

Claire gazed at the trophy. "He sees Dad . . . He sees me as . . ."

Wendall took over. "Your son-in-law is a class act. That paragon of privilege rode roughshod over Claire's feelings, in my presence, I might add. He said, 'I thought I married a pedigree. It turns out I married a mongrel.'"

"*He whaaat!*" Babs gasped. "How dare he?"

"That's not all," Wendall said bluntly.

"Wendall, don't," Claire pleaded.

"Claire." Babs sounded thoroughly incensed. "Unlike your father, Colin isn't ill. If he said those horrible things, I demand to know every word."

Her face a picture of misery, Claire stared at the floor. "He thanked God we didn't have children. He said it's a foregone conclusion I'll pass on bad genes—criminal genes. He'd always wonder when the criminal element would come out."

"I smashed the son of a bitch's jaw!" Wendall said.

Babs shook with indignation. She threw her arms around Claire as if she could provide a protective barrier. Claire shuddered. She eased out of Babs's embrace. "I'm fine."

"I'm not. How could we have misjudged him so? We trusted him to care for you."

"Don't blame yourself. No one put a gun to my head. I loved him."

Babs was every inch the patrician mother venting her considerable wrath. Claire was her child. *Hers*. From the moment she had held the infant in her arms, felt her little fingers curl over hers, the baby owned her heart.

Babs spied Colin's trophy. "He finally won the bloody championship." Her arms braced on the mantelpiece, she read the inscription on the trophy's base.

"Yes, he did. Mom, please, can we talk about Dad?"

Ignoring Claire's entreaty, Babs's blue eyes darkened in anger. She crossed to the windows facing Central Park South.

"Washington Irving headed the commission that planned the park. Frederick Law Olmsted designed it with Calvert Vaux. It took nearly ten years to complete at a cost of nine million dollars. A drop in the bucket by today's standard. In acreage the park is double the size of London's Hyde Park."

"Won't you please discuss Dad?"

"I am," Babs said enigmatically, and Claire looked helplessly at Wendall when Babs seemed to deliberately block any discussion of their serious situation.

"If Edward lived at the end of the Civil War and had ten million dollars then, he could have paid for Central Park."

Claire felt a tightness in her chest. If she couldn't make Babs face facts, she didn't know what she'd do. Bringing her back to the topic, she asked, "What will you say to Dad?"

Babs arched an elegant brow. "I'm not sure. I need time to think. He kept me in the dark for more than a quarter of a century. Now I learn I knew his parents. I had no idea who they were. This is too much. Don't expect me to come up with a decision in two seconds."

It was warm in the room, but Claire's teeth chattered. The comforting hand on her shoulder made her look helplessly at Wendall.

After a lengthy time, when they sat watching Babs's back, she heaved a sigh, then turned around. "Claire, you've known this longer than I. It's clear you're paying a heavy price. What have you decided? Are you prepared to stand by him?"

She touched her wedding ring. "A circle of diamonds lit by the fire of love," she had said when she wore it for the first time as Mrs. Colin Brice. She had thought she would wear it forever. "I dream I'll wake up and find out it's been a horrible nightmare. Until Colin's trophy reminds me this isn't fiction. He said I should leave, that I don't owe Dad a thing."

Babs leaned against the wall. "Do you owe him anything?"

She answered without looking up. "I don't have a simple answer. I can't equate love with a balance scale the way Colin can. It's easy to condemn Dad. I don't approve of what he did, yet if I abandon him the way Colin abandoned me, what makes me better than Colin?" She lifted her eyes. "I guess it all comes down to one thing. Whatever you decide, I'll stand by him. Despite everything, I love him. He's still my father."

"He's still my husband," Babs said, her tone unequivocal.

"You're taking this better than I expected," Claire blurted out. "I thought you would go to pieces."

Babs brushed a strand of hair from her sleeve. "Is that why you're here, Wendall? To pick me up from the floor?"

"Let's say I'm here to help you to a chair should you need

it. Would you like hot tea or coffee? I don't think you need a tranquilizer."

"I prefer white wine." He poured her a glass. She sipped it, then said, "Claire, it's time I told you why I've never had children. When I was sixteen, a doctor removed my cancerous womb."

The admission surprised Claire and caught Wendall's full attention.

"I healed physically, thanks to it being an encapsulated tumor. My emotional scars lasted far longer. I had fallen in love with a man. I was in my early twenties when we announced our engagement. I made a huge mistake. I waited until after he put a ring on my finger to tell my fiancé why I couldn't have children. After he recovered from shock, he accused me of leading him on. We were of the same rigid social code. I, of all people, should know an heir to a large fortune required his own heir. Adoption, he said flatly, was out."

Claire reacted with angry loyalty. "He was dumb! Mother, don't put yourself through this."

"No, darling, I'm fine. His mother had sent out the invitations to his family to celebrate our engagement party. At the time, I wanted to die of humiliation. Later, I resigned myself to spinsterhood."

Wendall rose. He took his coat from the back of a chair where he dropped it. "I'll wait downstairs."

"No, stay. Truly, this is old news." When he sat down next to Claire, Babs continued. "Between my charitable interests, my sponsorship of the ballet, attending the Met, I fashioned a life. Each year I treated myself to a vacation. The year I met Edward, I was on summer holiday in Gstaad."

She smiled. "I love Gstaad. It's a magical Alpine valley. One day as I was coming out of Union Bank, I spotted a virile man with dark, roguish good looks, pushing a baby carriage. You know I normally avoid strangers. Magnets controlled my feet. The truth is your father could turn any woman's head. And you were adorable. You cooed and gurgled, showing off your baby tricks. Your father beamed.

I was delighted. You, my darling, provided the introduction.
You gave me a reason for speaking with Edward, then and
on subsequent days. So you see, you chaperoned us. A
rather unique courtship."

Claire leaned forward, caught up in the story.

"We walked and talked for miles. You thrived on attention and the fresh mountain air." Babs smiled. "The mountain air put you soundly to sleep."

"Mother, you're terrible."

"Yes, I was, wasn't I? We never called our walks dates.
Without telling Edward, I extended my holiday. He fascinated me. By then I knew that I had fallen deeply in love
with this appealing, sexy, intelligent man. Of course I never
let on. What was the point? I saw our friendship as an
interlude. Two lonely people—friends—reaching out for a
moment in time, exchanging confidences. We took you
everywhere, even to Sir Yehudi Menuhin's Beethoven
concert."

"Beethoven," Wendall said reverently.

"Do you like his music?" Babs asked.

"He's my favorite. What did Claire do at the concert?"

"Mine, too. She slept or she sang to the music. The day
before I was due to fly home, Edward and I dined at the
Palace Hotel. You, my perfect angel, snored through a
five-course meal."

"I never snore, and you eat like a bird!" Claire cried.

"I picked, I admit, but five courses take a long time. I
hated to see the evening end. We said good-bye at my
chalet. You awoke, I held you. You scrunched up your tiny
face, and you sobbed as if you knew it was our last time
together. I cried. Edward's eyes were suspiciously damp.
He returned later. He had dressed you in a pink dress with
lace ruffles. You had a pink ribbon in your hair. You kept
pulling at it."

Babs laughed softly. "He was a nervous wreck. He laid
you on the bed, propped pillows on either side of you, and
stuck a pink pacifier in your mouth."

"Then what?" Claire asked, enthralled.

Babs blushed. "He held me in his arms. He said he loved

me for myself, not for my body parts. Could I possibly see myself married, with you for my child? Silly man. He granted me my life's dream. Of course, I said yes." Her eyes shone.

"Wendall, Claire knows this, but since you know the rest, you might as well know this, too. When my father died, I insisted he commingle the Denison funds. Claire, do you remember hearing us argue? Your father didn't want to do it."

Claire nodded. "I do remember. It was one of the few times I've heard you two go at it."

"I prevailed. Grandma lived her remaining years without pressure, in her customary gracious life-style. Your father has managed our financial affairs with scrupulous honesty. The way he manages his business. What you told me about his parents proves what I've always known. He couldn't deny them or you the pleasure of knowing each other. I just wish he had told me." She tilted her chin proudly. "Who knows? Maybe he thought he'd endanger my life, too."

"It worried him," Wendall said. "I'm sure he thought his silence protected you."

"In some quarters, I'd garner sympathy if I left him. But, I ask myself, will that ensure my happiness? Not one iota. Not at Edward's expense. The time to show love is when it's needed most. I wouldn't trade my life with your father and you, Claire, for all the money or so-called status in the world. I've had both. Trust me, being a lonely member of high society is cold comfort in an empty bed. Yes, Edward has a lot of explaining to do. Sticking by him won't be easy. I'm sure I'll falter. Except for loving him, I can't give guarantees. So there's my answer. Our lawyers will advise us, but I'm staying, too. That's all I have to say."

She had said a lot. Leaving Wendall in deep respect of her, and Claire misty-eyed, she set the wineglass on a table and crossed to the fireplace.

"Now I want to examine Colin's gorgeous trophy." She took it down from the mantelpiece. "I collect Baccarat," she told Wendall. "It's plain to see why Colin treasures this. Not only for its symbolic value—he's strived for years to win—

but see how the light catches the prisms. Excellent work-manship, excellent."

Wendall and Claire exchanged puzzled looks. She barely contained her irritation. "Colin phoned. He forgot it. He wants it packed carefully."

Babs held the trophy higher. She looked back over her shoulder with clear blue eyes. "I don't blame him. Have you decided to give him the divorce?"

"Yes."

"Then I think you should return to California as soon as possible. Hire a fine attorney."

"Now that you're home, I will. I'll leave the day after tomorrow."

"That soon. How long will you be gone?" Wendall demanded, bringing Babs's attention to his scowling face.

"I'm not sure. As long as it takes," Claire replied.

Babs raised the trophy higher. Turning and tilting it, she examined the craftsmanship from all angles. "The sooner she puts this nasty business behind her, the better. Don't you think so, Wendall?"

He grimly agreed.

"This is absolutely exquisite Baccarat," Babs said. "Very lovely. Very pricey."

Without warning she dropped it on the marble outer hearth. It smashed and broke into chunks.

Claire stared at the shattered crystal. Her mother had dropped *Baccarat*! *On purpose!*

"How terrible of me." Babs smiled archly. She wore a grin of pixieish satisfaction. She turned devilish eyes on them.

"Dear me. It's totally ruined. What a pity! Pack it with meticulous care, as Colin wished. You can't trust the mail nowadays, can you?"

Wendall roared. His admiration for her grew stronger by the minute. His shoulders shaking with mirth, he found a plastic bag beneath the bar. "Let me do the honors."

She toed a chunk of glass nearer to him. "Thank you. Claire, you're officially released from duty. You attend to your affairs. I'll take care of Daddy. Don't let Colin or your in-laws give you grief. You're better than they are."

A visibly relieved Claire bounced up to hug her. "You're amazing. It's easy to see why Dad loves you. Give me a minute to change, then we'll go to the hospital."

"Are you Ron and Kitty Everett-Lawson's son?" Babs asked when Claire left.

Wendall's wary gaze shot to the bedroom door. His expression cautious, he nodded.

"I've met your parents. At first I didn't make the connection. Why do you keep looking at the bedroom door?"

He dropped the last piece of broken crystal into the plastic bag. "I'd just as soon you don't tell Claire. We met at my South Bronx clinic. She assumes I'm a hometown boy who made good. My detective friend, Vito, looked into Colin's background. Both his parents grew up in a protected, privileged environment."

"Not quite as protected as you think." Babs laughed. "Angie's parents wanted her to marry a friend's son, a man who shared the same Spanish background as they did. Naturally that left out Simpson, whose ancestry is English. They didn't reckon on his ingenuity." Babs giggled. "Guess how he overcame their objections?"

Wendall dutifully asked, "How?"

"He impregnated their virginal daughter."

His brows shot upward. "How do you know?"

"One night Simpson drank more than he should. He confided in Edward that there are all ways to reach an objective. Colin came into the world eight months after the wedding, weighing eight pounds, not exactly a preemie's weight, is it? Angie's family told everyone she was too delicate to carry full term."

Wendall howled, then sobered. "With the way Colin flaunts his heritage, I'm afraid if Claire knows about my family, it'll spook her. I'll tell her in due time."

Babs's soft mouth curved in a smile. Wendall lacked Colin's charismatic movie-star quality. His face was leaner, his physique lankier, and his thick auburn hair, she guessed,

was once a bright red before a smattering of gray had toned
it down. His eyes, however, were spectacular, a blue that
pierced a woman's heart. She glanced at the hands he'd
raised in her daughter's defense. Claire was right. Wendall
inspired trust.

"Don't wait too long," she cautioned. "It could backfire.
Thanks for punching Colin. Do you fight often?"

He laughed, welcoming an ally. "Claire asked the same
question. No, I don't. In his case, I'd gladly make it a habit."

"My daughter's in good hands," she said. "For the record,
is the Pontiac your only automobile?"

He grinned. "Nope. I own a white Corvette. Neatest
number you ever saw. I call it Ludwig."

"No candy wrappers on the floor?"

"Bite your tongue."

At her request, Babs saw Edward alone. Claire and
Wendall understood her need for privacy. "Here's where
we'll be. Call when you're ready to leave." Wendall gave
her Harry's phone number.

Vito was at Harry's when they arrived. He sat down at
their table. At first Claire felt awkward, but then he said he
was sorry he was the one who had discovered the truth.
He'd spent several hours that afternoon with her father.

"I've gotten to know him better, Claire. My sense is he's
a decent person. I can assure you he wasn't involved in
Carmine's murder."

"I know, but it still leaves the IRS, the bank, and the press
to come after him."

She was so glum that after Wendall consumed a pizza
burger on Irish soda bread and devoured an order of crisp
fries, he patted her shoulder. "I'll play piano for you. That
will cheer you up."

Vito scraped back his chair, hastily claiming he already
had indigestion. Claire dabbed her lips and put down her
napkin. After hearing so much from Wendall about his piano
prowess, she looked forward to the entertainment. The room
became quiet as he rose. A sense of pride rippled through

her. She noticed Harry and his son passing out steins of beer to everyone.

Wendall's first number had her wondering. By the most generous standard, he was an enthusiastic novice. Baffled by the audience's politeness, she glanced at Harry, who gave her a broad smile. Wendall ended the selection. The audience clapped. A few whistled. It was as if they acted on cue, then resumed eating and talking. Puzzled, she wondered whether she was the only one with good hearing.

Harry sauntered over to her table. "Terrific, isn't he? Everyone's happy. The booze is Wendall's treat. He pays for two rounds. Don't tell him I told you."

Claire's eyes widened. So that's how he did it! She loyally suffered through his . . . concert. His hands hit the keyboard. She grabbed a stein of beer. He mutilated Beethoven's *Fur Elise,* and then, thank God, it ended. She considered joining Vito outside. She remembered Wendall's many kindnesses and clapped the loudest and longest.

Wendall winked at her. He bowed. He closed the piano and hopped off the stage. "See, I told you I could make you forget your troubles. Did you enjoy my playing?"

She tilted her head to the side, appraising his face over the flickering candlelight. "I've never heard *Fur Elise* played quite like that," she said, not having the heart to tell the truth.

Wearing a devil's grin, he came to her side. Leaning down, he cupped his hands on her face. He peered intently into her eyes, then he kissed the top of her nose.

Laughter erupted from him. "No one else has either. Harry snitched. I learned today Harry told Vito I pay for the drinks. I see he's told you, too. I can't bribe Vito. If you noticed, he's taken a hike."

She giggled. "Wendall, you're a—"

"Don't say it. Unless you want to be an adorable liar."

She burst out laughing. "Why do you do it?"

"I love it. I think I'm tone-deaf. Have I told you that you're very alluring and very desirable? I love when you blush. I want to see your whole body blush."

"Be quiet." Her eyes darted nervously around the room.

His voice carried. She was sure her whole body was beet red. "People can hear you."

He kissed her lips. "You know I want to make love to you. I want us very close, very naked, very involved."

"Wendall!"

He tweaked her nose and sat down, acting as if he hadn't said anything shocking. She was grateful for his brazen irreverence, his teasing brand of psychological support.

Vito came back from his "walk." The time flew. She found herself caught up in the details of one of Vito's cases. When her mother phoned saying she'd seen Edward, and to come get her, Claire had forgotten her troubles for a little while.

Two mornings later an uncharacteristically silent Wendall drove her to Kennedy Airport. Her comments about the clear weather for flying went unanswered. Attempts at small talk failed. Resorting to the radio, she found a talk show. The guest psychologist's topic: marital counseling.

"Counseling should be a legal requirement before granting a divorce decree. Counseling saves and strengthens even the most troubled marriages."

Wendall switched to a different station. He crossed the Belt Parkway, staying on the heavily trafficked Van Wyck Expressway. "The man sermonizes as if it were gospel. No two cases are the same."

Jet planes roared overhead. A steady stream of aircraft took off from different runways. She tracked one, then replied, "The psychologist speaks sense. Why should people divorce if they can save their marriage?"

"Are we talking about you?" he asked bluntly.

She studied her fingernails. Her mother had asked the same question before they said good-bye. *If he asked, would she reconcile with Colin?* Could he change? Given his rigid beliefs, she didn't see it happening.

She looked straight ahead, yet she could feel Wendall's heated gaze riveted on her, pulling at her until she looked at him fully. She knew nothing about his private life.

"I'd rather not discuss me. Let's talk about you. Why

aren't you married? I've seen you with children. You'd make a wonderful father."

Taking the off ramp, he joined the flow of cars entering the airport complex. "I never met the marvelous mommy to make me a fabulous father. The truth is I never felt the urge to marry. Times and situations change."

She bent forward and picked up her purse. "Are you close with your parents?"

"Yes. They're good people. I respect their values."

"How long have they been married?"

"Thirty-nine years." His voice smiled along with his eyes.

"A lifetime." She let out a wistful sigh. "In today's world that says a lot."

"It says their marriage isn't based on selfish gain. Basic character doesn't change with marital counseling. Once a bastard always a bastard. Like Colin."

He flashed her a dazzling smile. She felt it clutch her heart. *It's his sea blue eyes.* He could charm a woman right out of her clothes. She suspected he did. Often. She found herself growing intensely curious. He had taken to throwing his arm around her shoulders, giving her gentle squeezes, asking for hugs.

Switching lanes, he headed for the American Airlines departure terminal. On the busy ramp, an airport policeman waved cars forward. He fed the car a small amount of gas.

"Just let me off," Claire said. She was dressed for comfort in a denim jacket, blue jeans, a red cotton ribbed sweater, red knee-highs, and sneakers. She had left her fur at the Plaza for Babs to take to Connecticut.

Wendall squeezed between a van and a limo. He shut off the motor, hopped out, deposited her suitcase with the sidewalk ticketing agent, and said he'd be right back.

She scampered out. "Don't feel you have to stay with me. I'm fine. Go to work. I know you're busy."

A vein throbbed at his temple. "Claire, I'm not too busy for this. I'm doing it for me." He took off before she could protest.

A stiff easterly breeze ruffled her hair, whipped at her legs, stopping her reverie. She watched long lines of cars, vans, and limousines pull up to the curb, depositing passengers and luggage. Wendall loped across the street, taller than most, his red hair windblown, his navy peacoat open and flapping.

The went inside, lining up to pass security inspection. Given permission to continue, Wendall took her hand, and they strode down the long corridor to the waiting area. Bypassing the seats, he switched right. He rapped on a door opposite her departure gate. When no one answered, he knocked again. He tried the handle. The door opened. "We can go in," he said, holding the door open for her.

Hot air blasted down from the overhead heating ducts. A speaker piped in boarding instructions. The room contained a beige metal desk, a four-drawer beige filing cabinet, a beige push-button phone, an overflowing gold ceramic ashtray, and a wall map of the United States, dotted with colored push pins.

Wendall took her coat and put it with his on a chair. "This office belongs to a friend of mine. We'll wait here."

Riveted by the lines of impatience creasing his features, his brooding stance, his broad shoulders blocking the exit, and mindful of their discussion in the car, she asked him, "Why here? What's wrong?"

He tunneled his fingers through his hair. "Plenty. For one thing, I want to be alone with you. For another, I don't like you facing that bastard alone. Colin wouldn't dare try anything if I were with you. I wish you could have stayed until after New Year's."

The holidays no longer held appeal. Nothing did. Rejected, adrift, an empty void in her heart, she wondered when the hurt would dull.

When she said nothing, he asked, "Does Colin know you're coming?"

She shook her head.

"Is that wise?"

She drew a ragged sigh. "I feel as if I'm watching part of me die. I don't know how to stop it from happening. This is the worst time of my life, yet I'm supposed to make vital decisions with a clear head."

"I have a better idea. Think of us."

"Wendall, you haven't been listening."

"I love when you say my name all prim and proper. I'm a very determined man. I'm also a lot smarter than Colin, but you're allowed one mistake for poor judgment. He never learned the word *we* in *wedding* means two people facing life together, the good and the bad. Hold still and let me read you."

She gave him a dubious look. "Read me?"

"It's a tactile exercise."

"I'm in no mood for games."

He drew her close to him. "I assure you this is no game. All you have to do is trust me. Keep your arms at your sides. Do it for me, if not for yourself."

With infinite tenderness he used his fingertips as magic wands, closing first one eyelid, then the other. He traced her eyebrows, tilted her head from side to side, touching her cheeks, her chin, her ears. His left hand on her back brought her closer, and his right hand touched her neck. He kissed it for a long while. He kissed her eyes, traced kisses across her cheekbones, and over her eyebrows.

"It's like playing piano," he murmured.

She giggled merrily. "I've heard you play."

He chuckled. "You hurt me to the quick. Get ready for my virtuoso number."

Then his lips grazed hers in erotic, tantalizing arpeggios. He settled his mouth on hers, lightly rubbing from side to side. He twined a hand in her hair, locking her in place.

"Wendall," she whispered, "I know why you're doing this. You're trying to make me feel wanted."

He nibbled her chin. "I'm glad you appreciate my selfish motives. Put your arms around my neck." Saying that, he helped her. "Good girl. Now fasten your lips on mine. Like this."

He brought his mouth over hers. He slid his hands down her back, flattening them across her hips, clasping her buttocks, fitting her flush to his distended front. She felt his shudder even as his clean, fresh breath fanned her face.

From the day she had met Colin, she let no other man

arouse her passion. With heightening awareness, Wendall's
scent, the taste and texture of his mouth, imprinted itself on
her brain. She leaned into him, into the strength of his
thighs, into the urgent mating motion of his hardened body.

A moan escaped her, parting her lips, giving his questing
tongue entrance, unleashing his hunger. Knowing she
should pull away from him, she clung to him instead, her
rapid heartbeat matching his.

He drew back, his eyes hotly aware of her rising breasts,
her quickened breath. He tipped up her chin. "Claire, I don't
seem to be able to help myself where you're concerned. On
principle, I don't make love to married women. So as far as
I'm concerned, you're not married. Colin doesn't deserve
you. If I hadn't stopped, it's quite evident I wouldn't be able
to. The way I feel now gives new meaning to the word *hurt*.
I won't lie awake wondering how it will be for us. I can
drive myself insane knowing if I can get you out of a damn
airport, I'll prove it. You're a person of worth. Remember
that."

Her heart somersaulted. "Dear, kind, generous Wendall.
You know the right words to keep me from feeling embarrassed. Don't you have any faults?"

"None whatsoever," he teased with absolute conviction.
Then his eyes hooded. His voice throbbed with intensity as
he told her he'd miss her. He nestled her in his arms. For
long minutes they stayed that way—she burrowed against
his chest, dreading her encounter with Colin, the pain of
divorce, Wendall selfishly dreading Colin might have a
change of heart and might convince her to reconcile.

Her flight was announced. The airline agent started
calling rows. Hers was called first. She lingered until
everyone else had boarded.

"It's time," she said quietly.

His eyes a bleak blue, he cradled her face, kissed her
mouth, then whispered fiercely, "I'll phone you so you
won't forget me."

As if she could. His taste and feel remained with her as
she found her seat, as the plane taxied down the runway and
lifted skyward in a surge of energy, the morning sun

bouncing off the wings. She gazed out the window. The dazzling ribbon of cars grew smaller and smaller. One car was Wendall's.

The time since her father's accident seemed unreal. God alone knew what dark days lay ahead for her, her father, and for Babs. She had a terrible present to live through before she achieved independence. It could take years. But she wouldn't forget Wendall. Or her body's heated response . . .

Twelve

EDWARD JAMESON'S DAUGHTER arrived home by limousine. The shiny black Lincoln glided past the Beverly Hills Hotel into Claire's exclusive neighborhood, where bulldozers recently leveled several multimillion-dollar mansions to make way for more opulent showplaces. When the limo slowed before a pair of graceful, scrolled iron gates, she lowered the smoky glass window, identified herself to security, sat back as the chauffeur—a twentysomething blond-haired Adonis—guided the car past manicured lawns, stopping on the circular driveway before her palatial home. A home soon to be for sale.

Once inside the cool interior, she was met by silence. She mounted the stairs to her bedroom. Essy was in Palm Springs. Before unpacking, she phoned Babs.

"Cee-Cee's coming home for Christmas," Babs said, "then she's coming to you."

Cee-Cee, bless her, didn't waste time. She was a true friend.

"Don't worry about us," Babs said. "Do what you have to do. I'll tell Wendall you called. Any messages for your father?"

Family and friends. They were as important to her as breathing. "Give Dad my love. Tell him I'll phone when I can."

"And Wendall?"

"Tell him . . . tell him thanks for me."

Claire unpacked, showered, changed. Minutes later, wrapped in a lavender silk robe, she unlocked the safe bolted behind a false wall in her closet. Her hand reached in. It found empty space. Perplexed, she looked in. An empty shell! Her jewelry wasn't there. Racking her brain to think if she'd put it elsewhere, she raced into her bedroom. But why would she do such a thing? She never had. She always removed her jewelry, put it immediately into the safe.

She tossed the white eyelet Frette bedspread aside, sped to the closet, yanked boxes from shelves, upending them on the bed. Nothing! Telling herself to stay calm, she rechecked the closet. Her hand skimmed over the shelves, her fingers touching a box. She sniffed the air. Over the cedar aroma, she caught the faint scent of orange and cloves. Closing her hand over the floral patterned tin, she lifted the lid.

"So this is where you've been hiding."

She'd found her grandmother's pomander! With careful fingers, she took the hard scented ball from its cushioned bed, touching it to her cheek. She kissed it, then tenderly pushed a loosened clove back into its tiny hole. With little time to spare, she placed the pomander on her desk.

Like a whirlwind, she emptied lingerie drawers, almost certain she wouldn't find her jewelry there, but afraid not to look. For this reason, she removed the drawers, searched the cabinet's shell. Nothing.

What did it mean? She had counted on the money from the sale of her jewelry—personal gifts—to purchase and furnish an apartment, money to tide her over while she searched for a job, money to live on until the lawyers divided their joint property.

The room looked ransacked. Racing downstairs, her heel caught on a step. She tripped. Her hand lunged for the banister, grabbing it in the nick of time to prevent an accident. *Calm down,* she warned herself.

In the dining room, she checked the silverware cabinet, opening each wine-colored velvet lined drawer. Golden Winslow by Kirk Stieff, service for thirty-six, all accounted for. As was her fine bone china English Renaissance pattern, her Royal Doulton Dickens figurines, the collection Babs started for her when she was little. She searched each room, her critical eye looking for signs of thievery. She dialed security. No robberies. All quiet. She called their insurance broker. He and the police reported no thefts.

Who would steal her jewels? Who, as Vito said about a case the other night, had motive, method, and opportunity? Not Essy. Whatever else she thought of her for her blind devotion to Colin, Claire knew Essy was honest.

Unnerved, she tried to think who had motive, method, and opportunity. And then she knew. Colin. Every instinct pointed the finger of blame at him. But why would he take her jewelry to his office safe? It was hers, gifts from her family and from Colin, but hers. She prayed she'd made a mistake, prayed the man she'd loved and married for life wasn't vindictive, vengeful.

Seated at the desk in the bedroom, she wrote feverishly from memory, listing the missing pieces: a diamond and gold pin; an opal, ruby, and diamond necklace; a sapphire ring surrounded by diamonds; an emerald and diamond cocktail ring; opera-length, seven-millimeter pearls; diamond and pearl reducer.

Colin appeared at the door. She'd been so engrossed, she hadn't heard him. Dressed in a navy blue Polo sport jacket, striped blue and white shirt, navy trousers, and Bruno Magli loafers, his blond hair was slightly mussed as he strode into the room. His gaze swept over her, taking in her flushed face, her bright eyes, the parted lavender silk robe, the glimpse of cleavage. She quickly drew the robe together, but not before she saw his flash of interest. He watched her beneath hooded lids. She'd seen his heated look thousands of times.

"This is a surprise. You might have told me you were coming," he said, his tone flat. "When did you get back?"

She expected cordiality, if for no other reason than his desire to proceed with the divorce without her giving him trouble. She expected him to comment on the messy room.

"A while ago. What happened with Sam Yamuto?"

"He promised to sign as soon as the lawyers iron out the last kink. The Yamutos left for Japan."

She rose. "Then you've gotten everything you want."

"Not yet. I'm working on it." He stepped closer. His hand brushed her robe. "Did you let Lawson fuck you?"

She recoiled from his crude remark. His breath smelled of liquor. "I won't dignify your insult with an answer. Did you empty the safe?"

Colin picked up the pomander. "Yes. The trophy arrived broken. But you knew that, didn't you?"

"For your information, I didn't pack it. Put down my grandmother's pomander. Now that you've had your spiteful revenge, where's my jewelry?"

"I sold it."

She catapulted off the chair. "Tell me that's a joke."

"It's not. I sold the jewelry."

She gaped at him in disbelief. His action was beyond petty, beyond mean. Who was this man she'd married? What did it say for her judgment?

"I need it. Buy it back."

He sniffed the pomander, then put it down. His brows set in a straight line. "Even if I could I wouldn't."

A knife twisted in her stomach. "You bastard!"

"I told you once, watch who you call names," he said angrily. He was pacing, his hand punching the air, his finger jabbing at her. "I acted in our interest."

Her anger matched his. "Stealing my jewelry is not in my best interest!"

He whirled around, bearing down on her. "Why can't you listen? I told you I prepaid suppliers. Where did you think the money was going to come from?"

"Where it's always come from. The business."

He snorted. "It would have, but thanks to your father's monumental theft, my counsel expects a heavy financial fallout. I've had to divert cash to defray future legal expenses. Blame your father for selling your jewelry, not me."

"You're assuming he'll be charged."

He snorted. "It's a safe bet he will be."

"You've been busy. Who is your counsel?"

"Brian Hickman. You gave me the idea. I figured if he bled Marybeth dry, he's the man I want."

She seethed. *Hickman.* Her palms grew damp. Nicknamed "Barracuda," the barrel-chested barrister had himself married four times, leaving a wake of vengeance-seeking exes. Joining forces, they had penned an exposé about Hickman, telling the "Geraldo" audience he left them penniless.

"The man's a sleaze."

"He wins cases."

He did. Hickman sued the publisher of his wives' book. He settled out of court. The women didn't collect a dime. "I'm charging you with jewel theft. Even if Hickman tosses it out of court, Marybeth will have a feeding frenzy."

Colin's enigmatic eyes narrowed. "Fine. We'll have a drag-out fight in court. The attorneys will win, not us."

"Us. There is no us. You killed us. You mean you."

He grabbed her wrist. "I'm willing to pay you a small amount of alimony."

Wincing in pain, she twisted away, so upset she felt herself losing control, but couldn't seem to stop. "How generous! I'll bet you were paid a huge sum for my jewelry. With the money you stole from me, you're willing to pay me a small amount of alimony. Not only do I pay myself, I cheat myself!" The words left her mouth in a hiss.

His hand shot out. His fingers dug into her upper arm. "Let me go!" she yelled.

"Not until you listen." Breathing in angry spurts, he kept his face close to hers. "I could charge you and lover boy with adultery. Act sensible, and I won't." He let her go.

She rubbed her arm. "Wendall isn't my lover. Tomorrow morning I'm *sensibly* calling a Realtor. I'll *sensibly* list the house. It'll fetch a good price. From the proceeds, I'll *sensibly* deduct the amount you received from my jewelry. If you don't produce the receipts, I'll use the higher insurance estimates. If you refuse to act *sensibly,* get ready for a fight."

Unconcerned, he walked to a table that held a silver tray and poured a liberal shot of Chivas Regal into a glass. He tossed it back, poured another. "You can't sell the house."

"Read the law. California's a community property state. This house belongs to both of us. I want my half."

He lifted the glass to his lips. "Forget it. My parents own the house. The deed is still in their names. Do you think they'll sell the house and give you half the proceeds?"

She felt ill. She took short, panting breaths to stem her rising panic. How could she be such a patsy? No wonder Colin sounded sure of himself. He lost nothing. She had assumed her in-laws had deeded them the house. Words didn't exist to describe her stupidity. She learned a bitter lesson. *Never assume!*

In her romanticized version of marriage, she had handed Colin her trust along with her hand. The chip in her perfect marriage started on their honeymoon when Colin urged her not to think of starting a family for years. She had been foolish enough to feel flattered that he wanted her for himself. That was before she realized why he coveted all her attention. Now he informed her she couldn't hope for an equitable distribution.

She touched the gold charm at her neck. "Sell the yacht."

"Can't. The corporation owns it. Ditto the automobiles. I plowed our money into land in the corporate name. You forget the money I spent to cover the suppliers."

"Sam is going to sign the papers."

"I promised the suppliers immediate payment."

"So unpromise them. You're good at making up alibis."

"Not for this, Claire. My reputation is on the line. My word is gold. It got me the discount. I had a sweetheart deal until I read your father's letter."

She tasted bitter bile. "Do you enjoy hurting me?"

"My dreams died in New York. Do I enjoy hurting you? Hell, no. Your father tricked me. On both counts, I lose. Do you think I like the whole town getting off on Marybeth's columns? Whenever I pick up a paper, she's got a reference to us. Thank goodness Yamuto left the country. I'll go ahead with the mall, recoup the money, and we get a quiet divorce."

Without his halo, stripped of her idealized vision, she saw past Colin's handsome mask to his rotten core, to the man so consumed by ambition and his ingrained sense of high society that he'd throw away his marriage in order to survive.

"I spent five years living with a superficial man. You insult me, now you set down the rules for my behavior. You appeal to what? My good nature? My genetic breeding? It won't work. I'm not afraid of Brian Hickman. What can I lose? I'll sign the divorce papers gladly, providing I receive my rightful share."

Colin slammed the glass down on the dresser. "If you persist in this, you'll make a costly mistake. Don't play hardball with me. I didn't ask for this raw deal."

"Did I?"

He shrugged. "No. I'll grant you that. Look, I planned for Hickman to tell you this, but since you're here . . ."

A chill raced down her spine. Whatever bomb he was about to detonate, Colin put space between them, crossing to the other side of the room.

"I stopped your credit cards. They're in my name."

"You can't!" she cried, her voice shrill with shock.

"It's done," he shot back. "Hickman figured you'd pull a credit card stunt. He checked the accounts' status. You went on a designer shopping spree in New York. Return the clothes. Unless you want to pay for them yourself." His glance slid to her diamond solitaire.

"Sell it." His tone suggested she heed his advice. "It'll help you get started. You harped about a career. Now's your chance. We shouldn't sleep under the same roof, so you can stay here while you clear out your things. I'll use my parents' condo."

Rage scalded her throat. In a torrent of resentment, words spewed forth. "Do you seriously think I'll let you get away with this?"

His expression hardened. "You have no choice. I've lost this much, I won't lose more. You've never lived on a budget, and I don't need you running up revenge bills."

"This from the man who told me not to stay in the hospital room, to go out and buy a wardrobe."

"That was then, this is now."

He turned on his heel. She heard the front door slam behind him. There was a sulky meanness about Colin she had never seen before. He reminded her of a wily, dangerous animal who, if backed into a corner, struck swiftly without warning.

With her jewelry gone, without a job or a car, she owned next to nothing she could turn into cash. She couldn't go to her parents for a loan. They'd need money for legal fees, living expenses, salaries for Ruth and Jimmy.

Her stomach churning, she sat on the edge of her chair. Colin's debasing manner, his vile denunciation, made her realize her only recourse. Fight fire with fire.

She'd hire an attorney of Hickman's stature. She knew exactly who to call—Richard Parish, Brian Hickman's rival for being the most feared divorce attorney on the West Coast.

Spectacular office buildings line Wilshire Boulevard in Beverly Hills. Building codes restrict the height of the glass-and-steel edifices, mirroring the sky. One lone, eight-story redbrick building looked out of place bracketed between two of I. M. Pei's finest designs.

Once people learned Richard Parish owned the building, they understood why he ordered the design. The shrewd legal showman, one of Stamford University's most famous graduates, grabbed attention. The flamboyant Parish lived for legal warfare. When Claire Brice phoned saying she had selected him, that her husband had retained Brian Hickman, Parish squeezed the socialite into his busy schedule. He'd read the *Carrier,* but hearing Claire's reason for being in New York iced the cake. He admired Edward Jameson's perspicacity.

Parish's brown custom-made suit matched his mocha eyes. The introductions long out of the way, he leaned back in his chair, studying his new client. Her sultry mouth, riot of dark hair, green eyes, and fabulous form did wonders for a pencil-slim white pantsuit. He didn't mix business with pleasure. If he did, she'd be numero uno.

"Colin is right," he said. "You can't sell what you don't

own. If he unloads company assets, the government could suspect his father knew about your father's financial roots. The result could cast a shadow on Colin, too. I spoke with Hickman this morning. I agree. Why hand the IRS ammunition? Make the bastards earn their keep. Colin's offered to deposit ten thousand dollars into your account. He feels the money should tide you over until you get a job."

"He feels!" she said, then forcibly controlled her vehemence. "And my jewelry?"

"He's contending that you granted him permission to sell the jewelry. In short, between the time you met in New York and now, you've reneged on your word."

Her voice was heated, intense. "That's a lie! We never discussed jewelry."

Parish placed a malachite pen next to a yellow legal pad. He gave her a kindly look.

"The yacht?"

He shook his head. "Like Colin said, it's company-owned."

"Will I see any money?" Her lower lip trembled.

"I told Hickman we expect full remuneration, but don't hold your breath. Lawyers specialize in delaying tactics."

"What can you do?"

"I'll force Colin to sell assets not in the company name. Before you get too happy, you should know the government is first in line with its hand out. I'll go after the rest."

She shuddered. "Like carrions picking at a carcass, except this carcass is my life."

"Don't worry. We won't give away the store without a fight."

Easy for him to say. It could take years. Years of mounting legal bills, without guarantees.

Disconsolate, her gaze shifted to Parish's law diploma and his string of honorary diplomas. His luxurious suite occupied an entire floor. He employed seventy-three attorneys. She didn't doubt he billed more in a day than most people earned in a year. Acutely conscious of Parish's outrageous fee, Claire heard the soft incessant pinging of a walnut grandfather clock that seemed to count down his five-hundred-dollar consultation fee. What good would his high-priced reputation do her? Colin held her financially hostage.

With this rude awakening, she could forget buying an apartment, furnishing it nicely, and taking time to find the right job. She'd take what she could for now and consider herself lucky to have a steady income and a rental. While she never felt at home in Beverly Hills—the city the Chamber of Commerce hyped as the sister city of Cannes, France—she never dreamed she'd bring her designer clothes to Ritz II on consignment.

"Colin and I weren't alone in my suite. I won't let him get away with his lie."

Parish fired up a cigarette, took a deep drag, waved away the smoke. "Who was the man with you in your hotel room?"

He zapped the question like an electric bolt. It took her by surprise. "Who was the man in your hotel room?" he repeated.

"I heard you. Isn't my word enough? Why can't you pass this information on to Colin? That should stop him."

"He's a witness. We may need his deposition. Please answer the question."

"Wendall."

Parish blew out a stream of smoke. "Who?"

"Dr. Lawson."

He picked up his pen. "What time?"

She tossed her head. "I don't know. After midnight. Colin was in the suite when we returned."

Parish jotted it down. Claire fidgeted. "Wendall is my father's doctor. Naturally we keep in touch."

"Why?"

"I told you why," she said, hiding her irritation. "He's my father's physician."

Parish flashed her a quick smile. On a naiveté scale of one to ten, he ranked her an eight. "You're a married woman. You bring a man to your room after midnight. Your husband surprises you. How does it look? Incriminating or innocent?

What were you and Wendall doing before you brought him to your room?"

She bristled. "Eating."

"Nice restaurant or quick bite?"

"Nice place."

"Cozy ambience?"

Realizing he made it seem as if she and Wendall had engaged in illicit acts, she clasped her hands so tightly her knuckles whitened. Her knees went weak, and she was glad for the chair. "It wasn't cozy in the way you mean. It's a lively place. I sang with the waiters."

"Where?"

"Asti's."

He jotted the name of the restaurant on the pad. "I know the place. You're right. Asti's is a lot of fun. Not the sort of place you visit when you're worried sick about your father. Then what?"

Her lips thinned. She could hear her voice rising. "Is this necessary?"

He took a deep drag on his cigarette. Exhaling, he nodded. "Then what?"

Her lips thinned. "Then nothing."

"That's not the way I hear it."

Disgusted, she erupted angrily. "If you knew about the fight, why ask?"

Parish tamped out his cigarette. "I didn't know. You fell for an old lawyer's trap. Lead 'em and bleed 'em. Is Lawson your doctor, too?"

"No. He's a plastic surgeon. What would I be doing with a plastic surgeon?"

He smiled. The pen tapped the legal pad. "My point exactly. Lawson isn't your doctor. Regardless of the words you use, Colin says you two dated. He claims his unexpected arrival merely prevented you two from hopping in the sack."

Her hand came down on the desk. "It's not true."

Parish raised his palms in a gesture of peace. "I'm not accusing you. I'm on your side. Bear with me, please. I am trying to get all the facts, not casting blame. Now you know what to expect from Hickman. Okay, the men fought. I take it Colin saw red and threw the first punch."

Her mouth felt like mush.

Parish's brows furrowed. He leaned forward. "Claire, no lawyer likes surprises. Me least of all. Give me a complete account."

"It wasn't a full-fledged fight. Wendall socked him."

The pen jiggled. "Where?"

"On the jaw. Colin went down. Colin got up. He swung. Wendall ducked. Wendall told him to leave."

Parish recorded the information. "Told or ordered?"

She shifted on the seat, crossed her legs in one smooth line, and glared at him. "Ordered. Colin left. Believe me, there was provocation."

Parish's eyes flicked downward. "Wendall packs a pretty good wallop to drop Colin. I've met Colin. He's a big man, in excellent shape. What caused the fight?"

She repeated Colin's statements about her genes.

Parish's head shot upward. A soft look of sympathy came into his eyes. "Claire, your husband is an unmitigated fool. Still, Dr. Lawson took an oath as a healer. Society frowns on a man who decks a husband after he's caught with the man's wife in her hotel room in the middle of the night. Or day, for that matter. Nighttime is worse, however. People go bump in the night. On beds. No one will buy the excuse this was Dr. Lawson's normal visiting hours. Especially when Hickman proves you two dined at Asti's, where waiters confirmed you sang and had a marvelous time. How long were you at Asti's?"

Parish saw the flush creep up her neck and stain her cheeks. He sighed. "I'm not trying to hurt you, Claire. The Brices and the Garcias are famous California families, high-society dynasties. Consider Colin's viewpoint. Unbeknownst to him, his wife's father and his business associate committed grand theft. This smooth con man tricked him and his family into thinking his bride was a member of high society, like his family."

Claire squirmed uncomfortably. Her father's past shocked her, too. "Must you?"

"Yes," Parish said. "Colin will hold fast to the idea that his father-in-law duped him. He'll use the truth. Your father evaded the law by taking the drastic measure of surgically altering his facial appearance. He deviously adopted a new persona, married a socially correct second wife, Barbara Denison, and if this accident hadn't happened, would sleep safely laughing up his sleeve at everyone's gullibility. Marriage is an important step in a man's life. Colin had a right to his dreams."

Hearing Parish's spin on the facts, Claire's face darkened. "What about my broken dreams?"

"We're discussing Colin's offense. Hickman will portray him as the hardworking, attentive husband, true to his heritage, an innocent lamb led to the slaughter, not the ambitious, self-righteous bastard he is. Hickman will say your father promised Colin the union would lead to great financial benefits. Colin claims he arranged the introduction, then encouraged his courtship."

"That's preposterous! Colin knew it was Babs's idea for me to meet the right sort. He knew I treated it as a joke."

Claire paled. She realized how damning that sounded.

"Let's hope Colin forgets that. We're a target-oriented society. When Colin's father retired, it put Colin a heartbeat closer to company president. The man's obviously driven by his own demons. He hates seeing his name in the gossip columns."

"Stop it!" she snapped. "Colin's building the largest shopping mall in America for my father's friend Sam Yamuto. Isn't it ironic that while Colin scurries to a lawyer, crying foul, *he* claims I ruined him, *he* lies about Wendall and me, *he* kicks me out, *he* steals my jewelry, *he* cancels my credit cards, *he* stands to earn a bloody fortune, thanks to my father! Colin's banking on the mall attracting Asian investors. He can't lose."

Parish thought her fury magnificent. Compassion swept through him for the young woman with the golden skin, quivering red lips, and hurting emerald eyes. Colin, the ass, was throwing away a desirable, passionate woman. Unfortunately the truth didn't matter worth a damn. "You forget Colin's father's and the Brices' standing in the community."

"How does this affect my father-in-law? He's retired," she said, her teeth clenched.

"In cases of fraud, the IRS audits a business's records with a fine-tooth comb. There's no limitation on how many years back it searches. The IRS will look for a link between your father and Colin's."

"They won't find it. My father assured me he acted alone, never told Colin's father."

"He says. Why should the IRS believe a thief?" Claire winced. "The IRS assumes smoke behind the partnership mirrors. It loves flexing its muscles, setting examples in celebrated cases. I can imagine what the strain is doing to your father. By the way, how is his health?"

They'd spoken that morning. He sounded nasal. He said he couldn't shake his cold. When she asked if he'd seen their local family doctor, he offered his famous line, "A cold takes three days coming, three days staying, and three days leaving, with or without medicine."

Babs cited endless hours closeted with his attorneys. "How would you expect him to be? He can't shake his cold, and his attorneys give him rotten news."

The grandfather clock ticked the hour. She gnawed her lip. "Can Colin get away with stopping my credit cards?"

Parish watched the myriad emotions shifting expressions on her lovely face. All women should learn the rudiments of financial protection prior to applying for a marriage license.

"Yes, he can. He filed for a legal separation. Hickman said you charged twenty designer outfits. The salesclerk said you didn't try them on. Don't let Hickman's tactics surprise you. All lawyers hire foot soldiers."

Her heart sank. One knee-jerk reaction, and look where it got her! "Mr. Parish, you've painted a dismal picture. Can you help me?" she asked hollowly.

"I'll do my best," he replied easily. "Incidentally Marybeth Frankel is getting her own syndicated gossip column. She's had an offer from Louis Marx," he said, naming the powerful owner of a nationwide tabloid. "He hates Charlie Frankel, for personal reasons. Tit-for-tat rag journalism at its ethical peak."

Claire twisted her hands.

"Have you ever caught Colin with another woman?" Parish asked suddenly.

Her eyes shot upward. Her own attorney made her sound cheap. Sordid. "No, and neither has Colin caught me with another man! Not that it's your business, but my husband is the only man I've slept with."

Pity. Parish notched her naiveté level to nine. He stared in sympathy at the anguished young woman. Before this was over he had to toughen her up. "Colin will claim he was a faithful, loving husband. Was he attentive sexually?"

Claire felt her cheeks burn.

"Please understand my role is to clarify your position. It's my duty to protect your interests, not give Hickman unnecessary ammunition. Stay away from Wendall."

Resentment boiled up in her. "Do you propose I hide in a closet when he examines my father?"

"I advise you to stay in California until we hammer out an agreement."

"This isn't about Wendall as a third party. My husband's proven his true character. How do you think I feel knowing I was a possession? Now that I'm no longer a valuable asset, he's exacting his pound of flesh. He's incapable of loving anyone more than himself. I pity any woman who marries a man in high society, unless she's an equal, financially and through a blue-blooded line of ancestors. As for Wendall, what you suggest is insulting. It assumes a personal relationship exists."

"It assumes the appearance of a sexual liaison. Is there a friend you could invite for a visit?" he asked, moderating his tone.

Claire sat tall. "I am expecting my closest friend, Cee-Cee Evans. She'll stay a week, perhaps longer. But don't expect me to hang around California. I've got a future to map. A life to lead. I'm going to New York."

Parish extended his arms on the desk. "Claire, your father

has his full mental faculties. Your mother provides moral support. He'll see Dr. Lawson in his office. If you're not having an affair, there's no reason to see him. If you're thinking of having one, don't. It won't hurt the doctor. It will hurt you."

She hated Richard Parish. Hated his perspicacity. What would he say if he knew Wendall had slept at the hotel, in her bed, holding her in his arms all night while she cried? What would he say if he knew Wendall had barged into her room in Connecticut and kissed her, that she'd kissed him back? What would he say if he had witnessed them in the airport? She'd destroy her already weak case. Parish was right. She'd give Wendall a wide berth.

The clock chimed the hour. Rising quickly, she snatched her shoulder bag and slung it over her shoulder.

"Mr. Parish, if a marriage dissolution boils down to legal chess playing, I think the game you lawyers play stinks. Divorce is demeaning. It's mercenary."

The attorney's brown eyes held hers in a level look. He notched her naiveté level to ten.

"Welcome to the real world, Claire."

"You can keep it," she fired back.

Parish grinned. She might make it after all.

Wendall sat a listless Juanito on the examining table. For once the boy wasn't shouting or making demands. The child ran a fever of one hundred three. His worried mother and an anxious Daria leaned on the wall, ordered by Wendall for the third time to stay put. Juanito clutched Piggy's hand.

Wendall told Juano to say "Ahhh."

Jaunito complied with rare cooperation. Wendall examined his throat, felt his neck, checked the child thoroughly.

"You'll live, Juano. It's your tonsils."

Daria promptly said, "They have to come out."

Wendall rolled his eyes heavenward. "Do you want me to assist you, or shall we try to get rid of the infection with antibiotics?"

"Ant . . . botics," whined Juano.

Piggy shot Daria a disgusted look.

"Whatever you and Juano say, Doc," Daria capitulated.

Wendall smiled inwardly. "All my consults should be this easy. Thank you, Daria. Thank you, Piggy. Don't forget your gun on the way out."

After his last patient left, Wendall shut his office door and dialed Claire's number. If Colin came on the line, he'd hang up. Claire answered.

Happy to hear her voice, he asked how her day went. She told him everything, including Parish's advice that she not see him.

"If money is the problem, forget it. I'll lend you whatever you need."

"Absolutely not. It's sweet of you to offer, but I've seen your car. I know you pour your money into the clinic. Besides, I'm not destitute. I'll sell my ring, rent an apartment, find a job, and before you know it, I'll be fine. I'll treat this as a bad dream."

He heard the quiver in her voice. "Do you think you could manage to do all that by tomorrow? Come back, I miss you."

"I'll be there after Cee-Cee's visit."

Claire hung up feeling better for having unloaded her anger. Wendall felt worse. This wasn't the time to tell Claire the Everett-Lawsons could run financial rings around the Brices and the Jamesons combined.

Thirteen

ON JANUARY FIFTH, Cee-Cee Rittenhouse Evans breezed into Claire's house, acting and sounding like a mother hen bent on cheering her chick. Three months Claire's senior, she had dark brown eyes, fair skin typical of redheads, and a feast of freckles that marched across the bridge of a slightly upturned nose.

"Whatever your father did or didn't do in the past, the man I know is one hell of a guy who raised one hell of a daughter." Cee-Cee eased a potentially difficult reunion. Primed by tales of Colin's treachery, she preached that the best defense is a good offense.

"Drastic insults, Clarissa, require drastic measures." Cee-Cee reverted to a childhood habit of using variations of Claire's name. "Parade your puss. Flaunt your finances. Shop till you drop. Haute couture and ready-to-wear. Later you can send the clothes back. Don't alter them. We'll dine at Ma Maison, the Polo Club, Spago. Whatever's hot."

"Sorry, that's the last thing on my agenda. Colin canceled my credit cards. I made the awful mistake of going on the revenge shopping spree of my life."

"What a shit!"

They ate in the sunroom. Cee-Cee declared one misery at a time, celebrating with a diet moratorium. The women devoured poppy seed rolls piled sinfully with ham and Swiss cheese, washing them down with creamed coffee.

Pots of giant mixed hyacinths in redwood tubs lined the

217

floor, scenting the room with a delicious fragrance. The Sunday *New York Times* Employment Section lay open next to five linen-embossed invitations to A-list parties Claire didn't plan on attending. She didn't want people gawking at her.

About fifteen feet away, a bare-chested man positioned a large red hibiscus over an immense hole. His sun-bronzed torso rippled with powerful muscles. A checkered headband soaked up sweat from his nutmeg brown hair.

"Wow! Male beauty in motion. I love his tight jeans. Can you imagine what's beneath them?" Cee-Cee teased. "Let's invite him in to play."

Claire swatted her. Her zany pal was crazy for her husband, Tom. She loved Cee-Cee's tale of how she had met and fallen in love with Tom Evans. Late for a date, she ran down the hall in the BBC studio. Rounding a corner, she crashed into the bespectacled, sandy-haired scholar, knocking Tom off balance. With David Frost, who'd just interviewed him, watching, Tom landed on his rump. Mortified, she stammered an apology and thrust out a helping hand. Fascinated by the tall girl with cropped red hair and warm brown eyes, he sat on the floor, his knees bent, pretending a mortal wound. Hearing her American-accented apology again, he twisted the guilt, saying his devastated parents deserved an eyewitness account of his imminent demise. A laughing, astute David Frost wished him luck in the hereafter, winked, then magically disappeared.

Captivated by Tom's deviltry, twinkling blue eyes, and droll humor, Cee-Cee let him hang on to her all evening. They spent four hours in a Jolly Roger pub, drinking, talking, making eye contact, while awaiting his last earthly gasp. Then they spent another three hours in a nightclub, slow dancing, making body contact, and the rest of the night making wild love, during which he emitted a series of gasps, uttered for a far different reason than drawing his last earthly breath.

The third time, gasping chorally, Cee-Cee massaged a body part that sent him into a crescendo of heavenly eruptions. Tom asked if she'd like to prolong British-

American relations. They spent the weekend in bed, emerging to shower and to eat. Three months later a deliriously happy Cee-Cee asked Claire to be her matron of honor. After four years of wedded bliss the Evanses were as happy as honeymooners, presumably gasping on regular and frequent occasions.

"Is sex all you think about?"

Cee-Cee swiveled for a better view of the sweating hunk. "I'm not asking for myself. He's for you. Look at his steel buns. Imagine exploring his wicked mouth. Look at the shape of it. Elvis incarnate. Clara, my pet, you mustn't go through life sowing one oat. Consider it therapy."

"If I listen to you, I'll need a couch. For a shrink." Claire giggled.

"Why is Colin stalling on the divorce agreement?"

"He claims I gave him permission to sell my jewelry."

Cee-Cee whirled around, serious now. "Son of a bitch! Don't you let him get away with it!"

Claire flicked her head sideways. "I'm not. I pulled a page from your book, Cees. Hickman demanded an itemized inventory of what I'm shipping home. I mailed him a list of my lingerie. I said I'm not certain if Colin wants people knowing he cross-dresses, but he's welcome to half my bras and bikinis, especially the red lace set, since I bought it for him. Colin wasn't amused."

Cee-Cee whooped. "What a talented devil you are! First the smashed trophy, now this."

"Give Babs credit for the trophy. Colin had a bird. It's a shame when a thing is more valuable than a person."

She tapped the *Times*. She hoped to line up interviews before flying to New York. "I wish the right job would jump off the paper."

Cee-Cee grabbed it. "You don't know how to look." She ran a Manchurian red manicured fingernail down column after column.

"Dental assistant?"

"Yuck!"

"Insurance?"

"Boring. Ditto banking."

"Telemarketing?"

"Nope. I don't intend to sit on my ass."

"X-ray technician?"

"Not qualified. Not interested."

"Real estate?"

"Not licensed."

"You're tough. Okay. Trade on your looks and your personality. With your fashion flair, how about a TV star?"

"In your pipe dreams."

Cee-Cee attacked the columns. "Aha! Here's one. Liaison and assistant. World Cruise Line. Flexible assignment."

"Promising. Sailing off into the sunset is one way of escaping. What about my father's health? As much as Mom and I are glad Wendall removed the wires from his jaw and sent him home, Dad's wearing himself out. Despite the freezing weather, he insisted Jimmy take him out on the boat."

Cee-Cee bit into her roll. "You need a job. You can't sit and hold your father's hand. He's got Babs. You said yourself the legalities take a year. Tom knows the owner of World Cruises. He'll put in a good word for you."

Claire held her coffee cup away from her lips. "It sounds tempting, and I appreciate it, but first tell me how my father looked. Mom's worried about his weight loss."

Cee-Cee noted Claire's tension, the stiffening of her shoulders as if preparing for bad news. "Claire, relax, please. He's pale, but it's wintertime. He spends hours cooped up with lawyers. That's enough to kill anyone's appetite. As for his hair turning white, that's not unusual after an accident, and remember he is getting older, so it's part aging, too. Give him time."

Claire fretted. "We've always been honest with each other. You medicate bacteria, not viruses. Viruses are self-limiting. If he's improving, why is Wendall making the trip to Connecticut so often? He's his plastic surgeon, not his family physician."

Cee-Cee picked up the carafe. She refilled her cup and took a sip of coffee. "Maybe so, but this way Wendall stops by on his way home, so it's perfectly logical."

"What do you mean?" Claire asked, puzzled.

Cee-Cee gave her a quizzical look. "Just what I said. He's not going out of his way."

"Of course he is. Way out of his way. He grew up in the Bronx. He lives in New York City."

"Wendall was born and grew up in Groton, Connecticut. His parents still live there."

Baffled, Claire asked, "Is this a joke?"

"Why would I say it if it weren't true? I know you're friends. I liked him, too, when I met him. He asked zillions of questions about you. He cares for you and hates Colin with a passion. Your mother's his fan. Ruthie's in love with him."

When Claire still didn't look convinced, Cee-Cee continued, "His name is Wendall Everett-Lawson."

A frown marred Claire's forehead. "No, it's not," she insisted. "It's Wendall Lawson. I have his professional card in my purse. Everyone calls him Dr. Lawson. His best friend, Vito Malchesne, referred to him as Dr. Lawson the first time we met. The nursing staff calls him Dr. Lawson. You're mistaken."

Cee-Cee covered Claire's hand. "I wish I were. His full surname is Everett-Lawson. One of his ancestors led the Connecticut forces in the Revolutionary War. Another was in the whaling industry out of Bridgeport. Wendall's bloodline is completely blue. On the Everett side, the bulk of the money came from railroads. On the Lawson side, it came from steel. Wendall has taken his family into the twenty-first century. He owns a computer plant in the Silicon Valley."

Claire was shocked. The idea that he wasn't from the South Bronx had never dawned on her. To learn that his prestigious family background surpassed Babs's and Colin's, and all it entailed from a financial standpoint, was daunting. The sound of her cup rattling on the saucer brought Cee-Cee's hand out, steadying it.

"He never said a word. How do you know this?"

Cee-Cee gave her a pitying look. Owing allegiance to her

dearest friend, she said, "My mother told me. I'm sure Babs knows, too."

"How?" Claire asked, devastated. A cloud passed over the sun, shadowing the room. Babs, her society-born step-mother, had withheld the facts. She assumed Babs had done it to protect her feelings, for she surmised Wendall's parents adhered to the same rigid social code as Colin's. If Colin's parents had rejected Edward Jameson's daughter, so would Wendall's. She felt numb. The Everett-Lawson lineage, according to Cee-Cee, dated back to the founding fathers.

"He graduated from college and med school in New York," Cee-Cee said. "He left Connecticut to live and work in New York. While we were growing up, he carved his career."

"Does he have siblings?" Claire asked softly.

"No."

Claire paled. "I see." She knew of Wendall's closeness to his parents, his respect for their values. In the airport, he'd kissed her, said he considered her single, spoke of the future. He said he loved her, but love, she learned, was fragile, fleeting, and often expressed to achieve a goal. Wendall's happy bachelorhood suited his life-style. Without realizing her actions, she shredded her napkin.

"Don't jump to conclusions," Cee-Cee advised.

Claire's lower lip quivered. "I'm okay. There's no reason for Wendall to give me his biography."

"I'm sure he was trying to spare you."

"From what? More castigation? When will I learn? He drives an old heap, hangs around with a detective from the South Bronx, splits his time between his office and his clinic, befriends inner-city people, gives them jobs, food, and clothing, and God knows what else. What must he have thought when I congratulated him on doing good work for *his* people? He offered me a loan, and I refused. I said after seeing his car and knowing he financed the clinic, he needed his money. What a fool I am. When he said he lived on the Upper East Side near Sutton Place after his friend moved to San Francisco, I complimented him on coming up in the world."

Cee-Cee let out a low whistle.

"What else do you know about him?"

"He's comfortable in all spectrums of society, never flaunts his money or his status. He's a nice guy who managed to escape the clutches of all the women who want to marry him."

Claire lowered her head and sighed. "Who told you?"

"My mother's friendly with Wendall's parents. She likes them very much. They're anxious for him to settle down so they can play with grandchildren."

Claire's brows flew together. Wendall hobnobbed with all facets of society. She recalled their conversation Christmas Day, how he chatted about Piggy and Daria, the kids, saying everyone missed her and sent their love. She laughed when he said he'd dressed up as Santa Claus, but forgot the pillows. He made such a skinny Santa that Daria stuffed rolls of toilet paper down his costume.

Three days ago he'd visited her parents. He and Ruthie exchanged more recipes. He stayed for dinner, insisting on preparing the entrée, while Ruthie fixed an endive and cherry tomato salad. Babs made instant chocolate pudding. Claire asked what he made for an entrée.

"Polpettini di Vitello con Salsa d'Aglio e Peperoni. Veal patties with garlic and red-pepper sauce." Then he offered to make her Cosce di Rane Ritte con Salsa Tirolese sometime.

"What is it?"

"Deep-fried frog legs with Tyrolean sauce." She laughingly told him to forget it.

Her heart raced. He'd phoned at midnight, saying he was lying in bed thinking of her, couldn't wait for her to live in New York, and the hell with Parish's objections. No wonder. As Parish said, he had nothing to lose.

"I'm sorry," Cee-Cee said.

Claire felt something twist inside her. "Don't be. You've done me a favor. I've decided the last place I'd move to now is New York."

Cee-Cee looked her in the eye, at the granite determination on her face. "It's Wendall's family, isn't it?"

Claire shrugged. A strong sense of detachment filled her.

"Partly. Class clings to tradition. Wendall is a decent man. I suppose he and my mother thought not telling me was a kindness. It's better that I know. I need time to get my act together. The worst mistake I can make is going from one doomed relationship into another. I've experienced lust, ambition, betrayal, and passion in less than a month."

She tapped the newspaper. "I'm applying for the cruise ship position."

Cee-Cee didn't miss a beat. "Good. You need to get away. Dress nautical for the interview. I'll call Tom."

World Cruises hired Claire, who, on Cee-Cee's advice, dressed in a blue suit piped in white, a red blouse, and navy shoes.

"I could have been naked," she said later, showing her a cutaway of the recently commissioned thirteen-deck, sixty-three-thousand-five-hundred-ton *Sea Voyager*.

"If you were naked you wouldn't need Tom's recommendation. Tell me about the job."

"I'm permanently assigned to the purser, Giancarlo Valustre. His office is between the chief steward's and the executive chef's, who also has a small office in the galley. I'm a glorified temp. It's Executive Chef Hans Aldred's last contract. I'm uncertain how many sailings his contract entails, but I'll find out. I'll escort groups to the galley for his tour. The chef orders supplies through Chief Steward Robert Briani, who will train me to assist him on their computer program. I could hostess if the maître d'hôtel is shorthanded. Giancarlo said with my figure I'll be asked to model in the fashion shows, too."

"Wow! You won't be bored, thank goodness."

"That's why I took the position."

"Your brain's clicking. What's the purser like?"

Claire grinned. "Cute." She described him as medium height, with a tight compact body, gray eyes, dark hair, sporting a close-cropped beard.

"Cute single?"

"Forget it. I see your brain whirling. Giancarlo is cute

married—eighteen years to an Australian, and he lives in Sydney. He's sailed for twenty years. That's all I know."

"It's too bad about him, but the job sounds ideal. You won't be confined. You can check out the various occupations, find one of interest."

On their last night the friends talked into the wee hours of the morning. The following afternoon, Claire would fly to Connecticut to visit her parents, before starting her six-month contract. In the morning, Cee-Cee flew home to London.

Both cried when they hugged good-bye. "You'll see Tom and me on the ship. I promise."

Claire walked into the garden she'd built with love. In the weeks since her return, not one member of Colin's family had contacted her. Her in-laws had ostracized her, considered her persona non grata.

The *Carrier* lay on the table. Claire read Marybeth's column, now in syndication via the Marx chain. She devoted today's installment to Richard Parish and Brian Hickman, citing the personalities of the two legal giants on opposite sides of the lurid Brice-Jameson divorce.

"The case," Marybeth wrote, "involves Colin Brice's divorce action against his wife, Claire Jameson Brice. The root causes for the bitter breakup contain the elements of high drama: murder, theft, intrigue, duplicity, society marriages, sex, and greed."

She embellished an article first printed in *USA Today*. What the Brices knew or didn't know regarding Jameson's past, Marybeth left to the reader's imagination, clearly avoiding a libel action. She did, however, cleverly insinuate that the Brices knew everything but hated getting caught.

Claire read the skillfully written trash, then threw it out.

The phone jangled. Colin snidely accused her of dragging her feet. "Drop your countersuit. I'll deposit one hundred thousand dollars into your account."

"The jewelry's worth far more."

"All right. Suppose you tell me and my folks how much it will take for them to rid the family of vermin."

Claire slammed down the phone. She dialed Richard Parish and repeated Colin's remarks.

"He shouldn't call you."

"You're right. Tell Hickman two hundred fifty thousand. Not a penny less."

"I'll try. Where will you be?"

"On a ship, working." She quickly told him her plans. "Mail the divorce papers."

Babs ushered Sam Yamuto into Edward's study. Her eyes focused on the frail man who stood at the window gazing at the Sound, where a stiff January wind sent waves crashing to the shore.

Babs tucked her hand in Edward's. "Darling, it's drafty near the window. You'll catch pneumonia. Before you scold, look who's come to visit."

Edward's thin face brightened as he smiled. "Sam," he said, shaking his hand, "it's good to see you. Babs loves to boss me. I should have married an obedient Japanese wife like Lia, instead of this warden."

Sam's dark eyes hid his shock as he took in Edward's snow white hair and fragile body. Only the fire in Edward's eyes burned brightly.

"Lia's no better. I'm afraid we're stuck with kindred spirits. Let's sit. I don't know about you, my friend, but I'm tired from my trip." Babs sent him a grateful smile, then left them alone, saying she'd return with a tray lunch.

Educated at Oxford, Sam Yamuto spoke impeccable English. "I've always liked this room," he said. The walls were deep coral. Inside the warmly masculine retreat, the coffered ceilings and parquet floors glowed to a darkly rich shine. Bookcases lined two walls. Oil portraits of Claire and Babs hung on the wall behind Edward's massive desk. A pair of early Louis XV side chairs, separated by a coffee table, flanked a rose quartz hand-carved fireplace, where a log crackled on the grate.

Edward poured sake into delicately scrolled cups and handed one to Sam. Beneath his Irish cable-knit fisherman's sweater, corduroy pants, and thick woolen socks, he shivered and perspired. He'd lost his appetite and his chest hurt, but he kept those facts from Babs.

"Don't mind me." He mopped his brow. "This damn condition brings on the sweats. I'm anxious to hear your news."

"I did as you asked. If you change your mind, I'll honor my pledge and sign the final papers."

"That's exactly what I don't want you to do," Edward rasped. "Don't get caught up in this legal mess. Use Farrar Brothers, they'll do a fine job. Babs and I agree. There isn't enough money in the world to compensate for Colin's betrayal. He isn't entitled to a penny's profit. When will the banks revoke the loans?"

Sam loosened his tie and stretched his legs. "Soon. I thought I'd give Colin a few more days to dangle. When I spoke with him today, I told him my people raised another question. He asked if he could help me, but I said no, we'll take care of it. His voice shook. The man's worried."

Edward smiled grimly. "Good. Let the bastard stew. What about the various building permits? When will they be rescinded?"

Babs brought a tray of roast beef and tuna fish sandwiches, shirred eggs, and carrot sticks. She set it on the coffee table. Ruthie followed with a pot of tea and a dish of lemon.

"Right after the banks notify Colin they're not granting the loans." Sam helped himself to a tuna sandwich. He took a bite. "I shall personally inform Colin he committed an unpardonable sin."

Edward folded his hands. "How does this affect your timetable?"

"It helps it. My company is heavily involved in projects in Hong Kong and Japan. We struck, as you Americans say, while the iron was hot. Colin's treachery affords a perfect excuse to wait for a more auspicious time to build."

"I could strangle Colin," Babs said heatedly. She handed Edward a plate of food.

"If she had a gun she'd shoot Colin."

"After I break his paddle tennis racket over his head." She

told Sam that Colin had sold Claire's jewelry. Muttering a curse beneath her breath, she sailed regally from the room.

Edward sombered. "It kills me knowing I caused my loved ones unhappiness. Both women have an infinite capacity for forgiveness."

"They love you. They know you didn't do this with malicious intent," Sam said kindly. "Colin is a spineless dog. He deserves to hemorrhage. Claire's better off without him."

Edward coughed. "I blame myself for introducing them, for not seeing the man behind the face. He crushed her dreams, my friend. At what price will she make new ones? Babs worries about us. I worry about them. Once Claire sails, I'll feel relieved, although we'll miss her terribly."

"Are you getting proper rest, Edward?"

"Babs insists I nap each day. In the beginning I argued, but now I go meekly, mainly to escape investigators breathing down my throat. The DA's office for the Southern District of New York sent a team of attorneys. Then there's the FBI and the IRS."

He coughed into a tissue and took deep breaths. "Forgive my manners. How are Lia and the children?"

"All well. Lia is enamored with Clint Eastwood, Paul Newman, and Mel Gibson. I run a distant fourth. She sends her regards and to say her heart is with you."

Sam drank his sake, put down his cup, then leaned forward. "What else can I do?"

Edward took out a roll of lozenges and placed one in his mouth. "Nothing, thanks. I pop these things like candy. That and using a vaporizor. Claire's coming home for a brief visit, but if she hears me hacking, she won't go."

"Drink tea with honey."

"Honey! Babs is turning me into a tea bag. My family physician advises a long vacation in the sun. Dr. Lawson, my surgeon, dropped by last week. He reamed me out for risking pneumonia for a boat ride. I'm inundated with advice from all sides. That's why I don't tell them everything. Frankly I wish they'd stop."

"You must follow orders," Sam chided.

"Why?" Edward waved his hand. "Who knows more? Doctors or God? God, of course. In the hospital I lay awake pondering the meaning of life, asking myself why I hadn't used my seat belt. At night I dreamed of death. I'm not a religious man, but I believe God put me here for a reason. I'm damned if I know what that is. When I came home, the dreams stopped. But this week they started again. I spend hours trying to figure out why I dream of death. It's not a death wish. I love my family and I certainly want to stick around."

Sam understood the dream as his subconscious locked in a struggle. In death there's no shameful publicity, no long drawn-out trial, no certain jail sentence. His family would carry on with their dignity intact.

Rising, he patted his friend's bony shoulder. "It means you're getting old, like me. You're under the weather. Therefore, you and your subconscious brood. It will pass."

"You're a wise man, Sam. You mastered the art of sounding brilliant while spouting bullshit."

Fourteen

AS VITO'S COMPUTER course on photographic superimposition and computer process detailing ended for the day, he became engaged in a serious discussion with Daria and Piggy.

"Of course I've noticed the change in Wendall. Who hasn't? He's glum, grouchy half the time, a pain in the ass all the time. He doesn't touch the piano. Harry's customers drive Harry crazy. They count on Wendall for free booze."

"What's wrong with him?" Piggy asked.

"An advanced case of hormonal imbalance," Vito offered.

Daria set three brown mugs on her desk. Despite attempts to attract Peter Ramirez, Wendall's new assistant, she'd failed. The beehive hairdo disappeared in favor of a more fashionable blunt cut. The green eye shadow and kohl-outlined eyelids remained, Cleopatra fashion.

Holding a coffeepot in one hand and a bottle of cheap whiskey in the other, she poured equal portions of liquids into the mugs, adding peppermint swizzle sticks left over from Christmas. The men helped themselves. The sound of crunching candy punctuated the conversation.

"You're wrong for a change, Vito. It's Wendall's gonads. His primary sex gland's drying up from lack of use," Daria said.

"Christ!" Piggy cried out. In the throes of his first real romance, he gasped in pitying horror. Motivated by love, he considered applying for the police force, and asked Wendall to remove his facial scar. Hearing his idol had fallen on hard times visibly upset him.

Daria came around to the front of her desk and perched on its edge. "Look, guys, when a man's gonads dry up, it's bound to affect his personality. It has to. Especially Wendall's. Everyone knows that."

At that moment, Wendall stormed out of his office. The aroma of barley soup wafted into the reception area. He slapped a stack of manila folders on Daria's desk and glared at her outfit.

"What the hell kind of fashion statement is that?" he barked, disapproving of her tight green leather miniskirt and her plunging neckline. "This isn't a goddamn whorehouse. It's a medical facility. Cover your tits and ass!"

He whirled around, retreating to the sanctity of his room, and slammed the door shut. In seconds, he opened it and stuck his head out. "I didn't mean to insult you. Wear the blouse Claire sent you for Christmas. You look terrific in it."

He slammed the door again.

"See what I mean, guys?" she said. "He's in worse shape than I thought. We've got to help him."

"I'll talk to him." Vito carried his mug with him. He sauntered into Wendall's office and closed the door behind him. He cleared a chair for himself. Wendall sat at his desk, his arm covering a report.

"It's obvious you've lost your irresistible charm. Harry's worried. Dust is piling up on the piano. His business is down thirty percent. The customers miss you butchering Beethoven." He jerked a thumb toward the reception room. "We both know I'm not Daria's greatest fan; however, you shot your mouth off for nothing. She claims your gonads are drying up. Are they?"

Glowering, Wendall scraped back his chair and stalked around to the front of his desk. "Get the fuck out! Can't you see I'm busy?"

Vito didn't budge. "I guess Motor Mouth's right about your shriveling gonads."

Wendall pulled his brows together. "Jesus Christ! Go solve a murder, will you? I can't believe you three idiots don't have better things to do than discuss me."

Vito put his legs on the edge of the desk. "Nope. You're the star idiot. Lawson, you're a sorry sight. Cheer up."

"Give me one good reason," he demanded.

"I'll give you several, which in my exalted position gives me inside information. On Edward Jameson's say-so, Sam Yamuto cancelled the shopping mall. Ditto the building permits and the bank consortium's loans. Mr. Yamuto is going with a second choice—Farrar Brothers—on Jameson's recommendation. Jameson is one smart cookie. He's furious with Colin. When he learned Claire has no claim on the house, cars, and yacht, and that Colin sold her jewelry, he set financial fires like lightning in a dry forest. While the IRS is slapping liens on Jameson's holdings, he's getting revenge on Colin. He's squeezing his balls, screwing him in Colin's Holy Grail: his pocketbook."

Glad to hear it, Wendall reserved his opinion. His reaction depended on how it affected Claire, who stopped answering her phone. Frowning, he asked, "When did this happen?"

"Over the last several days. This morning I received a call from a woman named Marybeth Frankel. She's a syndicated columnist for the Marx newspaper chain. Said she's a friend of Claire's, asked for background material."

Wendall's hand came down on the desk with a solid whack. "She's the viper who poisoned Claire. What did you tell her?"

Vito sipped his coffee. "Nothing. What do you take me for? If she's Claire's friend, she'd call her, not me. This is an official police and government investigation. I never discuss confidential business, present company excepted."

He took a green lollipop and dropped the wrapper on the desk. Wendall scooped it up, tossing the wrapper into the trash.

"You're a slob."

"Thank you." Vito tipped back his head, the lollipop's stick dangling from the corner of his mouth. "This is a first, me giving you advice, but if I were you, I'd see Claire."

Wendall's stomach rumbled, reminding him he had skipped lunch, and at eleven P.M. still hadn't eaten dinner. "Flying to California is out of the question. I scheduled surgery every day next week. Plus, Peter's going to a meeting, and the workmen are about to start the new kitchen. How do you propose I drop everything?"

Vito drained his coffee. "What does this have to do with you driving to Connecticut?"

"Why should I go there?"

"Don't be a dunce. Claire's in Connecticut."

"What?" Dumbfounded, Wendall felt as if he'd been punched in the stomach and had the wind knocked out of him. He opened his mouth, then couldn't speak. Claire home! Within driving, touching, kissing distance, and she hadn't said a word. Why not? Why wouldn't she tell him? Surely Parish didn't believe he'd compromise her case if he saw her in the privacy of her home.

"How do you know?"

"It's my business to know everything going on in the Jameson family. Claire's taken a job on a cruise ship. She's home for a final visit. She leaves soon."

Wendall's mouth went dry. "Why didn't you tell me?"

"I thought you knew," Vito said, seeing the hurt in Wendall's eyes.

Wendall rose. "I didn't. She didn't say a word." A surge of fierce determination gripped him. He put on his coat, had his hand on the doorknob, and was half out the door when he pivoted.

"You don't mind if I cancel dinner tonight?"

Vito pocketed a red lollipop and stuck another in his mouth. "I'd be disappointed if you didn't."

Silence cloaked the huge Jameson house when Wendall pulled into the driveway a little before one A.M. The cold night air nipped at his face, but he was too angry to feel its bite. His footsteps crunched dead leaves scattered on the gravel road.

Like a fool, he imagined a reunion with Claire, drawing out a scenario of a heated embrace, her arms open in welcome, her green eyes glowing. For him. In one of his scenarios they didn't make it past the hall to the bedroom. So much for a frank and open relationship. She had used him.

His temper rising, he rang the doorbell. After several minutes he leaned on the bell. If he woke the whole house, tough! This had nothing to do with Parish or with Colin. Claire owed him an answer.

Behind the door, a bright light clicked on, casting a roseate glow through the stained-glass transom. In seconds porch lights illuminated the outside. A grumpy male voice demanded to know who was there. Wendall identified himself.

The door swung open. "Wendall, for goodness' sake! What are you doing here at this hour?" A barefoot pajama-clad Jimmy clamped the sides of his bathrobe together and stepped aside to let him enter.

"I want to see Claire. Don't tell me she's not here. I know better."

Jimmy read his resolute face. "She's asleep."

"Wake her. If you don't, I will."

Jimmy nodded. "Wait in the study."

Wendall removed his coat, dropped it on a chair and thrust his hands in the pockets of his navy slacks. He was gazing at her portrait when he sensed her presence, smelled her elusive scent even before he turned around, his face grim, unsmiling.

"Hello, Wendall."

He felt as if the space between them were thin ice, so cool and matter-of-fact was her greeting. Wearing a silk bathrobe and slippers, her face scrubbed clean, her lustrous hair tumbling around her shoulders, her green eyes luminous, she extended her hand.

He ignored it. His eyes probed her. "Now I know why you didn't answer my calls. Since I've served my purpose, you decided to sneak out of the country without giving me the courtesy of a call. Thanks a lot."

She clasped her hands to her breast. Her voice faltered at first, but then grew stronger. "I wasn't sneaking out. I simply had to leave. I thought it best."

He snorted.

She felt her cheeks blazing with cowardly color. From the moment she'd made her decision, she recognized she cared for him. A quick, neat, surgical cut was the best way to ward off trouble. She couldn't any longer. Without preamble, Wendall, his blue eyes full of pain, his brow tight, his mouth thinned, had wiped out her choice. She wrapped her arms around her waist to keep from hugging him.

"Would you care to sit?"

"I prefer to stand," he said bluntly.

"A drink, then?"

"I don't want a drink. I don't want to sit. I don't want small talk. I want the truth. Why didn't you tell me? Why did I learn this from Vito? Why are you running away from me? I thought we had gone beyond this."

Nervous, caught in an awful dilemma, feeling his eyes boring into her back, she swept past him to the French doors. As she switched the terrace lights on, the sudden brightness aroused a flock of sea gulls. Tied up at a private dock, the Hatteras's bow rose and fell in rhythmic slumber. A hundred times her hand had hovered on the phone to tell him she'd taken a job, but she couldn't bring herself to make the call. She knew intuitively that he'd wear down her defenses. Now he was here. Behind her, surrounding her, his tension a tangible thing.

"We can't go beyond this. Ever."

He whirled her around and looked into her eyes. "What are you saying? You need time? It's okay, I understand."

"No." She shook her head. She considered the pros and cons, always coming up with the same damning reason. His parents' shadows loomed in the background. "It won't work." Her voice caught. "We have different goals."

He cursed. "It's Colin. He wants you back. You're considering it?"

"Never," she retorted so quickly that some of the tension eased from his face. "Never."

"Then why, damnit?" His gaze was searing, relentless. "I drove like a freaking maniac. I broke every speed law on the books. It's a wonder the cops didn't haul me in. What changed your mind? Don't hedge. I'm not leaving until I get the truth."

"All right. I know your last name is Everett-Lawson. Cee-Cee told me. Then I went to the library. I read about your family, your long line of distinguished ancestors. I can't handle more denunciation. What's more, I won't," she said, her tone belligerent, her chin jutting forward. "Even if it doesn't matter to you, it matters to me."

He ran his hand through his hair. "You matter to me, not your name or your family. Why should mine matter to you?"

She spoke quietly and directly, her eyes looking straight into his. "You overlook one important truth. You had ample opportunities to tell me about yourself, and you didn't. Neither did my mother. The reason is clear. Both of you were born into high-society families. Both of you know its code, or have you forgotten my mother talked about it that night at the Plaza?"

"She also said it didn't matter."

"Please! I'm not naive. It matters. If you and she concealed the truth to protect me, I'd have to be a glutton for punishment to repeat the same mistake twice!"

He blanched. He realized he should have told her. By not saying anything right away, he had unwittingly confirmed her suspicions.

"Judging from your expression, Wendall, I'm right. You love your parents. You, yourself, said your mother wants grandchildren."

Desperation tinged his voice. "All mothers say that. It's a conspiracy. They have nothing else to do with themselves," he said wildly, and Claire smiled in spite of herself. "In case you haven't noticed, I'm a grown man."

"The same grown man who withheld vital information."

"Crap!" he said succinctly. "I didn't tell you for fear you'd react exactly this way. Okay, I should have taken my chances, but I didn't."

"You're an Everett-Lawson. A son, regardless of age, as I'm my father's daughter. I love him, you love your parents. I refuse to enter a room and know I'm responsible for the sudden hush. I won't put myself in an untenable position."

He ran a hand through his hair again, disheveling it. "What untenable position? How do you know so much? You never met them," he said, reaching out to touch her.

She became awake of his nearness, of his warm hand pressing her arm. She released it. "Please don't make this harder. Sympathy stops at the front door when a son—the only heir to a great fortune—is involved. Then it's hard-scrutiny time. Can you guarantee your parents would condone a liaison with a felon's daughter? Of course not. Would you in their place? I'll be brutally honest, Wendall. If it were my child, I'd have reservations. My father's lawyers expect he'll be brought to trial next year. The media will be out in force. They'll badger us. What will you do? Fight on our account? You've already punched Colin. Go back to your life. People depend on you. In time you'd resent me."

"For God's sake! How could I?" he exploded, overcome by the totality of her mistaken beliefs. Her anguish tore at his heart. "I've waited a lifetime to fall in love. Do you think I'd let your objections stop me? What sort of man do you think I am?" Agitated, he gave himself a moment to calm down. "Answer me honestly. Do you feel anything for me besides gratitude? If you don't, I'll leave you in peace."

She cast down her eyes, but he wouldn't have it. His finger tilted her chin up. "All you have to do is say yes or no."

She opened her mouth to lie, had every intention of lying. The challenge in his eyes kept her honest. She thought Colin had killed all sexual desire. He hadn't. He'd killed it for him.

She drew a deep breath. "I care for you," she whispered, miserable at her admission.

Wendall breathed a sigh of relief. He crushed her in his arms. "Thank God," he murmured, his hand sweeping her spine. "Then it's all right. We'll see this through together."

She shook her head and eased from his embrace. "It's not all right. I don't want to see you again."

"That's crazy!"

Assailed by guilt for trampling on his feelings, she tried

to explain. "I cherish your friendship. You've been a constant source of strength. I waited for your calls. You have no idea how much they meant. You're the most giving person I know."

He gritted his teeth. He had this mad desire to shake her until her teeth rattled. He hadn't driven to Connecticut to hear a thank-you-good-bye speech. This fight represented his life. His future.

He touched her face with his fingertips. "If I'm this marvelous paragon, give me one night. One night. I love you. I love everything about you. Including your invisible genes. Don't you know that?"

A taut silence fell between them. She gazed into his blue eyes, darker, more intense than she'd ever seen. "Oh, please, stop looking at me like that. I can't think straight."

As her plea penetrated his tormented brain, a river of misery slid from his shoulders. He smiled, a dawning smile of delight, melting her resistance. He swooped her into his arms.

"No," she wailed, but gave up the useless struggle and wrapped her arms around his neck. "Don't hug me. You have the most potent hugs. They're dangerous. They sneak up on me."

"Do they?" he said, hugging her tighter.

Her fingers threaded his hair, and her breasts pressed to his chest. "Yes, you awful man. You know what happened in the airport. Please," she beseeched him, her voice quivering. "Please turn off the charm."

Chuckling in relief, he buried his face in her hair, his long fingers curling around her nape. He lowered his head, whispering, "Not in a million years."

He pressed his mouth on hers. He kissed her deeply, his hands sliding up and down her back, cradling her in his embrace, urging her response as if by the force of his will he could eradicate each separate hurt Colin had inflicted.

She did respond. Slowly at first, then as her better judgment clouded, as he avidly rained kisses on her face, nibbled her ear, caressed her breasts, murmuring her praise, a sweet ache built in her heart, chipping away the ice around it. He kissed her until she was breathless, until he was all she could think about. Until his want became her want. His need. Her need.

He cradled her face. "Will you come with me?"

She looked in his solemn eyes that mirrored her desire. How could she say no to him or to herself, when she, too, wanted the memory of one night? He was so beautiful, and as he looked down at her with his wondrous eyes, she could feel his coiled tension, feel him rigidly holding his breath, waiting for her answer. And then as she nodded, a wondrous smile lit his blue eyes.

"We'll use the guest cottage, but I don't want to mislead you. It won't change anything."

The corner of his mouth lifted in a lopsided grin that spread wider until he was beaming. He pushed stray tendrils of hair away from her cheek. He kissed the tip of her nose.

"That's what you think, sweetheart."

Babs couldn't sleep. From her second-floor bedroom window, she saw her daughter and Wendall. She smiled. Maybe there was some justice in the world after all. She slipped back into bed, snuggling next to her husband. She put her ear to Edward's back. She didn't like the rattling noise in his chest. Tomorrow she'd take Wendall aside and ask for the name of a pulmonary specialist. She didn't want Claire knowing how worried she was. If she knew she wouldn't leave, and she wanted Claire at sea as much as Edward did. Away from Colin's clutches, away from the tabloids. Just last week a reporter snuck onto the grounds and snapped Edward's picture. Jimmy wrestled with the man, grabbed the camera, and destroyed the film. This time they were lucky.

The temperature in the low thirties, moonlight guiding their path, Claire and Wendall hurried to the white Cape Cod cottage, its dormers and shutters painted Wedgwood blue. She unlocked the door, turned up the thermostat on the wall, and ushered him into the cozy living room. Putting the house key on a wicker table, she switched on a hurricane lamp. Wendall shed his coat, helped her off with hers, and hung them up in the closet nearest the chintz-covered sofa.

"Cee-Cee and I used the cottage for our hideaway." She started babbling about marshmallow parties and Jimmy building fires in the fireplace for them and how once when she and her friend invited five others for a slumber party and they roasted fat wieners on the same sticks as the marshmallows, and the hot dogs split, came out gooey and sticky, but they loved it, and decided they had invented a new food. "Ruthie took one look at it and was aghast."

"You don't say." He kissed her chin.

"I do," she murmured, tilting her neck to give him better access. "Jimmy leaves logs on the grates. Once Cee-Cee and I forgot to check the flue. We caused a puff-back fire that damaged the furniture, walls, and the carpet. The place needed an airing for a week. We were scolded, let me tell you. Of course, we deserved it. Carelessness could have killed us. That's one of the reasons my mother didn't replace the carpet. Would you like a fire?"

He kissed her neck. "There's not much point in starting one down here, is there?"

Claire's pulse leaped. His tone sounded conversational, but she felt the sparks igniting between them. *"Sewing one oat is going to come back and haunt you,"* Cee-Cee had warned.

"Would you like to see the downstairs? It's a lovely cottage. I love the golden oak floor, don't you?"

"The floor is beautiful," he said, not taking his eyes from her face.

"When the sun streams through the windows, the floor sparkles," she prattled. "It's hard to believe a floor can sparkle. Most shine in spots. Trust me, this one glitters. I think it's the grain of the wood. Oh, and see the 1860 grandfather clock in the corner? It works like a charm. We have a book on the shelf about the man who designed it. He's an Englishman. Would you like to see it?"

His eyes were gleaming sapphires. His right hand cupped her cheek. "I'd like to see the bedroom."

She knew her face was scarlet. "I . . . I should have changed first. This is an old flannel nightgown."

"I'm not interested in your clothes."

Her heart slammed in her ribs. She dropped her head to his chest. "Look at me. I'm a grown modern woman, and I'm scared out of my wits. Nothing's going to happen, I'm Jell-O."

He chuckled. He lifted her chin, dipped his head, and kissed her neck. "Mmmm. I love eating Jell-O."

She jumped backward. "Don't say that!" His hands on her shoulders caught her back, slipped over the soft round globes, caressed her buttocks. He nibbled her ear, sending shivers to her toes. "Oh, what are you doing?"

He brushed his lips on hers. "I'm getting started. Don't mind me. Go on with your list of objections." His hand cupped her breast, his fingers teasing the nipple to a nubby peak.

"I'm not objecting. You've built up this image of me," she chattered, trying to balance a fit of nerves and the tide of rising desire. "I've never. Cee-Cee warned me. I mean it's one thing to discuss——"

He smiled into her eyes, then kissed her lips shut. "If it helps, I'm scared, too."

"You?" she cried, her eyes wide with astonishment. "You're a doctor. You see hundreds of naked women."

"Hundreds of thousands." He kissed the silky curve of her neck. She closed her eyes. His hands slid to her waist, keeping her where he wanted her. "Daria told Piggy and Vito my gonads are drying up."

Claire's eyelids popped open. "You're kidding. She said that?"

The corners of his eyes crinkled. "Yes, she did." He lifted her hair from her nape. He licked the rim of a delicate earlobe. "I love your scent."

She squirmed deliciously. His warm breath made her spine tingle. "It's Arpege. You were saying . . ."

His hands encircled her waist. "Can you imagine how I felt walking in on three nosy-bodies discussing my shriveling gonads? Daria said they need oiling. The fact is, she's right."

Amusement lit her eyes. His teasing disarmed her defenses. Her eyes wide in sham sympathy, she touched his cheek in a gesture of compassion. "I couldn't live with myself if I let you go through life with pruney gonads."

He grinned. "I hoped you'd see it my way. Do you have a bottle of wine?"

She nodded. She left the room and returned in moments with wine and two glasses. Taking the bottle from her before she battled another case of nerves, he put his other arm around her shoulders. They mounted the stairs to the master bedroom.

A pair of tall bay windows with window seats overlooked the Sound. The walls, painted mauve to match the carpet, had a wainscot of white. A light-marble fireplace had been set into the wall opposite Claire's four-poster canopy bed. An old English ash chest of drawers and a chintz wing-backed settee gave the room an added touch of charm.

"This is nice."

Wendall placed the wine and the glasses on the dresser. "Would you like a fire? I promise to check the flue." She nodded. "While I do this, you pour the wine."

He checked the flue, then lit a match to the kindling wood. In minutes a rosy heat filtered through the room. Claire handed him his wine.

"To us," he said huskily. He urged her to finish her wine, which she did. He put their empty glasses on the dresser and gathered her in his arms.

"You'll never be sorry. I swear it."

Her heart fluttered. "I know, darling," she said, responding to the tender urgency in his voice.

He bent his head down, pressing his mouth on hers for a long, deep kiss. He tasted the warm, wine-sweetened recesses of her mouth, unleashing a fever of desire. "God, I want you."

He pulled off the rose-patterned bed comforter. He shed his clothes until he stood naked, revealing a magnificently proportioned physique. She watched him, knowing he had undressed first, making himself vulnerable for her.

Her gaze roamed lower.

She wet her lips unconsciously as a different kind of pressure begin to build within her. With her eyes on his, her fingers went to the row of pearl buttons at her neck. One by one she slid them open. In one graceful motion she raised the gown above her head.

Wendall thought he'd never seen a more natural temptress. Her movements were slow, sensual, evocative. Her body was slim, softly curved with gently flaring hips and firm, high breasts. She shook her head, sending a riot of dark hair in a swirling halo around her face. The gown fluttered to the floor. With her eyes on his, she put her nerves behind her and walked straight into his arms.

The first electric contact of flesh upon flesh had him quivering, not from cold but from heated anticipation, flaming through his loins. The softness of her in his arms, the touch of her breasts against his chest, the feel of his hands caressing her set off sparks, almost more than he could bear. He pulled down the comforter, then he lifted her up and lay her gently on the moonlit bed.

"You're glorious," he said, gazing at her.

Nothing in his life could equal the feeling of love she evoked in him. He had been dreaming of this moment, and now it was here. He ran his fingertips over her skin. He wove his fingers through her thick hair. His hand molded and shaped a breast, sensitizing her with his touch. He dipped his head to cover the nipple, suckling it with his mouth. She moaned as he left one breast and treated the other to the same ministrations.

"We have the rest of the night for discovery. For me to give you pleasure."

Her heart expanded with gratitude. She began to realize he wasn't taking. This first time he was the giver, the healer, assuaging the pain. She did not stop him, but lay in his arms, her body trembling in his embrace as Wendall worshipped her with his mouth and hands. She saw his face, tender yet taut with passion. Each separate part of her surrendered to his touch. As if in a dream, she heard herself moan as he continued kissing her, his tongue mating with hers, his fingers stroking her secret prize.

Thrillingly attuned to his masculine grace, her restless hands traced the corded muscles on his arms. Her fingers dug into his shoulders. She was coming apart inside.

Instinctively her hips raised and, for one heart-stopping minute, she thought she would burst. Her eyes were hot emerald green. A faint sheen of sweat dotted her brow. The pleasure Wendall promised had become exquisite torture.

"No more," she begged, eager for him. "I want you inside me. I want you sharing this feeling."

His heart thudded. He bent his head and kissed her damp forehead, then he rose above her, the tight rein he had kept on himself showing in the harsh planes of his face. A groan of ecstasy escaped his lips, and with one thrust gave her what they both wanted. Her muscles sheathed him like a velvet glove. His eyes smoldering, he took her hand and brought it down to where they were one.

"I believe in our destiny. You may not accept it yet, but trust me, darling, this is meant to be."

She gave a low moan. They were safe as long as she kept the world outside her door. Tears of regret misted her eyes. If only it could be true, but it couldn't. Not now. Not ever.

"Shhh," he soothed. "It's all right. I love you."

Stroking the sensitive nub of flesh, he waited until she put her arms around him, then he moved. Slowly at first, taking her ragged sighs of delight as a signal. He thrust deeper, harder, wanting to be a part of her forever, to blot forever the cruel stigma Colin cast upon her, to never let her leave his side. Claire's pulse thundered. Giving him her absolute trust, she could feel his throbbing intensity. Their bodies moved as one, in a union beyond flesh, reaching into their hearts and souls. Her back arched upward. Crying out, she joined him at the pinnacle, sharing his dream in perfect harmony.

If only for a little while . . .

Blissfully content, Claire couldn't rouse herself. Neither did she care to abandon the cocoon of tangled sheets.

Snuggling closer to Wendall, she opened her eyes with a happy sigh. What an incredible night! All through the night they made love, drifting off sleepily, then coming languidly together, fondling and kissing, building to soul-shattering orgasms, as one or the other took the initiative.

Claire experimented. She learned his preferences, massaging and kissing him all over until he clutched the sheets in near delirium. With her newly acquired knowledge of him, she declared herself his sex therapist.

"You're more like a hooker," he grunted.

She yanked his hair. "What do you know about hookers?"

He turned her over on her back, spread her thighs, and lifted her legs. He moved his hips forward. "In case you haven't noticed, Madam Therapist, I'm hooking you right now."

They laughed themselves silly, made passionate love, then fell asleep.

The sun blazed a stream of light. Claire lay with her head on Wendall's chest, his arms cradling her. He asked when she was leaving to start her job. When she replied she was scheduled to leave the following day, he gathered her tightly to him. His eyes were sad, and this time his loving was bittersweet.

They didn't conceal their affair from her parents or the Fortunes. Wendall couldn't take his eyes from her. Her parents approved of the man who knew everything there was to know about them and still loved Claire. Claire snapped rolls of film. Pictures of the family, Wendall, Ruthie, and Jimmy. She recorded each room in the house, plus the grounds.

Her father suggested she use the name Denison for work. She considered it, then decided against it. She told Wendall later that it was up to her to help restore honor to the Jameson name. That afternoon they left in a flurry of good-byes and good wishes, before the rush hour traffic. She'd spend the night in Wendall's home. Her flight for Tokyo left Kennedy Airport at seven in the morning, connecting with Cathay Pacific for the final leg to Hong Kong. She would fly through several time zones, reaching her destination at close to nine at night the next day, a twenty-hour trip.

She thought his house charming. It had a large dining room with an oval table, and a huge high-ceilinged living room. Warm earth tones covered the sofa and deep armchairs. Wingchairs flanked a Vermont stone fireplace. Prints of Chopin, Mozart, Beethoven, Hayden, and Strauss hung on the wall behind the Kawaii baby grand.

She loved his cheerful yellow-and-white kitchen. What appeared to be a bookcase lined with shelves of books above a work desk was actually wallpaper. The spines of the faux cookbooks quoted titles by Julia Child, James Beard, and others.

"I bought this house from my former roommate, David Orchin, who moved to California. The man he sold it to couldn't get a loan. I'll fix one of my famous omelettes."

Working together in the bright, airy room, Claire set the table, found the wineglasses, and heated dinner rolls, while Wendall made the omelette.

"This is delicious," she said after finishing her generous portion. She raised her wineglass. "Do you know restaurant tables are usually set in a diamond pattern so people don't bump into each other when they move their chairs? That fine-tuning a table refers to the glasses and dishes being symmetrical and opposite mirror images?"

He bathed her in smiles. "Really. How do you know?"

She grinned. "Bum! Tom helped me get the job. I don't want to disappoint him, so I'm studying pamphlets the purser and the chef gave me. Dueces means a table for two. Guests prefer a table overlooking water."

"What happens if they don't get one?"

Without pausing, she said, "We toss them overboard, what else? Shall I tell you about the Vulcan?"

"Is it a bird?"

"Silly! It's an overhead system of pipes. It washes out grease, prevents fires. I memorized the pamphlet. I want the chef to think I'm smart."

"I hate to put a damper on your bragging rights. Vulcan is the brand name for stoves and cooking surfaces, beneath which are low boys. You're referring to the Gaylord system."

In high good humor, she overlooked her mistake. "Why would a short boy stand beneath a stove?"

"Claire, Claire, Claire. A low boy is a refrigerator. It saves the cook steps."

She batted her eyelashes. "Wendall, Wendall, Wendall. Who gives a hoot?"

"Cooking is serious business." He chuckled.

"Oh my god!" She giggled. "You mean I've failed pamphlet!" She kissed his palm, licking tiny circles with her tongue. He groaned. "Mmmmm. Good reflexes, Doctor. Is there anything you don't know?"

"Very little. Being a brilliant chef, naturally I'd have to know my way around a kitchen, restaurants, too. Did you know the best caviar contains the proper amount of grains?"

"Stop!" she shrieked. "If you think I'd stink up my hands counting slimy grains, you're nuts." She glanced at his plate, then at him, and their gazes locked. Both stopped smiling. She reached for his hand. "Why aren't you eating?"

In less than twelve hours she'd leave him. Wendall bleakly ran his hand over his chin. He looked at her through the sadness in his eyes. "I'm not hungry for food. It's selfish of me, but I don't want you to leave. What good is being smart if I can't convince you to stay?"

The urge to give in was so strong that Claire bit her lip to keep from saying the hell with it. She'd find a job in New York.

"Darling, you're usually so levelheaded. I'm struggling to find my identity. If I had a profession, it might be different. Since I don't, and with my father's trial coming soon, this position is doubly important. It's a lab course, on-the-job learning with room and board."

"It's the luxury-liner romantic setting that worries me," he grumbled.

She carried their dishes to the sink, washed them, then held her hands out to Wendall. He stood and looked down into her eyes. His eyes full of misery, he tried to sound noble for her sake.

"Don't mind me. How about a hug?"

She slipped her hands around his waist. "I've got a better idea. Make love to me, please."

Beethoven's bronze bust sat near the phone by his king-size bed. She put her purse on his desk and wandered into the other bedrooms and bathrooms while Wendall checked his messages.

When she returned, he had his tie off, his arm propped on the mahogany triple dresser. "I didn't use a decorator. I brought most of these things from home, which accounts for the mishmash of styles."

Her eyes warm with desire, she slipped her arms around his neck, molding her body to his. "Shall we discuss furniture?" she whispered huskily.

Holding himself back from pleading with her to stay, he crushed his lips on hers. . . .

At five A.M. they drove to Kennedy. Not caring who saw them, she clung to him, savoring the warm body contact, patting his chest, touching his hair, kissing his mouth.

He wanted to tell her there was still time to change her mind; her inconsequential husband didn't matter, she could find a job in New York.

The loudspeaker announced her plane. The line moved toward the gate.

"Don't forget me," he said hoarsely.

She hugged him fiercely. "As if I could. As if I'd want to." In her suitcase she'd packed mementoes: pictures of her family, the Fortunes, her home; her grandmother's pomander; in her purse, Wendall's picture.

They announced the boarding of passengers with her row number. He framed her face in his hands. "I despise all trips beyond a fifty-mile radius."

Blinking back tears, she privately agreed with him.

Fifteen

CLAIRE FIXED UP her cabin to look like home. It was smaller than her dressing room in Beverly Hills. But she didn't mind. She'd brought a favorite pillow from her room in Connecticut, hung pictures of her family on the wall, set her grandmother's pomander on her dresser, and placed Wendall's picture by her bed near his growing stack of letters which she tied with a red ribbon. Three months after she'd left home, she could honestly say she loved her work.

While Marybeth Frankel gleaned sadistic satisfaction spotlighting the Brice-Jameson travails in her syndicated gossip column, she saturated her brain with daily treasure troves. Supported by her father's advice that sound business practices apply across the board, Claire used the food-service industry as her business model. Food per se didn't interest her. Business did. She discovered she had a real flair for time management. When Hans spoke of prep kitchens where basic sauces, stocks, and garnishes were prepared in advance, she converted time saved into man-hours saved, which increased productivity and job performance.

She had three excellent teachers, although blustery, Austrian-born Chef Hans Aldred was her secret love. He appointed himself her surrogate father. The childless widower had lived in the United States for five years, teaching at the Culinary Institute in Hyde Park, New York. He discussed quality and food presentation.

The chief steward, Manolo Gittari, trained her first to

track par stock, then to keep the rest of the inventory on the computer. The maître d'hôtel, Vincenzio Verde, treated her as a favored niece. He discussed dining-room management and wine merchandising. Long after their workdays ended, the three sat with Claire, which flattered her. "The more practice I get, the more I'll be prepared to run a business," she said.

The men's special fondness for Claire stemmed from an incident in Australia two months after she had begun working on the *Sea Voyager*. Quayside for the loading of fruits and vegetables, she accompanied the local purveyor into the dockside warehouse. Her critical eye spotted limp, dry vegetables hidden under top rows of fresh vegetables.

After a quick check of the purveyor's dilated pupils, she asked Hans and Manolo to come outside. "He's on drugs. He's dumping garbage on us, using the money he'd pay for fresh produce to support his habit."

An investigation proved her right. The chief steward switched purveyors. She not only saved World Cruises money, she helped Hans maintain the line's reputation for excellence.

"Business fascinates me," she wrote her father.

On the computer she designed a model company, item-izing and adding up all expenditures, figured her cash flow, doubled it as the entrepreneurs suggested in the business and financial magazines she subscribed to, and showed Hans the chart.

"What do you think?" she asked, biting her lip as he checked each item.

"It looks good."

"But?"

"Dishes break. Don't spend so much on dinnerware."

"Back-door costs," she said, remembering. Hans smiled. She revised the figures.

In early May, Wendall called Claire after he operated on her father's nose, repairing it with a successful skin graft. "Your mother is fine, too," he assured her, asking if she still liked her job.

"More and more," she answered honestly, knowing he'd prefer it if she said she hated it and wanted to come home. "I'm never bored. If I'm not working, I'm studying. Each sailing is like a Broadway opening. Passengers care about efficient, prompt, courteous service."

"Me, too," he quipped. "The prompter the better."

She giggled. "I'm serious. We have seven, ten, or fourteen days to make a fabulous impression. Yesterday I modeled the latest fashions and accessories."

"What about single men?" Wendall asked.

"What single men?"

"Don't be coy. How much mingling is involved? Do men hit on you?"

"Well . . ."

"I knew it! They see a beautiful woman, the first thing you know they dream of making love to you. I ought to know."

"Wendall, you lovable old goat, you're jealous."

"Green with envy," he groused. With no claim on him, she reluctantly suggested he date.

"Don't tell me what to do. If that's a segue into saying you want to date, forget it!"

Claire remembered their lovemaking, and she could feel herself grow moist, wanting. He seemed to know her better than she knew herself, caressing her with an insatiable passion that triggered her own, as she cautioned herself not to guard her heart.

Wendall filled her in on all the news at home. Vito had met a model who wanted to write mystery stories. Wendall had his fingers crossed. Juano's mother's latest pregnancy didn't please Juano. Daria promised to love him the best. He said he was going to Boston for a two-day medical conference. Daria wrote glowingly about Dr. Peter Ramirez, and she asked for advice. Claire suggested she tone down the eye makeup.

Knowing Wendall loved cooking, she wrote about Hans, a natural showman. His booming voice could be heard scolding, "*The bacon is burning! Asparagus tips on the rim of the dish! Spinach is lighter, it goes on the bottom. Sauce on the dish, not the meat!"*

Her personal favorite, Hans's artistic seal of approval, came after his eagle eye checked the presentation of a fish dish for color. *"Gentlemen, present your pompanos!"*

Claire's days hummed with accomplishment. She filled journals with notes, phrases, and single-word memory jogs to transcribe onto the computer during her free time. All for one purpose—to learn all she could as fast as she could.

Wendall said for a woman who didn't know her way around a kitchen and couldn't care less, it was her just deserts to use foodservice as a business model.

Burned from Colin's cruelty, she mistrusted her feelings. Wendall was the exact opposite of Colin, relaxed in his informal attitudes toward people, slipping easily from one group to the next. But despite those qualities she believed his parents would have the same objections as Colin's did.

"High society," she told Cee-Cee, "looks unfavorably on daughters of bank robbers for marriage material." Every time she thought the news would die down, the tabloids resurrected all or parts of the story, subjecting her father to ongoing malicious scrutiny.

She concentrated on business, selfishly glad to be at sea. A natural sailor, she'd loved water from her earliest childhood.

In August she flew home on a weekend medical pass to see her father. He discounted his pale appearance.

"You spend your days with a suntanned crew, men in top physical condition. Don't judge me by them. I'm stuck in the house with lawyers."

His happiness at having her home was touching. Tears filled his eyes when he took her hand in his and asked if the name Jameson had caused her trouble.

She glanced at a misty-eyed Babs who sat with them on the sofa, then cupped her father's thin face. "I'm proud to be your daughter."

Later she phoned Wendall. "You're in Connecticut!" he said. "Why didn't you let me know you were coming home? I'm swamped with patients. There was a bad accident on the

George Washington Bridge involving two buses headed for Atlantic City. I'll be in surgery. Look, there's no way I can get away before tomorrow night. Can you come down tonight?"

She pictured him pacing his office, or sitting on the leather chair, or glancing out his window. She steeled herself from getting into her car, driving into the city, and stealing an hour or two. "Wendall, I wish I could. I can't leave my father. He's so glad to see me. I need to be here."

She thought he'd argue, but he didn't. "All right. I'll drive up tomorrow after work."

Her breath caught. "Darling, my plane leaves in the morning."

As September passed to October, she spent time in Hans's office, where he proudly displayed a glowing review written by Bryan Miller, the powerful restaurant critic for the *New York Times*. Mr. Miller awarded Hans's shipboard cuisine his highest rating of four stars.

Claire bragged it was his just due. Both mentor and student looked forward to her lessons.

"A flow pattern is like a super highway," Claire remembered during one of their private sessions.

"What else have you learned?" he asked.

"Maintain superior quality, buy the best for the least amount, eliminate waste, charge high prices, and hope the waiters don't bang into each other or drop food on a customer."

He winked at her. "You pass with high marks. What interests you?"

She'd given this a lot of thought and spoke with no false modesty. "I'm good with people. I'll find a business where I'll meet the public part of the time and run the office most of the time. I won't relinquish control of the books. Whatever I decide on, the employees will share in the profits."

"Why?"

"For a very practical reason. Good help is hard to find, harder to keep. If you own shares in a business, or know you'll receive a percentage of the profits in bonuses, you'll work hard for it. That translates into less employee absences, more job satisfaction."

Claire hadn't seen Wendall in months. The onset of October brought a fresh wave of longing for him. His busy days grew busier. He explored the advisability of setting up a mentor program in the South Bronx, where skilled people could teach the unskilled one-on-one.

"If it worked for me," she wrote encouragingly, "it will work for others."

Wendall phoned three times weekly, chatting about the clinic, Daria's gaga attitude toward Peter Ramirez, but mainly to hear her voice, worried she might forget him, that he occupied a transitory place in her life. He was negotiating for a site for his second clinic. Thanks to Vito's influence, Piggy considered filing an application for admittance to the police academy. Their lives were busy. And apart.

One day a passenger named Nancy Scott came to Claire's office. Obviously unhappy, the plump, honey-eyed blonde glumly said her parents had sent her on the cruise for a college graduation present.

"That's bad?" Claire asked.

"Awful. It's a present from hell. I graduated in June. I put this cruise off as long as I could. I know I sound ungrateful. My folks aren't rich, and their gift means a lot. This boy I like—Kenny—prefers skinny girls. He made fun of me for gaining weight, so I'm trying to lose. Will you tell me how I can lose when food's the Holy Grail around here? I lack self-control. I'm weak. I know it's my fault. I'm a sucker for fattening sauces. I'll go home a blimp. Do you realize you people push one hundred thirty-seven meals in one week, counting the midnight buffet, snack buffet, pizza bar, afternoon tea and sandwiches, and God knows what else?"

Claire knew better than to argue. "You're right," she commiserated. "Unless you're into yogurt and fruit, cruising can be a nonstop food orgy. If you wish, you can preselect your meals. It reduces temptation." Nancy latched onto the idea. She would feel in control.

"Since when do I make special sauces?" Hans scolded. "It's a given. If you don't gain ten pounds on a cruise ship, a person thinks the food's lousy." But he kissed Claire on the cheek and gave her a smile. "You're right, *liebling*, you're a natural negotiator. You made the customer happy and conned me. You'll do well in business."

"Be open to new ideas," she jotted in her journal.

Thinking of Kenny, Nancy's insensitive boyfriend, Claire thought of Colin, who had frowned if she put butter on her bagel, his look enough to make her eat it dry.

She checked the passenger list and spoke with the maître d'hôtel, who arranged for Nancy to switch to the second seating. She sat with three bachelors. By the end of the cruise, Nancy and a Canadian accountant had paired off. When he heard this girl from Utah couldn't ski, he offered to teach her. After seeing Claire model swimsuits in a fashion show, Nancy asked her advice about clothes. Kenny became Kenny Who?

"And this," Claire wrote Wendall, "is how I found myself a dating service, model, fashion coordinator, and diet guru. Incidentally I modeled swimsuits."

"Cover up!" he replied. "Men get horny at sea."

So do women. Just thinking about seeing him next month during her vacation set her motor running. This time nothing would go wrong.

Her sultry looks, dazzling smile, emerald green eyes, and her throaty laugh had more than one man wondering how she spent her off hours. They'd be surprised if they knew this pretty woman spent them familiarizing herself with the myriad occupations on board the floating city. It boggled her mind that a computerized laundry system washed, dried, and pressed twenty thousand items a day.

Hans found her pacing her small office one day, steaming mad. That morning she'd gone ashore. A stack of tabloids sat on her desk. She had purchased every damning copy. He picked up one of the papers. Claire's likeness stared back at him. Without saying a word, he read Marybeth's latest blast: Colin Brice's Estranged Wife Toils in Ship's Kitchen.

Claire broke down. No matter how hard she tried, she

couldn't escape. With Hans's arm around her shoulders, she told him about her father's past.

"This woman doesn't know the difference between a galley and a kitchen. She's stupid."

"Stupid or not, she's out to have me fired."

Homesick, Claire showed Hans pictures of the Denison estate, the house and the rooms, describing it in detail. He studied the snapshots of the gracious interior, the terrace, and grounds.

"It's a fine waterfront location, an ideal place for a restaurant. Ask your parents if they'd consider selling."

Claire didn't have to. "Out of the question," she replied forcefully. "My mother inherited the estate from her parents. She'd never sell, nor will I after I inherit it. It's home to Ruth and Jimmy Fortune," she said, reminding him of the caretaker couple.

Worry for her father, loneliness for Wendall, and her reaction to Marybeth's article depressed her. Feeling blue, she curled up on her bed with a stack of Wendall's letters.

Oddly enough, the overall tone of friendship, feeling a part of his world, captivated her interest more than the paragraphs filled with messages of love. Peter Ramirez now spent three days a week in the South Bronx clinic, which overjoyed Daria who religiously read fashion magazines and finally toned down her eye shadow.

Daria sent Claire a snapshot. Without piles of makeup and wearing a flattering dress, her dainty loveliness shined through. Claire hoped Peter noticed.

Wendall's fertile brain moved into high gear. His mentor program would start by aiding prospective single-family home builders to erect houses in the South Bronx. Tutors—building contractors who had fled after the fires of the previous decade—formed a cadre of assistance. Wendall met with the mayor, who spearheaded a coalition of tutors, bankers, and city officials. Wendall called a news conference, committing the city to its word. He sent Claire a picture of the first house completed under the new program.

Richard Parish mailed the divorce papers. Under California law, a divorce is granted in six months. She stared at the legal document, the paper erasing five years of marriage, and she started to cry. She wept for the proud, happy young bride who had glided down the aisle on her father's arm. If she had known the awful price she would pay for that happiness, she would have remained single.

Colin had started his own company. His contracts, Parish said, were small pickings, for Sam Yamuto cast a long shadow. He dropped strategic hints in financial circles that he had conducted a thorough investigation of Brice-Jameson following the accident that impaired her father. His sudden cancellation of Colin's dream mall, with hints about nefarious doings, fed the financial rumor mills.

And helped Marybeth's career.

One morning in early November, Claire was standing on Aloha deck watching passengers disembark in Barbados. In her hand she held Wendall's latest letter. She missed him and couldn't wait until she saw him. Tomorrow they'd be in St. Thomas, their final port before returning to San Juan. She intended to spend a few hours at Magens Bay.

Her beeper signaled. She picked up a deck phone for her message. Giancarlo wanted her. She entered the Galleria: a three-story lobby foyer surrounded by shops, demitasse bar, and wine bar. The area featured a spectacular centerpiece, a striking stainless steel sculpture suspended over a dramatic sweeping stairway.

She descended the staircase to Giancarlo's office. He greeted her, then told her a passenger had boarded earlier that morning. The man had reserved a luxury suite. Six months ago she wouldn't have batted an eye at the price he paid for his weekend extravagance, but now her brows rose.

Located on the upper decks, the spacious accommodations were divided into a lounge area, bedroom area, dressing area, and bathroom with bathtub. Each suite contained two television sets, a patio door, and a big verandah complete with loungers. Complementary pastels completed the decor.

"He doesn't like wasting time," Giancarlo said. "He jotted down a list of his needs."

She tore open the envelope, scanned the list, then read the

note. She felt her face heat, her heart pound. "Oh my god!" She started giggling.

"Something wrong?"

Her eyes twinkled. "Something's right," she said as she danced out the door.

Leaving him confused, and passengers wondering what caused her rush, she raced to the elevator; when it didn't come immediately, she climbed five flights of stairs. On the tenth deck, she took a deep breath, sped down the long hallway, and finally skidded to a stop.

A man hauled her inside and threw the double lock. "What took you so long?"

"Wendall!" she screeched, flinging her arms around his neck. She looked at a face brimming with joy, into summer blue eyes sending such a heated message that she tingled. His hands swept the whole length of her, securing her into his embrace like a starved man. She pressed herself against him, reveling in the feel of his body on hers. She felt his hands lift her hair away from her neck, his lips brush a bouquet of kisses over her face and throat. He wasn't an apparition, but actually here, sporting a mile-wide grin. Looking tall and lanky in jeans and a tan shirt, his open collar gave her a glimpse of burnished chest hairs.

"You magnificent man." She squealed. "I can't believe you're here!"

He lifted her up and swung her around, sliding her slowly down, rubbing her against his hard shaft. Cupping her buttocks, he held her tightly to him. His heart pounded wildly in his chest. "I couldn't stand it." He thrust his tongue into her mouth, kissing her, smearing her lipstick. She kissed his ear, spreading the lipstick over it.

"You've reduced me to a basket case. Use your wildest imagination, darling. I spent the entire flight fantasizing. By the time we landed, I could barely walk."

She kissed his neck and breathed in the lingering aroma of after-shave. She nibbled her way back to his mouth. He crushed her lips in a fierce kiss, and she tasted faint traces of coffee. A breeze carried the salt tang of the sea, mingling with the scent of fresh-cut flowers in a vase on a table.

Neither noticed or cared. They kissed greedily, groping madly like a couple of frantic teenagers, who didn't know what to do first.

"Please." He held her away only long enough to plead. "Darling, it's been months. Then I missed you when you came home. Please tell me you don't have to go back to work."

Her eyes sparkled. Her hands slid up his arms, slipped over his shoulders, her fingers threading through his thick hair.

"I'm yours, darling." He smiled in relief. "For an hour or so."

He stopped smiling. "Christ. I've only got the weekend. We're wasting time."

He yanked off the bedspread. His sneakers hit a corner of the room. His shirt and socks landed on a chair. His hand went to his zipper, sliding it downward with difficulty.

Her eyes widened appreciatively. "Yummy. I see why you found it hard to walk."

He glanced at himself. "Your fault." He shucked the jeans, flipped them and his briefs behind him. "I'm in serious danger of going blind. Unless you want me never to perform surgery again, I suggest you show a huge amount of pity. Take off the damn blouse. I hate clothes on you almost as much as I hate taking you to airports. Here, let me help you."

Peeling away her lime skirt and matching blouse, he unhooked her bra, sending her clothes sailing. He lifted her up, dropping her unceremoniously on the bed. She propped on her elbows, shaking her head, laughing.

"I'm glad I'm amusing you," he said, pulling off her black lace-trimmed panties, and tossing them over his shoulder. "I'm serious, and you're laughing."

"If you knew . . ." She collapsed in a fit of hysteria. "If you knew how I dreamed of us coming together again. I had so many versions, Rhett. Not once did I picture you hopping around like a crazy man."

He bent over her, placed his open mouth over hers, and

gave her a hot moist kiss. "Oh, yeah, well let me show one of my versions, Scarlett."

He gathered her in his arms, his eyes glowing with desire. His hand slid up her smooth leg to her inner thigh. "I dreamed of you, of loving you. Like this . . ."

He knelt down. Claire stopped laughing. She gasped. This kind of kiss made her unable to think straight. His clever mouth feasted on the gifts she freely offered—the softness of satiny skin and womanly curves, the perfumed passion of secret places. He worshipped her with unwavering skill, lingering at her sensitive breasts and nipples, kissing the pulse point at the base of her throat, while his finger slipped into her liquid heat.

Her hands sought him. She felt him shudder, heard his groan of ecstasy. The months of separation, of abstinence, fueled his starving appetite. No other woman compared with her. He'd been faithful with his body, his heart, and his soul. He wanted her by his side every night. Damning time, he cursed each passing minute.

Passion ignited her entire body. She quivered beneath his touch. She breathed rapidly now as she arched her hips. In the moment of joining, thickly lashed eyes as blue as the sea gazed at her with the sensuous smile she'd come to love. She wrapped her legs around him. They moved as one, straining to be closer. Then closer still. Every exquisite touch, every loving word, every song their naked flesh sang was as if for the first time. A time of rediscovery. When she thought she couldn't take more, he slowed, only to rekindle his tender assault, loving her more, riding her harder, pouring out his passion with a fiery fervor that left her stunned.

A single blazing image burst upon her brain. "Wendall!"

His climax had been as shattering as her own. She clasped him to her bosom. Breathless, she waited for her heart to beat normally, for the world to stop spinning. When it did, her lips curved in an impish smile.

"So tell me, Doctor, how's your eyesight?"

He kissed her mouth, rolled over, and looked at her. "Much better. Not perfect. I need a lot more treatments, but there's a definite improvement. Care for a permanent job?"

Thoughts of his family's rejection kept her from saying yes. She glanced at the tangled linens. "We're not very neat, are we?"

The bed looked as if it had been hit by a tornado. So did he. His hair was mussed. Lipstick smudged his face, chin, chest, and neck, where she had nipped him with love bites.

"I'm glad your gonads were drying up," she said, quoting from his outrageous note. "It shows you're true."

"I've been a hell of a lot more than faithful." His tone grew serious. His fingers stroked the back of her neck. "Daria and Piggy say I'm unfit company. Vito offered to buy me a ticket. Harry's business is off. I can't play piano. You're responsible for my condition. My secretary at Columbia thinks I'm losing my sanity. She's right. In the middle of dictation I stare off into space, wonder how you are, what you were doing. If you had met anyone."

She pressed her lips over the steady thump of his heartbeat. "You're the best thing that's ever happened to me. Without you, I couldn't have survived the scandal, the divorce. Don't you know that by now?"

He brushed damp strands of hair away from her neck. "My patients tell me without me they couldn't have made it. This isn't a cure we're discussing. A cruise connotes moonlight and romance. You're a beautiful, desirable woman. Don't you get lonely?"

She kissed his furrowed brow. "Yes, but I'm here to work, learn, and save money. Nothing more."

"I love you," he grumbled. "Letters and phone calls are lousy substitutes. I need lots of major hugs." He stroked her back. "We can't make love long distance. I missed your scent. I missed *us*."

"It's hard for me, too," she said quietly, threading her hand in his. "Revenue agents impounded my father's books. They exercised their right to go back more than three years. My mother said they went back to day one. Between the taxes and interest, there's no way Dad can afford the astronomical fines. He's facing an indictment for fraud. He can't shake his colds. He gets one after another. Mom blames it on stress. Just when we think the tabloids have had their fill, Marybeth triggers another landslide. This month alone she wrote that I'm losing my eyesight slaving over a computer, and I'm burning my fingers in the kitchen. The dope doesn't know to call it a galley. If the Brices say we're vermin, can you imagine what others say?"

Wendall braced himself over her. He lifted a lock of her hair. "The hell with them. You can stand on your head and whistle Dixie, and still you won't change narrow-minded thinkers. Why let a bunch of strangers control your life? You're a unique, wonderful person."

The scent of sex lingered on the sheets, on Claire and Wendall. He created magic. Alone with him, away from family ties, she could almost pretend they had a future. She gazed at his sensuous mouth.

"I memorized your face," she said in a husky voice. "This is much better, isn't it?"

"Infinitely." His hand drifted up her inner thigh. Her pulse quickened. She pressed her hips forward, glorying in the now.

Afterward, they spoke in whispers, in broken sentences, the spell between them strong, yet each tested it, touching, kissing, assuring themselves they shared a real dream, proving it with caressing hands and bodies entwined.

Wendall dozed. Sighing happily, Claire gazed her fill upon his virile physique. His gentleness excited her in ways she had never imagined.

"You're a lovely man," she murmured, kissing the flat planes of his belly. Her tongue flicked over his nipple, circling the tight bud. He seemed to purr in his sleep. She watched his rib cage expand. Smiling, she nuzzled his furred chest, raining tiny kisses along her path.

"Mmmm, nice." He came awake with a slow stretch. "Don't leave."

Their eyes met, and in his she saw compassion. And tenderness. And the leap of desire. She saw eyes shining with love.

"I won't leave. Darling, now that I've saved your

eyesight, not to mention your surgical career, would you please make love to this uniquely wonderful person again?"

He smiled. At his touch, she uttered a soft little cry. She closed her eyes and felt the enchantment begin. . . .

Sixteen

CLAIRE INTRODUCED WENDALL to Hans. He shook hands with a man of better than average height and build, salt-and-pepper hair, and penetrating gray eyes. Taking his role of surrogate father seriously, Hans trained his eyes on Wendall. Out of politeness, recalling Claire said Wendall cooked, he escorted him on a private tour of his galley. By the end of the tour, Wendall's honest reverence for culinary arts, coupled with his inquisitive nature, and his ability to listen avidly, won Hans's approval.

He autographed one of his cookbooks, handed it to Wendall, and beamed at Claire. "She works too hard," he said gruffly. "She eats too little. Do something about it. I can't."

Wendall waited until they were alone in her compact cabin to agree with Hans.

"I have to work hard," Claire said grimly. "I'm making up for lost time, plus my father's trial date will be set soon."

"Looks like you're writing a book." Wendall's gaze rested on a stack of computer printouts.

"My Bible."

"May I?" he asked. She nodded. His face grew thoughtful. Page after page denoted a woman in a hurry to master each day's learning. For a long time he was lost in the maze of papers. Impressed by her intense drive, he saw how much she'd changed. He touched her cheek. The shame heaped upon her father cut deeply; more, he suspected, than she knew.

"They go with these." She handed him loose-leaf notebooks. "What it amounts to is a syllabus in how to operate a restaurant." She shrugged. "While each business is unique, they share things in common. Overhead, location, a good product, an advertising budget, employees, benefits, state and federal laws, that sort of thing. It's amazing what you can accomplish when you have to."

Wendall pulled out a blue envelope from his breast pocket. He handed it to her. "Go ahead, it's yours."

Her expression quizzical, she skimmed her hand over the envelope. It had no writing on the outside. From the feel of it, it contained a light sheet of paper. Opening it, she removed a signed blank check. Claire felt a chill race up her spine.

"What's this for?"

Wendall put his arms around her waist. "To help you get started in whatever business you decide on."

She put the check back into the envelope and handed it to Wendall. There was a deep silence. Her expression remained serious. "Thank you, but I won't take your money."

"There are no strings attached."

"There are always strings attached," Claire said quietly. The divorce decree she'd shown Wendall lay on the table.

He saw the hint of pain in her eyes, the pride stiffening her spine. Without another word, he pocketed the envelope, knowing he'd made a major blunder. An expression of tenderness came into his eyes. "I'm not Colin. If you change your mind, it's yours."

During the night the ship sailed to St. Thomas. They awoke to perfect weather: brilliant blue sky, warm breezes, and a lazy golden sun. Wendall leaned over and kissed Claire's lips. She moved languidly into his arms, then stroked his head. She'd made love to him frantically as if with her body she could show him how much he meant to her. She'd made great strides in overcoming the past. The key was independence. No matter how she tried to find a place for Wendall in her future, she failed. He belonged to a closed world.

Her hand slipped over his shoulder, down his back, cupping his firm rear end. "To think I never appreciated redheads."

"Better make that singular, or I'll put on my boxing gloves. What's on your agenda today?"

"After I escort a group on a tour of the galley, I have a few hours off. In your honor, I won't coop myself up with the computer. I'm declaring a holiday."

Wendall dressed quickly and arranged to meet her downstairs. He nearly destroyed her composure when she led a group of guests to the galley only to find a sign cancelling the morning tour. Hans gave her a broad wink.

Wearing swimsuits beneath their shorts and T-shirts, driving a rented car, Claire and Wendall bypassed Charlotte Amalie, the shoppers' paradise of the Caribbean, and headed for the heart-shaped beach on the north shore of St. Thomas.

Magens Bay was a living painting. Beneath a tropical deep blue sky, backdropped by a necklace of shade trees, picture-perfect soft white sands curved along a crystal-clear natural cove to meet a sparkling turquoise sea. A regatta of pastel-colored sailboats crossed the horizon.

Claire had visited the Bay many times with her father. Her thoughts grew melancholy, and she sighed. Wendall, sensing its cause, stood behind her and wrapped his arms around her waist.

Shaking off her sad mood, she turned and kissed him. "Last one in is a chicken." Shedding her outer clothes, she gave him a first glimpse of her in a hot pink bikini.

He let out a wolf whistle. "Let's go back to the ship."

She stuck out her tongue. "Come one, I'll race you."

They splashed sloppily into the water. She was swimming like crazy when she glanced over her shoulder. She was swimming alone.

"You cheat!" she shouted.

Wendall floated on his back, close to the shore, waving his hands at her. When she swam back, he declared himself the winner, since he reached the beach first. He claimed his prize, a long kiss that left her breathless. He glanced around, then pointed to a secluded cove away from prying eyes. They swam toward it.

So overwhelming was their hunger for each other that when he pulled down her bikini, wrapped her legs around his waist, and thrust himself inside her, he banished the world from their thoughts. As his powerful loins and hands held her prisoner, she surrendered gladly, kissing him, clutching his shoulders, bursting apart in wave after wave, drawing his own shattering orgasm into her.

At a covered picnic table they shared a box lunch: carrot sticks, smoked turkey on toast points, and Oregon Tillamook cheddar cheese, which Hans said was twice the price of other cheddar cheeses and worth it, washing it down with sparkling water. Afterward they rented a sailboat. When they returned to the beach they built a giant sand castle. Feeling rested and at peace, Claire hoarded the idyllic hours.

Until Wendall said, "I want you to meet my family."

Claire sucked in her breath. Her heart sank. "Darling, it's such a beautiful day, and we have so little time. I'm so happy you're here. Please don't spoil it."

He tossed the tube of sunblock into his beach bag. His face wore an expressionless mask. Kicking sand, he walked to the water's edge.

She ran after him. "Talk to me," she pleaded, hating to hurt him.

"Claire, I'm not your enemy. Give me credit for some sense. Stop mixing my family's values with the Brices'."

"I'm not," she lied. Love colored Wendall's views. His parents would have no qualms about saving their son. She wasn't a Denison. She was Edward Jameson's daughter. A pariah. An undesirable. They might not openly defy a grown man—but she'd know. People send subtle messages with body language, an inflection, a raised brow, a laugh, a barb directed at others but meant for her, or the cold shoulder.

Meeting Wendall's parents spelled disaster—the end of their relationship. Why couldn't Wendall understand?

"Do you ever intend to marry me?" he asked bluntly.

No! For both our sakes. "Please. It's not you. I can't deal with the thought of marriage. It's too soon."

They made up, but avoiding the issue during his visit created a temporary strain. She wrote Cee-Cee, who answered bluntly. "You refused his money. You won't discuss marriage. You're telling him you don't trust him. He needs to know he can look forward to a future, too. How long do you think he'll accept the status quo?"

Claire couldn't answer. She didn't know, nor could she understand her father's continuous colds and his weakened resistance.

"Dr. March, the pulmonary specialist, says it's stress-related allergy syndrome," Babs said when she phoned. "I don't think doctors know a thing."

Claire urged Wendall to pressure her father into seeking a second opinion. He said he would.

Daria wrote letters sprinkled with general information; Vito still dated the model, but not as much. She wrote mainly about her crush on Peter Ramirez. Peter was young, handsome, single. He came from the barrio. She politely added she'd miss Wendall when he moved on.

Playing Cupid, Daria wrote Claire that Wendall pined for her. Subsequent letters added such flowery descriptions as *yearned, languished, hankered after, thirsted for,* and *carried the torch for.* Wendall said Daria had bought a thesaurus.

"It's your influence," he said when Claire phoned. "She dresses better, too. You're there for everyone but me."

Worried by his remark, Claire mentioned her concerns to Cee-Cee.

"Honey, he's anxious to settle down. Don't forget he's no kid. Yes, I know your marrying a stupid snob spooked you. You've got to put it behind you."

Claire clung to her resolve. "Spooked is too light a word. Why does Wendall say he understands when he doesn't?"

"He's in love. It's a powerful emotion. What do you

expect? One of these days you'll stop punishing yourself and Wendall for Colin's and his parents' stupidity."

Claire hung up feeling awful. On the one hand, she felt guilty; on the other hand, her resolute position shielded her. After all she'd been through, she didn't want to get involved with Wendall's parents. Why put either of them through needless misery?

Then a letter arrived from Wendall which disturbed Claire. Piggy's girlfriend had left him suddenly, with no explanation or note. It crushed him. He'd changed his mind about removing his facial scar and applying to the police academy.

Claire wrote him a long letter. She wrote of Wendall's and Vito's love and faith in him. The pride Vito felt when Franklin said he wanted to pursue a career in law enforcement. That Wendall was thrilled to have a small part in helping him attain his goal, that he'd wanted to remove the facial scar so people could see the real Franklin. Then she wrote a little about what she'd been through since the breakup of her marriage, telling Franklin that although they faced different personal journeys, they were lucky to have second chances.

"Franklin," she wrote, "Wendall said you've changed your mind about applying to the police academy and also about having him remove the scar. Don't throw away your plans because of one person." She added that any woman who didn't value him wasn't worth his love. As she sealed the letter, she realized how far she'd come in her quest for independence.

A month later, Piggy sent her his picture. His skin was smooth. Thrilled for him, she phoned him, saying he looked like a movie star.

Shortly afterward, Wendall flew out for a second weekend.

Claire wanted to surprise him with an omelette, so she asked Hans for instructions.

Hans handed her a balloon whisk and told her to crack the eggs, put the whites into a copper bowl, the yolks in another, and beat the whites stiff. Easier said than done. She'd never used a balloon whisk, or any whisk.

"No flecks!" He pointed to the yellow flecks with a rubber spatula. She ruined two dozen eggs.

"Yolks in one bowl, whites in another." He threw up his hands and turned to speak with the pastry chef.

Claire made the mistake of dipping the whisk into the egg whites without drying off the whisk from the yolks. She'd been at it so long that a group gathered to watch. She cracked more eggs. Once in a while she heard a snicker, but when she looked up, she saw serious faces.

Gnawing her lower lip, she whisked until she thought her arm would break. Finally she announced she'd gotten it right.

"Turn the bowl over your head. If you've done it correctly, the whites stay in the bowl." Hans repeated what Wendall had once said about testing the egg whites. She thought he was nuts, just as she now thought the same of Hans.

She glanced up to find Wendall standing nearby. So much for her surprise. He coughed, looking pointedly at Hans, then at the bowl. He started to say something. A stern look from Claire warned him to keep quiet. He closed his mouth.

"Wendall, I'm making you this lousy omelette if it's the last thing I do."

She didn't see his lips twitch.

Clamping her hands on either side of the copper bowl, she raised it above her head, and flipped it. A chorus of male glee hit her ears at the same time she let out a screech. Bathed in egg whites, the goop slid down her head, oozed past her forehead, slithered over her face, and dripped down her chin.

Sputtering, she grabbed the whisk, aiming it at Hans, who was doubled over. "You knew, you devil!"

Others rushed over for a hilarious peek. "Wendall, you louse, you're no better!"

Hans held his sides. He wheezed with laughter. "You used enough eggs for an army. I wouldn't have missed this for the world," he roared, wiping his eyes. "Stay out of the kitchen!"

Wendall parted the frothy white curtain. Egg whites clung

to her brows, her eyelashes, and her lips. He licked her lips, grinningly accused her of not having the knack for making things stiff.

"Oh, really."

That night she proved she could make *things* stiff.

"You can't leave me this way!" Wendall howled.

"Poor baby," she crooned, giving him an extra, expert massage. "Take a shower."

He dragged her in with him. They came out smiling, exhausted, but squeaky clean.

The following day she whipped up four egg whites, passed the head test, then smugly accepted congratulations.

Two months later, Cee-Cee and Tom spent their sixth wedding anniversary aboard the *Sea Voyager*. Wendall arranged his schedule to join them for his third weekend. Exhaustion written in his eyes, he flopped down on Claire's bed and slept for four hours.

Both he and Claire knew he couldn't keep up his grueling schedule, which now included teaching for a semester. She planned a private dinner party, entertaining them by rattling statistics. "How many omelettes can you make from thirty-nine thousand six hundred eggs?"

"It depends," Wendall quipped. "If it's you, *one*. If it's me, I'd have to know how many bottles of champagne you're bribing me with."

She lifted her champagne flute. She glittered in a green-and-gold minidress with translucent shine and spaghetti straps. "One thousand seven hundred fifty."

"Smart ass. I dare you to tell us how you make coffee."

Claire raised a smug eyebrow. "Easy. You dump sixty pounds of regular—"

"Stop!" Cee-Cee looked radiant in a flowing green chiffon dress that enhanced her vibrant coloring. "You lovebirds quit fighting. Now then, Tom, my lean, mean, British sex machine, what time is it?"

He gave her a conspiratorial wink. "Precisely eight thirty-five."

She patted her flat stomach. "A toast to my tummy. We're three weeks, one day, and forty-five minutes pregnant."

Claire screeched. She threw her arms around Cee-Cee. Wendall pumped a beaming Tom's hand.

"We have one thousand three hundred twenty gallons of milk on board," Claire said. "Feel free to drink, Cees."

"Will someone shut the statistician up," Tom joked.

"Here," Claire quipped, having a glorious time with the people who meant so much to her. "Have a beer, Tom. It's one of over fourteen thousand cans on board. We can spare it."

"Wendall," Tom barked good-naturedly. "Save us."

"The sacrifices I make." Wendall pulled her into his arms.

"Aren't you jealous?" he asked later in bed. "Don't you want to see our child's picture on the clinic wall?"

She did, more than anything. She harbored no illusions. But that wasn't meant to be. Not with Colin during his misguided marriage, nor with Wendall. Who knew better than she that when you marry, you marry a family. She leaped off the bed, recent witness to their lusty sex. Her heart fluttered in her chest.

"I thought we settled it. I thought we had a deal."

"Deal!" He pummeled a pillow. "What deal? Where is it leading? You're carrying this lineage crap too fucking far!"

Claire arched one brow. "Apparently not far enough! Apparently sex is all you care about!"

"And what about you?" he shouted, venting his frustrations.

He scrambled out of bed. He jerked a thumb at the disheveled linens. "I don't recall begging you."

She gave him a frosty look, picked up her comb, and yanked it through her thick hair. The plastic snapped in two. Disgusted, she hurled the comb at the wall.

Glowering, Wendall put on his trousers and grabbed his shirt. He yanked it over his head. "Damnit! I passed my thirty-seventh birthday in January. I'm ready for marriage. Kids. Every time we have sex I wonder what our child would have looked like if you weren't on the Pill. Would it have been a boy or a girl?"

That floored her. She gasped. Wendall had tapped into her inner thoughts. She had wondered the same thing many times. If she was pregnant, would the baby inherit Wendall's features or hers, or would it be a happy combination, her dark hair with his blue eyes?

Her gaze strayed to his open wallet where he kept a small picture of them taken at the Captain's Ball. She kept an eight-by-ten color copy in a silver frame in her cabin. Sentimentally she put it near her bed next to his other picture, so his would be the last face she saw before she retired, the first she saw when she awoke. For the gala, she'd worn a strapless aquamarine sheath, its shade reminding her of Wendall's eye coloring. The picture portrayed a tall, vigorous, proud man looking splendid in a tux, his hand possessively over hers.

She suppressed a sob. "I'll save you the bother of wondering. I don't blame you. Find someone else. Get married. You deserve a family. You'll make a wonderful father. You won't have trouble finding a suitable wife, one whom your parents will welcome with open arms."

He gave her a disgusted look. "Stop reducing me to a child who needs his parents' permission. It might surprise you to know they trust my judgment. I wish to God you would. Would you marry me if I were a poor, starving orphan?"

Yes. In a heartbeat. "You're deliberately trying to provoke me."

"You think I'm provoking you? Well, pardon me!" he shouted, his temper on a short fuse. "I suppose I should be grateful—relieved—you've mapped out my future. Answer the question. If you didn't know about my family, would you marry me?"

Claire's lips trembled. Unable to lie, she avoided a direct answer. "Your question is moot."

He looked at her a long time, knowing he shouldn't pressure her, yet unable to stop himself. He couldn't break the barrier, couldn't get past her steadfast determination.

"I love you, Claire. Humor me," he said quietly. "Answer the question."

She lowered her lashes. She balled her fists at her sides to keep from throwing her arms around his neck. "I prefer not to."

He cupped her chin, forcing her to meet his eyes. In hers he saw a familiar wariness. "Coward."

She batted his hand away. "I'm not playing word games with you."

Wendall sighed deeply. His gaze flicked to the picture. Muttering a curse word, he swung around on his heel and strode onto the verandah. Claire was afraid to say she loved him, but he knew she did, just as he knew he didn't want to live without her. Could he settle for a life with no marriage or children? No binding commitment? Was a piece of paper important? Yes, to him, yes. Knowing Claire, she wouldn't bear children out of wedlock. When he turned to argue his position, he found himself staring at an empty room.

CNN reported that the government expected to indict Edward Jameson for fraud and tax evasion within the week. Claire heard the news in her cabin. Her father had prepared her, but hearing it on TV, knowing the vast viewing audience heard the news, too, made her feel worse. She valued her anonymity. The ship was a giant refuge, with only Hans knowing about her father. Most staff and crew members were Italian. Passengers boarded for fun. She doubted if anyone drew a connection between the hostess who helped solve their problems and the woman who faced a painful period, perhaps for years to come.

She ached for Wendall. She loved him, but what choice had she? His parents were bound to hear the news about her father. Her head held high, she made her way to Giancarlo's office to ask to be relieved of her duties.

Pondering how to break the deadlock with Claire, a pensive Wendall stood on the verandah, staring at the cresting waves. Innocent, she had suffered Colin's verbal abuse. She was gentle, delicate, yet exhibited the strength of many when it came to withholding herself from him. Would he ever win her complete trust? he wondered.

There was a gentle northeast breeze; the temperature was a balmy seventy-two. A perfect night for romance. From several decks below, a steel band played calypso music. Going inside for a drink, Wendall flipped on the TV. He caught the CNN telecast that mentioned Edward Jameson's trial. Wendall listened, shook his head, then went to find Claire.

In their suite, Cee-Cee flicked on the TV and heard the tail end of the CNN news. "Tom, I should go to her," she said, flipping back the covers.
"Not tonight. Tonight she needs Wendall."

In Connecticut, Babs switched the TV off. Reporters had hounded the house all day, phoning, disguising themselves as workmen, making nuisances of themselves. The Fortunes got rid of the pests. She had more important things on her mind. Edward's cough sounded worse. It worried her that he wasn't improving. He'd rally, then come down with another cold. She couldn't understand his refusal to seek a second opinion from a pulmonary specialist. Sighing, she decided to ask Wendall to try again.

In her new Coldwater Canyon ranch, Marybeth Frankel lay on the deck by her pool, planning her next column. She'd lunched with Louis Marx, munching daintily on chilled shrimp and endive salad, while she really wanted to dig into Louis's Texas roast beef.
Shaded from the sun's rays by a huge, closely woven, multicolored umbrella, her eyes were closed, her baby-moist skin protected by an aloe cucumber facial masque. She ordered the product shipped from its Key West, Florida, manufacturer. Her pink tongue licked an ice cube. She was half listening to the radio, tuning the newscaster in and out of her consciousness. Suddenly she froze. "Yes!" she cried, bolting upright. She grabbed the phone. When she hung up, she hurried inside to shower and change.

At two forty-five A.M. Eastern Standard Time, Edward Jameson told Babs he felt better sitting up with the pillows

propped behind his back. His harsh coughing brought up
blood. He agreed to drink a cup of chamomile tea and honey
to ease the soreness in his throat. He asked her to open the
safe in his study and bring up an envelope with her name on
it.

She put on her white satin-trimmed silk bathrobe and
slippers. Downstairs for about fifteen minutes, she prepared
a pot of tea. She let the chamomile steep, covering the
Limoges teapot with a whimsical tea cozy she had purchased in a little shop in London. She used the bathroom,
then went into the study for the envelope Edward had
requested from the safe. With everything she needed on a
silver tray, she mounted the stairs.

Edward slept.

Glad of it, she put the tray on a table, switched off her
lamp, and crawled into bed.

Babs awoke three hours later. The room was dark from
the drawn drapes. Edward was still asleep. Good, she
thought. Her mother used to preach that sleep was the best
medicine, nature's way of healing. Babs thought about a
nice, hot soak in the bathtub.

She treated herself to bubble bath, adding drops of
Frangipani bath perfume, a present from Claire. She luxu-
riated in the soothing oils, wishing for the day when she and
Edward could sail with Claire. She dried herself with a thick
towel, applied moisturizing body lotion, dabbed Frangipani
perfume behind her ears. Not too much.

Slipping on her robe, she sat at her lighted dressing table.
Peering into the mirror, she turned her face right, then left.
Not bad for an old broad. At least she didn't have a sagging
neck or a waddle beneath her chin. She brushed her hair,
leaving it loose. Edward preferred it loose. She left the
bathroom door ajar and padded into the darkened bedroom
for a cup of tea. She'd drink it cold, cool, or lukewarm. She
just wanted a cup of tea.

She glanced at Edward. A prickling sense of foreboding
gripped her. She stubbed her toe in her haste to open the
drapes and flood the room with light.

"Oh, God."

His head lay at an angle. His eyes were open, staring. Tracks of blood ran from his nostrils to his upper lip. Bloodied spittle oozed from his mouth.

Panic squeezed the air from her lungs. Her heart roared in her ears. Her hands trembled. Petrified, she tapped his shoulder. When he didn't respond, she placed her hand on his forehead. It felt very cool. Too cool.

Using her meager knowledge of CPR, she held the heels of her hands over his chest. She pumped. She pumped like a mad woman. When she failed to rouse him, she begged, "Get up! Please, darling, wake up. Oh, please. Please, wake up."

She grabbed his shoulders and shook him. In escalating horror, she saw her efforts fail. A torrent of tears streamed from her eyes, splashing on his face, falling on his eyes, making it look as if he, too, were crying. While she had slept at his side, or leisurely soaked in a perfumed tub dreaming of them taking a trip, or sat brushing her hair to look nice for him, she didn't know which, her beloved husband had passed away.

Drawing a ragged breath, she returned to the bathroom. Wetting a corner of a towel with warm water, she tenderly washed and dried Edward's face, then closed his eyes. She had lost her best friend. She brushed his hair from his forehead, adjusted the blanket, pressed a kiss on his mouth. Bringing a chair to the bedside, she sat with him a long time. Numb, she spotted the envelope he had asked for. She put on her new reading glasses. The letter was dated the previous day.

My darling wife,
  First and foremost, I love you. I wish to God that I hadn't taken the money. I was young and tempted, but stupidity is no excuse. When I wanted to give it back I couldn't without tipping off the authorities. Yet, if I hadn't taken the money, if I hadn't had facial surgery, if I hadn't stayed on in Gstaad, I wouldn't have met you, and Claire and I wouldn't have been blessed. So you see, even filled with remorse, I'm selfish.
  I thank God for you, Babs. If we could have met

another way, I'd have chosen it, rather than have you face an ordeal you don't deserve, and not of your making. The thing is, I don't feel like a thief. I don't know what a crook is supposed to feel like. I told Sam Yamuto I was trying to figure out the meaning of life. I was searching for esoteric insight when all along I should have known. It's family. You and me and Claire. The rest is bullshit. You can't buy love.

Sweetheart, before Wendall did the skin graft, my blood-clotting time was okay. Both he and Dr. March hoped the operation would ease my breathing. Recent blood tests confirm why my breathing hasn't improved, why I'm getting so many colds. The tests came back positive for a rare form of fast-spreading blood cancer. I swore Wendall and Dr. March to secrecy. I don't hold them or Vito in any way responsible. No one caused my condition. Make sure Claire knows that. The truth is I dreaded the trial. It would have ended in a jail sentence—more shame and disgrace you and Claire don't need.

Strange the way life works. Nancy's accident led me to you. Mine led Wendall to Claire. She's a fine young woman. She takes after you, Babs. Nancy gave birth to her, but you're her mother. I love you. Now and forever.

Edward.

"Forever," Babs whispered, cradling his lifeless body to her bosom for a final embrace.

Seventeen

SIX SUNDAYS AFTER Edward Jameson's ashes were scattered at sea from the dock, the IRS impounded the yacht and seized his accounts; two weeks after Babs accepted Lia and Sam Yamuto's invitation to visit them for a well-earned rest, Claire slammed her father's desk drawer shut. How could she stave off the IRS-mandated auctioneer's gavel? It loomed as an insurmountable task. She couldn't find one scribbled note, one faded letter, one bill of sale to prove that her grandfather Denison had bequeathed the contents of the house to Babs, along with the estate. Without documentation, Mr. Morrisey of the IRS assumed Edward Jameson had purchased everything. If it weren't so serious a contention, it would be ludicrous.

Babs could live on the income from a small trust fund inherited from her father, a trust that hadn't provided for an option to alter its terms. But, the Fortunes' salaries, upkeep on two houses, garages, and dock, maintainence of the lawns and gardens, miscellaneous expenses, and high taxes on the exclusive waterfront property, would seriously deplete her finances in the next several years. Babs could either move to smaller quarters or, if the property could produce income, remain. The dilemma weighed heavily on Claire's mind and heart.

Wendall offered money. Claire thanked him and refused. "Mother needs a permanent solution, not a loan."

"Marry me," he implored, his voice deeply reassuring. "That's permanent. I'm rich. We'll help your mother."

She panicked at the thought of his family's reaction. *Gold-digger tricks, son!* Resorting to one of her many diversionary tactics, she said, "Darling, you know Mother wouldn't allow you to help her."

He clenched his teeth in frustration. If he dared mention the *M* word, she pulled from a list of creative excuses, thanks to her father's legacy and the Brices' castigation.

Hating to quit her job, but feeling she must in fairness to her employers, Claire had said good-bye to her friends on the *Sea Voyager*. "I'm needed at home," she cried, pouring out her heart to Hans.

He asked her to reconsider a restaurant. "It could work."

She didn't stop him when he spoke about a restaurant. He reminisced fondly of friends at the Culinary Institute in Hyde Park, New York, where he'd once taught. He told her of his love for the East Coast, reminding her he'd lived in America for five years. He offered to commission a Connecticut firm to do a feasibility study of the area, to check if the area warranted another exclusive restaurant. Claire left open the possibility, not wanting to close any doors.

"If you send me dimensions of the first-floor rooms, including the bathrooms, I'll draw up a blueprint. You have nothing to lose."

They parted knowing that if he gathered information, and she agreed, the final decision must be Babs's.

Claire's eyes zeroed in on Wendall who sat on the couch taking a break. What a way for him to spend a sunny Sunday, rummaging through moldy boxes dragged up from the cellar, dusty cartons lugged down from the attic, hoping to uncover proof that her grandfather had purchased even so much as a fork!

The IRS posted auction notices in government buildings and newspapers. In two dreaded weeks she would be powerless to prevent a carnival atmosphere from descending on her home, powerless to stop a locust of bidders from stripping her mother of family treasures, priceless antiques, paintings, rugs, silver, televisions, lamps, and the piano. The list was endless.

Frazzled, Claire dropped into an armchair. Her arms dangled over the sides. "How could the revenue officer think my grandparents lived in a bare house?"

"Did you ask him?" Wendall said.

"Yes." Her voice shook with bitter resentment. "He sympathizes with mother's plight, but the IRS is obligated to recover all the money it can. When I asked him why the rush to auction, he said if revenue officers feel the property is in jeopardy—meaning Mother might sell in a rush now that her husband is dead—they can speed up the date for the public sale."

Wendall gave her a quizzical look. The strain showed in her eyes, on her face. He had purposely avoided talking about the auction. The sea of tagged items infuriated her. A week after her father's death, ten overzealous IRS revenue officers drove up in two vans, rang the doorbell, stated their business, then proceeded to record and tag everything of value.

"The IRS can't do anything on this property without Babs's permission. She inherited the estate from her parents. She's the legal owner. There's no law saying she has to be a party to her own demise. The IRS is trying to save moving fees."

Incredulous, she stared at him. As his statement sunk in, the tight lines at her mouth and the stormy look in her eyes disappeared. Her face broke out in a wreath of smiles. She rushed over to Wendall and threw her arms around his neck, knocking them both flat on the couch. She rained kisses all over his face.

Laughing, he hugged her tightly. "I like the way you say thanks." She squirmed back and forth, simulating sex. "Let's go upstairs," Wendall said.

"Nope. Let's live dangerously." Sitting back on her haunches, she unzipped his trousers and pulled down her panties.

"Better?" she asked, lowering herself on his swollen shaft.

"Jesus Christ! You want someone to see us?"

Claire giggled. Ruth and Jimmy had gone shopping and wouldn't be home for at least an hour. But why tell Wendall?

"Chicken. Of course I do." She pumped for good measure.

That convinced him the Fortunes were away. "You're outrageous," he said, playing along with the charade. "Anyone can see you're attacking me."

He raised her blouse, unhooked her bra, and brought her voluptuous juicy breasts down for his delight. His finger found her clitoris. He hadn't done anything like this since he was a teenager, when he screwed a girl in his car in the park and a policeman shone a light in his face and told him to find a motel. With Claire, his incandescent sprite, it was ten times more chancy—the Fortunes might return at any moment!—a thousand times better.

"Having fun?" Claire teased. She wantonly curled herself over him to browse on his marvelous chest, nuzzle his neck, inhale his fragrance, claim his lips. "All male," she purred, her thighs making him a willing prisoner.

She tightened her pelvic muscles. When he groaned, she licked the corners of his mouth. "Darling, do you think we *should* stop? Do you think we *dare* continue? Darling, answer me. Do you think we *ought* to stop?"

Wendall suppressed a shudder. "Minx," he said wryly. "Vamp. We both know I couldn't stop now if an army of IRS officers trooped into the room."

"Goodie. I wanted to make sure." She licked his ear, bathing it with her tongue, blowing whispers into his ear, naughty, delicious promises of heaven.

Wendall held the firm globes of her buttocks, easing himself almost all the way out then tormenting her with the tip of his penis before bringing her all the way down. She moaned as he brought her higher and higher, climbing up and up the maddeningly intoxicating peak of sexual gratification. His common sense dazed by lust, his reward came just as her muscles clutched him in a violent orgasm.

For long minutes they lay drained of speech.

"As I was saying," he said when he could talk. Claire lay on top of him like a satisfied cat. "Most women keep their treasures in secret hiding places."

She giggled. "You found mine."

"Be serious. My mother hides things behind the basement ceiling tiles. I recall once at Christmas we were about to sit down to dinner when she realized she wasn't wearing her mother's bracelet. She feels about it the way you feel about the gold charm your father gave you."

"Did you find the bracelet?" Claire reluctantly rose.

"Yes, but not before we all trooped down to the cellar and tore apart a section of the ceiling tiles. She hid the pouch on one of the metal cross-runners. Another time an electrician was fixing a wire behind a section of the tiles. He came upstairs holding a bag filled with jewelry. He advised her to put it in a safe."

"Oh my god." Claire rearranged her clothing and followed him into the bathroom.

"That's what my father said." He made room for her at the sink. He handed her a towel. Their eyes met in the mirror. They broke out laughing.

"As I was saying, Mom doesn't trust a safe. She hates wasting time going to the bank, so she hides things. She told us that if something happens to her, Dad and I are sworn to unfold every scrap of paper, every item of clothing. Search! Do you remember my telling you she names furniture for previous relatives?"

"Yes, and I said you tell the nicest lies."

"I wasn't lying. Uncle Charlie is the piano bench. Uncle Frank is the rocker with the bottom falling out. Aunt Harriet is the wingchair. She's having her springs repaired. Uncle William was an eighteenth-century lecher. He's a footstool Mom kicks around. God's truth."

Wendall's mouth curled in a lazy grin.

"One hundred years from now I'll be a stick of furniture. A bed, no doubt. It's very reassuring."

Claire giggled. She loved watching the light playing in his eyes. "What's your father like?"

Wendall mentally crossed his fingers, hoping Claire

would change her mind about meeting his folks. "He's active. In his spare time, he builds powered model airplanes. He started an aviation club in a local school. The kids love flying the planes, and so does he. He fishes, but he won't take more than he can bring home to eat. Isn't it time you met my folks?"

Family stories aside, his parents wouldn't accept her. Under the circumstances, she wanted no part of them. What Wendall also refrained from saying was that his father had parlayed the family's fortune tenfold.

Claire had spent a second evening at the library, learning still more of his roots. Starting with *Who's Who in America,* she plowed her way through tracts on early Connecticut landowners. She read chapters on famous American business tycoons, and current magazines. The Everett-Lawsons emerged as people accustomed to power and prestige. They were individual thinkers, not followers.

Architectural Digest devoted five pages of pictures and description to the prime Long Island Sound property deeded by King George to one of Wendall's ancestors. The house passed down to the eldest child in each generation. The rambling mansion had grown from thirty-eight rooms to its recently added wing, bringing the number of rooms to fifty. Beneath the elaborate shingled roof there were enough mullioned windows to maintain a staff of window washers. Wendall had spoken casually of the home he would inherit, but he never mentioned the Degas, Monets, Renoirs, and Rembrandts gracing the walls, or the centuries-old tulip poplars, silver maples, red maples, mighty oaks, and weeping willow trees that formed a towering honor guard to flower-laden parks within parks. She could only guess the numbers of workers needed to maintain the grounds, tennis courts, Olympic-size swimming pool with its eight-thousand-square-foot pool house, its latticed enclosed gazebolike pavilion, the nine-hole golf course designed by Arnold Palmer, and the one-hundred-forty-foot yacht docked in their private cove.

She'd sworn never to place herself in the firing line of family approval again. Wendall loved her. There lay the difference. His parents didn't—and wouldn't—not with the baggage she carried: her father's legacy, Marybeth's unwarranted attacks, and the public IRS auction.

The Brices were small potatoes compared to the Everett-Lawsons. Wendall's mother might sound like a lovable eccentric, but she was far from that. She entertained presidents, governors, visiting royalty, and organized charity functions to benefit children and who knew what else?

Wendall's gaze narrowed. Claire's fingers clinched her denim skirt. Keenly aware of the workings of her agile brain, he knew he'd lost another round, that she was casting around for an excuse not to meet his family.

"Forget I mentioned it," he said irritably. "Does Babs squirrel things away like my mother does?"

She heard the annoyance in his tone. Why couldn't she say what he wanted to hear? The guilt she felt was in her eyes, and she forced herself to concentrate on Babs.

"Mother's cardboard boxes! They're on a shelf in the closet in my old bedroom. She and I both forgot about them."

There were five cardboard boxes, double the size of shoe boxes. She untied the strings holding them secure, lifted the lids, then spread the contents onto the wooden floor. The Abusson rug lay rolled and tagged for auction at the base of the opposite wall.

Babs saved dried flowers, bows, letters from old girl-friends, birthday cards, anniversary cards, Barnum and Bailey ticket stubs, and report cards. Claire knew Babs would forgive her for reading private documents, but saving her property from the auctioneer's gavel ranked ahead of privacy.

Quiet descended as they unlocked a treasure trove of Babs's family chronicles. In their healthier days, the elder Denisons had swooped over Europe—wealthy birds of prey—alighting with a practiced eye on various countries, collecting art, antiques, paintings, mirrors, and furniture. The letters documented and detailed their passion for acquisition while reminding Babs to be a good girl.

"Here's proof!" Claire cried excitedly. "My grandparents

bought the fireplace grilles at the flea market in the Porte de Clignancourt, the Marché aux Puces near Paris. Here, look at this letter! They're in Aix-en-Provence. There they acquired the *fauteuil à tabatière,* my grandfather's smoking chair—the one with the compartments for his pipes and tobacco, and the *bureau plat,* the writing table my mother uses."

He put down the letter he was reading. "I didn't know Babs plays piano. In this letter, her mother's reminding her they bought the Steinway for her, that they expected her to practice for a recital."

"She rarely plays, but these letters prove they bought a lot of things that are still here."

With the sunlight streaming on the patch of floor where they sat, Claire's proof mounted, and with that her spirits soared.

"I'm calling the IRS tomorrow. Wendall, you're a genius."

Their gazes met. *Not genius enough to get you to marry me,* his message read.

In a much relieved frame of mind, she gathered her evidence, putting it into one of the boxes. He returned the others where he found them. Downstairs they sat at the dining-room table, listing each item, cross-referencing it to a specific letter by its postmark.

"I've heard from Hans and Mother," Claire said. "You know I worried about her staying here. We've decided to go ahead with the restaurant." Her green eyes glowed with delight, now that she'd found a way to save her mother's possessions.

He stiffened in alarm. "I admire what you learned on the *Sea Voyager,* but that was a lab course. This isn't. For every ten restaurants that open, only one is operating at the end of three years. The attrition rate is horrendous. Have you any idea how much a good chef earns? The size staff you'll need? The heavy insurance you'll have to carry? Will the town allow you to zone your home as a business? You saw Hans's galley. It cost a small fortune, but he didn't pay for it, World Cruises did. Oh, God, I worry about you. Please, if you need money, take mine. It's piling up in the banks anyway."

Her eyes filled with gratitude. "I don't have much choice. I'm a fatalist, Wendall. There must be a reason I took the job at World Cruises, worked in foodservice, and had three wonderful tutors. You know I found it fascinating."

"Claire, you were ready to find anything new fascinating. If you worked in a garage, you'd have found it wonderful. This is the real thing. I don't want to see you get hurt."

"I love you."

"That's no . . ." Expecting a debate, her words stunned him. He checked himself in midsentence. She'd never said those words to him before. She was too cautious, too scared after Colin's betrayal.

A smile touched his eyes. "Do you realize this is the first time you said you love me?"

Claire caressed his face. "I've loved you for a long time," she said quietly. "It's impossible not to love you. You're the kindest, most generous man in the world. I'll love you till the day I die, but I won't take your money. I'll never be beholden to a man again."

His smile evaporated into a scowl. "That's some qualified love. You love me, but you won't marry me. You're broke, but you won't let me help. You're going into a chancy business you know nothing about. Don't tell me about the *Sea Voyager*. I could throttle Hans for ever mentioning this as a solution. He loses nothing but time. What about you?"

She held her fingers over his mouth. "If I went into this venture by myself, I'd agree with you. Hans is taking the bigger risk. He's got the reputation and the experience. I'll get practical experience under his tutelage. I've proven I'm a quick learner. As for money, I have the money from the jewelry settlement. I've arranged to sell my wedding rings and my sable. I don't need them."

He refused to be put off. The light played over his drawn face, highlighting the rugged contours of his set jaw.

"Hans never owned a restaurant."

"He's famous. He received two individual gold medals with the Austrian Culinary Olympic Team in 1976. Two

years later, he was awarded an individual gold medal and
the coveted silver trophy from the Société Mutualiste des
Cuisiniers de Paris, for the most outstanding platter of the
show. In 1979 he received the Goldene Ehrennadel—
Golden Honor Needle—from the Austrian Chefs Associa-
tion."

"I don't care if he received solid gold knitting needles.
Talk to Harry. He'll tell you how hard it is to operate a
restaurant, and I'm not talking haute cuisine. His time is
never his own. He's up well before dawn. Small as his place
is, his entire family works there. What about a liquor
license? Your kitchen isn't set up for this. Where will you
put provisions? What about the special areas for hot dishes
and soups, another for salads, appetizers and cold foods,
pastries and breads? You'll need freezers for fish and meat,
institutional-size refrigerators. Christ almighty! This is
Hans's dream, not yours."

"Wendall!" she said sharply. "It's my responsibility to
keep this estate intact. My options are limited. There's no
mortgage on the house, no rent, only overhead: utilities and
normal maintenance. The location is ideal. Eventually we'll
provide dock space for people to come by boat, too. Hans
has a friend who trained in Germany at the famous
Baden-Baden Restaurant. He's agreed to be the chef-
saucier."

"You need more than a chef-saucier."

"Hans plans on hiring talented graduates from the Culinary Institute. There are nice rentals in town."

Wendall wasn't convinced. "Where's the money coming
from to pay their salaries in the beginning? What will Hans
live on?"

"Money he's saved. He'll pay the salaries until the
business can support it. We've discussed this in detail. If
we offer excellent cuisine, fine service, advertise and
promote Hans's name, we'll draw people. I sent him the
dimensions of the rooms, including hallways and bathrooms. He's drawn up a blueprint. This isn't happening
overnight. He has to finish his contract. He's ready for a
challenge. If I take a regular job, whatever income I make

wouldn't be enough. This makes sense. Besides, if you think it through, I have no other choice."

Wendall paced the room, then halted. He leaned a shoulder against the doorjamb. "What will you do?"

"I'm the maîtresse d' and reservationist, office manager, bookkeeper. I'll do what's necessary, keep computerized records. I'm sure I won't lack for work. Colin accused me of not knowing how to balance a checkbook or run a house. A lot he knows. I'm good and I know it."

Wendall gritted his teeth. "It's not Hans's house you're turning upside down, or his privacy he's losing. He'll rent a place, but what about Babs? She's a new widow in shock. How could you ask her to make a decision this drastic?"

"To save her home, that's why."

"Why should she take the risk? She doesn't need the money for a few years. Why rush? Why not give her a chance to explore other options? If necessary, sell some acreage."

"She knows and agrees," Claire said with finality. "Hans won't wait around a few years. And, please, don't bring up marriage. It's no solution. I can't handle more problems."

He hesitated, amazed she could spark such anger in him so shortly after saying she loved him. To her the words *marriage* and *beholden* were synonymous. If marriage symbolized problems beforehand, and it was clear it did, then it left him with a bleak future.

Wendall sat down in a chair, his eyes glued to her stubborn face. Facing defeat, he said, "I wish you luck. What will you call your restaurant?"

"Then you're not angry?" she said, coming to sit on his lap.

He grinned at her. "I'm furious. Kiss me anyway."

She rocked back and forth, rubbing her bottom, enticing him. "I thought," she said, raining kisses on his face, "we'd name it Pomander's, in memory of my grandmother."

Monday morning at nine, Claire phoned the IRS and asked to speak with a Mr. Morrisey. The phone call was short, to the point, immensely gratifying.

"No, Mr. Morrisey. You don't have my mother's permission to hold the auction on the Denison estate. You neglected to explain that you have no legal right to do it. Also, my mother won't allow you to cart her property off the premises. . . . Yes, she has proof. Ample proof. . . . Yes, I do think it's wise if we review your list."

Wendall and Claire welcomed 1987 in bed, a celebration she carefully orchestrated to the accompaniment of flutes of Dom Perignon and the Big Apple countdown on TV. She lit bayberry-scented candles and snuggled in Wendall's arms.

They occupied the guest house, which Claire considered theirs. With the picture of them taken at the Captain's Ball on the *Sea Voyager* occupying a place of prominence on the dresser, novels on nightstands, bedroom slippers on the floor at each side of the bed, her clothes moved over from the big house in her closet and his in his closet, and his toiletry kit in the bathroom, they settled in. She stocked the refrigerator with ingredients to prepare Sunday omelettes. They were a weekend couple—without benefit of a marriage certificate.

It suited her.

It irked him.

Wendall instructed Jimmy to buy back the guest house furniture at the auction. He wouldn't tolerate a stranger sleeping in their bed.

"It's only a bed," Claire said. It was nearly midnight, and she had on a New Year's Eve party hat and nothing else.

"It's not a bed," he said, his hands drifting on her supple skin. "It's ambience. Atmosphere. Memories of my finest performances." The clock bonged the hour.

She opened as a flower to receive him. "Happy 1987."

His eyes darkened by passion, his lips traveling down her sweetly feminine form, he lingered over her until she writhed in his arms, then he settled himself in her honeyed warmth. "Happy New Year, darling . . ."

Afterward she asked him what he wanted for his upcoming thirty-eighth birthday. "I'll grant you whatever your heart desires."

"Do you mean that?" he asked, the husky timbre of his voice hoarse from tenderness. She had trembled with exquisite ardor, giving herself up completely and naturally. Maybe now, he thought.

Her face alight with emotion, she stroked his cheek. "I wouldn't say it otherwise. Whatever I have is yours."

He searched her clear green eyes, his fingertips tracing the curve of her spine. "All right, then. I want your hand," he said, taking one and turning it over to kiss the palm.

"Such a small request. Only my hand?" she asked softly.

"In marriage," he said solemnly.

She stilled. "Anything but that," she said gently.

The words were barely out of her mouth when he muttered, "Here we go again." Dropping her hand, he studied her in a lengthening silence. "I sound like a broken record, don't I?"

"That's not true," she protested.

He snorted. "You wouldn't know it by me. I'm getting goddamn tired of you using me for stud service!"

"How can you say that when we just made love? It's ridiculous."

He looked at her flushed face, at the jumble of messed hair, at all the delicious secret hiding places of her luscious body that he knew by taste, heart, and mind. "Is it? Can you honestly say that you trust me?"

"Of course," she said, her voice rising in protest. She tore off the party hat.

"Not enough," he said flatly. "Not nearly enough. Dangle Wendall with your body, that's okay, but God forbid if he asks for a commitment. In my book that's not trust, love, or commitment. That's a weekend fuck!"

Stunned by his incendiary charge, Claire swung her legs off the bed and fled to the other bedroom. Slamming the door behind her, she stared out the window into the darkness. Feverish, she relived each vile thing he'd said. Damn him. And damn her for saying she loved him. She knew with horrifying clarity she had set him off with her offer to give him anything his heart desired.

Shivering, she crawled into the bed. She felt raw, lifeless

in body and spirit, when only a short while ago she'd felt his surge of life pouring into her. The facts were crystal clear. She'd finally run out of excuses. A hopeless situation.

A fog-shrouded dawn heralded the first day of the year. In his room, Wendall dressed. He left Claire a note saying he had work to do in the city. It wasn't true.

That Friday, he phoned. Swallowing her pride, she asked his weekend plans. He said he'd come to Connecticut but didn't feel like staying in. He mentioned a popular supper club. She wore a slim black dress with a multicolored beaded bolero jacket, completing the outfit with the gold charm necklace and drop earrings.

They paid attention to their orders of chicken cordon bleu, wild rice with mushrooms, a medley of julienne vegetables, and the music from a six-piece band. They danced, gliding around the small dance floor. She stared at his worsted woolen blue suit jacket, at the Adam's apple in his throat, his blue silk tie, silently inhaling his scent. From time to time he gazed down at her, his bearing proud, his eyes devoid of their usual teasing warmth.

Neither mentioned the New Year's Eve disaster. The fragile truce festered beneath the surface. On the drive home, he turned up the stereo, preventing a discussion that she didn't want anyway.

In bed they turned to each other as if they couldn't help themselves. Wordlessly, urgently, they made love—straining in animallike copulation. Without tenderness, kissing, or foreplay. Without satisfaction.

Afterward, they faced opposite sides of the bed: Claire wretched, empty, curled in a tight, protective ball of misery and from Wendall a muted sigh as if he knew the day would have to come soon when he found the guts to break off their relationship.

Claire was almost grateful when he said he was leaving for California to attend a board meeting of his microchip plant in the Silicon Valley. He said he'd stop off to visit his friends, Samara and David Orchin, in San Francisco.

Upon Wendall's return, he called to say he had too much work to catch up on to see her that weekend. The next weekend an emergency came up at the hospital. The weekend after that he said his mother was having a family dinner.

For two days? She quelled the thumping of her heart. There was nothing she could say or do.

On a windy day in March a thinner, quieter, more introspective Babs returned home to a house stripped of Edward's purchases. Thanks to the proof Claire and Wendall found for the IRS, she retained many of her lovely pieces of furniture, fine antiques, Venetian mirrors, and the Steinway piano, but there were gaps. Empty spaces and ghostly outlines marked the walls that had once held oils and watercolors. Edward's desk and chair no longer occupied a place of prominence in his study. Jimmy reported one person purchased Claire's bedroom furniture. Another purchased Cee-Cee's childhood bedroom furniture, including the gumdrop dispenser. Kitchen appliances sold as one lot. Claire had sent Jimmy to the auction to buy back her parents' bedroom set.

Babs dried her teary eyes. "The IRS can't sell my memories."

In Japan she had spoken to Hans on several occasions. With his contract concluded, he rented an apartment in Stamford. He treated Babs with the utmost respect and consideration. Learning she enjoyed the European tradition of afternoon tea, he set a beautiful linen-covered table and served her tea sandwiches, scones, tarts, and tea biscuits. He joined her, knowing she needed company. As they shared tea, he spoke about the loss of his wife, saying he missed her and that he was sorry for spending so many years at sea. Babs spoke about Edward. Their common loss forged an understanding only one who had loved and lost a spouse could fully comprehend.

Hans created a state-of-the-art restaurant kitchen, complete with the automated Gaylord safety system hanging from the ceiling. His blueprint called for fifty-two continuous assigned stations, among them storage, dishwashing, baking, hot and cold food preparation, undercounter refrigeration, and the pickup of food. As April came and went, trees budded, flowers sprouted, and equipment arrived.

Unable to change Wendall's thinking, Claire lived with growing tension. Work afforded her respite. It alleviated some of her tension. Staying busy became her palliative. She bought a computer system designed for restaurants. It plotted table positions and assigned a number for each chair, tracked orders for food and liquor, and sent printed copies to the kitchen and bar. The system helped her control back-door costs.

High expenditures could spell disaster for a fledgling operation. Profit was the name of the game in business. As Claire told Hans, "Watch the pennies, and the dollars will take care of themselves." Wendall had been right. Compared to the lab course she'd set for herself aboard the *Sea Voyager,* this was far harder and deadly serious. She didn't have World Cruises' money backing Pomander's. She learned to include security, inventory yields, receiving, purchasing and storing, operating expenses, menu pricing, repair and maintenance, food costing, equipment purchasing, holding down employee turnover. She was a jack-of-all-trades tap-dancing her fastest not to be a jackass of all trades.

She hadn't seen Wendall in two weeks.

Eighteen

ONE AFTERNOON AS Claire unpacked an order of pots and pans, she heard Wendall calling her. "I'm in the storage room."

He picked his way around empty cartons. Her heart thudded. He was wearing a three-piece navy blue suit, white shirt, blue silk tie, and gold tie tack, not his usual attire when he planned on staying for the weekend.

"Claire, let's go outside."

Alerted by his not kissing her, by his serious tone, she wiped her hands and followed him onto the terrace.

His eyes a cool, assessing blue, he faced her. The sun blazed down on his head, making his hair a fiery auburn. He leaned a palm on the balustrade.

"There's no easy way to say this. I've done a lot of thinking." He squared his jaw. "I want out of our relationship."

Her insides plummeted to the pit of her stomach. She wasn't surprised. Ever since New Year's when she refused for the umpteenth time to marry him, she had felt the pressure between them building.

"I see," she said, swallowing hard.

"I'm tired of having the Brices in bed with me," he said as if she'd asked for a reason.

She gasped. If he had hit her over the head with a massive frying pan, he couldn't have shocked her more.

"When did I ever mention Colin in bed, or his parents for that matter?"

"Constantly. Not outright, but they were there. In bed and out of bed. I have simple human goals. I'd like to marry the woman I love, make a home with her, and make babies with her."

An arrow pierced her heart. She sniffed furiously to hold back the tears. "I've never tried to hold you."

"That's my point, you never have," he said with emphatic brevity. "It's been the other way around. You're so self-absorbed you didn't see what was happening with us, or if you did you didn't care."

She felt the air change, the wind kicking up as if to hurl its vengeful assent. "Why now? Why couldn't you wait until after Pomander's opened?"

Anger sparked in his eyes. "We'll never synchronize our time. You'll never make up for your father's theft."

The wind slapped her hair into her face. "Is that what you think I'm doing?"

"Yes. I think you've subconsciously given yourself a mandate to atone for your father's crime. Do you remember saying it was up to you to restore honor to the Jameson name?"

"What's wrong with that?" she said immediately.

"When it's your prime motivation, plenty's wrong. It's exhausting to look backward and forward at the same time. Why can't you put the past behind you? Why has Babs handled her husband's theft better than his daughter? If you find the answers, you'll know why I said the Brices were in bed with us."

Babs is a Denison. "You're cruel."

"Am I?" he replied with resignation. "What about you? Babs isn't a pauper. She had options—options you took away from her."

"I did not!"

"Who made the decision to turn her home into a restaurant?"

"She did."

"You railroaded her!" he insisted, implacable.

"She agreed to Pomander's!" Claire argued, indignant.

He didn't give an inch. "Sure she did. You convinced yourself it was your only option, then you convinced her. Babs was a traumatized widow. You're damn lucky she and Hans get along."

She seethed. "It's easy for you to say. You don't live my life!"

"I don't share it either," he said shortly. "You're determined to restore your father's good name. He made the mistake, not you."

"I know that! Just as I know I can't restore his good name." She pummeled his chest. "Only my name. Only my reputation. Only mine, damn you!"

Wendall spoke slowly, enunciating each word with precise deliberation. "You never lost your good name or your reputation, Claire. You only think you did. From the start, ours has been a one-sided relationship. I took a good long look at where my life isn't going. I need more than playing house on weekends. I wanted us to give each other joy. To be there for each other for the tough times, not program our lives for Saturday and Sunday. I have needs, too. I am who I am. Me. I'm not an orphan, I'm not poor. I'm my own man. The hardest thing I've ever done is come to this decision, but I can't forever accept conditions based on your lack of trust in me."

"I don't need to hear this," she said, weeping. "If you're going, go."

"I'm not letting you off the hook so easily. I want you to know precisely what you've given up. We could have been happy. Contraceptives aren't foolproof. If we stayed together and you became pregnant, then what? Babs, Hans, and the Fortunes see the baby whenever they want, but I'm to sneak off with our child to show it to my folks? That's obscene. You refused to meet my family. In St. Thomas I asked you if you ever intended to marry me. You asked for time, which you deserved. Well, I've passed two birthdays since I met you. As far as I'm concerned, it's time to get out."

"I never meant to hurt you." She swallowed hard to kee[p] from crying.

He glanced at his watch. "I know. One of these day[s] you're either going to have to drop the protective barrie[r] you've built around yourself, take a risk and trust a man, o[r] stay alone for the rest of your life. Good-bye, Claire."

Her eyes blurred by tears, she watched him stride out o[f] her life, get into his sleek Corvette, and speed out the gate[.] Wretched, his death-knell good-bye reverberating in he[r] head, she walked inside to the study and shut the door. Th[e] room was bare except for a dented metal bridge table an[d] folding chairs the revenue agents had passed over, saying i[t] wasn't worth the auctioneer's time. A phone sat on the table[.]

Forsaken, abandoning herself to a mountain of misery[,] she pulled out a chair and sat. She sobbed until her eyelid[s] puffed and she could barely open them. Then she dragge[d] herself into the bathroom, turned on the tap, and doused he[r] face in cold water.

He was wrong, she told herself wrathfully. Couldn't h[e] know when she heard his car in the driveway her heart lifte[d] with anticipation? Couldn't he see it in her eyes when sh[e] threw her arms around him, feel it when she kissed him[,] when she made love to him? Couldn't he see when h[e] smiled at her with his to-die-for blue eyes she went al[l] mushy like a giddy teenager? Couldn't he know when the[y] lay in bed holding hands and talking that she treasured thos[e] moments as the sweetest, most cherished times in her life[?]

Apparently not.

She wandered through the house to the storage room[,] looked at the pots and pans, shook her head, and left for th[e] house she'd shared with Wendall. The house she'd occup[ied] alone. She made her way upstairs, sat on the bed, and crie[d.] Her hand fell on the phone. Her fingers drummed the plasti[c] case. Penny-pincher or not, she needed to speak wit[h] Cee-Cee. They had seen each other through every joy an[d] catastrophe in life. If Wendall was right—his accusation[s] held just enough of a kernel of truth to be frightening—i[t] meant she had usurped her mother's rights; not for the pur[-] and noble reason of saving the estate, but for her own selfish motive: proving the Brices wrong.

She dialed London.

"Oh, Lord!" Cee-Cee exclaimed when Claire completed her tale through a tidewater of tears. "I was afraid of this."

"Have I really been mean and shitty?"

"Clarissa, none of us is perfect."

"Oh, God," she wailed piteously. "I love him. But what else could I have done?"

"Meet his parents. He didn't ask you to move in with them, merely to meet them."

"In other words," Claire said, "I dug my own grave. Is he right about the restaurant, too?"

"Are you asking for the truth or what you want to hear?" She groaned.

"He raises an interesting theory," Cee-Cee said carefully. "Personally I wouldn't have thought of it. Then again, he's the one with the brilliant, analytical mind."

"You're no slouch either."

"Thank you, Clarabelle. On the other hand, his distraught state could impair his judgment. My advice is to have a mother-daughter chat. Lay it out, hear what Babs says. Give her the chance to change her mind."

Claire shuddered, a cowardly chill creeping up her spine. "Hans will sue me if she stops Pomander's at this late stage."

"No," Cee-Cee said cheerfully. "Hans will *murder* you. Then he'll mince you up in a grinder, add spices and some of his haute-cuisine delectable fungi called truffle. He'll list you on the menu—a one-night delicacy—Claire Pâté de Foie aux Truffles Stamford."

Claire laughed in spite of her miserable state. "Very funny. You really think I should give Mom a chance to change her mind?"

"I do, Claresta. Please find the courage to speak with Wendall's parents. I need a happy ending for the book I'm going to write about you two. I'm through with soaps."

After asking about Tom and the baby, Claire hung up. She took stock of her situation. She'd lost Wendall, permanently and irrevocably, but she owed it to Babs to have the opportunity to decide if she wanted Pomander's to open.

Claire combed her hair and repaired her makeup. She found Babs in the dining room. She took one look at Claire's ravaged face, put down the swatches of materials she was testing on the chairs, and asked what was wrong.

Claire told her she'd broken up with Wendall.

Babs took Claire's hands in hers. "Why did you refuse to meet his parents?"

She bit her lip and clenched her hands. "I had to. From the minute Colin learned about Dad, he and his family cut me dead. It was worse than if I'd never existed. I'm the wife he and my in-laws supposedly loved for five years—until I brought shame to them. Colin said they called me vermin. It wasn't for anything terrible I had done or deserved, but simply for being Edward Jameson's daughter. Marybeth Frankel carved out a career for herself capitalizing on our family, specifically on my hide. Wendall's a good man. He sees me for myself, but he can't swear for his parents. He loves them, they love him. He wants marriage, children. I can't give him that without causing a breach in his family."

"What a burden you've taken on yourself," Babs said compassionately. She remembered Wendall's concerns when she had guessed Kitty was his mother. "How can I convince you I disagree?"

"You can't, so please don't try. What about Pomander's? Would you prefer not to go ahead?" If Babs said yes, she would speak with Hans, explain her terrible error, arrange a payment schedule to cover equipment she couldn't return. She'd be in debt forever.

Babs nodded. "All right, I'll answer you as honestly as I can. When I came home, I looked at the house and I thought how can I turn my family home into a business? My God, what have I done?"

Heavy with guilt, Claire stood up immediately. "Don't worry. I'll speak with Hans."

Babs gently but firmly coaxed her down into her chair. "You'll do nothing of the sort. That's what I thought then. With or without Pomander's, my life isn't the same without your father. Wendall's right. I could sell off acreage, live here alone, wait for old age to creep up on me. Or, I can keep busy and productive. Pomander's keeps me busy. I'm in my familiar beautiful setting."

"Then you're not sorry?" Claire asked, sounding hopeful.

"Not any longer. I get up in the morning looking forward to getting out of bed. I didn't for a long time. I was furious with Edward for lying to me, for dying on me, for not aggressively helping himself to good health. I had so much anger in me, I raged with it. Then Dr. March set me straight. He said Edward only had a month or two left. While I was in Japan, I left you to deal with the IRS. Throughout this awful period, you've borne the brunt of our troubles while I worked through my problems."

She asked Claire to wait. She left the room, coming back with Edward's letter. "Read this. Then you'll know why I don't give a fig what others think. I'll love your father until I die, but until then I have to go on—for my sake and yours. Thanks to you and Hans, I have problems to solve. I'm needed. I feel productive. Hans discusses each day's events with me. Just yesterday he asked me what kind of soufflés I like."

"They can be marked up five times cost," Claire interjected, in her habit of retaining facts. "I'm sorry. You were saying?"

"Jimmy drags me into the hothouses to see the new shoots. Ruthie's Ruthie, bless her. It will never be as before, darling, but it's a new chapter."

Claire read her father's last words. She set aside her anguish to ask one last question. "Has what Dad did made you leery of people?"

Babs hesitated briefly. "You know the saying: Today's headlines become tomorrow's garbage. The spotlight moves on. In other words, nobody cares, not that I advocate this unpleasantness, but the time I was leery—scared—was after my fiancé dumped me, and my mother canceled the engagement party. All Dad and I ever wanted was your happiness. We thought . . . we hoped and prayed it would be Wendall. I still do. You're right for each other."

That night Claire sat in the window seat in the guest house, in the bedroom she had shared with Wendall. He had forgotten his clothes, shoes, slippers, toilet articles, books. All his belongings. She sat with his yellow cashmere sweater, her birthday present to him. His scent clung to the fibers. When she could no longer keep her eyes open, she fell asleep hugging his sweater.

Over the next few months Claire survived by working until she dropped into bed at night too exhausted to think or to dream. She blessed Pomander's for keeping her busy.

The town council approved Pomander's license to operate. The local newspaper printed the zoning change, duly noting the names of the partners. The local newspaper profiled Hans Aldred, the world-famous chef. It led to an article about him in *Bon Appétit* magazine.

They expected a full house for the gala opening and took reservations for the seven P.M. and nine-thirty P.M. sittings. Hans invited friends from the Culinary Institute. He sent Bryan Miller a handwritten invitation. Favorable mention in his *New York Times* column would be tantamount to royal accreditation.

Marybeth Frankel phoned Pomander's to find out the date of the grand opening. Hans took the call and jotted down her reservation.

When Claire read her name in the book, she saw red. "I'm not letting her in here. She's determined to ruin my life."

"Do that and you'll play into her hands," Babs said.

"You're telling me I should let her reservation stand?"

"I never tell people what to do. I merely suggest," Babs said, gliding from the room.

Claire stared at her back. Her mother had echoed Wendall's favorite phrase.

On Wendall's last day in the clinic, Vito popped into his office. He dropped a file folder on the desk near a half-filled bottle of Dewar's and an empty glass.

Wendall aimed a pushpin at a corkboard that had previously held snapshots of his young patients. The pin bent.

joined a litter of bent pushpins in the wastebasket near his right foot.

"My, my, we're busy today," Vito said. Daria had given him an earful.

"What's in there?" Wendall peered over his shoulder at the manila folder on his desk.

"A copy of a file a private-detective pal got for an irate client. It's for Claire."

Wendall zeroed in on the corkboard. "It's none of my business."

Vito helped himself to a red lollipop. Wendall gave him a bleary-eyed look but said nothing. Vito worried about Wendall. Since breaking up with Claire, he wore his misery on his sleeve—a human Vesuvius on the brink of eruption.

"That's where you're wrong, buddy. In your abysmal state you're incapable of making a logical decision. I'm doing you and your sad gonads a favor."

"Did she ask you to show me the file?"

"Nope," Vito replied airily. "Claire doesn't know about it. You look dreadful. You're growing red mold."

Wendall ran a hand over his fuzzy face. Clumps of curly red hairs stuck between his fingers. "This beard is my new fashion statement."

Vito snickered.

Wendall fixed him with a resentful glare. He laid two heavy hands on Vito's shoulders. "You're a fucking busybody. Take the file and get out."

Vito sniffed. His head reared backward. "Christ! You're soused."

"I am not inebriated. Yet." Wendall tilted left. "I am, however, close. I'm the doctor. I'll let you know when I arrive."

"Crap. I'm the law. You're not driving. I'll take you home."

"Why this interest in my welfare?"

Vito rolled his eyes upward. "I'm your friend. I'm trying my level best to break the deadlock between you and Claire. Read the file."

Wendall dropped down into his chair. His rational mind

condemned him for scolding Claire. That sweet girl. It wasn't her fault she'd lived through hell. The loss of a father. A man's entitled to one mistake in life. So what if it was for filching a measly ten million dollars that with taxes, interest, and penalties for twenty-seven years must be a billion dollars by now! Did Claire turn on her daddy when he stubbornly refused to communicate with her at first? No. She bought a VCR and played his beloved Abbott-and-Costello movies to cheer him up.

"I do not like them," Wendall announced thickly.

"Who?"

"Abbott and Costello, dummy. I like the Ritz Brothers."

He closed his stinging eyes. Poor Claire. Saint Claire. She had faced the agony of her shit husband and his shit parents and that shit Marybeth while the lot of the shits defamed her good name. Beatific Claire. Did she give up when her shit-turd husband broke her heart? No. A lesser woman would wallow in a woe-is-me mentality. Did his precious Claire? No. She got herself a job, used it as a lab course, and impressed everyone with her quick mind and ability to learn.

She stood up to the fucking IRS!

"Why do you think Babs is sleeping in her old bed?" he asked.

Vito sucked a red lollipop. "I know you'll tell me, fried brains."

Wendall chortled. "Claire spent the money Colin—the shit—coughed up for hocking her jewels."

"Take a peek at the file."

Wendall tossed it off his desk. "Claire's a closed chapter."

"Says who?" Vito muttered, getting a firm grip on Wendall's elbow, leading him out the door. Piggy helped him get Wendall into the car. He dragged him up the stairs into his home. He left Wendall draped at the piano, battering a Beethoven sonata. At least Vito guessed it was Beethoven. It was hard to tell. Wendall could thank his lucky stars he didn't live in an apartment with thin walls. If he did, the neighbors would kill him for sure.

Vito returned to the Bronx. From there, he sent the file by overnight courier to Claire.

"Exquisite." Claire cast her decorator's eye of approval on her mother's peerless taste. She had transformed the ballroom into a series of tasteful dining areas, selecting splashes of pink and red peonies on a white background for the table skirts, valances, and drapery fabric; green-and-white-striped fabric for the chair cushions. The room resembled an English country garden, with windows gracing a terrace romantically lit with amber lights, shining on large Chinese porcelain blue floral jardinieres filled with yellow tulips.

Months of frenzied preparation had included expanding the downstairs bathrooms, hiring and training staff, selecting menus. Everything had been planned down to the last detail to ensure the success of tonight's gala opening; even the buckets of Siberian irises lining the path to the front door would be perfect. The guest list included CEOs and local businessmen and -women, invited gratis at Claire's suggestion.

"There's nothing like word of mouth. It's an investment," she said to Hans, who agreed. She suggested they present the ladies with a pomander, boxed with the restaurant's name.

Since Wendall's abrupt departure, Claire had struggled to maintain her outward composure. Not even Colin's betrayal or her subsequent divorce had affected her so deeply. Wendall was more than her lover. He was her soul mate.

She refused all attempts to unburden her heavy heart, saying, "It happened for the best."

Babs, Hans, and the Fortunes disagreed. Since discretion was the better part of valor, they kept a watchful silence, missing the congenial doctor's upbeat presence. At least once a day, Claire slipped out of the main house for a breath of air. Unaware that Babs observed her heading for the dock, she returned with eyes red from crying, blaming it on allergies.

Claire smiled at Babs. "We closed tonight's reservations
We're booked solid."

Babs squeezed her hand. "Thanks to you."

"We can all take a bow." By making the decision to ru
a pool restaurant, the employees shared the tips. It fostere
harmony, while discouraging slackers.

With five hours left before Pomander's official opening
Hans joined them in the dining room, followed by the staff. H
had trained them like a corps de ballet, rehearsing, serving th
staff's families complete meals. Claire had tested the comput
erized ordering system and ironed out unforeseen problem
with vendors. Hans waved his spatula like a baton, called fo
attention, then delivered a pep talk. When he finished, h
turned the meeting over to Claire.

She raised her hand, signaling the busboys, dining-roo
captain, wine steward, and kitchen staff. On the downbea
everyone chorused, "Present your pompanos."

An emotional Hans dropped the spatula. His eyes mois
he wrapped his arms around a misty-eyed Claire. "Goo
luck, partner." He formally shook Babs's hand.

"You can do better than that," she said, giving a flustere
Hans a hug.

Then the moment arrived. Pomander's opened for busi
ness. Her dark hair styled in a French braid, and wearing
shawl-collar tangerine silk, her father's gold charm at he
neck, Claire glanced at her watch. They were four hours old
She observed the filled-to-capacity restaurant with grea
satisfaction. Except for one person. Marybeth Frankel.

She sat at a window table near the terrace.

"Mom, take over the hostess duties, please."

Babs wore a classic black Chanel suit, off-white sil
blouse, and a strand of pearls. She followed the direction o
Claire's tense stare. "I hope she chokes. Not here, Go
forbid. I don't care if Hans took her reservation. Shall I as
Jimmy to throw her out?"

"No. I'm fine. There's nothing more she can do to hur
me." Claire threaded her way to Marybeth, who looked lik
a wax dummy. If she smiled, she'd crack. "Is everything t
your satisfaction?" Claire asked with detached coolness.

Marybeth ate the last bite of caramelized apricots with almond cream, and put down her napkin. *Eat your heart out,* she thought. The plastic surgeon charged an arm and a leg, but he was worth it. She didn't need a bra. Her derriere sat up nice and high. Her tummy was still a little sore from the liposuction, and she wasn't too crazy about the outline left by the collagen injections around her lips, but all things considered, she was a new woman. Too bad Louis couldn't make the trip to see her shine. He was going to love her new look. Perhaps, she thought, peeved at Claire's sultry beauty, she should have chosen different clothing for tonight.

"My compliments to your chef. The Fillet of Beef Balsamico with Red Onion Confit was superb. I scarfed down the dessert, too." She smiled to show there were no hard feelings. "Have you time for an interview?"

"I didn't think you'd come here for the food," Claire said dryly. "Why don't we get it over with now?"

Claire handed Marybeth her bill.

"Most places comp," she said, affronted by the bill.

Claire turned her back, leaving her to grab her purse and follow her to the register. Claire took Marybeth's credit card, did the necessary work, then handed her back her card and a copy of her receipt. "Follow me." She walked outside.

Marybeth's spiked heels clicked on the stone path. Claire would pay dearly for her insult. "Where are we going?"

"To my house."

"That's very nice of you. But then again, you're a smart girl. You know the power of the press."

"I know the power of scorned wives, too."

Claire ushered her inside. She stood with her back to the fireplace.

Marybeth glanced at the surroundings. "What a smart idea to mirror the staircase wall below the banister. Most mirrors are on the other wall. I'll have to remember that. You don't mind if I steal your idea, do you?"

"Help yourself."

Marybeth sat on the couch. She opened her large purse and waved a small black tape recorder. "Recognize this?"

Claire eyed it with disdain. "How could I forget? It launched your career."

Marybeth smiled her pearly white smile. "Yes, it did."

"Shall we begin? I have to get back to work."

Marybeth pursed her lips. Let the bitch wait. This was payback time. "Working for a living is a new role for you. How do you like it?"

"I love it."

"Still, it's quite a come down. Colin has a new love. She resembles you. But she's the genuine article. Very rich, very Social Register. He checked her out first. His parents are delighted. I understand he's bought a new house. A bigger one."

Claire felt nothing. Not for Colin nor for Marybeth, who was trying her hardest to get her angry. She opened her desk drawer and took out Vito's folder. Tapping her fingers on it, she gazed at the shallow woman, then walked over to her.

"Why did you do it? Why did you write those horrid articles? Why did you try to destroy me?"

The moment Marybeth waited for had come true. She briefly closed her eyes, savoring her sweet victory.

"I did destroy you."

"That's a matter of opinion," Claire said without raising her voice.

"You invited me to your party, then you said you canceled it. I phoned your caterer. You lied to me. I wasn't good enough to hobnob with you snobs. Colin refused my interview. His secretary gave me the boot. I saw his face when he picked you up at the restaurant. He looked right through me, as though I didn't exist. When June Lamont called me, she gave me the ammunition I needed. Now you know how it feels when your husband throws you out, when you have nothing and have to work like the rest of us."

"So you did it for revenge," Claire said brusquely.

"For justice!" Marybeth reprimanded with a toss of her head.

Claire nodded. "I misjudged you."

"We all learn, don't we?"

"I guess we do."

Claire dropped Vito's report into Marybeth's lap. "Read that. You'll find it interesting." She poured herself a Coke, sipping it slowly, while listening to Marybeth's gasps.

"Dynamite, isn't it?"

The wax doll face collapsed. "Who gave you this? How dare you spy on me?"

Claire laughed shortly. "Coming from you, that's a riot. Aren't you wondering whether I'll ruin you, the way you tried to ruin me?"

"Louis never told me his wife owns the majority stock in the chain. I didn't know that's why he married her."

Claire shrugged her shoulders. "You're not a thorough reporter. Greed got in your way. That and your desire for revenge."

Marybeth's right eyelid twitched. From the neck up she'd turned a blotchy red as if she'd had an allergic reaction from shellfish. "You gloating bitch! You tricked me! You brought me here to ruin me!"

She was right. After Claire had read Vito's report, she couldn't sleep for nights. She dreamed of dragging Marybeth into her home, threatening her with dire consequences, watching her squirm, saying whatever ugly things popped out of her mouth. So why wasn't she doing just that? Who would blame her? She'd been brought to her knees by Marybeth's vindictiveness. But she'd also found herself as a result. With dawning certainty, she realized that Cee-Cee and Wendall were mistaken. It wasn't her lack of trusting Wendall that had finally sent him away. Losing Wendall had resulted from her not trusting herself.

If she trusted herself, his parents, or anyone's for that matter, couldn't harm her.

Good God, what a turn of events. How did other women manage revenge? All she had to do was tell Mrs. Marx. Overnight, Marybeth's career would be squashed. There'd be a For Sale sign on the lawn of her secret hideaway in Coldwater Canyon. She could accomplish the same thing by calling Louis Marx. He wouldn't voluntarily relinquish his power base. The only way he'd leave his powerful position, she felt certain, was if his wife kicked him out.

Claire handed Marybeth a box of tissues. "Stop sniveling."

"You bitch," she wailed. "First Charlie, now you. You're out to destroy me."

"Blow your nose."

Marybeth honked.

Claire surprised herself. She walked over to the window and gazed at the Sound. The ticking grandfather clock reminded her of sitting in Richard Parish's office, shunned by her husband, her in-laws, scared and weighted down by worry for her father, anxious for her mother. She had been so nervous and miserable that day. How different she felt now. She'd come full circle. No, she'd gone beyond the old circle. She'd stepped into her own new circle, found untapped strengths.

Marybeth was stuck in a time warp. A value system as false as Colin's. By Claire's hurting Marybeth, who stupidly equated social ranking with success, it had led to this. Marybeth hadn't caused her marital troubles with Colin. She exacerbated them, yes, and in a horrible way. But the truth was Colin suffocated her, manipulated her so he could feel superior. Was she better off now? Decidedly yes. Was she happy? Without Wendall she'd never be completely happy, but she'd go on, a better person for the time they had spent together.

"I'm sorry," Marybeth howled.

"No, you're not. You're sorry I know. You're scared I'll tell Louis's wife. You know if I do, you'll lose your house, your syndicated column, your power base, your standing in the community. Your ex, Charlie, will gloat. So will Colin. That's why you're sorry. You haven't learned a thing from your divorce. You let it eat at you, just as I almost let you win over me. You're a desperate, neurotic, needy person."

Marybeth blanched. She buried her face in her hands. *Charlie would gloat.*

"You had the power of choice. You still do. We all do," Claire said gravely, the words meant for herself as much as Marybeth. A weight lifted from her shoulders. She'd come into her own at last.

"How?" Marybeth demanded. "You had it easy all your life. I didn't."

"Easy," Claire muttered under her breath, thinking of what she'd lived through, of how she'd lost Wendall. "We're judged by our own character, by our own actions. I'm sorry I lied to you. Happiness isn't exclusive to elitists. It doesn't equate with money and power. Be your own person."

"What do you want me to do?"

Good question. Vito didn't say who ordered the investigation into Marybeth's background. For all she knew, Louis's wife had hired a private detective, yet if this was true, why didn't she act on the report? Then again, she didn't know Mrs. Marx's state of mind or whether or not she was a healthy woman. If Claire brought her misery for the sole purpose of getting back at Marybeth, she'd be no better than Marybeth.

Still, under the circumstances, a little blackmail for a good cause could be excused.

"I suggest you break off your affair. If I ever read or hear of you maliciously browbeating another person, I'll phone Louis's wife in a heartbeat. If you move to another newspaper chain and you attack someone, I'll send the tabloids your pictures in a flash. It's a nice juicy story. Most newspapers prefer reporters to gather news, not make it."

"You want me to give up Louis?" Marybeth asked, incredulous.

"It's your choice. I never tell people what to do. I merely suggest," she said, repeating Wendall's statement, a phrase even Babs had adopted. He'd affected all their lives. She wondered how Wendall was, whether or not he hurt as much as she, or if he'd been able to put their affair from his mind.

Marybeth wiped her eyes. "All right. I promise."

"Who did your face-lift?"

"My friend Horty's doctor. She swears by him."

Claire tsked. "She should swear at him. He does awful work. Wendall could do a better job any day in the week. Blindfolded."

Marybeth's hands flew to her cheeks. "God, help me!"

"God hasn't time for vain women. I suggest you get started," Claire commented.

Marybeth flew out the door before Claire added to her demands.

"Good riddance," Claire muttered. She returned the file to her desk drawer, then dialed the main house. She spoke with her mother.

"Marybeth's gone. She won't bother us again. I'll tell you about it later. Would you mind taking over the hostess duties? I'll be back soon."

She emptied Wendall's closet. It took four trips to load the Volvo. Before she declared herself healed, she had one more thing to do. She had to prove she trusted herself.

Nineteen

THE EVERETT-LAWSON MANSION blazed with light. Claire parked in the circular driveway, cut the motor, dropped the keys in her large shoulder bag, and stared at the house Wendall called home.

It sat on the crest of a sweeping lawn, its expanse sloping to the water. For all its grandeur, the house was a venerable, solid, sheltering structure, home to generations of Wendall's ancestors. She could imagine his bringing his wife and children here for weekend retreats, one day living here with his family.

Hit by an attack of anxiety at the horrible thought of him making love—making babies!—with another woman, she gave herself a hard mental shake. *Don't wallow. Do what you came to do, and leave.*

Suddenly a flashlight shone in her eyes. Startled, her hand flew up, knocking over her purse, spilling its contents onto the seat and floor.

"May I help you?" a male voice asked.

"I'm not trespassing," she stammered, realizing he was a security guard.

The man leaned his head into the car. "I didn't say you were. Well, I'll be. Did all this stuff come out of your bag?" he asked, astounded at seeing a package of tissues, lipstick, comb, hairbrush, house and car keys, spiral notebook, pencil, pen, checkbook, small calculator, yellow chalk, paprika, oregano, and food coupons.

Paying more attention to him than what she was doing, she shoveled the items into her purse.

"I understand most of it," the man with the twinkling brown eyes said chattily. "I can't figure out why you're carrying a large can of paprika and a jar of oregano. If I'm not too nosy, mind telling me why?"

She looked at the floor. She stared at the paprika and the oregano as if seeing them for the first time. She didn't have the foggiest notion how they had gotten there. She'd kept her car keys in her shoulder bag's outside pouch.

All of a sudden she knew! The last time she used this purse was when she and Wendall had gone grocery shopping. When they came home, he dropped one of the bags in their driveway, ripping it. She helped pick up the groceries, and when the remaining bags were too full, she dropped the items into her purse. She'd forgotten about it. This was the first time she'd used the purse since then.

She glanced at the house. Any minute the door might open. "It's a long story. Look, I'm sorry, but I'm in a hurry. Would you mind helping me carry these clothes to the front door? They aren't mine."

"I can see they're a man's," he said pleasantly. He peeked into the back. "Aren't these Wendall's?" She nodded "Excuse me, miss, what is your name?"

"Claire. There's a lot more in the trunk. Books and things."

"In that case, we'll need help."

"No!" She spoke more sharply than she intended. "I'll do it."

He came around to her side. She stepped out. He was tall, with brown hair. "Claire," he said gently, putting his hand on her arm. "You drove here for a reason. I don't think it had to do with returning Wendall's clothes. Don't you think it's worth your seeing it through?"

She stilled. She gazed into a pair of kind, compassionate eyes, and sighed. "I mistook you for a security guard. You're not, are you?"

"'Fraid not," he said cheerfully. "I'm Wendall's dad, Ron. You're Edward Jameson's daughter, Claire."

"How do you do?" she said. "You're one of the persons I came to meet."

"Is that so? Well, I'm glad to meet you. Who's the other person?"

"Your wife. I'm taking the cure." She clucked her tongue. "I didn't mean that. I meant I'm proving something to myself. I won't stay long." Damnit, she was babbling. Whenever she was nervous, she babbled.

"I understand completely." He gathered Wendall's suits.

The front door swung open. A woman—Claire guessed she was Wendall's mother from her red hair—stood under a halo of light. She saw the woman lock gazes with Ron, stare at her.

Claire told herself not to panic. Why should she? What could Wendall's mother do to her? Nothing. Not one damn thing. A fast introduction, a courtesy of time, then she'd be off. Why she thought she had to prove anything was beyond her. She was due back at Pomander's.

"Mrs. Everett-Lawson, my name is Claire Jameson. I came here to meet you and to bring Wendall's things. Now that I've done it, I'll leave."

Vito rushed to the door. "Hello, Claire. Please excuse us. Kitty, it's Wendall."

"Is Wendall worse?" Kitty wrung her hands. She gave Vito her complete attention. He nodded.

"What's wrong with Wendall?" Claire asked.

"Ron, hurry!" Kitty shouted. "Wendall's taken a turn for the worse."

Ron dropped his armful of clothes. He clipped past Claire, racing after Kitty and Vito.

"Hang on, my boy. I'm coming."

Wendall sick! Wendall taken a turn for the worse! For all she knew, Wendall could be dying!

She ran into the house, racing after the others into a huge salon. It contained so much furniture she didn't see Wendall.

She heard him.

A mournful note brought her eyes to its source.

"Oh my God!" she screeched. "What happened to him?"

Hunched over the keyboard, his handsomeness buried, looking like a god-awful mountain man with the scruffiest red beard she'd ever seen, Wendall sat on a piano bench. Vito stood behind him, supporting his back. His hands braced Wendall's shoulders.

"Don't come closer," Vito warned sharply. "He's in shock."

That ranked as the understatement of the year. Wendall's eyes nearly bugged out. By some miracle, Claire, so gorgeous he couldn't wait to get her alone, had come of her own volition. Madman Vito had heard a car, glanced out the window, and recognized the driver. He'd raced into the bathroom where Wendall was about to shave off the beard he'd grown during the last month, hauled him into the salon, forcing him onto the hard bench. Vito had said that if he so much as opened his fucking mouth without his permission, he'd personally shoot him. *Dead.*

Wendall lifted his forefinger and struck a B flat.

Claire hovered near his distraught parents. She raised her voice to be heard. "Wendall, darling, talk to me."

"I . . ."

Vito's hammer thumbs dug down. Wendall struck an A minor with his pinky.

Claire turned to his parents. "He's ill. Why isn't he in bed?"

Kitty said, "He won't listen. Not to me nor his father."

Claire was astounded. To think she'd been afraid of his parents. This was how they cared for their son!

"He's ill. How can you shirk your duty? I don't understand either of you. Or you either, Vito." Claire condemned her audience en masse.

"Darling," she called to Wendall, "if you don't tell us what's wrong, how can we help you?"

He opened his mouth. Vito's knee shot forward, striking the small of Wendall's back. Yelping, Wendall's fist banged a full chord.

"Oh, God, Vito, he's crying from pain. I think I see tears in his eyes. Darling, Wendall, sweetheart, talk to me. The hell with everyone else."

His Claire had said the hell with his parents! What a

wonderful phrase. Wendall opened his mouth. Vito's fingers dug in. Wendall let out a pitiful sound.

Claire couldn't stand it. "Never mind, darling. It's hard for you to speak in your condition. What exactly is his condition?" she demanded of his parents.

Ron glanced at Vito. "We're not sure."

"Not sure?" Claire said, incredulous. "What does the doctor say?"

Kitty said, "Nothing. We haven't called one."

Claire was shocked. "How long has he been like this?"

Vito answered. "About a month—give or take a few days."

"A month! You let him suffer for a month and you haven't called a doctor?"

"We think it's emotional. He hasn't been happy," Ron said.

"He's very difficult to live with," Kitty added.

Smiles poured from Claire's heart. "Oh, darling, I know how you feel. I couldn't stand it either. The more I tried to forget you, the more you stayed in my thoughts. Sweetheart, you were right. I was afraid to trust you. No, that's not true," she amended with a shake of her head. "I was getting there at my own speed, but you've always been hasty where I'm concerned. It's not a complaint, mind you. I'm merely saying you fell in love with me first. It's understandable. You had nothing else on your mind. I did."

Wendall loved being called empty-headed as long as Claire did the name-calling. He opened his mouth.

"No, darling," she said, saving him another one of Vito's acutely painful messages. "You're so gorgeous. *Were* so gorgeous. It breaks my heart to see how rotten you look, how low you've sunk."

Behind her Wendall's father coughed. Kitty covered her mouth. She collapsed onto "Aunt Harriet," whose springs still squeaked.

"It wasn't you I didn't trust," Claire babbled. "I love you. I didn't trust myself. You can't blame me entirely, either. Everything crashed on me at once. But I'm a strong woman. Pomander's is going to be a success. I feel it in my business bones, just as I know I can't live without you."

Wendall started to rise. Vito pinched his neck. Claire's recital was far from finished.

"No, that's not entirely true," she certified. "I can live without you. But I don't want to. My mother is lonely, but she isn't alone, if you know what I mean. She's interested in life again. I'm over my fears. Oh, darling, you look wretched. I could weep."

"So could I," Kitty said, crossing her legs.

"Me, too," Ron said.

Wendall hit a C sharp.

"He's been doing that all day," Vito added. "One sickly sour note at a time, and we all know what a lousy piano player he is."

"He's a wonderful pianist!" Claire gave Vito a glacial glare. Awash with guilt, sick at heart, she flew to Wendall, pressing his face to her breasts.

He sniffed her perfume, shifted his face from side to side, and groaned. Hanging on for dear life, his arms lashed her. "I think you're a wonderful pianist," she crooned, smothering him, stroking his hair.

"You do?" Ron asked, perched on "Aunt Harriet's" arm.

"The girl's got extraordinary taste," Kitty murmured to her husband. "Do you think she's tone-deaf?"

"I certainly hope so," he whispered.

Claire wasn't paying attention to them. "Sweetheart, Marybeth came to Pomander's tonight. Would you believe her nerve? I could destroy her with the file Vito sent me. Thank you for trying to help, Vito. I didn't use it. I can't sink to her level. I blackmailed her a little bit—a lot—but only to make sure she never hurts anyone the way she hurt me. Wendall, precious, whatever is wrong with you, we'll see it through together."

Wendall couldn't get a word in edgewise. Claire was on a roll. "Mr. and Mrs. Everett-Lawson," she said, releasing him. He grabbed her back. As far as he was concerned, she could rattle on until she was blue in the face as long as his face was buried between her breasts.

"I love Wendall. Desperately. We love each other. He loves you. You must be wonderful people if you raised so fine a son. I hope you'll learn to love me one day, too. I thought you'd like to know we want a large family. My goodness! I forgot." She stood back to give Wendall air. In a voice that trembled for fear he would refuse her, she asked, "Darling, will you marry me?"

He responded in a heartbeat.

"I accept! I do. I will."

In his haste to stand and kiss her, several things occurred: His right heel crunched Vito's right foot. He knocked over the piano bench. Vito lost his balance and landed on the floor with a thump. Wendall did not apologize.

He was too busy kissing Claire.

Giving himself a lot of credit, a grinning Vito sent a thumbs-up sign to Wendall's parents. If Wendall was smart, he wouldn't tell Claire he had started growing his idiot beard as a fashion statement, that he was on his way to the bathroom to get rid of the damn bush when she arrived. Ron and Kitty, bless them, played along with his hurriedly makeshift plan. They were geniuses for not needing coaching. Wendall owed him his address book for shoving his skinny ass on the piano bench. If Daria married Peter—she was working on it!—and Piggy—no, *Franklin Paggliani*,—got into the police academy, and if he, Vito, found himself a wife who worshipped him the way Claire loved Wendall, life would be great.

Ron and Kitty looked at each other and smiled. They knew all about the proud young beauty parting the corona of hair surrounding Wendall's mouth to kiss their son as if the sun hung directly above his head. (Which it did.) *Isn't this nice,* Kitty thought, approving of his choice.

Ron stood up. He cleared his throat. "Claire, when you have a minute, would you tell us if you've thought of a name for our first grandchild? Kitty's hidden a book around here somewhere with the names of our ancestors. Unless, of course, you prefer naming him Edward. Assuming you and Wendall have a boy first."

"Then you approve?" Claire asked, blushing deeply from the circle of Wendall's arms. Suddenly she was embarrassed by how her nervous babbling must have sounded, but once she'd gotten started she couldn't stop. Not with Wendall's health at stake.

"Naturally he approves." Kitty got off "Aunt Harriet." "Edward Ronald Wendall Everett-Lawson is a fine name. Wendall, kindly remove the hideous fur coat from your face. You look like a red wolf."

Wendall laughed. "Excuse us."

Giving Claire a look of pure bliss, he grabbed her hand, leading her from the room, racing past portraits of his ancestors, hauling her into a bathroom, locking the door, and crushing her in his arms.

"You can't back out. I accepted your proposal in front of my parents and Vito. I'll sue you for breach of promise if you do."

She playfully tugged his ridiculous beard. "You can't live without me, can you? This disgusting thing proves you're miserable without me."

"Would you have married me with it?"

She didn't hesitate a second. "Yes. But I would have chopped it off while you slept."

He cupped her cheek in his palm and lifted her face so that his eyes looked directly into hers. "Have you any idea how much I treasure you? I'm so proud of you."

She linked her arms around his neck and tilted her head back. "I love you."

He thought of the picture he'd seen in her father's wallet. "Not more than I love you."

"Yes," she said softly, her glowing eyes letting him know she recognized the words.

"No."

"Yes! Yes! Yes!"

"Impossible," he said, meaning it. "When shall we start our family?"

She reached for the doorknob, testing the lock. The gleam in his eyes told her he was ready now. "Nah. We better wait until we're home."

* * *

Wendall and Claire were thirty-three minutes late for their wedding two Sundays later. The fault was entirely theirs. Making love as often as possible to get a head start on the next generation of Everett-Lawsons, neither noticed the time. Finding a loving baby-sitter wouldn't pose a problem. Babs, Ron, Kitty, Ruth, and Jimmy each said, "You do your part, we'll do ours."

They were trying.

Ron, Kitty, and Vito entertained the guests, keeping them in hysterics recounting the story of how Claire had proposed to Wendall.

Harry arrived with his wife and sons. In Wendall and Claire's honor, he had closed his restaurant for the day. He brought a giant poster of good wishes from Wendall's cult fans.

Hans outdid himself with a sumptuous meal.

Babs, stunning in an Oscar de la Renta gown, fussed over the floral arrangements.

At one A.M. the previous night, Babs, Ruthie, and Jimmy completed the last of the two hundred pomanders each guest received for a keepsake. Their fingers smelled of cloves and oranges.

A radiant Claire made sure Daria caught the wedding bouquet.

Franklin . . . Franklin showed up with the Warriors. Dressed to the nines in a rented tux and tails, the Warriors patrolled the Denison estate, making certain tabloid journalists stayed off the property.

Tom and Cee-Cee Evans were thrilled. Cee-Cee excitedly said she thought Claire's story would make a great mini-series.

After a two-week honeymoon cruise aboard the *Sea Voyager*—with a stop at Magens Bay—Dr. and Mrs. Wendall Everett-Lawson returned home with twenty rolls of film and presents for everyone. Gradually they settled into a routine. Claire worked at Pomander's where she kept an eagle eye on back-door costs. As a result of Bryan Miller's rave review, the restaurant quickly became popular. Wendall divided his time between his second clinic in Bridgeport and his private practice in New York. At night the newlyweds gleefully hit the sheets, continuing what they did best:

Happily trying to make Babs, Ron, and Kitty grandparents.